BLUE MOON

A HOWARD MOON DEER MYSTERY

Books by Robert Westbrook

Howard Moon Deer Mysteries
Ghost Dancer
Warrior Circle
Red Moon
Ancient Enemy
Turquoise Lady
Blue Moon

Coming Soon!
Hungry Ghost
A Howard Moon Deer Mystery

The Torch Singer Trilogy
An Overnight Sensation
An Almost Perfect Ending
The Saint of Make-Believe

Left-Handed Policeman *series*
The Left-Handed Policeman
Nostalgia Kills
Lady Left

Other Books
Intimate Lies:
F. Scott Fitzgerald and Sheilah Graham – Her Son's Story
Journey Behind the Iron Curtain
The Magic Garden of Stanley Sweetheart

BLUE MOON

A HOWARD MOON DEER MYSTERY

Robert Westbrook

SPEAKING VOLUMES, LLC
NAPLES, FLORIDA
2020

Blue Moon

ISBN 978-1-64540-009-7

for Gail, again, always

Prologue

He ran hard, his lungs gasping for air, plunging through the forest, slapped by branches, tripping over roots. He scrambled up the hillside like a four-legged beast, his hands and feet clawing his way ever higher into the mountains

Terror drove him, animal terror. He ran harder, faster.

The summer night was dark. A crescent moon flickered through the branches, cold and impassive. There were three men behind him, possibly four. He didn't know if they had dogs. He hadn't heard barking, but he wasn't certain. If there were dogs, they would rip him apart.

The air was thin at this altitude and the mountain was steep. He struggled to breathe, but there wasn't enough oxygen. It was like drowning, craving air and never getting enough.

He came to a rocky stream and jumped across to the far bank. He could hear the men behind him thrashing through the brush, but they were some distance away. If he could lose them, he might be all right. He had been a long-distance runner in his youth. The track team at Cambridge University. But that was a long time ago

The branch of a pine bough sent him tumbling backward onto the ground. He lay for a moment sucking air in raspy breaths. The lower part of his leg throbbed with pain. Not far away he heard a whoosh of wings as a large bird swooped down through the trees onto its prey. There was a high squeal of terror from the creature who was caught. The night was full of death.

They say a drowning man sees his life flash by in an instant, but he saw only disconnected shards.

His mother holding his hand, a summer day in Hyde Park.

A girl he had seen for an instant in a café in Paris . . .

A shout from the forest below brought him out from his stupor, a human voice calling to someone, more of a sharp yelp than actual speech. He couldn't stay here. *Get up!* he told himself. *Get up and live!*

He picked himself up and ran.

The shout came again, closer than before.

I'm going to die, he thought.

Was there a cave? Somewhere to hide?

He stumbled out of the trees onto a mountain meadow. The tall grass was silvery in the moonlight. A pair of glowing eyes peered at him from across the meadow. The eyes weren't human. These were animal eyes. His heart nearly burst with fright.

Three enormous elk stood in the meadow. His sudden appearance worried them and they ambled away into the trees.

He couldn't go further. He was seventy-one years old, he had nothing left. It was too much to ask.

He sank to his knees with the certainty that this mountain meadow was the last place on Earth he would ever know. The animals would eat his flesh, scatter his bones.

He had always imagined death differently. A car crash in California. A coronary in London. His trans-Atlantic flight plunging into the ocean. You never knew where death would find you.

And now, here it was.

There was a disturbance in the sky. A vibration in the air. He wasn't sure at first because his rasping breath was so loud. But the vibration increased until it seemed to be everywhere, the omniscient thrum of a great beast.

The sky burst open with light.

He raised his eyes and saw only brilliance.

"Oh!" he cried.

The ladder of heaven unfolded above him.

"Come!" said a voice.

The arms of the universe reached down and took him.

Chapter One

Howard Moon Deer's backpack bulged with everything a wise person might need to survive in the wilderness.

There was a cooking pot tied to the outside strap and a folding camp chair he had bought at REI. A French baguette and a salami stuck out horizontally from the top flap like wings. Two half-bottles of French wine protruded from the side pockets, perfectly balanced.

Howie stood in the gravel parking area alongside his Subaru at the foot of the trail and hoisted the pack onto his shoulders with a grunt. He adjusted the straps and jiggled the pack up and down attempting to find a more comfortable position, but no matter what he did, it was heavy.

Seriously heavy.

The forest service sign at the head of the trail said: Dawson Peak Summit 15.8 miles. This wasn't an especially great distance except for the fact that Dawson Peak was the third highest mountain in New Mexico, 13,137 feet, and the trail was steep.

Luckily, it wasn't too late to lighten the load. He went through the contents of his pack in his mind, wondering what he could jettison. Not the tent, certainly. Nor the one-burner stove, foam pad, inflatable pillow, ground cloth, sleeping bag, change of clothes, rain poncho, water filter, water bottle, hunting knife, hatchet, Gortex shell, sunscreen, waterproof matches, or extra socks.

It was the food, he decided, that was adding all the weight. Howie planned to be in the wilds for four days and three nights and he had considered his culinary needs as carefully as though he were heading off to Antarctica for a month.

Tonight the menu included salmon, a potato to bake in foil in the campfire, cold asparagus in a vinaigrette already prepared in a small plastic container, and a chocolate bar for desert. This was the first night, a kind of Welcome to the Wonderful World of Trekking indulgence.

But for the rest of the trip, it would be strictly dried camping fare from REI, little bags of Chicken Couscous and Pasta Primavera that you could cook right in the bag, adding water.

Breakfast and lunch had likewise given Howie a good deal of thought. Along with the salami and the baguette, he had a box of English water crackers, several cheeses—a wedge of Jarlsberg, a slice of sharp white cheddar—two oranges, breakfast bars, six hard-boiled eggs, and a small jar of peanut butter. Coffee was especially welcome on a camping trip and Howie had a plastic one-cup dripper with three paper filters and a small bag of Starbuck's French Roast.

There was nothing in itself that was particularly heavy, but one by one, the items added up. He debated leaving the wine behind, along with a book of poetry that was stuffed into the front pocket, *100 Poems from the Chinese* translated by Kenneth Rexroth.

But what was a camping trip without wine and poetry? Why even go?

Was there anything else he could leave behind?

Yes, he decided. He didn't need the collapsible camping chair that was tied to the back of the pack. He would sit on the ground.

By God, he would rough it!

***

Howie was trekking up the third highest peak in New Mexico due to a broken heart. His girlfriend, Claire, had left him. She was in love with somebody new.

This hurt. It hurt a lot. And he was determined to sweat her out of his system with every step upward, lugging his heavy load of anger and regret along with the pack.

He'd received her Dear John email four days ago.

Dear Howie, she wrote from London, *I don't know how to say this so I'll just come out with it as best I can. I met someone. I didn't mean for it to happen. I didn't WANT it to happen. But it did and I'm so confused . . .*

He hadn't answered and each day afterward he had received additional emails from Claire detailing her emotional muddle. Frankly, Howie didn't want to hear about it. That was almost the worst part, that she still needed to confide in him.

She had been living in London the past six months, using the city as a base as she and her classical music ensemble toured the major world capitals.

Claire played the cello and her group, the Boston Chick Quartet, had become very successful—four attractive young women who played with "dazzling power" (*The New York Times*) and "intense sensitivity" (*The Guardian*). Howie had managed to spend a month with her in Tokyo last year, and early this spring he had met her in Paris for a week. But there were long separations and in the world she inhabited—culture, talent, money—Howie always knew this "someone" would eventually appear.

Unfortunately, in this case he was more than a mere someone, he was a world-famous conductor, Sir Richard Watson-Fowles, a charismatic white-haired maestro three times her age who she had met while performing the second Shostakovich cello concerto with the Berlin Philharmonic under his baton.

Claire was still a member of the Chick Quartet, but her career had progressed to the point where she was performing solo engagements with the great orchestras of the world. She had done the Elgar cello concerto with the London Philharmonic. The Dvorak in New York. The A-minor Schumann in Moscow.

Sir Richard had taken her under his wing in Berlin.

He brought out something in my performance that I can't describe, she had written in email #2. *A passion I didn't know was there.*

Right.

Somehow he made me see I was holding back, that you must surrender completely to the music to be a true artist! Once you've mastered the technique, you have to let yourself go and give, give, give!

Howie had always known that Claire was an exceptional musician. He had encouraged her. But she had never before written awful babble like "true artist" or "give, give, give." The Claire he knew would never have put exclamation marks at the end of every sentence. In the old days—the days she had spent with him—she would have laughed.

He had met Claire during a time when she was in New Mexico at loose ends, at the end of a bad marriage. He had loved her. He had helped put her back together. And now, put together, she was touring the world to thunderous applause while he remained the same old Howie Moon Deer in San Geronimo, a small-time private eye with a dangling PhD dissertation he had never managed to finish: a Lakota Indian who had been lured from the rez by generous scholarships to fancy universities, and now didn't quite belong anywhere—not the white world, nor the native world he had left behind.

Simply put, there was no possible way for him to compete with the wonderful Sir Richard Watson-Fowles, world-famous maestro.

Howie had just turned thirty-four and he felt he should have figured out life by now. But he hadn't.

Why aren't I more ambitious? he asked himself.

Why didn't I finish my doctorate?

I could have been Professor Moon Deer by now, a famous intellectual.

But I'm not, not, not . . . probably because I didn't give, give, give . . .

Meanwhile, it was a perfect summer morning, the second week of July, birds chirping, blue sky overhead, and Howie climbed the steep mountain trail with a vengeance, glad for the heavy backpack.

Claire!

He felt her in his soul with every step.

If you love somebody, let them go . . .

Was that a line from a song? Or just some stupid cliche?

How about: *Once you have met her,* never *let her go!*

That *was* a song. "Some Enchanted Evening."

There was always the possibility he would find another woman, of course. San Geronimo was a small town with a limited gene pool where any male who wasn't a penniless drunk was considered a catch. Howie was decently employed, decently attractive, and he supposed he was now officially single. Women often gave him a looking over. Very nice women, too. But none of them gave him the zap that Claire did.

Should he wait for Claire? Maybe she would get over her fabulous white-haired maestro. But maybe not.

Keep climbing, his body told him.

Up, up, up . . . until you're so worn and exhausted, Claire will seem a hallucination of the thin air.

A woman you never really knew.

***

Howie arrived at his first camping place, Lost Horse Lake, after a steep six-hour climb which had taken him above tree line to nearly 12,000 feet, then over the top of a ridge and down the other side into a wooded canyon.

The lake sparkled in the late afternoon light, the surface rippling in the breeze. It was only a small lake, hardly more than a pond, but few people camped this high up in the mountains and he had it all to himself. He had met only two other hikers the entire day, a man and a woman who were coming down.

The solitude was profound. As soon as Howie had his tent set up, he stripped off his sweaty clothes, dove into the shockingly cold water, and swam furiously for five minutes before hurrying out onto the bank with goose bumps up and down his body. He was so tired he barely had the energy to remember his broken heart.

He managed to cook himself dinner and drink a single glass of wine. There were bears in these mountains, so he cleaned up carefully, washed his dishes in the lake, and hung his food in a nylon bag from a limb of a tree. Then he crawled wearily into the tent, snuggled into his sleeping bag, and fell asleep almost immediately.

The next morning, he repacked his gear and set out in an optimistic mood. He had slept well, waking to a perfect summer morning. Birds chirped, the sky was blue, chipmunks scurried about cheerfully, and Howie was starting to think this wilderness trek had been a very good idea.

By noon, his body was in a pleasant rhythm as he hiked along the narrow trail. He was above tree line for most of the day with the world spread out below him, mountains all around as far as the eye could see. For several hours he went along the top of a high mountain ridge, occasionally descending into the trees, passing in and out of green forest grottos, miniature worlds with streams running through.

Howie was feeling good. The mountains, the sky, the exertion of his body, the sun on his face. This was the real life, the life of the planet. In the huge expanse of nature, his personal drama no longer seemed so important.

For the first time since he had received Claire's email, Howie suspected he was going to be okay. He didn't need to compete with a famous maestro. Despite his many faults—no PhD, little money, even less ambition—the fine July day made him feel he was alright just the way he was.

He would love Claire forever. But he would let her go . . .

There was an Indian saying he remembered from his childhood: *As summer follows spring, and autumn follows summer, and winter follows autumn, we are born, we live, and we die. It is good to be a part of this!*

"I am part of this!" he said aloud to a flock of big-horned sheep he saw through his binoculars on the next hill over.

The perfect summer morning ripened into a perfect summer afternoon.

He stopped for a moment to set down his pack and take a drink of cold, clear, clean mountain water. It tasted good.

Howie was a happy camper.

An enlightened camper.

Until the first black cloud appeared on the horizon.

***

The lone black cloud soon had company. A host of black clouds drifted across the sky from the east.

The wind came up, the sun disappeared, the temperature dropped nearly twenty degrees.

Thunder rolled across the mountains, each peal louder than the one before. Without warning, a zig-zag bolt of pure electricity exploded in the blue mist not far ahead. Howie counted the seconds. *One, two, three, four* . . . five seconds later a great boom of thunder shook the land like an earthquake. Which meant, by Howie's reckoning, the lightning was approximately five miles away. Not far enough when you were above tree line at 12,000 feet.

Luckily, the rain held off. Maybe it was coming, maybe not. Summer storms were unpredictable in northern New Mexico. Often they simply passed over, dissipating as quickly as they appeared.

This storm, however, looked like it planned on staying around. Howie glanced at his watch and saw it was a quarter to six. Normally this time of year, there would be daylight until nearly 9 o'clock, but with the storm nightfall would come much earlier. He wasn't optimistic he'd get to his next camping spot, Angel Creek, while he still could see.

According to the online information Howie had researched, Angel Creek was an undeveloped site, a clearing in the trees with a fine view of Dawson Peak less than a mile away, an easy hike the next day. There would be nothing at the campground except a fire ring and a year-round stream where he could refill his water. The ground would be flat and if he could set up his tent before the rain began, he would be alright. But he still had a hike ahead of him of at least two hours. Possibly more.

Howie quickened his pace. The trail had become sketchy, barely more than a hint of a path, and it was often hard to see the way forward.

FLASH! . . . the sky exploded with electricity. The thunder followed almost immediately, no time to count the seconds. Howie flung himself onto the ground and sprawled face down on the rocky grass, trying to make himself a small target.

The lightning flashed again and again with great percussive explosions of sound. Every muscle in Howie's body tensed as he readied himself for instant annihilation. He wondered if there would be time to know he was dead. There would be an immense sizzle, he imagined. Then nothing.

Being part of nature was wonderful on a sunny afternoon, but not so lovely now.

With each thunderbolt, Howie was certain he was barbecue. But then, unexpectedly, the storm cell passed. He sat up cautiously listening to the sky. The wind had died and, for the moment, it appeared safe to continue on the trail. But he knew this could change in an instant.

Howie got to his feet and set off at a jog. His backpack hadn't grown any lighter and it jumped up and down uncomfortably on his shoulders as he ran. He kept going at a quick pace for more than an hour, hoping to outrun the next installment of cosmic terror.

The first raindrops began pelting down at close to 8:00 and there was still no sign of the Angel Creek campground. A new deep growl of thunder shook the air. The trail took a dive, descending below tree line into a dense forest. The rain was coming louder now, plipping and dripping through the high canopy of branches overhead. The sky once again flashed without warning. A great shock of thunder nearly threw him off his feet.

He crouched fearfully until the lightning appeared to move off to the south. *One, two, three, four, five, six, seven, eight* . . . twelve seconds later there was a more distant *BOOM!*

He found his rain poncho in his pack, slipped it over his head, and continued jogging. Night was coming on fast and the trail was getting harder to see. The rain fell in bursts. The branches creaked dangerously overhead, something more to worry about.

Suddenly the rain became a deluge, like some angry god had turned on a faucet. Just as Howie was thinking his best option was simply to crouch in his poncho by the base of a tree and stay put, the trail turned a corner and came to a small grassy meadow where there was an established fire pit. The creek nearby wasn't more than a foot wide, but it was deep, gurgling on its way down the mountain. Howie was at Angel Creek.

He hurried to get his tent out of the pack and set up before everything was soaking wet. The tent was new and tricky. This was the second time he had set it up, but it was still a challenge. There were poles that needed to be extended and put into the right grommets. The rain fly was particularly difficult to understand, how it was attached to the frame. If this were an IQ test, Howie figured he'd fail it.

The tent billowed and blew as he worked to get everything in its proper place. He didn't bother with pounding the stakes into the ground. He figured his own body weight would keep him from blowing away. As soon as he had the rain flap attached, he tossed his pack inside and zipped the door closed. He was walking a few feet off with the intention of a final pee when a flash of lightning lit the meadow with intense clarity.

Howie cried out in astonishment.

In the flash of light, he saw a figure, an old man walking into the clearing. He was ragged and barefoot and bare chested, dressed in filthy trousers and no shirt. He had long white hair that was slick from the rain, plastered close to his head.

The lightning flashed again, a jagged bolt that seemed to burst upward from the summit of Dawson Peak. The old man drifted closer, a ghostly silhouette with the mountain lit behind him in a corona of fire.

Howie had never seen such a ferocious show of nature. He was beyond wet. He was stunned. And the old man kept walking closer. Howie wasn't sure whether to offer help or run for his life.

He decided to offer help, but be prepared to run.

"Hello!" he called cautiously. "Are you . . . lost?"

The old man didn't seem entirely real. There was no color to his face. With his long wet hair, he looked like an Old Testament prophet.

He raised a hand.

"Greetings!" he said. "Are you an Earthling?"

Howie couldn't think of a decent reply.

Chapter Two

The rain fell steadily from the cold black sky as Howie and the old man regarded one another.

"I say, dear fellow, were you able to get a photograph?" the man asked. For a ragged wraith—more a hallucination than a human being—he was remarkably polite. He spoke with an upper class British accent Howie associated with the BBC.

"A photograph?"

"Of the ship. You saw the ship, didn't you? In that intense burst of light?"

"The, er—"

"The flying saucer. You saw it, I hope? The one I came on."

"Well, no."

"But you couldn't miss it! Ye gods, it was the size of a football stadium! Impossible to miss, I should say. Shaped more like a giant hot dog than a saucer, actually."

"No, there was no giant hot dog in the sky," Howie told him firmly.

"But there was! How else could I have gotten here?"

That was a question Howie was unable to answer. The old man's appearance at Angel Creek Campground was inexplicable.

He didn't look good. He was shivering spasmodically. He was a small, frail person and he didn't appear dangerous. But Howie kept his distance anyway, not taking any chances.

"I escaped, you see," the man explained.

"Aha!" said Howie.

"No, please hear me out. The porthole opened and I ran down the gangplank. Princess Zora helped me get away. What a beautiful girl!

Blue eyes, black hair like a raven, a complexion smooth as marble. A shame she wasn't real!"

Howie sighed.

"You see, they only take human form to make us feel more comfortable. What they *really* look like, I can't say. I suspect they don't have bodies at all. Ye gods, the things I've seen! Alpha Centauri! Are you sure you didn't get a photograph of the spacecraft? No one will believe us otherwise!"

Howie shook his head.

"But you saw the burst of light?"

"There was lightning . . ."

"That wasn't lightning, that was *them*!" the old man exclaimed. "That was the ship arriving! Ye gods, man, you didn't think that was *lightning*, did you?"

"Actually—"

"No, no, that was us emerging from the wormhole! We had to go backward in time to get here! You see, that's the secret! Time has no specific direction!"

The old man was getting more and more excited. "You see, Einstein only got it partly right! Spacetime not only bends, you can go backward or forward in it, either way! It's all so simple!"

This was becoming a problem. Howie had no idea what he was going to do with a half-naked lunatic who had appeared out of nowhere at his high mountain campground. At least, the rain had slackened but it was still wet and cold.

"How long have you, er, been wandering?" he asked.

The old man threw back his head with a laugh. "Oh, ho-ho! All who wander are not lost, my lad! You've heard that saying, have you? No, no, I must tell you about the planet Klizmor and the marvels I've seen!"

15

"What we should do," Howie said, "is think about getting you warm and dry."

But the spaceman wasn't having it. "We've got to get to the Institute!" he cried. "You see, I know everything now! Wait 'til I tell them! It's all in my head! Don't you see? This will be the greatest breakthrough in physics since Newton!"

The old man was so excited he didn't seem to understand the predicament they were in.

"That's wonderful," Howie agreed, in the voice he used with small children. "But here's the situation. We're at 12,000 feet on a mountain without cell phone service, miles from help. And once the storm clears out, the temperature will drop down below freezing."

"We're in Nepal?"

"No, New Mexico."

"New Mexico!" The spaceman laughed extravagantly, even more wildly than before. "Of course, New Mexico! I should have guessed. They come here all the time! It reminds them of home, you see. Klizmor has high deserts just like New Mexico. No water, unfortunately. Ever since they lost their atmosphere, they've had to make their water telepathically. Not hard, really, once you know the trick."

"Listen, I have a one-person tent," Howie said, ruthlessly. "And a one-man sleeping bag. That's it. So I hope you have some camping gear nearby. Because you're going to need it."

"Camping?" The old man seemed baffled. "No, they don't camp on Klizmor. For holidays, they transport themselves to Zlaphzix—that's the largest of their seven moons."

Howie was losing patience. It had been a long day, he was wet, he was cold, and meeting a lunatic was the last straw. Meanwhile, crazy or not, his new acquaintance was going to die of exposure if Howie didn't do something. There would be no way to get him down the mountain until daybreak, and even then, it was going to be a problem. No shirt, no shoes, shivering, raving mad, it was going to be a serious challenge to get this goofball to safety.

Howie wasn't happy. A big part of him simply wanted to turn his back on the whole situation. It wasn't fair, that in all these tens of thousands of acres of wilderness he should have come across a lunatic while off trekking trying to forget Claire. It was a responsibility he didn't want.

But what could he do?

"We're going to have to spend the night up here," Howie explained. "Do you understand?"

"Can't we simply teleport ourselves back to the Institute?"

Howie shook his head. "No, we can't teleport ourselves to the institute," he said grouchily. It was the second time the spaceman had mentioned the institute, and Howie was getting the picture. "Institution, I believe, is what you mean."

"No, no, the Institute for Advanced Study! Princeton! Do you know it?"

Howie did know it, as a matter of fact. He had done his master's degree at Princeton and was theoretically getting his doctorate there as well. The Institute for Advanced Study had no formal connection to the university. Still, it was enough of a connection for Howie to give the spaceman a closer look. In fact, he seemed somehow familiar. If you dried him up and put him in decent clothes, he was the sort of dreamy intellectual you could imagine floating around Firestone Library with a distracted look on his face.

"Look," he said, coming to a decision. "I'm going to give you some of my dry clothes to wear. They're going to be large on you, but at least you'll be warm. You can sleep in the tent."

"How very kind!" the old man said.

Howie shook his head. He didn't feel even slightly kind, but he couldn't see any other option. He couldn't let the old man freeze.

He unzipped the tent, got out what he needed for himself, and let the old man crawl inside. He gave the fellow his spare shirt and sweater and retreated back into the cold and wet.

"Damn!" he said, feeling very sorry for himself.

Howie took his pack and flashlight and arranged himself against the trunk of a tree beneath his rain poncho, dressed in every piece of warm clothing he hadn't given away.

This was no longer the camping trip of his dreams. But at least the rain had stopped, the sky was clearing, and the storm seemed to have passed.

Overhead, a star twinkled through a break in the trees, laughing at him.

***

The night went on forever. Cold, wet, and miserable.

Howie was so exhausted, he managed to sleep for an hour or two propped up against the tree, dozing and waking, experimenting with different positions. He woke at one point to find a small furry rodent sniffing his hand.

"Get lost!" he told the creature.

When morning finally came, he was so stiff he could barely unbend his body and stand. The sky was clear overhead, cloudless and blue. Except for the dripping branches, there was no sign of last night's storm. But it was cold at 12,000 feet, bone chilling. Howie considered making a fire, but this would take some doing as everything was wet. He could use his knife to shave kindling from one of the dead branches on the forest floor. But he decided to put this off until he figured out a plan for the day.

Somehow, he had to get his spaceman (as Howie had begun to think of him) down the mountain. But it wasn't going to be easy with only a single pair of shoes between the two of them.

There was only one way to do it. He would give the spaceman his boots. This would leave Howie barefoot, but he thought he could manage. He would make the descent wearing the two pairs of thick hiking socks he had brought along, using them as slippers. It wouldn't be fun, but there was no other option.

They would make the descent slowly, that's all. Take plenty of rests. With luck, they might run into some other campers who could help. With more luck still, there was already a search party out looking for the fellow. Surely someone must know he was missing.

Howie unzipped the front of the tent intending to explain his plan. But from the first glance, he knew there was no way he was going to get the old man down the mountain today. The spaceman was lying on his side breathing convulsively in loud gasps, in much worse shape than when Howie had left him the night before. He had part of the sleeping bag covering his feet but had thrown the rest off. He was burning with fever.

"How are you feeling?" Howie asked hopefully, poking his head inside the zippered door. A ridiculous question since the answer was obvious.

The old man was too weak to answer. Howie saw he would need to climb down the mountain by himself and get help. At least that would solve the problem of one pair of shoes. Once he got down, he would return with a stretcher and volunteers. A helicopter would be better. Either way, his spaceman needed to be evacuated as soon as possible.

The old man opened his eyes and tried to sit up. He collapsed back onto the sleeping bag with a sigh.

"Here's what we're going to do," Howie told him. "I'm going to climb down the mountain and get help. I'll leave you water and food, but you're going to be alone for a while. Do you understand?"

The fellow muttered incoherently. Howie brought his head closer.

"I'm going to have to leave you by yourself while I get help," he repeated. "We're a long way from anything, so it's going to take some time."

The old man's lips moved.

"What?" Howie asked.

"I was raving, wasn't I?" he said weakly. "They gave me something."

"It doesn't matter," Howie said, leaving the question for another time of who it was who gave him what.

"Psychedelics," the man said. "Maybe lysergic acid. But stronger. I'm sorry if I babbled."

"Don't worry about it. The main thing is to get you help. Will you be okay on your own for a few hours?"

"Wait," said the man. "Help me sit up. I feel terrible. But I need you to do something. Do you have paper? A pencil? Anything?

"You shouldn't try to move."

"No, I'll manage. Find me paper and something to write with," he said again.

Howie helped the old man sit up, propping the pillow behind him to give him some support. He had a pen and a small spiral notebook in one of the outer pockets of his backpack. But when he produced it, the man shook his head.

"Larger," he said. "One page will do, but it needs to be larger."

Howie had nothing else to write on except the paperback book of poetry he had brought along, *100 Poems from the Chinese*.

"That will do," said the old man when he produced it. He took the book and the pen and began scribbling on the blank page inside the front cover.

"I have to write this out while I still can remember. You're going to need to be quiet so I can think . . ."

For the next ten minutes Howie sat cross-legged in the doorway of the tent watching the old man bent over the book in his lap scribbling intently, muttering to himself as he worked.

"Finished yet?" Howie asked after a while.

"No! Be quiet! I need to think . . ."

At last the old man finished. He thrust the book at Howie and sank back onto the sleeping bag, exhausted by his effort.

"Take it!" he said weakly. "Give it to Dr. Henry Sachs at the Institute for Advanced Study. No one else. You'll need to deliver it in person. It's too important to put in the mail. Whatever you do, don't give it to Brandon Eckehart or anyone else at LANL. They'll be all over you, but don't give them the equation."

"LANL?" Howie repeated skeptically. "The Los Alamos National Lab?"

"Yes, yes . . . LANL. It's where I've been the last six months. Don't let anyone there have it. Don't even let them know it exists. They'll use it for war, that's all they care about. They're mad!"

Howie opened the book to see what the old man had written. It was a mathematical equation. A very long mathematical equation with sines and cosines and negative square roots and markings that looked to Howie like hieroglyphics. He had taken a required basic math course as an undergraduate at Dartmouth, but this left him in the dust.

"You're a physicist?"

"A*stro*physicist!" said the old man with a snort of irritation. "Ye, gods!" he muttered to himself.

"What's your name?"

"My name's not important. All you need to remember is Dr. Henry Sachs in Princeton. And watch out for Brandon Eckehart at LANL. Repeat that back to me!"

"Dr. Henry Sachs, Princeton," Howie repeated reluctantly. "And watch out for Eckehart at Los Alamos."

He was liking this less all the time. LANL had a dark history in New Mexico. The birthplace of the atomic bomb. A place of evil enchantment where you really didn't want to go.

The old man gave Howie a sly look. "It's the Theory of Everything!" he said with a strange glint in his eye. "I finally got it!"

He began coughing so hard Howie was afraid he was going to give up the ghost.

"Go!" he said when he could speak again. "But be careful. There are people who will kill for this . . ."

Howie knew what the Theory of Everything was. TOE, for short. Einstein had spent the second half of his life looking in vain for the illusive Theory of Everything, along with every ambitious physicist who had followed after him. One simple, elegant mathematical equation that would explain the entire universe. Good luck! No one had found it yet. And it was hard to believe this sick raving old man had discovered the answer.

Howie watched as the old man closed his eyes.

"Go!" he whispered more faintly than before.

Howie shook his head. He wished he could pretend the spaceman had never walked into his camp.

"Damn everything!" he thought in frustration. "Damn Claire! Damn Sir Richard Watson-Fowles! Damn this ridiculous old man and his crazy story!"

But he didn't have a choice, and that was the most damnable thing of all. He couldn't just let this frail old fellow die in the wilderness.

Chapter Three

Howie had come to Angel Creek Campground the long way, along the established trail. But there was no time for that now. The short way down the mountain was more direct. Straight down. Down steep hillsides of scree and through dense forests, with no trail as a guide.

The downward climb was dangerous and hard going. Howie often ran into natural barriers that forced him to turn back and find another route. Occasionally he found himself helplessly lost and had to climb upward again to get his bearings, losing precious time. He had a trail map on his phone, but it had no information about this area of the mountain. He figured it would take at least six or seven hours to get down to somewhere with cell phone service, but that was only a guess.

At least his pack was light. He had left most of his food and water with the old man, along with his tent and sleeping bag and cooking equipment. He had only enough salami, cheese, and crackers for lunch and a single liter of water that he had filtered into his bottle from the creek.

Climbing down the scree was the scary part, steep hillsides of loose rock that could slide at any moment. You had to be careful not to get moving too fast or you wouldn't be able to stop. Howie descended the steepest parts on his butt, crab-like, using both his hands and his feet to steady himself.

He passed through valleys where he had to cross fast-moving streams and then climb up the other side. He went up, down, and sideways. He didn't have a compass so he kept an eye on his wristwatch and the position of the sun, judging as best he could the direction he needed to maintain.

To amuse himself and scare away the bears, he sang old Lakota walking songs until his voice was hoarse. When he ran out of Indian songs, he turned to the Beatles. He stretched out "Hey, Jude" to half an hour. Bears didn't like to be surprised.

In the mid-afternoon, he came at last to an official Forest Service trail, which made hiking a great deal easier. He followed the trail for another two hours until he came to where he had left his car. It was a relief to see his dusty Subaru, thirteen years old, battered and bruised, but a loyal friend. He unlocked the door, threw his pack into the back seat, and collapsed into the driver's seat with a sigh.

He tried his phone but wasn't surprised to find there was still no service. Huge portions of New Mexico had no service. No anything. He needed to drive closer to town along the unpaved forest road before he got a signal. That took another twenty minutes. At last he pulled over onto an overlook with a view of San Geronimo in the valley below and saw the magic bars on the screen of his iPhone.

The 911 operator answered promptly. Howie described the bare bones of the situation, the disoriented hiker he had left at Angel Creek Campground who wasn't able to make his way down the mountain on his own. To keep things simple—and sane—he left out the flying saucer and the planet Klizmor. It seemed best to mention only an elderly hiker at a high elevation who needed to be rescued.

Howie's next call was to San Geronimo Search and Rescue. The head of the volunteer group, Tim Scarborough, agreed to meet Howie at the foot of the Dawson Peak trail. Unfortunately, it was already late afternoon and there wouldn't be much daylight left by the time the team was assembled and the rescue could get underway.

Howie drove back to the trailhead and waited. A Sheriff's deputy arrived first, then Tim Scarborough a few minutes later. Before long, there was a small army of cars and vans parked precariously on the side of the forest road. The vans were full of Search and Rescue volunteers, as well as ropes and radios and other specialized equipment. Two rescue dogs were along for the operation, each with a special doggie vest that had SAN GERONIMO SEARCH & RESCUE written on the side.

Howie knew Tim from a winter rescue a few years back on San Geronimo Peak—an unwise skier who had ducked under a boundary rope to get fresh tracks and got lost instead. Tim had a large fold-out Forest Service map of Dawson Peak spread out over the hood of his car which he and Howie examined together, discussing the fastest route to Angel Creek. The big question was whether to attempt the rescue tonight or wait until morning.

"You think your guy will make it until then?" Tim asked.

"I don't know. This morning he could barely sit up. He's exhausted and disoriented, probably suffering from hypothermia."

"We'll go tonight, then. There's going to be a three-quarter moon, no cloud cover, and everybody in my team has a good headlamp and extra batteries."

Now that Howie had set the rescue in motion, he found himself superfluous. Tim said he could join the operation if he liked and climb back up the mountain with them, though frankly he didn't recommend it. Howie was tired, he wasn't provisioned properly, and he would only be in the way.

"Can you bring down my tent and stuff?" he asked Tim. "I left a few things up there with the spaceman."

"Spaceman?"

Howie hadn't meant to say that. "He was a little spacey," he said, backtracking.

Howie watched as the rescue team assembled at the foot of the trail, got their equipment organized, and began the climb back up the mountain. The team consisted of four men and two women and they operated with military precision. It was a volunteer organization, but they were all gung-ho and in terrific shape. Howie had once described Search and Rescue to Claire as the left-wing version of a militia. Instead of shooting off guns, they did yoga. But it was an elite group. They practiced their skills nearly every weekend, each one of them was a certified EMT, and they took the job of saving lives seriously.

Howie was happy to wait at the bottom of the trail. He'd had more than enough hiking for the day, and he knew the group would be able to get to the campground more quickly without him.

The long summer twilight deepened into night. There was now an ambulance waiting at the bottom of the trail parked alongside the Sheriff's car, but it would be at least several hours before the rescue team reached the campground and radioed with news. Howie knew the deputy, Ed Gomez, who had been in the Sheriff's Department for a long time.

"Look, I think I'll mosey on home, Ed," he told the deputy. "To tell the truth, I'm beat. But I'm concerned about the old guy. Is it all right if I phone you later for news?"

"Go home, Moon Deer. You look like something the cat dragged in. I'll call you," he promised, "as soon as they reach him."

Howie made sure Ed had his cell number. Then he drove off home.

He was so exhausted he didn't bother with dinner. He took a quick shower, washed off three days of dirt, then crawled up the ladder into his loft and fell into bed.

He was asleep so fast he didn't even have time to miss Claire, who had once been in this bed beside him.

***

Howie slept later than he had intended, to nearly ten o'clock the following morning. He got out of bed quickly, sensing that life was rushing ahead without him and he needed to catch up.

He checked his phone messages while his coffee was dripping into the glass carafe. There was nothing from Ed Gomez, no word on the spaceman. But there were two new texts from Claire.

The first read: *Howie, please answer and let me know how you are. I'm so worried about you! Please tell me you're all right. You'll always be my best friend!*

She had put a little smiley face after friend. Howie scowled at the screen.

The second message: *I'm in Bonn waiting to do a concert tonight. The Elgar. I have an idea. Why don't you come to London in August. I'll have the use of a house in Chelsea where we can stay and talk things over. I feel there's so much unfinished business between us. And Howie, I miss you so much! I'm so confused I can't stand it. Please answer. I'm going crazy not hearing from you!*

A small growl of exasperation escaped Howie's lips. Chelsea was a particularly expensive part of London and he sensed the house in question belonged to Sir Richard. If Claire missed him so much, what was she doing with this creep three times her age?

Honestly, he didn't want to think about it. Instead he punched in the number for Deputy Ed Gomez who answered on the first ring.

"I didn't want to wake you, Moon Deer," the deputy said. "The rescue team got to the campground a few hours ago. They found your tent, but there was no one there."

Howie was stunned. "He was gone?"

"It was empty. Nobody."

"I hope they're looking nearby. I don't think he could have gone far, considering the shape he was in. He was out of his mind a bit so he may have wandered."

"They've spread out and they're still searching. But they can't find him. They've looked all over. To tell the truth, Moon Deer, some of them have started to wonder . . ."

"Wonder what?" Howie asked.

"Well, you were the only one who saw this supposed guy. Up there by yourself at 12,000 feet . . . you can imagine what they're saying."

"Ed, that *supposed* guy was real! I put him in my tent, I left him with food and water, I nearly killed myself getting down the mountain to get help!"

"Moon Deer, calm down. I believe you. So does Tim. But whoever this guy was, he's gone."

Howie sighed with frustration. He had become invested in the polite little fellow with his British accent. It was worrisome that he had wandered off. But he had done his best to help him. And sometimes with crazy people—as with ex-girlfriends—you just had to let them go.

He hung up and found his backpack with the book of Chinese poetry, just to make sure he hadn't dreamed the episode. Sure enough, the long mathematical equation was still there, written out on the blank page inside the cover. Howie certainly hadn't written it himself. He didn't even understand ninety percent of the symbols.

He snapped the book shut, finished his coffee, and stood up from the table with sudden resolve. It was time to do some detecting.

Before leaving home, he sent Claire a reluctant reply, very brief, knowing it would be cruel to leave her hanging with nothing.

"I'm sorry you're feeling bad but I'm feeling worse," he wrote. *"I'll write in a few days when I've had time to digest."*

He couldn't help adding: *Good luck tonight with the Elgar.*

It was awful how much he still loved her.

Chapter Four

Howie drove into town with Jerry Garcia and David Grisman playing loudly on the stereo, *The Pizza Tapes.*

Jerry Garcia had an awful voice and Howie wasn't sure why he liked this album so much. Maybe because it was authentic. Authenticity had become a rare quality in the modern world of spin and anxiety and trendy fashions.

Town was crowded with summer tourists in shorts and gaudy shirts meandering from store to store in search of junk to take back home. San Geronimo was a scenic place, nestled against the Sangre de Cristo mountains in a high desert valley. Tourism had become the mainstay of the economy, along with skiing in the winter, bringing prosperity as well as the usual ills and irritations. Traffic moved at a crawl and the parking situation was even worse. Luckily, Howie had an assigned parking spot at the rear of the Wilder & Associate office, an old adobe building in the historical district.

Jack Wilder, Howie's boss, was in Hawaii for ten days with his wife, Emma. But it wasn't a vacation. Their fifteen-year-old nephew, River, had been killed in a surfing accident on the North Shore of Oahu, drowned in a huge wave when his head slammed down on the board. Jack and Emma were there for the funeral and to comfort River's anguished parents. The agency had no ongoing cases at the moment and Jack had decided they could afford to close shop for two weeks.

It was Friday and Howie hadn't planned to return to the office until Monday, but his visitor from the planet Klizmor had changed that.

"I wasn't expecting you," said Ruth as he walked in the back door. Ruth was the new part-time secretary Jack had hired, saying the agency was doing well and they could afford it. She was a crisp old lady with a hard-ass attitude and Howie wasn't certain that she approved of him.

"My camping trip got cut short," he told her. "I had a small adventure."

She glanced up from her computer screen. "I heard Search and Rescue got sent out last night after some lost hiker on Dawson Peak."

"He wasn't a hiker. He was a lunatic who claimed he'd been abducted by a flying saucer. You'll be glad to know that aliens regard New Mexico as a flying saucer-friendly state, which is why they keep returning here."

"No kidding?" said Ruth, giving him a hard look.

Ruth Sisak was in her sixties, a gruff, no-nonsense ex-New Yorker with short gray hair. She was a small woman, seemingly frail, but intimidating nevertheless. She reminded Howie of a strict third grade teacher he'd had long ago at Rosebud, the reservation where he had grown up. You never forget teachers like that. They haunt you forever.

As an ex-cop, Jack was big on paperwork and Ruth had been using the time the agency was closed to transfer their old files into a digital format.

"How are things?" he asked.

"We've had a few queries. The owner of the Hunter Gatherer wants to hire you to find out if his wife is embezzling cash from the restaurant. Also, a woman phoned who's trying to find her father. A Dr. Mia Bloom. She wants you to call her back as soon as you can. I told both of them that you and Jack were out of town until next week. I didn't say you were camping and Jack was in Hawaii. I didn't want them to think you're lazy bums and take their business elsewhere."

"There is no elsewhere," Howie reminded her. "Not in San Geronimo, at least. When it comes to private detecting, we're it."

"Hmph!" Ruth huffed dismissively. "No competition!"

"That's true. But we're pretty good. We almost always get our man. Or woman. Except for the times we don't."

Howie glanced at the message slips. The Hunter Gatherer was the new paleo diet restaurant in town, a place he avoided. He didn't even want to imagine cave man *haute cuisine.* As for Dr. Mia Bloom, he had no idea who she was or why she should be missing her father.

For the last several years, the agency had been receiving more requests for investigations than they could accommodate. With a few high profile cases behind them, they had been picking up business far beyond San Geronimo and Howie suspected they would give these two queries a polite refusal.

Howie left Ruth in the reception area and went to his own office at the front of the building. Wilder & Associate occupied an historic one-story adobe that was two hundred years old. It was quaint: thick adobe walls, kiva fireplaces, uneven floors, and a lattice work of vigas and latillas overhead. It was also freezing cold in the winter and the plumbing didn't always work, but that was the price you paid for quaintness. Howie had the smaller front room and Jack had the big comfortable office in the rear.

Howie sat at his desk and turned on his desktop Mac thinking he would google UFO sightings in New Mexico. His fingers lingered momentarily on the keyboard, but instead of flying saucers he gave into a masochistic urge and typed in Sir Richard Watson-Fowles.

The Wikipedia photo at the top of the page showed a patrician white-haired man in his sixties with a sharp, hawk-like face and piercing eyes. In the picture he wore a white turtleneck sweater and stood on an orchestra podium with a baton in hand. His arms were raised as though he was about to flap his wings and fly away. There was an ecstatic expression on his face like he had just heard the mermaids singing, each to each, and he could barely stand the beauty of their song.

"Asshole!" Howie murmured.

"Did you say something?" Ruth called from the next room.

"Achoo," he called back. "Just a sneeze."

Sir Richard was Scottish, born in Edinburgh. His musical genius had been recognized early when at the age of nine he performed Beethoven's Third Piano Concerto for an astonished audience. At the age of twenty-two he had been hired to conduct the Royal Scottish Orchestra, the youngest person ever to hold this post.

One accolade followed another. As time passed, Sir Richard conducted all the great orchestras of the world. London, Berlin, New York, Los Angeles, Boston, Philadelphia, and more. He was known for championing the careers of young performers—young women in particular—whom he plucked from obscurity and turned into stars. He had been married four times.

Howie scowled furiously. He was scrolling down the page to the impressive list of discography when Ruth knocked on his door. This was a formality since in fact his door was open.

"There's a chick here who wants to see you."

"A chick?" Ruth liked to use slang from fifty years ago, believing she was very up to date. "Tell her Jack will be back next week."

Ruth rolled her eyes.

"Believe it or not, she's asking to see *you*. It's the chick who called the other day. Dr. Mia Bloom."

"The one who's looking for her father?"

"I guess. I should mention she's young and good-looking. Except she's dressed like someone who woke up this morning in a coffin in Transylvania."

"A vampire, you're saying?"

"Let's just say if she leans forward to give you a hug, don't offer your neck."

Howie sighed. If it hadn't been for the spaceman, he would still be up on Dawson Peak having profound thoughts on life.

"Well, I guess you'd better show her in."

* * *

"*You're* Howard Moon Deer?" said the woman as she entered Howie's office.

She said it with mild disbelief, as though a large young Indian with a moony face and long black hair tied in a ponytail down his back couldn't possibly be a private eye. He stood to shake her offered hand.

"Mia Bloom," she told him. "Dr. Bloom, actually. Caltech."

Howie had the same disbelief, only not so mild. She didn't look like any kind of doctor. For one, she looked about sixteen years old, delicately built, very pretty. A Goth Girl beauty. If there was such a thing.

She wore a tiny black cocktail dress, very summery, that showed a good deal of leg and arm. There was a single small gold ring in her left nostril. Her hair was jet black, cut in a short page-boy style with bangs, a straight line across her forehead. Her lips were red and her eyes a startling blue. Her fingernails were the same red as her lips and her complexion was smooth and pale.

It was the blue of her eyes, accented by the blackness of her hair, that unsettled him even more than her skimpy outfit. Her eyes were almost violet, a color he had seen before only at 30,000 feet from the window of an airplane. They had an intensity and depth that was almost other worldly.

"If you've finished inspecting me, do you think I might sit down?" she asked.

"Yes, of course," he said quickly. He moved the chair by his desk so she could sit more easily. It was an awkward gesture and not necessary. Frankly, she made him nervous.

Her smile was subtle and confident. She understood her effect on men. When she crossed her legs, her teensy dress rose, and Howie noticed a tattoo on her left thigh. It was a butterfly, beautifully done, intricately colored. The way she was sitting, he could only see the lower half of the butterfly. The upper half disappeared under the dress higher up on her thigh where his eye wanted to follow.

"Thailand," she said.

"I'm sorry?" He thought she had said Thigh-Land.

"Bangkok. That's where the tattoo comes from. Do you like butterflies, Mr. Moon Deer?"

"Well . . . who doesn't like butterflies?" he managed. He conquered the blush that was rising to his face and added, "So, Dr. Bloom, what can I do for you?"

"I left a message. But you didn't get back to me."

"I've been away from the office," he told her, glad to be on safer ground. "My partner, Jack Wilder, won't be back until the middle of next week. He's the person you should talk with if you have an investigation you'd like us to undertake. But I'd be happy to listen and give you any advice I can."

"No, it's you I want." Her violet eyes focused on him intently, like a shopper in a market deciding on what she's going to cook for dinner. "I want you to find my father."

"Your father is missing?"

"Yes. He's famous, of course, which makes it all more complicated."

"I see," said Howie, who didn't see at all. "If you don't mind me asking, what's he famous for?"

She raised a jet black eyebrow. "You don't know?"

"Well, no. How could I?"

"But you've met him. Grisha Bloom, the astrophysicist. He won the Nobel Prize in 1994 for the discovery of the Blue Moon quark."

"Blue Moon quark?"

"Do you know what a quark is?"

"Not really. I've known a quack or two. But never a quark."

She didn't laugh. Her delicately crossed left leg swung up and down meditatively, as though she were considering whether to give him a good kick or try an explanation. She wore sandals and her toenails, he noticed, were painted the same red color as her lips and fingernails.

"Quarks are subatomic particles, what we believe to be the most basic building blocks of the universe. Until my father, quantum physicists believed there were only six kinds of quarks. Charmed, Strange, Up, Down, Top, and Bottom. But then Daddy found a seventh quark. He saw it for only a billionth of a second in the CERN particle accelerator in Switzerland. He called it the Blue Moon quark because it pops into existence once in a Blue Moon, so to speak. But it's the key to understanding dark energy, which up to now has been the great mystery of Twenty-First century science."

"Dark energy!" Howie grinned. "Sounds like my boss, Jack, when he's in a bad mood!"

She ignored him.

"The Blue Moon quark is the point of intersection between our universe and the next dimension," she went on. "If Daddy's right, it's our door into the multiverse."

"I see," he said, trying to look halfway comprehending.

"Some physicists say there are nine universes, others eleven. But Daddy believes the number of universes is unlimited. The omniverse he calls it. I hope you see the practical applications of all this, Mr. Moon Deer?"

"Well, uh . . . no."

"If you find the doorway, you can travel from one universe to another and then back again, and end up in a different place from where you started. In theory at least, you could travel to the stars."

"Ah!" said Howie. Theoretical physics of this sort was way beyond him. But he was starting to have a notion about the human side of this conversation.

"Your father is the guy I met wandering around Dawson Peak on Wednesday night?"

"Didn't you know that?"

"He never told me his name."

"But surely Daddy told you what he was doing up there?"

Howie hesitated. He decided, for the time being, not to mention the planet Klizmor or UFOs shaped like giant hot dogs. Or the equation Daddy had written in his book.

"I'm afraid he wasn't entirely coherent," Howie told her. "My only thought was to get help. I got him into my tent, gave him dry clothes and food and water, then I climbed down the mountain to call Search and Rescue. We were up high in a very remote place, so this took a while. When the rescue team finally got back to where I had left your father, he was gone."

"And they still haven't found him?"

"As far as I know, they're still looking. But let me make a phone call and I'll get an update."

Howie picked up his phone and tried Ed Gomez but the Sheriff's deputy didn't answer. Probably he was off duty, sleeping. Next, Howie tried Dana Scarborough, the wife of the head of Search and Rescue, where he was able to get some new information.

"I'm sorry, they haven't found your father yet, they're still looking," Howie said to Dr. Bloom when he hung up. "They're planning to spend the night on the mountain and they'll keep searching tomorrow. They'll be able to get some air support tomorrow, a helicopter, which will help."

"Another night!"

Howie saw that she was tired and upset. Looking more closely, he also realized she was older than she had first appeared. Thirty, perhaps. It was her elfin appearance that made her look like a teenager.

There was something bothering him and it took Howie a moment to pin it down. "Do you mind if I ask you a question?" he said. "How did you know that was me up there with your father? It hasn't been in the news yet."

"Well, I've been looking for him for several days now. That's why I came by to see if you could help me. When I didn't hear back, I called the State Police to see if he'd been in an accident. They told me that you'd found someone matching his description wandering in the woods."

"Really? Who did you talk to?"

"I don't remember his name but I think he was the person in charge. He was very helpful. From his description, I was sure it had to be Daddy."

"I see," said Howie. Something about this didn't sound right but he let it go. "Your father's British, I presumed from his accent. He mentioned working at the Institute for Advanced Study in Princeton. Can you tell me why he's in New Mexico?"

"He gets more British by the year, I'm afraid," she said with a smile. "It's bred in the bone, as they say. He was at Cambridge University working with Stephen Hawking until they had a bit of a falling out over the omniverse. Five years ago he went to Princeton to work independently. He's been in New Mexico for the past six months as an advisor at Los Alamos. He's supposed to return to Princeton in mid-August."

"And you, Dr. Bloom, where do you live?"

"Los Angeles. As I mentioned, I'm an astrophysicist at Caltech. I flew to New Mexico last week after my father called me. He said he was worried about something and needed to discuss it with me."

Howie might have been surprised to find a Goth Girl with a butterfly tattoo at Caltech, except he was starting to suspect that theoretical physicists tended toward eccentricity. Like poets, the great ones also tended to be young. Isaac Newton was 23 when he came up with his world-changing theory of gravity. Einstein was 26 when he dreamed up $E = mc^2$.

"Did your father say what he was worried about?"

"He said he couldn't talk about it on the phone. Then when I got here, I couldn't reach him. I left voice messages on his phone, but he didn't get back to me. He's rented a house up in the mountains. It's an hour from Las Alamos but he likes the peace and quiet."

"Did you try him at LANL?"

"Of course. That was the first place I tried. But they gave me the run-around. Once when I called, they said he was in a meeting. Another time I was told he hadn't come in that day. I left messages but he couldn't have received them. Otherwise I'm sure he would have called me back. It's really very mystifying."

"Are you close with your father?"

She hesitated. "Yes and no. We haven't seen each other for a few years. My mother died when I was young and we were very close when I was growing up. But we've drifted apart in recent years. Mostly due to geography, living in different places."

"Do you know what your father was doing at Los Alamos?"

"You're kidding! Everything there is secret. Those people are tighter than clams!"

Howie was running out of questions. "And what's your field, Dr. Bloom?"

"I'm working on Heisenberg's Uncertainty Principle as it's applied to M-Theory. Do you know anything about M-Theory, Mr. Moon Deer?"

She did her best to explain her work. Unfortunately, it was like hearing Greek spoken backwards. He didn't get it at all.

He had heard of these things, of course, the names at least. String Theory, Superstring Theory, and now M-Theory, the latest. For Howie, the notion of multiple universes and multiple dimensions was beyond bizarre. Yet these concepts were taken seriously by some of the most brilliant minds on the planet.

It was said that until Einstein, physics was something any reasonably educated person could understand. But after Einstein, you needed an advanced degree in mathematics even to get a foot in the door. Or perhaps, be a mystic.

Dr. Bloom stopped talking when she saw the lack of comprehension on his face. She laughed and her blue eyes sparkled.

"I guess my ignorance is obvious," he admitted. "I'm good in the kitchen and I can even be funny at times. But astrophysics, forget it."

Her smile saddened. "Will you find my father? Can you find out what happened to him? I can pay you whatever you want."

"Let's wait a few days, Dr. Bloom. Hopefully, Search and Rescue will find your father alive on the mountain and then there won't be any mystery to solve."

"Alright. I'll be at the La Fonda Hotel in Santa Fe until Sunday night. I need to fly back to L.A. for work on Monday. I live in Pasadena. Let me give you all my numbers and email . . ."

Mia Bloom spent a few moments writing down her information then she left with a shake of his hand and instructions to call her night or day if there was any news of her father.

It wasn't until after she was gone, sitting alone at his desk, that the question about how she had known that he was the camper on Dawson

Peak who had helped her father resurfaced in his mind. It was the Sheriff's Department who had responded to his 911 call, not the New Mexico State Police, and it was hard to imagine how they had been able to give Mia Bloom such detailed information about her father. It was a small matter, perhaps, but it bothered him.

Howie walked out to the reception area.

"When did Dr. Bloom leave her message about wanting to hire me?" he asked Ruth.

Ruth consulted her calendar. She was meticulous about paperwork, which was why Jack had hired her.

"Thursday morning," she told him. "Just after I got here at nine o'clock."

This gave Howie serious pause. Thursday morning at nine o'clock he had just left Grisha Bloom in his tent at Angel Creek campground, saying he would return as soon as possible. It was at least seven hours later before he had reached his car and made his first call to 911 and Search and Rescue.

He went through the sequence of Mia's story in his mind. She flew to New Mexico because her father was bothered about something he didn't want to talk about on the phone. But when she got here, she couldn't find him at LANL, so she came to Wilder & Associate for help. Later she called the State Police to discover Howie had found someone matching Daddy's description wandering up in the mountains.

It could be, sure.

But it was off somehow.

Chapter Five

Howie sat lost in thought for some time after Mia Bloom left the office.

Eventually, he took his copy of *100 Poems from the Chinese* from his day bag and opened the book to the long mathematical equation.

Howie wished he were smarter. He knew he wasn't dumb. He was smart enough, for example, to understand that the scholarships he'd won to pricey schools like Dartmouth and Princeton hadn't been entirely due to his brilliance, but because he was a disadvantaged minority *du jour,* a Native American. He had benefitted from the white man's well-deserved guilt. However, once he was at these schools, he had worked hard and done well.

But the equation in the book was beyond him. He found it hard even to imagine multiverses and quarks—Charmed quarks, Strange quarks, and now a Blue Moon quark. Apparently, these subatomic abstractions actually did exist. You could shoot them at each other at the CERN particle accelerator in Switzerland and record their collisions. Despite the theoretical nature of nuclear physics, atomic bombs—dreamed into existence only a few miles away from where he was seated—actually exploded. You only had to ask the people of Hiroshima and Nagasaki.

At five o'clock, Ruth came by his office to say she was leaving for the weekend and would see him on Monday. He nodded distractedly at her from far, far away.

There finally came a time when his thoughts were flying in so many different directions that he stood up abruptly, deciding he needed some air. He locked the office behind him and walked outside into Calle Dos Flores, the narrow street that fronted the agency building.

It was a languid late afternoon, a hint of coolness in the air after the heat of the day. The summer streets were busy with pedestrians and cars, people moving slowly on the sidewalks, searching restaurant menus for dinner, drinks, and prices. There was a scent in the air of meat barbecuing from the Tex-Mex restaurant at the far side of the Plaza.

Howie wandered with the crowd, not certain where he was going, glad not to run into anyone he knew. He wasn't hungry and it was too early to drink.

At the corner of Dos Flores where the street came out into the Plaza, he passed a store that had a poster in the window advertising what was billed as a "UFO Festival" two weekends from now on July 27th and 28th. For Howie, the subject of flying saucers didn't come up often and it seemed odd to him that they now seemed to be popping up in his life from every direction.

Beam me up, Scottie!

Well, why not? Life on Earth was becoming less pleasant by the year and an escape into outer space had an appeal. He had read recently that the super-rich were already lining up to buy expensive tickets on private rocket ships that were only just being built.

Howie stopped to read the poster. The two-day UFO Festival promised prominent speakers including a retired state senator and "a World-Famous Ufologist." On Saturday night there would be a banquet with dancing afterward to a group that called itself the Space Cadets. The whole thing was presented half in fun, but also with great seriousness. The group organizing the weekend called itself the Little Green Man Society. Only $175 per person to attend.

Howie wandered into the Plaza and found a bench where he could sit and watch the passing scene. Mom and Dad in shorts and gaudy shirts with bored children trailing behind staring at their small screens as they walked, unwilling to be digitally disconnected even for a New Mexico sunset.

As Howie sat pondering the state of the universe, he became aware of an Indian sitting down on the far end of his bench.

He took a quick look hoping to fend off an encounter. The kinds of Indians who hung out in the town Plaza tended to be of the dysfunctional variety.

He looked away after a casual glance, did a double take, then turned back in surprise.

It wasn't just any Indian who had joined him on the bench. It was John Concha, the War Chief, one of the most important members of the Pueblo.

"How you doing, Lakota?" John asked.

The War Chief always called him Lakota. It was a taunt, but a friendly one. The San Geronimo Pueblo didn't much like outsiders, even Indians from other tribes, but Concha and Howie were friends of a sort. The War Chief's job was concerned mostly with traditional religious rituals that were kept secret. But he was also in charge of the Pueblo's security, overseeing the tribal police and keeping tourists from wandering into forbidden areas of the reservation.

"I'm good, John," Howie answered. "How about you?"

"Can't complain. Nice evening."

John Concha was a tall, powerful looking Indian in his late forties. He wore a loose cotton shirt and jeans with a traditional black apron around his waist. He was a vet, an Army helicopter pilot who had seen action in Afghanistan and Iraq, and had been elected War Chief upon his return to San Geronimo.

He wasn't the sort of person you would expect to find sitting in the Plaza.

"So what brings you to town, John?" Howie asked.

"Maybe to find you, Lakota."

"No kidding? And you knew you'd find me on a bench in the Plaza?"

"Hey, I'm psychic," he said with a straight face. Then he smiled. "Naw, I was walking up the street behind you just as you were coming out of your office door. I followed you here."

"Okay," said Howie. "I'm honored. But why?"

"I hear you were up on—" John said a name in Tiwa. It sounded like "Ko'a kee'a." But Howie wasn't sure. He didn't speak Tiwa, a language that was forbidden to be taught to outsiders.

"Dawson Peak," John continued. "That's not our name for it, of course. Dawson was an Army cartographer who passed through here in 1849 and he liked to put his name on things. I'm sure it never occurred to him that my people have been going up there for a thousand years."

"Really?" said Howie. "There were people here before Columbus discovered America?"

The War Chief didn't laugh. "You see my point, Lakota. What the White Man calls Dawson Peak is one of our most sacred places. Pueblo land extended there until 1914 when the folks in Washington decided to reduce our reservation by 94,000 acres. For the last two decades we've been fighting in the courts to get it back."

Howie nodded. He knew of the court battle but hadn't realized that Dawson Peak was part of the disputed land. In northern New Mexico, land disputes were common among both the Indian and Spanish populations due to a complicated history of broken treaties and old land grants. Today Dawson Peak was part of the Carson National Forest, which was another cause for unhappiness. Kit Carson wasn't a beloved figure among the Pueblo tribes.

"So what do you want to know?" Howie asked the War Chief.

"What do you think I want to know? I want to know what happened up there on Wednesday night."

"I was off camping, that's all. And I'm starting to wish I'd just stayed home!"

"Come on, Lakota. We got a court date coming up in September and this could help us. Part of our argument is that sacred Indian land is being misused by the National Forest."

"Well, okay, John. But I'm not sure my story will help you much."

He told it anyway, the saga of his trek up Dawson Peak. He left out only the reason for the trip—Claire—and the equation, which might (or might not) be the Theory of Everything.

The War Chief didn't laugh often, but he did laugh a little when Howie told how the spaceman—Grisha Bloom, he had a name now—said he had been abducted to the planet Klizmor in a flying saucer the size of a football field that was shaped like a giant hot dog.

"Man, these White Men sure are crazy!" John said with a shake of his head.

"You think they're crazier than we are?" Howie asked.

"Don't you?"

"John, I don't know. Before the White Man came, we spent most of our time fighting each other, one tribe against the other. That seems pretty crazy to me. If we had been united, we might have held them off for another fifty years. Maybe longer. Not forever, but long enough to make a better deal to protect our land."

"Maybe," the War Chief said doubtfully. "But what is, is. Will you come to Washington to testify if we need you?"

"Sure, I guess so. But I can't see how me running into a crazy astrophysicist in a thunderstorm is going to help your case."

"Well, I'll need to pass this tale on to our lawyers, but I think it might. White people running around in our sacred places telling crazy stories about flying saucers might be just what we need."

"Excuse me," a voice said from not far away. "Do you think the two of you could sit closer together for a photograph?"

Howie and John Concha looked up to see a large flabby woman with her smart phone smiling hopefully at them. Her skin was pale white, sunless, as though she rarely stepped outside. She wanted to take a picture of two Indians sitting on a bench in the San Geronimo Plaza. Without a word, the War Chief stood abruptly, turned his back on the woman, and stormed away.

Howie got up, too. He flashed an apologetic smile at the woman and followed after John. The woman appeared baffled. She didn't know what she had done wrong.

"Hey, she didn't mean any harm," Howie said, catching up with the War Chief. "You need to have a sense of humor about people like that."

"Do I, Lakota?" John Concha stopped long enough to give Howie an angry look. "No, I don't think so."

Chapter Six

Howie walked back down Calle Dos Flores toward the office, intending to turn on the alarm and make certain the windows and doors were closed up for the night.

As he approached the building, he was unhappy to find a homeless man slumped in the agency doorway. Howie knew the homeless had to sleep somewhere, but this was irritating nonetheless. In the last few years, there had been a noticeable increase of dysfunctional street people—men, women, sometimes entire families—drifting into San Geronimo, pushing shopping carts with their sad belongings, often accompanied by scruffy dogs.

The tourists walking up and down Calle Dos Flores in their vacation clothes gave the homeless man in the doorway a wide berth. They didn't look, they refused to acknowledge the disagreeable presence of poverty and despair. For Howie this was almost the worst part of the growing homeless crisis, the eyes that turned away.

There was a men's shelter now in San Geronimo, an old house that had been converted into a dormitory with county funds and donations. But it only accommodated twelve men each night and Howie hoped it wasn't full. He decided to wake the guy up—gently if possible—give him a few dollars and direct him to the shelter. If necessary, he supposed he would give him a ride. This was a human being, after all. You couldn't pretend otherwise.

"Hey!" he said softly, leaning over the sleeping figure. It was an old man with stringy white hair and as Howie leaned closer, he sensed this wasn't the usual sort of down-and-outer you saw begging for change outside the supermarkets. There was no smell of booze, no filthy sleeping bag, no dog.

The agency doorway was inset a few inches from the outside wall. The old man had arranged himself sideways in the doorway and was sleeping with his head partially turned toward the door.

"Hey, you can't sleep here, you gotta wake up," Howie said as politely as possible under the circumstances.

He hoped words alone would do the trick. But they didn't. He reached cautiously and shook the old man by the shoulder.

"I'm sorry, but you can't sleep here," he repeated, shaking the shoulder gently. "Hey, wake up . . ."

But the old fellow wasn't sleeping.

He fell limply out onto the street. Howie's shaking had dislodged him from the doorway.

He was dead.

Howie jumped back so abruptly that he tumbled into two French tourists. He stared at the dead man in astonishment.

It was the spaceman! Grisha Bloom, the famous astrophysicist who had already intruded on his life—and sanity!—far too much.

How he had gotten himself from Howie's tent on Dawson Peak to arrive dead on his doorstep in town thirty miles away was beyond Howie's brain power to compute.

* * *

Howie was shaken. He found his phone in his back pocket, but it nearly slipped through his fingers and he had to do some fancy juggling to keep it from dropping onto the pavement.

He fumbled to bring up the number pad, got his camera app instead, and finally, with further fumbling, managed to tap in 911.

Had he been thinking more clearly, he would have called Santo Ruben at the New Mexico State Police. Instead, the 911 dispatcher sent him a patrol car from the San Geronimo Police Department which took twenty minutes to get to him though the station was in fact less than five minutes away.

The local police force were poorly paid and weren't known for their brilliance. The patrol car arrived at last with a single officer inside. He parked in the middle of Calle Dos Flores with his roof lights flashing, blocking traffic, and sauntered toward Howie with a smirk of self-importance on his face.

"So, what's up?" he demanded.

Howie explained how he had discovered the dead man on his doorstep.

"Dead, huh?" the cop asked sagely. He was a young hispanic man, good looking, who seemed to think the world of himself.

"Look for yourself," Howie suggested.

The young cop bent over the corpse, put two fingers on his neck, felt for a pulse, then stood up slowly.

"He's dead."

"Exactly," said Howie. "Maybe you should call for backup."

"Are you trying to tell me how to do my job?"

"Not at all, Officer. I'm only trying to move this along."

"So what happened here? Did you assault this guy?"

"No, of course not."

"Then what are you doing here?"

"What am I doing here? This is the door to my office. I work here."

"You know, I'd better see some identification. Nice and easy, now. I want to see your hands at all times."

It wasn't going well. They had gotten off to a bad start. Howie knew it was his fault. He was exasperated, unhappy with the way life was buffeting him around, and he hadn't made an effort to show the proper respect. He was wondering how he could get things on the right track when a white van arrived at the bottom end of Calle Dos Flores, blocking off the street from that direction. With the patrol car on one end of the street and the van on the other, Howie was starting to feel like a fox in a trap.

A short middle-aged woman stepped out of the van and walked their way with a laminated ID held high in her right hand. Three very large men in identical gray suits, white shirts and ties, exited the rear of the van and followed behind her.

Feds of some kind, Howie decided. He wasn't sure if he had been spared from town arrest or if something worse was in store for him.

"I'll take over from here, Officer," the short woman said as she came closer. She wore glasses with tortoise shell frames and was dressed in a no-frills dark blue pant suit with a black handbag slung over one shoulder. She had an angry bulldog face. Her nose, eyes, and mouth seemed scrunched together toward the middle. It wasn't the sort of face Howie warmed to.

The town cop stared at her ID in confusion, trying to figure out where she came from and what authority she had to order him away.

"And you are —"

"You don't really want to know, Officer," she told him. "What you want to do, Officer, is beat it."

He looked up at the three large men in suits who stood behind her and decided she had all the authority she needed. He beat it.

Howie turned toward the woman.

"You're Howard Moon Deer," she informed him. It wasn't a question.

"I am," he agreed.

"You're in a shit load of trouble," she said. "I hope you know that."

Howie did.

***

"Inside!" she ordered.

"The body —"

"I'll take care of the body. Open the door."

One of the dark suits guided Howie inside the office toward the visitor chair in the reception room. He set him down onto the chair and kept him there with an iron-like grip on his shoulder.

"I'd like to see that ID again," Howie said to the woman. "You flashed it a little too quickly to get a look."

"You think you're a tough guy, huh?"

"No, what I think is I'm a person with legal rights."

She laughed. "Legal rights!" she said to the three men in suits who had swarmed into the office beside her. They laughed, too.

Howie shrugged. "Look, I'm a licensed private detective in the state of New Mexico," he told them. "Now please show me some ID."

"Alright, Mr. Legal Rights, have it your way."

She reached into her handbag and produced a laminated card. The ID had a photograph that didn't do her justice. She had been caught momentarily without a snarl, looking almost human.

THE UNITED STATES DEPARTMENT OF ENERGY was written at the top. A seal with an eagle on it was visible beneath the writing that followed. The eagle didn't look happy.

LORNA WOLF, SPECIAL AGENT, said the card next to her photograph. She had written her signature beneath her name. It was a hurried, arrogant scrawl, the kind of signature famous people make when they don't much care if their writing is legible.

Howie was surprised she was with the Department of Energy. He hadn't thought such a department would have a law enforcement arm.

But then he got it. She was from the Los Alamos National Laboratory. In America the nuclear laboratories were run by the Department of Energy.

"Satisfied?" she said, seeing the understanding on his face. "Now, shut up, Moon Deer, and listen up. This is serious. So please behave yourself and don't give me any trouble."

Howie took a deep breath.

"What do you want?"

"What I want is to impress upon you the fact that we take nuclear secrets very, very seriously. So let's start from the beginning. I want you to tell me everything. How you met Grisha Bloom, everything you did, everything you heard, everything you saw Wednesday night on Dawson Peak. We're going to go through it again and again until I'm satisfied you've told me everything you know."

Howie laughed mournfully, wondering why, *why* he had ever gone camping? He could have gotten over Claire with much less trouble sitting in a bar.

"This isn't a laughing matter, I promise," said Lorna Wolf. She moved her face closer. Her eyes, magnified by the lens of her glasses, held a fanatical intensity. She poked him hard in the chest with the index finger of her right hand. Hard enough to hurt. "Start talking and don't leave out a single detail."

Howie sighed. Then he did as she told him to do. He told all.

Well, almost all.

***

Howie was getting good at telling the tale of his hike up Dawson Peak and his meeting with the crazed astrophysicist who had been abducted in a flying saucer. He was getting a lot of practice with this story and it improved with each retelling, while at the same time becoming only an anecdote, less real.

Once again, he left Claire out of the story, the reason for the trip. She was nobody's business but his own. And he left out the equation.

This was more difficult to justify except he had liked Grisha Bloom, the polite little man, and he didn't like Lorna Wolf. Bloom had instructed Howie to give the equation only to Dr. Sachs at the Institute for Advanced Study, and specifically not to give it to anyone at LANL. Howie was inclined to follow his wishes.

The three large men in suits made a thorough search of the agency office while Howie was recounting his story. There was a bad moment when one of suits came across *100 Poems from the Chinese* on Howie's desk. The door was open from the reception area to Howie's office and he could see the man pick up the book and flip through the pages from the back.

Howie kept talking while also keeping an eye on what was happening in his office. Fortunately, he was facing the right way and didn't need to turn his head.

The agent in Howie's office was thorough. He held the book with the pages facing downward and gave it a good shake to see if any papers came floating loose. But there was nothing and he didn't notice the writing near the front. He put the book down and went on searching the rest of the room.

"And that's it," Howie concluded. "I climbed down the mountain and called for help. I never saw the old guy again until this evening when I found him dead on my doorstep. Believe me, I have no idea how he got down from Angel Creek campground to end up here."

"He didn't give you anything?"

"Not a thing."

"Did he say anything to you?"

"About what?" Howie asked innocently.

Wolf glared at him. "About nuclear secrets!"

Howie shook his head. "Look, I was just off camping having myself an idyllic time in nature. That's all. I tried to help an exhausted hiker and I've started to wish I hadn't. Quite honestly, I wouldn't know a nuclear secret from a . . . enchilada."

"Enchilada?"

"A figure of speech," he told her. It had slipped out unconsciously because he hadn't eaten since breakfast and he was hungry.

One of the suits came into the reception area and whispered something in her ear.

"Okay, Moon Deer, we found the safe. What's the combination?"

"I'm not sure my boss would like me giving that away."

"Look, either you give it to me, or I'll haul you down to a room in Los Alamos that you won't like. Then I'll get one of our techs up here and we'll open the safe anyway."

This didn't leave Howie much of a choice. Luckily, the office safe didn't contain anything important at the moment. They used it to store sensitive documents and evidence connected to ongoing investigations, sometimes cash, but now there were only a few business papers inside. The safe opened with a digital code and Howie gave it to her.

As he expected, the agent returned a few minutes later and shook his head.

Lorna Wolf and her team continued their search of the office for another two hours. But finally, finding nothing, they gathered in the front room and prepared to depart.

Before she left, Wolf sat down facing him. Her eyes bored into him through the thick lens of her glasses.

"Now listen to me, Moon Deer. Grisha Bloom was working on some very sensitive research. The sort of research certain people would give a great deal to know about. Are you getting my drift?"

"Research, certain people," Howie repeated. "I'm drifting with you, Ms. Wolf."

"So if anybody tries to contact you about this, anybody at all, I want to know about it immediately. No matter what they offer you, no matter who they are, no matter what they say. Are you paying attention, Moon Deer?"

"I am. I'm paying attention."

"That's good. Because this is a matter of national security and you seriously don't want to cross me. I'm going to leave you my card with a number where you can reach me day or night. You understand?"

"I do." Howie wondered if "certain people" might include the Goth beauty with the butterfly tattoo who had sat in his office earlier in the day. He imagined she might. But he decided to keep quiet about her anyway. At least until he had spoken with Jack.

"I'll be back," she said, rising to her feet. "I'm not done with you, Moon Deer!"

"I'll look forward to it," he told her.

***

When they were gone, Howie put the book of poetry into his daypack and locked up the office. He turned on the security system and walked out into the cool night air with a sigh of relief. He was glad to see that the body of Grisha Bloom had been taken away. He was sorry that the old fellow was dead, but it wasn't really a surprise. What was surprising, of course, was how Bloom had gotten himself from Angel Creek to San Geronimo.

Maybe a flying saucer had brought him.

Whatever. Howie was too tired to think about it.

Despite his exhaustion, he was tense, wound up. He was tempted to slip over to the Blue Moon Café and have a drink or two at the bar. But he looked at his watch and saw it was 3:23 in the morning and the bar was closed.

A good thing, he decided. He drove home and went to bed instead.

Chapter Seven

"Ugh!" Howie said on Saturday morning, peering into the mirror at his bedraggled self.

It had been nearly dawn by the time he'd gotten home and he hadn't had nearly enough sleep. His cat, Orange, had woken him before nine by licking his ear and purring as loudly as an alarm clock.

Orange was a large furry beast with ticklish whiskers. The vet had told Howie to put her on a diet, but he hadn't had the heart to do so. Minus Claire, Orange was the only creature in the whole wide world who truly loved him, and he spent a good deal of his life trying to please her.

Howie lived off grid on ten acres of land in a high tech eco pod that he had put together from a kit he'd purchased from Germany. Claire said the pod looked like a large metallic egg propped up on four chicken legs. Despite its unusual appearance, it had all the conveniences cleverly built in, including solar power and a satellite connection for his laptop.

After a large cup of coffee, Howie spent twenty minutes doing yoga outside on the small patch of lawn next to his vegetable garden. Yoga was Howie's latest attempt to transform himself into an enlightened being. Get flexible, he told himself. Take a deep breath and let it go. Twist yourself up like a pretzel and relax into the motherly arms of the universe.

In fact, he did feel better after his morning routine. He was particularly fond of standing on his head. The world looked better upside down.

After yoga, Howie showered, dressed, and drove into town. He intended to spend the day at the office working on the Internet, searching Google for the answers to a number of questions that were worrying him. He could have done this at home, but Ruth was gone for the weekend so he would have the office to himself. Plus, he liked his office desktop Mac with its large screen, and there happened to be a good bakery three doors down Calle Dos Flores where he could get an excellent bear claw and a cappuccino.

Lorna Wolf's goons, unpleasant though they were, had at least put the office back together before they left. Howie settled at his desk with his coffee and pastry and began by making a call to Lieutenant Santo Ruben at the State Police.

Jack and Santo were friends. They had breakfast once a week, which gave Howie special access to the lieutenant and some leeway. But there was a line that couldn't be crossed, cop to private detective, and Howie was always respectful.

The switchboard put him on hold for a long enough time that Howie wondered if he'd been disconnected. But then Santo came on the line with a blustery, "Howie, I only have a minute. How was your camping trip?"

"Sort of nuts, actually. I found this half-naked crazy guy walking around in a thunderstorm near the summit of Dawson Peak and the next day I had to hike down the mountain to get help for him. I didn't tell the whole story to Search and Rescue because I didn't want to complicate things. The guy claimed he had just been let out from a flying saucer. He'd been abducted to the planet, Klizmor, you see."

Santo laughed. "Well, that's San Geronimo for you! We've got our share of nuts."

"But here's the rub. When Search and Rescue got up to my tent where I'd left him, he was gone. Then somehow twenty-four hours later he ended up dead in front of our office in town. I have no idea how, and no idea why."

"I heard about the body on Calle Dos Flores. That was your flying saucer guy?"

"It was. I called 911 and they sent over a town cop. We were just getting started when a bunch of heavies from Los Alamos arrived and took charge. Do you know a woman by the name of Lorna Wolf?"

"The She-Wolf? I do, Howie. She's in charge of security at the Lab and she's someone to steer clear of. Tell me about the guy you found."

"His name is Grisha Bloom and he was a famous astrophysicist who won the Nobel Prize in 1994. His daughter contacted me yesterday wanting to hire me to find her father. I put her off, saying we should wait to see if Search and Rescue finds him first. Now I guess I'll have to tell her he turned up dead."

"That's never easy news to deliver."

"I'm not looking forward to it. But here's why I'm calling. She said she'd been looking for her father for a few days and she contacted the State Police to ask if he had been reported in an accident. This would have been yesterday. She said she spoke to somebody in charge and I was wondering if that was you."

"It wasn't me, Howie. I never spoke to her."

"Well, maybe she spoke with somebody else at the station. But it's been bothering me. Supposedly this person in charge told her that I was the camper on Dawson Peak who found her father in the rain and went down the mountain for help. It didn't seem likely that you would give out that kind of information."

"No, we wouldn't. Certainly not in this case," Santo told him. "I heard there was a search going on for a missing hiker, but that's all. I had no idea you were involved. Probably she spoke to someone at the Sheriff's Department instead of us. Outsiders sometimes confuse the different law enforcement agencies in New Mexico."

"I guess that's it," said Howie, not entirely satisfied.

"But what was a physicist doing wandering around Dawson Peak in the rain?"

"I don't have a clue, Santo. Bloom was at the Institute for Advanced Study, which is a very elite place in Princeton. The last few months, he's been doing some special work at LANL. Lorna Wolfe kept grilling me for hours last night wanting to know if he'd passed any nuclear secrets my way."

"You're going to need to watch your step, Howie. Nuclear weapons, plutonium cores—these are matters you want to stay clear of."

"Believe me, Santo, I don't want any part of this!"

"Well, you did what you could for the guy. You tried to help him. You did your best. Now tell me, have you heard from Jack in Hawaii?"

"I'm going to call him later today."

"Be sure to give him my best. Look, I've got to go. I have an ongoing situation, a nineteen-year-old kid who has abducted his fourteen-year-old girlfriend and is holding her at knife-point in his house."

Howie disconnected with a final promise that he would leave the mystery of Grisha Bloom for wiser souls to solve.

Of course, he would.

The guy had ended up dead on his doorstep. But why should he get involved?

***

And yet . . .

He was involved, like it or not. How could he pretend otherwise? Curiosity may have killed the cat, but Howie wasn't prepared to be an ostrich with his head stuck in the sand.

After a few minutes of doubt, tossing the question back and forth, he turned on his computer, googled Grisha Bloom, and found an astonishing one thousand two hundred and fifty-two hits for him on the Internet.

The majority of them, he saw, were academic discussions of his work written by other scientists. Many of the others were magazine and news-paper profiles from 1994 when he won the Nobel Prize in physics. In a side bar on the Google page there was a photograph of Bloom leaving Howie in no doubt that it was the spaceman he had encountered at 12,000 feet. The photo showed a younger, healthier man but the delicate, intel-lectual features and the dreamy eyes were the same.

Howie decided to start with the Wikipedia article, which began with a general description of the discovery of the Blue Moon quark. This had apparently been a big deal in the mid-90s, enough to send him to Sweden, but had become increasingly controversial by the two thousand teens. In 2017, an astrophysicist at MIT, a Sergei Isett, had said flatly that the Blue Moon quark was a fraud.

The second paragraph went to a more specific explanation of the quark. Apparently, there were thousands of tiny subatomic particles which appeared for a fraction of a second before they were annihilated by antiparticles. Howie was interested to learn that subatomic particles destroyed one another at a frightening rate, matter versus anti-matter. Quantum mechanics was a dog-eat-dog world just like everywhere else.

Howie thought he was doing pretty well for the first few paragraphs. He understood almost everything. But just when he was feeling smart, the discussion became increasingly arcane and he was soon lost. The prob-lem, as far as he could see, was that quantum mechanics really didn't make sense.

For example, Heisenberg's Uncertainty Principle, the notion that one subatomic particle could be in two places at once. Howie could only shake his head.

He moved on to the Wikipedia section titled Personal History. Here he discovered that Grisha Bloom had been born in London in 1949 and had been educated at Eaton then Cambridge. In 1969 he had married

British biologist, Martha Denham Bloom, who had died in 1998. There was one child born of this marriage, a Mia Bloom.

Howie continued reading for another fifteen minutes, following Bloom's academic career from Cambridge to the United States until finally arriving at the prestigious Institute for Advanced Study, all the while publishing numerous papers in important scientific journals.

Grisha Bloom was without doubt a towering figure. But his reputation had become tarnished in recent years by speculation that the quark he had discovered did not appear once in a blue moon, as Bloom had proclaimed, but rather not at all. The discussion of the science involved was too dense for Howie to absorb, but he got the general idea that theoretical physics wasn't a settled matter but a field that was in constant motion, with new ideas coming up all the time debunking what had come before.

Like quarks, modern science was also dog-eat-dog. The competition was intense. The rewards were great. If you were lucky, you could end up in Sweden. But if you missed a step, you could find yourself teaching high school math in Kansas.

The speculation that the Blue Moon quark was an outright fraud, resting on false data, had only surfaced in the past two years and it threatened to destroy what remained of Bloom's reputation. Howie might not understand the science involved, but fraud was a different matter. Fraud was the seamy side of winning and losing. Fraud was something he and Jack had dealt with before.

After an hour of dense reading, Howie decided he needed to take a walk to clear his head. He closed up the office and stepped outside, heading away from the busy Plaza toward a burrito cart he knew on the edge of the historical district.

He was wondering what it must be like for a man like Grisha Bloom to be accused of fraud—the embarrassment, the shame—when something began nagging at him, something he had read in the Wikipedia article that didn't make sense. He wasn't sure what it was that bothered him, but it had left behind a trace of wrongness. He continued toward the burrito cart until his steps slowed and he came to a stop.

He turned and walked back quickly to the office. He started up his computer and brought the Wikipedia article on Grisha Bloom back onto the screen.

It took him a few minutes of reading before he found what had bothered him. It was a date. In Grisha's personal history it stated that his daughter, Mia, had been born in 1971. That would mean that Mia was 49 years old.

But this couldn't be right. Howie knew he wasn't very good with ages, and women in particular were often hard to judge.

But there was no way the Goth beauty who had come to his office yesterday could be that old.

Thirty, maybe. Thirty-five at the most. But not forty-nine. That was impossible.

Combined with her claim that someone from the State Police had told her about his adventures on Dawson Peak, Howie was beginning to suspect that the woman who called herself Mia Bloom didn't always tell the truth.

***

Howie rifled through his desk and found the card that she had left with him on Friday with her contact information.

It was a nice-looking card, simple but elegant, good quality stock. In black letters against a white background, it said Dr. Mia Bloom, The California Institute of Technology, with an .edu email address underneath and a phone number with a 213 Los Angeles area code.

He returned to the Google search page and typed in "Caltech faculty." The Caltech website came up with a listing of departments and faculty members. Howie chose the Division of Physics, Mathematics, and Astronomy. A new page popped up with the names of the various professors who worked in these areas. They ranged widely in nationalities and ages, but they all looked brilliant, not a dud in the lot. And not one of them was Mia Bloom.

The home page of the Physics, Mathematics, and Astronomy Division had several sub-pages—Research Faculty, Postdoctoral Scholars, Visiting Associates, and more, each with more names and photographs and email contacts. Caltech was a large school and Howie spent the next twenty minutes carefully going through the different lists of scholars, assistants, project heads, and graduate students without finding Mia Bloom.

He exited the Caltech site, returned to Google, and typed Mia Bloom in the search box. He got several hits for a Mia M. Bloom who was a Professor of Communication at Georgia State University. The photograph showed a middle-aged woman who was the author of numerous books. But she was certainly not the Mia Bloom who had come to his office yesterday, the girl with the butterfly on her thigh.

"Hmm," hummed Howie, increasingly concerned.

It was difficult to imagine anybody these days who didn't have a digital footprint. Particularly an astrophysicist who was the daughter of a famous man. Even Howie had a digital footprint. He googled his own name, just to make sure he existed. And there he was, Howard Moon Deer, several pages of Google references, mostly concerning old cases that he and Jack had investigated.

So why wasn't there anything about his Mia Bloom?

He decided to phone her, punching in the number on her card. But she wasn't there either.

"This is Mia Bloom," her recorded voice said pleasantly. He was relieved to discover that it was indeed the voice of the woman who had come to his office on Friday, cool and precise. "I am not available now, but if you leave a message, I'll get back to you as soon as I can."

Howie waited for the beep.

"Hello, Dr. Bloom. This is Howard Moon Deer, the private detective in San Geronimo. Would you please call me back?"

He hesitated, not certain how much he wanted to say to a machine, and not sure how to say it. He settled on a cautious approach. "I have news about your father."

Howie put down his phone with a glum sense of incomprehension. The mysteries were adding up, one after the other, and Howie didn't know where to begin the unraveling.

There was only one thing to do. It was time to call Jack.

Chapter Eight

It was a quarter to noon in New Mexico, 7:45 in the morning on the North Shore of Oahu. Jack Wilder, Howie's boss, was 73 years old and, like many old men, he didn't sleep well. Howie guessed he had been up for hours.

Howie had met Jack soon after he and Emma moved to San Geronimo, to a house Emma had inherited from an aunt. At first Howie had worked simply as Jack's handyman and general helper. The work was meant to be only a part-time job, a way for Howie to earn money while he finished his dissertation. Until one night a year later, over a very decent bottle of zinfandel, Jack had proposed the fanciful idea that the two of them should start a private detective agency.

Why not?

Jack was a medically retired policeman from San Francisco who had worked his way up the ladder from patrolman to inspector, then on to lieutenant, captain, major, and finally commander, a rank just below the deputy chief of police. He was very good at his job and might have gone all the way to the top were it not for a police action gone tragically wrong: a hostage dead and a bullet that grazed his skull and caused him to lose his eyesight.

Jack was devastated at finding his career abruptly ended. He hadn't been ready for retirement. He was bored with nothing to do. And now, with Howie's help, he proposed to jump back into the game—as a private cop this time, but still a chance for him to return to the life he knew best. All he lacked was his eyesight. And this was where Howie came in. Howie would be his eyes.

"But, Jack, I don't know a thing about being a detective!" Howie had objected.

"I'll teach you," said Jack.

"You can do that?"

"Sure, I can. You're smart, aren't you?"

"Well —"

"Howie, let's do it."

And so they did. It was an odd partnership, but somehow it worked. During the first year, Howie didn't do much more than drive Jack from place to place and take care of various matters where eyesight was necessary. But gradually, as Jack passed on his knowledge—the means and methods of investigation—Howie's apprenticeship evolved and he began taking on a greater role. Eventually he got his own private detective's license in Santa Fe and his PhD dissertation was shoved once again to the side.

Howie found the work fascinating. All in all, it was a whole lot more fun than academia. Besides, women liked witty, ironic men-of-action more than they liked dithering intellectuals. Howie was reborn.

Jack was the boss, but he was a generous boss and a good friend. Despite the fact that it was Jack's money that had set up the agency, he insisted they split the proceeds of their cases fifty-fifty. The agency was doing well and for the first time in his life, Howie found himself earning a decent living. This was fun, too. He didn't mind saying goodbye to his years of being a perpetually half-starved graduate student.

Today, Jack answered on the first ring a world away in Hawaii, as though he had been waiting for Howie's call.

"Howie," he said in a flat voice. "I hope you're getting yourself a vacation."

"I wouldn't call it a vacation, Jack. How are things on Oahu?"

"Not really a vacation either. The funeral's on Tuesday and it's a damn mess. Both sides of the family have flown over and everybody's at each other's throat. Lots of blame and angst. Emma's devastated and I guess I am too. I liked River a lot. He was a sweet kid. I'll tell you all about it over a glass of wine some night. But right now, I'm up to my ears in misery and I'd rather hear about you. How are things in Glocca Morra?"

Jack said things like that. How are things in Glocca Morra. He was a little corny, which Howie imagined was a condition that came with age.

"Glocca Morra's not entirely peachy, Jack."

"No? Are you hearing any news from Claire? That girl's a keeper, Howie. You won't find someone like that every day."

A small sigh escaped Howie's lips. He hadn't told Jack yet about Claire and the fabulous maestro, and he didn't plan to do so today.

"Listen, the reason I'm calling is some odd things are happening around here and I might have ourselves a new client. A girl. A woman, really, but she looks like a girl."

"Really?" said Jack, not sure he liked the idea of a woman who looked like a girl. To Jack's mind that spelled trouble.

"She's an astrophysicist."

"An astro what?"

"Physicist, Jack. From Caltech. Or so she says."

"What do you mean, or so she says?"

"I mean, I can't find her on the faculty website."

"Well, there are some smart people at Caltech," Jack mused. "But they don't have a football team. They used to. The Beavers. But they stopped their football program in the Nineties. A shame, if you ask me. What's college without football?"

"Maybe the dam burst," Howie suggested.

"What?"

"It was a joke, Jack. Beavers, a dam . . . never mind. Let me tell you about my camping trip. That's when this odd stuff started happening."

"You went camping?"

"I did, Jack. The agency was closed so I went camping. But it wasn't exactly a weenie roast. Pretty much everything went wrong that you could ever imagine going wrong on a camping trip. Including a dead body that just showed up on our doorstep."

"Uh-huh," said Jack. "You'd better tell me about it."

Howie did.

***

Jack was a good listener. He asked a few questions, but not many. It was only after Howie had finished, that he began dissecting Howie's story.

"So this spaceman of yours, Grisha Bloom—he just ups and disappears from your tent? Maybe he wasn't as sick as you thought," Jack suggested. "Maybe he climbed down that mountain on his own and died in town."

"I don't think so. He really didn't look good. And he didn't have shoes. An old man like that, he wasn't going to get far barefoot in those mountains."

"But you found him dead on the agency doorstep? How did he get there?"

"That's what I'm saying, Jack. It's impossible."

"No, it's not impossible if it happened. There are two possibilities. Either he got down the mountain on his own and expired on our doorstep, which you say he didn't do. Or someone brought him down. *Voilà!* By the process of elimination, we've found the answer."

Howie sighed. He hated it when Jack said *voilà,* then proceeded to ride roughshod over any opinion but his own.

"Ever hear of Heisenberg's Uncertainty Principle, Jack? An object can be in two places at once. Yes doesn't automatically rule out no. You can be right and wrong simultaneously—"

"Howie—"

"I'm just mentioning it, Jack. The universe doesn't always make sense."

"Sure, Howie. But back on Earth, where most of us live, this is simply a matter of discovering who brought Grisha Bloom down from Dawson Peak."

"Well, it wasn't Search and Rescue," Howie told him. "They spread out over a radius of a mile and didn't find any sign of the guy."

"Let's start at the beginning. You're saying he walked into your campground barefoot and babbling? How did he get up on that mountain in the first place?"

"Jack, I don't know. I'm starting to think maybe the Klizmorians brought him."

"Sure, Howie. That must be it."

"Well, it's a mystery. And then there's the fact that his daughter seemed to know about my part in finding him before I was able to get down the mountain and call it in."

"Have you asked her about this?"

"No, but I plan to. If she really is Blooms's daughter. On the Internet the one reference I found about a Mia Bloom said she was born in 1971. But she doesn't look nearly that old."

"This is the woman who looks like a girl?"

"Exactly. Or maybe she's a girl who looks like a woman, I can't say."

"Did you say anything to her about the equation?"

"No, I didn't. Grisha told me not to. I haven't mentioned the equation to anyone except you, not even Santo."

"And you think this could be the mysterious Theory of Everything?"

"Jack, maybe it's the Theory of Nothing, I don't know. But whatever Grisha Bloom was doing at Los Alamos, it was important enough that I had a very unpleasant visit last night from the head of security there. A lady by the name of Lorna Wolf. She had fangs, believe me. She wanted to know everything Bloom said to me, everything he did. She just rolled on in without a search warrant with three big guys in suits and went through our office like a tornado from hell. She even opened our safe."

"You gave her the combination?"

"I didn't have a choice. The way she was going on, I thought I was an inch away from getting waterboarded."

Jack didn't like their office being searched and he made Howie repeat this part of the story several times.

"But she didn't find the equation?"

"Blind luck, I guess. If you don't mind the expression. One of the suits actually picked up the book and shook it to see if anything loose came out. He flipped through the pages. But somehow he missed the writing near the front. They spent a few hours going through everything until finally they left."

"Damn it, Howie, I wish you hadn't gotten involved in this! Nuclear secrets are something to stay clear of."

"So everyone keeps telling me. But Jack, I was off hiking, that's all. I was toodling up and down this idyllic mountain trail having all sorts of happy thoughts, when this whole thing came down on me like a . . . like a . . ."

Howie searched in vain for an apt metaphor, but found it impossible to come up with a description of the unfairness, the total random nature of his predicament.

He left the metaphor unfinished, dangling. And he hated that. He hated dangling metaphors.

"Calm down, Howie."

"It's too late to calm down. I'm never going camping again!"

"Okay, okay. But listen to me, the first thing you need to do is get that book somewhere safe."

"Yeah, I've been thinking about that. I don't want to send it to Dr. Sachs in Princeton, not until we have a better idea of what's going on."

"*We*? How did this become plural?"

"Hey, you've got to help me, Jack!"

"I will. But I can't leave Hawaii until after the funeral so you're going to have to muddle through on your own for a few more days."

"What if I put the book in the mail addressed to myself? That'll keep it safe until I come up with a better idea."

"No, don't put it in the mail. That's too obvious. It's one of the first places Wolf will check."

"But she won't be able to get at it. I mean, we're talking about the United States Postal Service!"

Jack laughed. "Howie, Howie, you're not really getting this. There's nothing more important to American intelligence than nuclear secrets. If they think a top physicist like Grisha Bloom gave you something classified, they'll tear apart the post office brick by brick to get at it. They'll dynamite the building if they have to. Is this getting through?"

"Yeah, Jack, it is. But look, here's an idea—"

Howie was about to suggest putting the book in a safe deposit box at the bank, but Jack cut him off.

"No, don't tell me. We've talked too much already."

"You think they're monitoring my calls?"

"It's a possibility. I should have stopped you earlier, but it didn't occur to me how serious this was until you told me about the Wolf woman."

"So what should I do?"

"I'm not going to say anything more. But think about it. Think hard. Leave me a clue, if you can. Then maybe get out of town for a while. Lie low until I get there."

"Vanish, you mean?"

"If you're smart," said Jack.

Chapter Nine

Howie woke Sunday morning at the civilized hour of 10 o'clock after a late dinner with a friend at Valentino's, an Italian restaurant in the foothills that had a spectacular view of the desert below.

His friend, Sergio, was a ski buddy who had just returned from Nepal and his tales of the Himalayas had left Howie longing for travel. They went through four courses, a good bottle of chianti, snifters of cognac, and by the end the evening, Howie was ready to chuck everything and head off to Asia. He saw himself on a high mountain trail with a trusty yak snorting along behind him . . .

Howie was sitting in the sun outside his home drinking coffee, enjoying his fantasy, when his phone rang.

He grimaced when he saw the screen. It was Claire. Should he answer? Yes, he decided. He couldn't put her off any longer. He said goodbye to Nepal and steeled himself for a difficult conversation.

"Howie, at last! I've been trying to call you for days! Where have you been?"

Howie was annoyed that she thought he should be available whenever she decided to call. But at the same time, he was pleased she couldn't do without him. It was the Uncertainty Principle in action. Yes and no were both the correct answer.

"I've been busy, Claire. Things have been a little hairy around here."

"You're on a case?"

"It's complicated. Where are you?"

"Copenhagen. We did a concert last night. The Mozart G Major Quartet, then some Beethoven and Dvorak. My heart wasn't really in it, but I gave it my best . . . oh, Howie, what are we going to do about *us*?"

"I didn't think there was an us anymore."

"Howie, you can't just turn a relationship off, like shutting off a faucet. I don't want to lose you!"

"Even if you've fallen for someone old enough to be your grandfather?"

"Richie's not that old, really. He's very spry for his age. Music keeps him young."

Howie ground his teeth. *Richie?*

"Tell me, Howie, are *you* seeing anyone?"

"Seeing someone? Well, nobody special. The usual one-nighters," he lied. "This time of year, there are always young babes in town looking to fill out their resumés."

"Babes! . . . oh, honestly, Howie, I know you too well to believe a word you're saying! Look, I don't want you to be lonely. I *want* you to meet someone. But if you do meet someone, I'll be miserable."

"Well, that's a paradox."

It was more than a paradox. It was a muddle.

It wasn't a satisfying conversation. In the end, they decided nothing except they were both unhappy. Even Claire was miserable and supposedly she was madly in love. Go figure.

In fact, Howie was sick of the whole thing.

He ended the conversation with a promise that they would talk again soon, but he wasn't sure he would. If she had met the love of her life, the fabulous Sir Richard, okay. It hurt, but he could accept it. But this waffling was driving him nuts.

For consolation, Howie made himself a small avocado omelette with Jarlsberg cheese and mushrooms. Only two eggs, because any day now he was about to go on a diet. After breakfast he changed into work clothes and set about transferring his five tomato plants from pots into the ground. He should have done this a week ago because the plants were getting large. But with his camping trip and everything else, he had put it off until now.

His garden was in a fenced clearing at the side of his pod, watered by a hose that was gravity fed from a nearby creek. The fence was necessary to keep out the deer and the rabbits. He had spent several days the previous summer building an attractive wooden gate. Claire had been visiting and she had helped him with the planting. It had been a happy time together, pre-maestro.

Howie liked gardening. And he especially liked good tomatoes, which bore no resemblance to the tasteless pulp you bought in the super-market.

His cat, Orange, was watching him sleepily from a grassy place in the sun when his phone rang from where he had left it on the outside trestle table.

Probably it was Claire calling back with more muddle and he wasn't sure he wanted to answer. But when he checked the screen, it was a number he didn't know.

He wiped his dirty hands on his shorts.

"Yeah?"

At first he heard only loud music, screaming guitars. Then a voice. "Is this Howard Moon Deer?" a man asked belligerently.

"It is. Who are you?" Howie asked in return, shouting over the music.

"You're Howard Moon Deer?"

"Yes, I am. Who are you?" he repeated. "Look, why don't you turn down your music. Better yet, why don't you just go away."

"Hold on, for chrissake . . . gimme a damn minute!"

Howie stared at his phone, agog with irritation. What was the world coming to, crazy people you didn't know calling you on Sunday morning? He listened as the music receded in volume to a background trickle.

The voice returned.

"Okay, Moon Deer, you've succeeded in crashing my bliss. Now, look, this is Brandon Eckehart. You and I need to talk."

"Do we?" Howie was immediately on guard. Eckehart had been Grisha Bloom's assistant at LANL, an individual Bloom had told him specifically to avoid. Not only that, but both Santo and Jack had warned him repeatedly to have nothing to do with Los Alamos. A wise person would hang up now. Yet curiosity tickled his brain.

"I don't know what we have to talk about," Howie said cautiously.

"Sure, you do. And it can't wait. Look, I'm busy all day, but let's meet tonight, 10 o'clock at the Worm Hole in Dawson."

"The *what*? Where?"

"The Worm Hole. Two words, not one. Is there something wrong with your hearing?"

"Tonight's not good for me, I have a date."

"Break it. This is more important."

"But where the hell is Dawson? You're not talking about the Peak, I hope?"

"For chrissake, not the Peak, the *town!*"

"I've never heard of it."

"Then look it up. You're a private eye. Find it."

Eckehart disconnected leaving Howie standing by his trestle table holding his phone. He was starting to wonder if all astrophysicists were psychopaths. Maybe it had something to do with spending too much time in other galaxies. Orange jumped up on the table and gave him a sympathetic meow.

"Damn!" he said.

Tonight really wasn't good for Howie. He had a date with a friend, a woman who was a chef at a local restaurant. The San Geronimo Community Center was running a film series, "The Ten Best Art Movies Ever," and they were planning to see the 1961 classic, *Last Year at Marienbad*, in which absolutely nothing happened. The movie was reputed to be so boring you knew it had to be profound. He supposed he could give it a miss.

Howie went inside and washed his hands in the kitchen sink. Then he sat at his laptop in the pod's communication nook and googled the Worm Hole.

He expected it would be a bar or restaurant. But there was nothing. Zilch. The Internet had plenty of information about wormholes, one word not two, a concept that sci-fi buffs found exciting. But there was no Worm Hole that one could actually go to at 10 o'clock tonight, or any other hour.

Next, he typed Dawson, NM into his search engine to see if such a town existed outside of Dr. Brandon Eckehart's fevered imagination.

It did. In a spectral sense.

"It's a ghost town!" Howie said aloud to Orange.

He continued reading. The ghost town of Dawson, New Mexico, was 17 miles northeast of Cimarron, the legendary Wild West town where Billy the Kid once roamed. Dawson had been a major coal mining town in the early years of the 20th century, boasting a population of 9,000, a golf course, a railway line, a fancy hotel, a swimming pool, even a movie theater. But there had been two major mine disasters—one in 1913 when 263 men were killed, and a second in 1923 that claimed 123 lives, and by 1950 the town was abandoned. Coal, sad to say, wasn't always beautiful.

Howie took a shower and put on his town clothes, a clean pair of jeans and what he classified as "a dress T-shirt." This one was from the Salvador Dali Museum in Paris. Claire had bought it for him because he was always late. It was the classic surrealist painting of a watch melting in the sun.

Now that he was properly attired, he had two things he needed to do before his 10 o'clock meeting tonight.

He had to decide where he was going to hide the New Directions paperback of Kenneth Rexroth's translation of *100 Poems from the Chinese.*

And he needed to get his hands on a gun.

Howie disliked guns. He didn't like the noise they made; he didn't like the hard recoil when they fired. In his journey through life, he had decided long ago that he wished to be armed with knowledge, insight, and humor. Not bullets.

But there were times you had to be realistic.

A late-night meeting in a ghost town in the middle of nowhere at a place called the Worm Hole didn't inspire a snuggly sense of security.

Chapter Ten

Howie stopped for dinner at the St. James in Cimarron, an historic hotel built in 1871 that was said to be haunted by the spirits of Jesse James and Billy the Kid. At least twenty-six murders had occurred here over the years and guests were especially warned to avoid Room 18, where a restless spirit still roamed. Apparently, ghosts were abundant in this far corner of New Mexico.

The restaurant had been recently remodeled, with the original Victorian decor replaced by cowboy kitsch that was designed to attract tourism. The room was crowded with young families on their summer road trips, eager to get an authentic taste of the Old West. Howie avoided the Mexican food on the menu, sensing that it would be bland, and settled for an authentic buffalo burger instead.

What could you do to a buffalo burger? he wondered. He soon found out. You could cook it to death and serve it with a cold bun that was falling apart.

From Cimarron, Howie took the narrow county road to Dawson 17 miles away. He was armed with a 9mm Glock from Jack's safe. This had been the easy part of his afternoon. Howie had the key to Jack and Emma's house in order to water the indoor plants while they were in Hawaii, and he knew the combination to the safe in Jack's study where the gun was kept.

It was the book that had been the problem, where to hide it—*100 Poems from the Chinese* with the equation written inside. Howie had spent hours considering this question, changing his mind several times. Part of the problem was how to let Jack know the hiding place, or at least leave him a clue of some sort, something that Jack would understand but nobody else. Above all, Howie didn't want the equation to be lost forever if he ended up dead. Not a happy thought, but he wanted to take precautions.

In the end, Howie believed he had found a pretty good hiding place for the book and a clever clue to leave for Jack, but uncertainty gnawed at him as he drove toward the old coal mining town of Dawson. Maybe he should have buried it on his property in a waterproof container. Maybe he should have left it in his ski locker up on San Geronimo Peak. Maybe, maybe, maybe . . .

The pavement ended after a few miles and turned into a dirt track that became bumpier and more deeply rutted as the miles wore on. Howie slowed to 25 mph to keep his Subaru from shaking apart.

The mountain West is full of ghost towns, places where the optimism of America once flourished and died. Gold, coal, silver, copper, as well as new metals like molybdenum had seen their days of glory come and go. Boom towns sprang up around the money until the money was gone, and then the people left as well.

Dawson, New Mexico, was ghostly with the wreckage of time. Howie arrived shortly after 9 o'clock when the last of the summer twilight had faded from the sky. His headlights showed a wide bare plain with mountains rising up beyond the ruins of the town.

Howie kept driving, passing the shell of a train station and a once prosperous two-story hotel. He continued along a darkened main street that was lined with fragments of stores and homes. He passed a cemetery where the headstones and faded wooden crosses leaned at haphazard angles.

Then he came to the strangest sight of all.

The road turned a corner and Howie's headlights shone on an old wooden building that had lights glowing in the windows. It was a saloon with several cars and motorcycles parked out front. After so much death, the presence of life was startling. The electricity had to come from a generator, though Howie heard nothing but the restless New Mexico wind.

A sign above the door identified the saloon as The Worm Hole Café. A second sign nearby: Food That's Out of This World!

Howie parked in the gravel area by the side of the building next to a pickup truck. He slung his day bag with the Glock inside over his shoulder and locked the Subaru up tight so that no ghost could come along and take it for a joy ride.

Outside the front door, a biker in a fringed buckskin jacket was standing by his shiny Harley, a great hog of a machine. The biker wore a cowboy hat and had a big droopy mustache. His face was gaunt and deeply lined. Howie wasn't sure if he was a ghost or real.

As Howie watched, the cowboy biker threw a leg over his Harley and straddled the machine like he was sitting on a horse.

"Hey, amigo," he said as Howie approached. "How's tricks?"

"Tricks are just fine," Howie said cautiously. "Is this really the Worm Hole?"

"You got it, amigo. You have arrived."

"Kind of off the beaten track, isn't it?"

"We're an eclectic bunch here," said the cowboy. "Folks who appreciate being off the beaten track."

"In a ghost town?"

The droopy mustache expanded as the man smiled. "The dead tell no lies. Some of us like that. Doug," he said, leaning across his bike to offer his hand. "Doug McKay. So what brings you out to this lone parcel of the universe?"

Howie shook hands warily. He supposed he should give his own name in return, but he didn't. "I'm supposed to meet someone here."

"Yeah?" Doug lowered his voice to a conspiratorial whisper. "Now, let me make an educated guess who that might be. The great Dr. Eckehart, I bet. Am I right?"

Howie moved back a pace and gave Doug McKay a harder look. Straddling his Harley, he looked like an easy rider with his droopy mustache and long hair. But there was something unsettling about his eyes.

Doug laughed when Howie didn't answer. "Relax, amigo, everything's cool. We all know each other here, that's all. Well, time for me to ride off home."

Howie watched the cowboy biker as he kick-started his Harley and roared off down the empty street.

In the distance a coyote howled.

Howie turned and entered the Worm Hole Café with deep misgivings.

***

Inside the front door was a bouncer stationed on a stool, but he wasn't like any bouncer Howie had ever encountered before. He was a large black man in a tight blue spandex outfit that clung to his body. His face was hidden in a rubber Yoda mask from *Star Wars*.

"A member, you are?"

"Well, no. Is this a club?"

"Twenty dollars, it is. If a member, you aren't. Sign the register, you must."

Howie brought out his wallet and took out a twenty-dollar bill. The register was a large ledger. There were columns for surname, first name, address, phone number, email. But otherwise the page was blank.

"You want all this information? I'm only going to have a beer."

"Sign it, you must. If inside you want to go."

Howie wasn't prepared to give out so much personal information. "Tonto, Joe," he wrote in the book. He gave a fictitious address in Santa Fe and a made-up phone number and email.

Yoda regarded Howie with hostile eyes through the holes in his rubber mask. He turned the book his way to see what Howie had written.

"Are you going to stamp my hand?"

"Remember you, I will. Mr. Tonto."

Howie sensed this sort of Yoda-talk could become tiresome.

The bar in the center of the room was circular, a ring of inch-thick transparent glass that was lit by colored lights from below, giving it a celestial appearance, like the rings of Saturn. The lights cast bizarre colored shadows on the faces of the few customers who were perched on the circumference of the ring with exotic looking cocktails set before them. The ceiling of the room sparkled with stars.

The bartender inside the glass circle was a large muscular man like the bouncer at the door, but he didn't wear a mask. Instead he had two antennae with green ping pong balls on the ends coming up from his head. It was like something children wore at Halloween.

There were three men at the bar, two on stools on the near side of the circle, and one by himself on the far side. None of them looked like they might be Dr. Brandon Eckehart. The rest of the stools were empty. They were white plastic disks the size of a frisbee each on a thin chrome stand. It was the strangest bar Howie had ever seen, in the strangest town.

To a stool Howie walked. Onto the stool Howie sat. The bartender nodded at him.

"I'll take a Guinness," he said.

"You kidding?" asked the barman.

Howie sighed. "I guess I'll have a Bud then. Unless you have something off-planet. From Pluto, maybe?"

"Pluto isn't a planet anymore. You should know that. It's just a chunk of rock in the Kuiper Belt."

Howie wasn't sure if the world had gone crazy on him, or he had gone crazy on the world. Either way he was feeling out of sync.

The beer arrived in a long-neck bottle and it looked pretty much like the standard Milwaukee product. Howie was grateful it wasn't green. He looked at his watch and saw it was ten minutes after ten and there was still no sign of Brandon Eckehart.

Howie listened in on the conversation of the men two stools over. There was a large man and a small man, a Laurel and a Hardy.

"No, they don't call it socialism up there," the large man was saying.

"But they share everything equally," the small man answered. "So in effect, it *is* socialism."

"Naw, you got it all wrong. They don't use money, you see. They don't even know what money is. The way I think of it, picture an aspen grove here on Earth. You know how aspens share a common root system? All of them connected underground? Well, that's how *they* are. They're all connected, you see. Sure, they're individuals. But really they're a single organism."

"And you're saying that's not socialism?"

"Come on! Sure, aspens are communal. But you can't call 'em commies. That's how *they* are."

Howie heard a loud unpleasant laugh from the single man on the other side of the bar. The man was hugely fat, three hundred plus pounds. He was reading a comic book, the Hulk, with the lurid cover partially obscuring his face. It was difficult to imagine how he managed to balance himself on the small round stool. Howie would never have taken this individual to be Dr. Brandon Eckehart from the Los Alamos National Laboratory, but he recognized the laugh from their phone call.

Howie picked up his beer and walked around the bar to him.

"Dr. Eckehart?"

"That's me. And you are Howard Moon Deer, I guess." He put the comic book down on the bar and slapped the open page with his huge, flabby hand. "I love this stuff!" he said. "Don't you?"

"Well, I used to like comic books," Howie told him. "Back when I was ten."

"Don't give me that crap!" Eckehart turned and looked at Howie for the first time. He had short ginger-colored hair, a big round babyish face, and several days of growth on his chin. For all his huge size, he couldn't be much older than his mid-thirties. "What are you, some guy who's misplaced his inner child?"

"My inner child is doing fine," Howie answered. "But the rest of me has grown up."

"Sure!" said the physicist in disgust.

"So what are we doing way out in the middle of an old ghost town?" Howie asked. "We could have met a whole lot easier in Santa Fe or San Geronimo. This place looks a little crazy to me."

Eckehart barked his unpleasant laugh. "I needed to get out of the house. My wife's been driving me crazy and we have a one year old who cries a lot. Anyway, I get a kick out of these ufologists. Sometimes I get an idea or two listening to them. Most of them would give anything for a ride in a flying saucer. Wouldn't you?"

Howie considered this. "I'm not sure. I'm the sort of guy who likes to keep his feet on the ground."

"Me, I'd go in a New York second," the physicist said. "Now tell me about Grisha. What the hell was he doing up on that mountain top?"

"Why do you want to know?"

"*Why*? He was my buddy, that's why. I've been with him on and off since my graduate days at Cambridge. I'm the reason he came to Los

Alamos, so we could work together on a theory he's been toying with. Up until ten days ago, I would have called him my mentor."

"What happened ten days ago?"

"He disappeared with all our lab notes, everything. Which isn't cool. The folks at LANL take a dim view of papers and laptops leaving the compound."

"He took documents from the lab?"

Eckehart sighed. "Listen, what gets worked on at LANL, stays at LANL. Them's the rules. What pisses me off is he took a flash drive with my work on it, too. It's going to set me back a few months, but I don't mind that part. What I mind is he's going to publish it and claim it's his."

This certainly gave Howie a different picture of Grisha Bloom from what he'd had before. If it were true.

"When's the last time you saw him?" he asked.

"The Friday before last. He didn't show up at the Lab on Monday and nobody's seen him since. Not alive, anyway. Except you," Eckehart added, giving Howie a meaningful look. "What happened up there on that mountain?"

"Why I should tell you, Dr. Eckehart?"

"Oh, come off it, Moon Deer! You wouldn't be here if you weren't looking for answers. Maybe I'm the guy who'll give them to you. Or maybe I won't. But you sure as hell aren't going to find anyone else at Los Alamos who'll even give you the time of day."

That was true, Howie supposed. He proceeded warily.

"Well, there's not much to tell. It was raining hard and I was hurrying to set up my tent when Bloom walked into the clearing from nowhere. He scared the hell out of me. He was barefoot, dressed only in pants, no shirt. He looked like some crazy prophet from the Old Testament."

Eckehart grinned. "The mad professor! That's Grisha, alright. Even on a normal day."

"This wasn't a normal day. He was in bad shape, rambling all sorts of nonsense."

"Rambling about what nonsense exactly?" Eckehart asked.

"How he had just come from a wormhole backward in time from the planet Klizmor. He said he'd been dropped off by a spaceship shaped like a giant hot dog. Really crazy stuff. I was worried about him."

"Klizmor, you said. Are you sure it was Klizmor?"

Howie gave Eckehart a deeper look. "Why? Have you traveled to Klizmor, too?"

Eckehart smiled. "Of course not. Klizmor is one of the hundreds of exo-planets we've discovered in the past few years. That's just the nickname we've given it. Its real name is A40-57M. It's in the Alpha Centauri system. We're finding these planets by their gravitational pull on other bodies. Klizmor is especially interesting to us because it's very Earth-like. It's in the Goldilocks Zone—that's what we used to call the zone where we believe there's liquid water and the possibility of life. Not too hot, not too cold. A planet that's just the right distance from a star."

"You don't call it the Goldilocks Zone anymore?" Howie was disappointed. As a fan of fairy tales, he'd always liked this designation.

"It's complicated. In recent years, we've come to accept the possibility that life might exist outside the Goldilocks Zone. Planets and moons where there might be subsurface water heated by tidal motion or by the molten core. Europa, for instance, one of Jupiter's moons. But you're probably not interested in stuff like that. As for Klizmor, it's all speculation—no one has ever been there, and no human ever will. It's much too far away."

"You don't believe in wormholes, Doctor?"

"No, I don't. And if there were such a thing, any life form as we know it would be torn apart, atom by atom. What else did Grisha tell you?"

Howie proceeded to describe how he got Grisha Bloom into his tent and how the next morning Howie hiked down the mountain to get help.

As Howie was speaking, Eckehart turned on his stool so that he was facing Howie more directly. He was so fat it wasn't easy for him to swivel on the stool.

"Look, Moon Deer, I don't care about the rain, I don't care about you hiking down to get help. You know what I do care about, don't you?"

"No, I don't," Howie answered.

"Did he give you something? Did he tell you anything?"

Howie shrugged. "Only what I've told you. He was rambling, suffering from exposure. How he got up there I don't know. But it was obvious I needed to get him down. He was a sick man."

"And that's everything?"

"What more could there be?"

"What more? You're kidding me! This is Grisha Bloom we're talking about, one of the top nuclear physicists in the world. Whatever he told you, anything at all, could be important."

"Tell me about the discovery of the Blue Moon quark," Howie countered. "Did you work on that with him?"

"Sure, I did. But he was wrong. That quark was in his imagination, nowhere else."

"You're saying it was a fraud?"

"No, I didn't say that. Grisha believed he'd found something, but he was mistaken, that's all. The guy was sort of innocent, really. Gullible. Not a fraud as much as a fool."

"So what did he find in the CERN accelerator if it wasn't the Blue Moon quark?"

"You've been doing your homework, I see. What did he find? Well, in my opinion it was an anti-quark. Do you know the six types of quarks, Moon Deer?"

"I think so. Up, Down, Charm, Strange, Top, Bottom."

"That's right. But remember, each of these quarks is coupled with an anti-quark. This is probably more complicated than what you want to know. But that's what I think he saw, the anti-quark that's coupled to the Strange."

Howie pondered this. A strange anti-quark. It made him glad to be a mere private eye. "So the idea of outright fraud—"

"Hold on, you gotta understand that there's lots of politics in science, just like everywhere else. Competition. People trying to one-up each other. Jealousy, ambition, greed—science isn't immune. That's where this whole fraud idea came from. With Grisha's discovery, there were some people who wanted to shoot him down. Which is why if Grisha told you something on that mountain—if he *gave* you something—you'd better come clean about it or you're going to find yourself in a whole lot of trouble."

"From who? Whom," Howie added, correcting his grammar.

"Use your imagination. Inquiring minds want to know. And some of these people aren't as nice as I am. They'll squeeze information out of you in ways you won't like. Fingernails, electric prods . . . you're playing in the big league now, Moon Deer, and you'd better think carefully about what you do."

"So I should come clean to you, Dr. Eckehart? Is that what you're saying?"

He laughed. "Why not? Here we are having a drink together. We're buddies, almost. And believe me, you'd rather talk to me than some of the other players in this game. The Chinese, the Russians . . . you don't want to get involved with this, Moon Deer. I could help you navigate some tricky waters you won't be able to navigate alone."

Howie put on his most innocent, blankest, dumbest expression.

"I wish I could help you. But all I know is this was a sick old man who was wandering around in the rain at 12,000 feet. I tried to help him, that's all."

It seemed to Howie that he had been saying the same thing again and again to different people ever since he had climbed down from Dawson Peak.

He wasn't sure why nobody believed him.

Chapter Eleven

Howie had the Monday morning blahs.

It didn't help that it was another pitch perfect New Mexico summer morning. Blue sky, the air fresh and cool and clean. On a morning like this, you should wake up happy. But he wasn't. He had gotten home late from the ghost town and had only slept for a few hours.

His meeting with Brandon Eckehart had left more questions than it had answered. Above all, he had liked Grisha Bloom, the modest and oddly endearing Nobel laureate, and he didn't like thinking of him as someone who might have stolen nuclear secrets from Los Alamos.

If that was true. And maybe it wasn't. Howie knew he was in a tricky game where people might lie.

He drove into town and sat in the office feeling depressed. Ruth wouldn't be in until the afternoon because there wasn't much work for her to do until Jack returned from Hawaii and the agency was rolling again with a new case. Meanwhile, they didn't have a client, and every-thing felt in limbo.

The more he thought about his meeting with Brandon Eckehart, the odder it seemed. He still didn't understand why they had needed to meet in a ghost town. Grisha had warned him to be particularly wary of Eckehart and he was starting to think it was a warning he should have taken more seriously.

And what now?

It seemed to Howie that he should Fed Ex the book of Chinese poems to Dr. Sachs at the Institute for Advanced Study in Princeton and be done with the whole thing. This would be unsatisfying, but he didn't see what more he could do.

Sure, it would have been interesting to discover if Grisha really had stolen something from LANL, but there was no way a civilian like Howie could get anywhere near an investigation like that. Los Alamos was closed to him and he hated to think what Lorna Wolf would do if she found him poking around.

So just drop it, Howie said to himself. Get on with life. Write it off as a strange experience. Send Sachs the equation and let him worry about what he should do with it.

In the spirit of moving on, Howie phoned Louis Gunn, the owner of the Hunter and Gatherer restaurant who had left a message for him about a possible investigation. It didn't seem like the sort of case Wilder & Associate would take on, but it was only polite to get back to him.

Gunn came by in the late morning and Howie met with him in Jack's office to listen to his woes. Gunn was a tall string bean of a man with a long pale face and a mournful expression. Sadly, the paleo diet hadn't caught on in San Geronimo and Louis didn't understand why. The restaurant wasn't doing well. Worse still, he believed his wife—nineteen years younger than himself—was having an affair with the chef and they were both stealing from the till.

Howie explained that Wilder & Associate didn't investigate cases of marital infidelity. It was a rule Jack had laid down from the start and which Howie supported. There would be no sneaking around bedroom windows with cameras.

Stealing from the till made this case more complex perhaps, but it was still a yucky situation, a love triangle, a sad melodrama that Wilder & Associate would leave for the players themselves to work out. Mr. Gunn, with his failed restaurant and failed marriage, looked so woebegone that Howie didn't quite have the heart to turn him down. So, he said he would talk it over with Jack when he returned from Hawaii. He would let Jack tell the man no.

By the time Louis Gunn left, Howie was feeling grumpier and grayer than ever. Fortunately, it was approaching the lunch hour and the prospect of a good meal always cheered him up.

He was debating his eating options—pizza, a burrito, sushi perhaps—when his phone chimed with an incoming text.

The text came from a blocked number. It read:

Come immediately need to talk urgently my house 1051 Isotope Rd soon as you get this Eckehart

It seemed strange to Howie that this had been sent from a blocked number since the previous call from Eckehart had come from a number that wasn't blocked.

Howie called back wanting more information. He was starting to feel fed up with astrophysicists and he wasn't in the mood for a wild goose chase. But there was no answer.

He read the text message a second time.

Come immediately need to talk urgently . . .

Well, what else did he have to do today?

He closed up the office and drove to Los Alamos as fast as he could without getting a speeding ticket.

Why not?

***

Los Alamos was a prosperous mid-American town that had been dropped down, seemingly out of nowhere, onto a New Mexican mesa.

There were no old adobe buildings with softly rounded corners. Nor were there double-wide trailers with pickup trucks parked outside. The architecture was sharp and square. Yet somehow the hyper all-American ordinariness—just a regular little town that had invented the atomic bomb—gave Los Alamos a feeling that you had just entered the Twilight Zone.

Brandon Eckehart and his wife lived in a modest one-story home with a two-car garage on a residential street about half a mile from the Lab. There was a small patch of lawn outside and a flower bed alongside the front of the house that didn't appear to have ever received much love. A scraggy rose bush near the front door needed a good pruning.

There were no cars in the driveway, and it didn't look as though anybody was home. He drove past the house and parked a few houses further down the street, sensing something wasn't right. He walked back along the sidewalk and rang the doorbell. From inside the house, he was surprised to hear a child crying. It was a grating sound. The crying was ramping itself up, feeding on its own misery, growing to an almost hysterical wail.

Howie rang the bell a second time and waited impatiently for someone to come. The wailing paused as the child stopped to take a breath, then continued at a louder pitch. Howie remembered Eckehart saying that he and his wife had a one-year-old. The kid certainly had good lungs.

Howie rang the bell a third time. The wailing was starting to worry him. It was a wrenching noise that made Howie tense all over. Someone—mom or dad—needed to pick the child up and do something. Howie banged on the door with his fist.

"Hello!" he called.

There was still no answer.

This was starting to feel very wrong.

Howie tramped through the flower bed at the front of the house until he could see in the picture window. The living room had been trashed. A black leather sofa had been turned upside down, a lamp was broken on the floor, a painting torn from the wall, a flat screen TV tipped over. Comic books were strewn everywhere—Dr. Eckehart's collection, he presumed. Howie still couldn't see the child, but the wailing had ratcheted up into hysterical overdrive.

Howie moved quickly around the side of the house trying to figure out how he was going to get inside. The kitchen window looked like his best bet, but it was closed and locked. He found a rake leaning against the side of the building and used the handle to smash the glass. It was a messy operation. He used the handle again to clear away as much broken glass as he could from the frame, but he was still going to need something—a blanket, a piece of material perhaps—to keep from getting badly cut.

He found a pad on a garden chair in the backyard that he thought might do. He put the pad across the bottom of the window frame and used an outdoor faucet as a foothold to hoist himself up onto the sill and halfway inside until he was peering down into a sink full of dirty dishes. Unfortunately, his butt was hanging out the window and he wasn't sure how he was going to get the rest of the way in. He managed to grab hold of the kitchen faucet and kick with his feet. Somehow with an oomph and a wiggle, he pulled himself head first across the sink and tumbled onto the kitchen floor with a grunt of pain.

Howie picked himself up, breathing hard from the effort. His arm was bleeding from a shard that had cut him while he was crawling through the window.

The child's crying was louder and more insistent now that he was inside the house. The kitchen was as much of a mess as the living room. Drawers had been pulled out and there were broken plates and glasses on the floor. Howie ignored his bleeding arm and followed the wailing through the house. He came to a bedroom where he found a small child standing upright in a crib, holding itself against the side. It was a girl, Howie thought, but he wasn't sure. She was red in the face and howling with all her might. She was dressed in a blue pajama top with a pattern of little yellow ducks and her diaper smelled like it was in serious need of a change.

"There, there," Howie said helplessly. There was no telling how long the child had been left alone in the crib, but it was clearly too long.

"Upsy-ducksy," Howie said in his best kiddie voice. He lifted the toddler from the crib into his arms. He didn't have a clue what to do next except jiggle the child up and down and make soothing noises as he walked around the room.

"There, there, everything's going to be okay," he lied. But there was no fooling a one-year-old. The child screamed in Howie's ear, furious that life wasn't going her way.

Howie was sympathetic.

"Whoopsie doopsie," he cooed as he rubbed the kid's back and walked with her into the hallway. "Let's see if we can find your parents, shall we?"

Where were her damn parents?

Holding the child in his arms, he made a quick tour of the house. There was a master bedroom at the end of the hall and a guest room turned into a home office. Everywhere he looked, the house had been pulled apart. Someone had gone through here like a tornado.

"Yeeaahh!" howled the kid.

Howie improvised a half-remembered nursery rhyme. "Little Miss Muffet sat on a puppet, drinking her chardonnay . . ."

The baby continued to howl. The blood from Howie's arm had gotten onto the plastic diaper but there was nothing he could do about that. The kid stank. The diaper was so full, some of it was getting on Howie's hand. Which didn't make, all in all, for a fun afternoon.

He carried the child back into the kitchen hoping there might be a bottle in the refrigerator, something to suck on to quiet her down.

There wasn't.

He managed to jiggle the screaming baby into his other arm and find the phone in his back pocket. The screen was cracked from his tumble on the kitchen floor. But the light came on when he pushed the button.

He was starting to punch in 911 when he heard the front door open and the sound of footsteps in the living room. His first thought was, thank God, Mom and Dad are home. He was about to call out when caution took over. There was no telling who this might be.

Howie listened as the footsteps moved slowly through the living room coming his way.

To his surprise it was the woman who looked like a girl who stepped into the doorway. The woman who had come to his office on Friday wanting to hire him to find her father.

Mia Bloom. Perhaps.

Today she wore black jeans and a loose long-sleeve black shirt. Her strange blue eyes studied him from beneath her fringe of black hair. Her cheeks were slightly flushed. Oddly, the child stopped crying at the sight of her.

"Moon Deer," she said thoughtfully. "Well, well!"

There was a gun in her right hand, a small revolver, silver, pointed at him with a steady hand.

Chapter Twelve

Howie held the child in his arms more tightly, not sure if he was protecting the kid, or the kid was protecting him. He was relieved when the woman who looked like a girl lowered her gun.

"Are you auditioning to be a father, Moon Deer?" she asked.

"Actually, I'm wondering where Mom and Dad might be," he answered. "I was about to call 911 when you arrived."

"There's no time for 911. Trust me, we have to get out of here."

"Who are you? You're not Mia Bloom, that I know. So why should I trust you"

"There's no time to explain. They'll be back any minute."

"Who are they?"

"Not now. Give me the baby. Let's go."

"We can't just take a baby!"

"Sure we can. We'll get rid of her later."

"*Her*? How do you know it's a her?"

"Her name is Juniper, Moon Deer. I know all about her. Now let's get going. I promise I'll explain everything later. But we seriously need to leave."

As they stood talking, there was the sound of a van door sliding open in the driveway.

"Too late, they're here!" she hissed. "Hurry! We'll duck out the back door!"

"Who the hell are you?" Howie hissed back. "I'm not going anywhere until you tell me who you are."

"Okay. I'm from the military. I'm Major Zoey Kelly, United States Air Force. I'm a Good Guy. Now let's go!"

***

Howie followed her out the sliding glass door to the backyard. Major Zoey Kelly had won him over. For the moment, at least.

The backyard was small and not well-tended. The lawn was uncut and there were plastic toys scattered around in the bushes and the grass. A shallow wading pool was half deflated with an inch of dirty water at the bottom. Zoey—it was going to take Howie a while to think of Mia by that name—hurried to the wooden fence that separated the Eckehart's backyard from the next yard over.

"Hand her over to me when I'm on the other side!" she commanded.

"What? I can't just . . ."

He had started to say you couldn't just toss a baby over a seven-foot fence! But she was already up and over into the next yard. Military training had obviously done Zoey/Mia some good.

With serious misgivings, Howie managed to lift little Juniper and hand her over the fence into Zoey's raised hands. Fortunately, the little girl seemed to think this was a great game and didn't wail in protest. Howie followed after her, scrambling up and over. But he had no military training and was far from graceful. The fence was constructed of 1 x 12 planks that had been screwed onto three rows of horizontal 2 x 4s. He used the 2 x 4s as a step ladder to hoist himself up until he was able to tumble head first into a bush on the other side.

"Ugh!" grunted Howie.

"Hurry!" she told him. She was already dashing with the baby toward the fence to the next yard over.

Howie pulled himself out of the brambles and followed. This yard was considerably neater than the Eckehart's and the fence they needed to climb was the chain-link sort with better footholds. They repeated the ritual, Zoey going first, Juniper second, then Howie following as best he could.

The new backyard was larger than the others and it had a swing set and a child's playhouse. Howie could see a woman and child sitting inside the house through a sliding glass door. They were on a sofa watching TV, mesmerized, facing the front of the house rather than the rear. This was a lucky break. A brightly colored cartoon flickered on the screen. Howie hoped Juniper didn't start crying and bring their attention toward the backyard. Many people in New Mexico owned guns and when they saw an intruder, they shot first and asked questions later.

"This way!" Zoey whispered.

Howie followed Zoey and Juniper along a path at the side of the house that led to the street. His arm was bleeding again. It had stopped earlier, but all the climbing and crashing into bushes had opened the wound. He felt punctured and sweaty and bloody and bashed.

He came up behind Zoey who had paused by the edge of the house to peer up and down the street. A white van with no markings was in the Eckehart's driveway two houses down.

"LANL?" Howie asked softly.

"We don't want them to find us here."

"Why not? We haven't done anything wrong. All you have to say is you're Air Force."

She turned to him incredulously. "Are you kidding, Moon Deer? We've taken a kid from the home of one of their top physicists, a place with papers scattered everywhere and all the furniture upside down! You think this is going to be easy to explain? You want to spend a week in a windowless cell answering questions?"

Howie saw her point. "Not really."

"Where's your car?"

"It's just up the street. I wasn't sure what to expect when I arrived."

"Okay, we'll use your car. Mine's across the street from the house and they would spot us. Let's go. We'll walk slow and casual, a nice young couple with their kid out for a stroll."

They left the shelter of the house, walked to the sidewalk, then continued toward Howie's Subaru a few doors down. He was glad to put some distance between them and the Eckehart house. He felt an itchy place in the hollow of his back where he expected a bullet any moment.

"You drive," she told him when they reached his car. "I'll hold the baby."

Major Kelly was a bossy woman. Probably that came with her rank. Howie wasn't sure how he had gotten into this predicament, but there didn't seem any choice but to go along.

He drove while she sat in the passenger seat holding baby Juniper across her shoulder. The baby whimpered and gurgled from time to time but remained remarkably calm. Zoey seemed to have a knack with children. The leaking diaper didn't appear to bother her.

She directed him along the back streets of Los Alamos until they gradually circled back to the highway that descended into the Rio Grande river valley below. The middle of the day was generally an ugly time in New Mexico, beneath the hot blaze of hard, shadowless sun. But it was now after four o'clock and everything was starting to be beautiful again. The shadows returned, the desert glowed with vibrant colors, the distant mountains and mesas were etched against the darkening blue of the sky.

"Where are we going?" Howie asked.

"Santa Fe. We need to stop at Walmart to pick up diapers and baby food."

"There's a closer Walmart in Española."

"Yeah, but we need to get as far from Los Alamos as we can."

"So we're on the run, I guess," he said unhappily. "With a baby that's not ours! You know, Major, when you walked into my office on Friday, I had no idea what an interesting woman you'd turn out to be!"

She smiled. Just a little.

"We need to avoid Lorna Wolf, at least until things are more settled. Here's the deal. She's determined to recover whatever it was that Grisha Bloom took from the Lab. This is the most serious breach of security at Los Alamos in years and it happened under her watch. Lorna is an ambitious woman and she's fighting to save her career. Which makes her very dangerous."

"So what did Bloom steal from the Lab?"

She gave Howie a look. "How do I know? Why don't you tell me?"

He shook his head. "I don't know either. I was just—"

"Oh, sure!" she said dismissively. "The innocent camper hiking up the mountain picking daisies. When all of a sudden, wham bam thank you ma'am, he finds himself involved in a high stakes nuclear intrigue."

"Well, yes," said Howie. "That pretty much describes it."

"Poor Moon Deer! You should be back at Princeton, finishing your dissertation instead of being here playing in a dangerous game where you don't even know the rules. What's your academic field? Oh, yeah—culinary psycho-sociology!"

Howie turned to her. "Okay, you know a lot about me. Now let's hear about you. You say you're with the Air Force. How about showing me some ID?"

"I'm afraid that's not an option," she told him. "You'll just have to trust me."

Howie groaned.

"I'm sorry, but I'm with a department I can't discuss."

"Sure, you can. I mean, here we are, kidnappers together. Partners in crime."

"Okay, I'm with AATIP. That's the Advanced Aerospace Threat Identification Program. It's a secret program that I shouldn't be telling you about. We've been investigating UFO sightings for the past seventy years."

"That's a long time."

"The Air Force takes this seriously. We have to. We don't like unexplained sightings in our skies, whether they're Russian spy planes or UFOs. I've been with AATIP for four years now."

"And you're an astrophysicist?"

"Of course. You think the Air Force employs a bunch of amateurs? I earned my doctorate at MIT when I was twenty-three. I'm considered something of a genius in the field. That's why the government headhunted me. It's my job to analyze sightings and decide what's possible and what is not."

"And is Zoey Kelly truly your real name?"

She didn't answer immediately.

"Well?" he pressed.

She turned and smiled sweetly.

"Of course, it is! We're partners in crime now," she reminded him. "Why would I lie to you?"

He had to laugh, he supposed.

***

Howie wandered lost up and down the aisles of the Super Walmart in Santa Fe in search of Pampers and baby food. The store was gigantic, an empire of cheaply made consumer goods. You just about needed a compass to find your way from the pet food to the diapers.

Zoey and little Juniper waited in the car while Howie did the shopping. He had thrown on a sweatshirt he'd found in his car so his bloody arm wouldn't alarm other shoppers. From the diapers and baby food section, he made his way to bandages and antiseptic ointment, knowing he needed to take care of his scratches and wounds.

Shopping at Walmart felt oddly domestic, with Zoey and the new baby waiting in the car. They could almost be an all-American family. But Howie would have been happier if he were certain Zoey was her real name. He liked uncertainty as much as the next guy, but there are some things you want to pin down.

He paid with cash, as she had instructed him so as not to leave a paper trail. Unfortunately, Walmart had more surveillance cameras and facial recognition technology than anywhere on the planet, and if someone was looking for them, they wouldn't be hard to find.

Howie waited outside the car in the parking lot while Zoey laid little Juniper in the back seat and changed her diapers. For somebody in the military, she knew her way around children. When Juniper was safely in her new Pamper, she handed Howie the old diaper out the window. He held it at arm's length and carried it to a trash receptacle where he was happy to see it disappear.

"Now where?" he asked as he slipped back into the driver's seat.

"We need to find ourselves a motel for the night. I want to keep a low profile and stay off the roads until tomorrow."

"A motel's not a good idea," Howie said.

"Why not?"

"Well, there are two reasons. First, Juniper seems like a nice little girl. But she's not our little girl. Wherever Brandon and his wife are, they're going to be worried about her. We need to get her somewhere she'll be taken care of."

"Totally my thinking," she agreed. "In fact, while you were in the store, I phoned someone at Kirtland Air Force Base who's going to drive up tomorrow and take her off our hands."

107

"Why tomorrow? Why not now?"

"Look, Moon Deer, Kirtland isn't a day care center. Plus, there are legal questions involved, figuring out this kid's status and what they need to do with her. They want a few hours. It's not a big thing. We'll keep her overnight. It'll be fine. So what's your second objection to a motel?"

"Take a guess."

"Oh, come on, Moon Deer! Are you scared to spend the night with me?"

"Scared isn't the right word. Try terrified."

"Moon Deer, stop being silly. We're professionals and this is a serious matter. I want to get an early start tomorrow. Bloom was renting a house up in the hills and I want to drive up there in the morning and look around. Maybe we'll find something that will give us a better idea of what this is all about."

"Okay, I'll go along with that. So look, I'll put you into a motel and I'll go back to San Geronimo, and in the morning—"

"Moon Deer, your home will be the first place Wolf will come looking for you. So stop being silly. We're on a job, we'll bunk down for the night and get an early start in the morning. No big deal. I won't bite, I promise."

Bunking down for the night. Two professionals on a job. Put like that, it sounded okay.

And she had promised not to bite.

Chapter Thirteen

Room 226 on the second floor of the Motel 6 on Cerrillos Road was no romantic Shangri-La for lovers. It was a stripped down, antiseptic, charmless cave with a TV bolted to the wall near the ceiling on an ugly metal frame so that it couldn't be stolen.

But it had a bed.

A double bed.

Howie sat nervously on what passed in a Motel 6 as an armchair while Zoey took a shower. He could imagine too acutely her body in the shower stall—lithe, naked—the water flowing over her small breasts, her flat smooth stomach, her thighs, legs.

Claire no longer had a claim on him, so what was he waiting for?

Pounce, said the voice in his lizard brain. Probably she needed someone to soap her back.

Juniper had eaten an entire four ounce jar of Gerber's Banana Blueberry Delight and she was fast asleep with a bottle of milk in her arms on the center of the bed, dead to the world. *So slip out of your clothes and join Zoey in the shower.*

Stop it, stop it! he told himself.

The fact was, Claire *did* still have a hold on him, whether she had a claim or not. He wasn't ready to give her up. And for what? For a girl who had lied to him? A very pretty girl, as it happened, but he wasn't certain he even knew her real name.

She could be anything, anyone.

She could be a wiggly wet body in his arms . . .

How long had it been since he had slept in a motel room with a stranger? Desire pulled at him like a rip tide. He wanted her badly. Yet he knew he would feel that he had betrayed Claire if he gave in, whether this was reasonable or not. He wasn't over Claire, that was the problem. Not by a long shot.

Howie turned on the bolted-down television set to the evening news broadcast. Thank God for the evening news! There was nothing like it to deflate a runaway libido. War in Syria, political shenanigans at home, the arctic ice cap melting. Howie was sitting in profound gloom pondering the state of the planet when Zoey stepped out of the shower with only a white towel wrapped around her body. Being a Motel 6, it was a very small towel.

There was no denying the fact that Zoey looked good in a tiny towel. Her bare shoulders were delicately sculpted. Her skin glowed from the heat of the shower. Her tattoo, protruding from the bottom edge, was fascinating.

"Your turn," she told him.

He hesitated, watching her as she stood only a few feet away watching him. Hormones danced in the air between them. It wasn't only Howie. The erotic vibrations between them were so thick it was hard to breathe.

"Go take your shower, Moon Deer," she said gently. "Maybe another time, another place, don't you think? But you'd better lock the door," she added, "in case I change my mind."

***

He was asleep in the morning when she woke him, tugging on his arm.

"Come on, Moon Deer, we have to get going."

He opened his eyes reluctantly. Juniper had slept between them, the perfect chaperone. The child had woken twice in the night crying. Zoey had changed her diaper the first time, and Howie had done it the second.

But he didn't see the child now. There was no sign of the baby anywhere. Even the box of diapers and baby food was gone.

"Where's Juniper?"

"Someone from Kirtland came and got her an hour ago."

"While I was sleeping?"

"I didn't want to wake you. I told you we would only have her one night. Now, let's get going. There's a lot to do today."

She was already dressed in her black jeans and loose black shirt, flawlessly put back together.

They checked out of the motel, picked up coffee to go at a drive-through coffee spot, and headed north into the mountains to the house Grisha Bloom had rented during his stay in New Mexico. Consulting the map on her phone, Zoey directed him. The highway climbed in altitude to the summit of a long grade, then dove down into a wooded valley alongside a fast-moving creek. This was an impoverished part of northern New Mexico with only a scattering of houses and doublewide trailers. The buildings sagged with age and neglect.

"In a hundred feet, make a left turn onto County Road B254 . . ."

She was as impersonal as the voice of a navigational guide. Whatever vibrations had flickered between them last night, were now gone.

"This seems kind of far out in the sticks for Bloom to live," he said as they drove. "A long way from his work in Los Alamos."

"According to Google maps, it's less than an hour to the Lab. That's not a bad commute. In L.A., people often drive two, three hours to get to their job."

"So you actually *do* live in in L.A.?"

"Didn't I tell you that?"

"You did. But you also told me that you were Grisha Bloom's daughter."

"Turn right in five hundred feet," she told him, ignoring the jibe. "We're looking for Santa Maria Road."

Howie turned right on Santa Maria. He crossed a river on a rickety one lane bridge and headed up a hill on a winding country road. Every now and then he glanced over at her in his passenger seat. She was deep in her own thoughts.

"Okay," she said finally. "I'm sorry I had to tell you some fibs, Moon Deer. It's not my style. But I didn't have a choice."

"I understand. So why don't you make a clean breast of it? You'll feel better."

"I've told you already, I'm with the Air Force. What more is there to say?"

"Then why did you come to my office pretending to be Grisha Bloom's daughter?"

"Because we don't talk about what we do at AATIP. I work in a top secret department, just like the people at LANL. Anyway, I wanted to find Bloom and I thought pretending to be his daughter would be a way to get you to help me. My data base said you're highly susceptible to damsels in distress."

Howie rolled his eyes. "Your data base!"

"Well, was it wrong?" she challenged.

He decided to let this question slide. He didn't like being in a data base. Especially when it had the goods on him.

"Why were you looking for Bloom?"

"Because he was an unusually credible person, and he was saying he was abducted by a flying saucer. Of course AATIP is going to check out his story. That's our job."

Howie turned his eyes from the road long enough to give her a hard look.

"But here's the rub. You came to my office the first time on Thursday morning and you told Ruth, our secretary, that you wanted to talk to me about finding your father. Great, I get it. But on Thursday morning I was still up in the mountains and nobody except me knew that I had met Bloom. At that time, nobody but me knew about him being abducted by a flying saucer."

"And you want an explanation, I suppose? You want to know how I knew?"

"Only if it wouldn't be too much trouble to tell me the truth for a change."

Zoey nodded slowly.

"Okay, I'm going to trust you with a secret, Moon Deer, and I hope I'm not making a mistake. Last Wednesday evening, July 10th, an experimental aircraft from Kirtland Air Force Base flying at 53,000 feet came upon a possible event in the skies over northern New Mexico."

"What do you mean, possible event?"

"I mean a possible UFO sighting. The pilot recorded an unidentified object moving at more than 10,000 miles an hour that made an impossible 90 degree turn and disappeared into the mesosphere. The pilot was able to record the flight of this object for thirty-seven seconds before it vanished."

"You have this on film?"

"On his digital flight recorder."

"And you've seen it?"

"Yes, of course."

"Did it . . ." Howie paused. "Did it look like a giant hot dog?"

"For chrissake, Moon Deer, you've been reading too many comic books! It was more an intense beam of light without any real definition. No matter what we do with the digital recording, we can't make it any clearer. It could be anything, of course. We've had these kinds of sightings before, particularly at very high altitudes. There are a number of possible explanations that have nothing to do with flying saucers. But combined with Bloom's story, it's of obvious interest."

"Why does the Air Force keep these sightings secret?"

"Think about it. There'd be global panic if these things got out."

"I'm not sure about that. Sometimes I think there would be global relief. But you still haven't told me how you knew that I'd met Grisha Bloom when you came to the office on Friday."

"I was looking for him, that's all. He had disappeared from LANL with some documents. I'm an astrophysicist, Moon Deer, not a detective. I thought you would be able to help me find him."

"But why?" Howie had listened carefully to her explanation, but it didn't make sense. "I still don't get why you were looking for Grisha Bloom on Thursday. Maybe later, sure. But not then."

"It's the documents he took. They had to do with . . . well, I'm not going to get into that. They're top secret, the highest classification. Let's just say that they're connected to my field."

"Hmm," said Howie. "Claiming something is classified covers a lot of sins. But okay, tell me this. How did you know these documents were missing? You don't work for LANL, do you?"

"No, I don't."

"Then how?"

"Moon Deer, you're backing me into a corner!"

"I hope so. Now, how did you know?"

"Okay, Brandon Eckehart told me. He came to me last week. He's my source at Los Alamos."

"The Air Force has spies at LANL?"

"Moon Deer, this conversation is over. I've told you much more than I intended. Now keep your eyes on the road."

Howie pulled off the road onto a gravel turnaround and came to a stop. He turned off the ignition so that there was only the sound of the wind and the running water.

"Listen to me, Zoey, Mia—whoever you are. I'm not going anywhere until I know what we're doing. Your story doesn't add up."

She reached over and took his hand. "Okay, okay, Moon Deer, you're right. Of course, it doesn't add up. It's because there are so many things I can't tell you. You have to understand the constraints I'm under. I could go to prison if I tell you certain things. You've just got to trust me. Look, I'll tell you what. Let's concentrate on getting a good look at Grisha's house. I'm hoping it will clear some things up. After that, I'll see if I can answer more of your questions. Okay?"

She gave him a very earnest look. Howie knew he was a sucker when it came to women giving him earnest looks. But she was hard to resist.

"Alright," he agreed. "Let's take a look at where Grisha's been living. I'm curious, too. But then you need to tell all."

***

In Santa Fe it was a hot summer day, but in the mountains the sky was dark with the threat of rain and the temperature was at least twenty degrees cooler.

"In one hundred feet, bear left at the next fork," Zoey told him. Except for reading out occasional directions from her screen, she had retreated into a moody silence.

Howie continued upward into the evergreens and steep valleys, past remote ranches and dilapidated trailers. He passed a crude straw dummy hanging by a noose from the beam of an entrance gate to a ranch that he couldn't see from the road. The dummy was dressed up like a woman with a sun hat and torn gingham dress. A sign around her neck said,

115

HILARY. Wrong spelling, but the message was clear. Isolated lives in remote rural places weren't always filled with joy and sunshine.

"I wouldn't like to break down around here," Howie admitted, patting the dashboard of his Subaru affectionately.

The girl made no comment. The moody silence had thickened between them, and he had no idea into what nook of her personality she had gone.

The roads in these mountains were circuitous because of the rugged geography, but Howie sensed he wasn't that far from either Dawson Peak or Dawson, the ghost town. He would need a Forest Service map to be sure—or a bird's eye view—but he believed he was simply coming at the Peak in a roundabout way from a different direction. It was one more odd thing, he thought, that everything brought him back to where he had started. Just like the T.S. Eliot poem.

He said the line aloud: "We shall not cease from exploration, and the end of all our exploring will be to arrive where we started and know the place for the first time."

It was one of the great lines of literature. Words that every private eye should have framed on his wall. But Zoey wasn't impressed. Maybe she didn't like poetry. Maybe it wasn't uncertain enough for her.

"The signal's gone," she said flatly, barely coming to life. She lowered her phone with a sigh.

"I'm surprised you had service this long in these mountains," he said. "So we're lost?"

"The last screen I had said turn left into the driveway in five hundred feet."

"Then that's what we'll do. God forbid we don't do what the screen commands."

"Don't be a Luddite, Moon Deer."

116

"I'm not a Luddite. I'm just not in love with my telephone. Now, my stereo system—that's another matter."

"Whatever."

Howie found the driveway and made the turn. It was a paved switch-back road that zig-zagged upward to the top of a hill until it came to a modern A-frame home with large decks and cathedral windows. It was the sort of ski chalet style that's ubiquitous in Colorado, but you don't see that often in New Mexico.

The house stood at the top of a high grassy meadow with a huge view of the sky. Howie was starting to understand why an astrophysicist would choose such a remote spot. On a cloudless night at this elevation, with no light pollution, the universe would blaze clearly in the heavens. There was a geodesic dome up a path a short way from the house that looked like it might be an observatory. There was no sign of life anywhere.

Howie parked in the driveway. They got out and walked up the steps to a large wooden deck. This was clearly a vacation home. Everything about it promised leisure time in nature for a city dweller.

But this was where the vacation ended.

The front door was hanging open and Howie saw that the living room with its cathedral ceiling had been trashed like the Eckehart home in Los Alamos. Sofas were turned over, lamps were scattered on the floor, artwork pulled down from the walls. It was a more expensive house than the Eckehart home, but otherwise the same malevolent force had blown through here. The only thing missing was the screaming child.

"This is getting old," Howie said. "Someone's looking very hard to find something."

"Right," she answered. "And you know what they want, don't you?"

Howie thought he did know. It was hard to believe that a hastily writ-ten mathematical equation could cause so much trouble. Yet apparently it had.

"Why don't you stay here and see what you can find," she told him. "I want to take a look at that geodesic dome."

"It looks like an observatory."

"It does," she said. "And that's why I want to check it out."

Howie walked through the living room toward a large modern country kitchen with an island in the middle and an expensive gas range with six burners and two ovens. There was damage everywhere, drawers pulled out and broken plates and glasses and silverware on the floor.

He explored a den and a bedroom on the ground floor and then made his way back to the living room. He was about to climb the stairs to the second floor when he heard a sharp high scream from outside.

He ran out the front door and saw Zoey further up the path near the geodesic dome. She was standing with her back to him.

"What's wrong?" he called.

"Come here!"

He jogged down the steps from the deck and up the path to where she was standing.

When she turned to him, her face was mute with horror. She was more than pale. It looked to Howie like all the blood had been sucked from her body. She didn't look human. The blue of her eyes seemed to belong to an alien race.

"There!" she said, pointing to the geodesic dome.

Howie went inside to investigate and wished he hadn't. The dome was a single room with a high ceiling. There was a sled with a large telescope that could be wheeled out the front door on metal tracks onto an outside deck. The telescope was black, a fat metal tube at least eight feet long and three feet in diameter with an eyepiece near the bottom. It was a very professional looking setup.

Howie's eye moved upward from the telescope to the man hanging by his arms from the overhead struts of the dome's frame.

It was Brandon Eckehart. His feet were dangling more than six feet off the ground. His arms had been pulled backward in their sockets in an agonizing position. His head hung limply forward, his mouth open in what looked like a final scream. Whatever had happened here, death had come as a blessing.

There was a second body in the observatory. It was a woman sprawled on the concrete floor on her back with one leg at an unnatural angle. In life she had been an overweight woman in her thirties with frizzy reddish hair. She was dressed in beige shorts and a red Spider Man T-shirt. Howie had never seen her before, but he imagined she might be Ashley Eckehart, Brandon's wife. It wasn't apparent how she had died, but her eyes were open, and several large blue-green flies had settled on her eyeballs, feeding on the coronas.

Howie turned away and hoped he wouldn't throw up. He stumbled outside into the fresh air where Zoey stood where he had left her.

"Look, my phone's in the car," he managed. "Let me see if I can get a signal . . ."

He ran down the path to his car and found his phone in the empty slot beneath the CD player. But when he turned it on, the screen announced the predictable words, NO SERVICE.

Howie walked back up the hill toward the dome hoping a higher spot would give him a signal. In New Mexico, sometimes a few feet brought you back into the modern world.

He tried the phone again, but it was no good. He was in a black hole.

A monsoon storm was moving in over the mountains, dark clouds carried on a strong wind. As he stood frowning at his phone, a beam of sunlight broke through a break in the clouds sending down a ray of golden light. Like God was about to make a rare appearance. Hopefully to solve the problems of the planet.

Howie was looking up at the narrow beam of heavenly light when he thought he heard something. A footstep? A whisper? He wasn't sure. He listened tensely, but now he couldn't hear it.

He was starting to relax when the sound came again.

Yes, there was something, he was sure of it. But it was subtle, like a whisper of air, nothing he could put a name to. The sound seemed to slip in and out of consciousness, disappearing then suddenly coming again. It was more a vibration than an actual sound. A disturbance in the sky.

But what was it?

"Moon Deer!" she called.

He turned and saw the girl standing where he had left her. She stood directly in the narrow beam of light, which gave her slim body a miraculous appearance. Her blue eyes seemed to glow with rapture.

The vibration was growing louder. The sky blazed with an unearthly intensity.

"Moon Deer!" she called again. "Look! They're here!"

"Who's here?"

"*They* are . . . they've come for us . . . they're real!"

Chapter Fourteen

Jack Wilder knew about death.

He'd seen mangled bodies, bodies riddled with bullets, decapitated, bloated, eaten by rats, drowned, buried.

He'd seen children who had been beaten to death, old men stinking up apartments before anyone found them, young women raped and strangled and butchered.

As a cop, you saw it all. You learned to shrug it off with gallows humor and acquired insensitivity. But he couldn't shrug off the death of fifteen-year-old River Eastman, who was the son of Emma's favorite niece. There was no dark joke that could make it go away. There was nothing to stop the terrible hurt.

River had been a golden child. Handsome and kind, sunny, eager for life, possessing a natural charm. Though they lived far away, he and his parents had come to San Geronimo a number of times—in the summer to camp, in the winter to ski. Jack wasn't the sort of man who automatically liked children. But there was something about River that had opened his heart.

On the morning of the funeral, Emma had left Jack on the beach beneath an umbrella with his German shepherd guide dog, Katya, by his feet. Proof of a recent rabies vaccination was the only paperwork needed to bring a dog to the islands, and Hawaiian Air had allowed Katya to ride in the cabin with them.

As usual, Emma had chosen Jack's wardrobe: shorts, sandals, a Hawaiian shirt that wasn't too gaudy, a straw hat, dark glasses. To the people walking by on the beach, he would be just another *haole* on vacation on the North Shore of Oahu.

Jack could smell the salt of the ocean and the heat radiating from the white sand. Without the sense of sight, his other senses were sharpened. He had been to Hawaii before and it had always seemed to him a paradise that wasn't quite. There was too much tension in the air. The tension of overheated tropical places where sex was the dominant engine driving everything. The sullen resentment of the native Hawaiians whose culture had been stolen and marginalized. The smear of tourism.

Despite the poster-perfect appeal of the islands, Jack wasn't sure he liked it here.

Emma's niece, Julia, and her husband, Todd, had a lot of money, far too much money in Jack's opinion. Their two-story house sat directly on the beach behind a line of swaying palms surrounded by fragrantly scented plumeria trees. They had nearly an acre of well-manicured lawn and garden. At the rear of the house was a swimming pool, which seemed unnecessary to Jack with one of the planet's most beautiful beaches only yards away. They also owned a high-rise condo in Honolulu, a ranch on Maui, and a ski chalet in Aspen.

Julia and Todd had met in the Peace Corps in Micronesia at a more idealistic time of their lives when Todd had hoped to be a novelist. But a few years of poverty in New York City had cured him of this fantasy and he became an investment banker instead. Unfortunately, all their money hadn't done their only child a bit of good when he drowned in the surf less than half a mile from the expensive location where Jack was sitting. Nor had it helped Julia and Todd's marriage.

Jack let Katya out of her harness and began throwing a stick for her, a piece of smooth driftwood that she had dropped optimistically onto his lap. She was an exceptionally well-trained guide dog, but a dog just the same. Jack had a good arm—a long time ago, he had played baseball on the San Francisco Police League team—and he managed to throw the stick a good distance.

With each throw, Katya took off running like it was the most exciting game in the world, tearing down the beach and returning the stick to his lap. Jack liked throwing sticks for her. It was rhythmic and soothing and mindless. It helped him forget the family quarrels in the large house behind him, the snipes and recriminations that tend to surface in stressful times.

Todd's parents, Dick and Sally Eastman, had flown in from Illinois. They were Christian fundamentalists who believed Jesus had visited punishment on the family because of Julia and Todd's secular lifestyle. River had died on a Sunday and Mr. Eastman had mentioned several times that, if the boy had been at church that morning instead of surfing at the beach, he would still be alive. Emma had taken to avoiding them altogether.

Meanwhile, Julia and Todd were fighting because she hadn't wanted to allow River to surf the huge waves on the North Shore, believing a fifteen-year-old boy was too young. It was Todd who had insisted their son shouldn't be overprotected. Julia didn't actually come out and say I told you so. She said nothing, which was worse. The looks she gave her husband were pure poison.

The memorial service had become an especially contentious issue. Julia wanted a simple ceremony with a few close friends on the beach near where River had drowned. But Todd had other plans. He insisted on a large wake at the fancy Turtle Bay Resort a few miles away, inviting business associates and several important Hawaiian politicians. As usual, it was Todd who got his way.

The marriage had been in trouble even before River's death. All that money, the expensive houses, the weeks apart when Todd flew to Hong Kong and London on business. Jack suspected Julia's husband had affairs. Julia, too, perhaps. Though of course grown children didn't necessarily tell their relatives such things.

"You know, Katya, I gotta tell you, I'm glad I'm not young any-more," Jack said to his guide dog when she returned the piece of drift-wood to him, only slightly slobbery. He and Katya often had long conversations together. "And you, my friend—aren't you glad you're fixed?"

He gave the stick another good throw, but this time she didn't run af-ter it. She remained by Jack's feet, tense and watchful. She had been trained to protect him.

"What is it, girl?" he asked affectionately, petting her thick furry neck.

Jack became aware of the slush of sandy footsteps coming his way.

"Well, my God! Jack Wilder! What a small world! How are you, Commander?"

Jack didn't immediately recognize the voice. It had to be someone from his police days since he had been addressed by his old rank.

"I heard you lost your eyesight," the man said coming closer. "But you're looking good, Jack . . . it's Burton," he added. "Burton Harris."

Jack nodded cautiously, not especially pleased. "Lieutenant Harris," he acknowledged. "It's been some years."

"Actually, it's Colonel Harris these days. I've been in Washington for quite some time, ever since the Presidio got turned into a damn park. A very bad decision. But there it is. Politics. Meanwhile, I'm stuck behind a desk at the Pentagon, which isn't as much fun as San Francisco in the old days. But you know how it is, Jack. You go where you're told . . . mind if I sit down?"

Jack did mind. But Emma had left her vacant beach chair under the umbrella alongside his own and there had never been a way to stop Burton Harris from doing what he liked, even when he was a mere lieutenant.

Harris had been the Deputy Intelligence officer at the Presidio, the Army fort that guarded the entrance to San Francisco Bay before Congress deactivated the base in 1994. Jack's duties in the SFPD had occasionally brought the two men into contact. There had been one particularly ugly case, an Army sergeant who had been running drugs out of the Presidio, that had strained cooperation between the military and local police. As usual, the military got its way, hushing up the incident, and the SFPD got nothing.

"So what brings you to Oahu, Burton?" Jack asked, hoping to keep the conversation short.

"To be honest, you do, Jack. I was thinking it might be a good idea to have one of my people come have a word with you. And then I thought to myself, Burton, old man, here it's July and you're stuck in an office in muggy D.C.—why don't you jump on a government plane and hop over to Oahu and speak to your old friend Jack Wilder? It would be fun to see him after all these years, and maybe even get in a few games of golf, and suck up a Mai Tai or two. You know how it is when you work for the government, Jack. You're always looking for the odd perk. I mean, a trip to Hawaii! What the hell!"

Jack nodded very slightly but didn't smile. "I'm flattered you came all this way to see me. But I can't imagine why. I've been retired for years."

"I understand you're running a detective agency in some New Mexican town?"

"That's right. Very small potatoes, I'm afraid. More of a hobby than a business."

"But, hey, a gumshoe! I like it, Jack! You and Sam Spade! I'm a little envious, in fact. It sounds like more fun than sitting in an office at the Pentagon. Though it must be a challenge. Being blind, I mean. A blind detective—that's not something you encounter every day."

Jack's face registered no expression.

"Yet you do very well, I understand. More clients than you can handle. You must be good, Jack. But then of course, you always were good. That's one of the things I remember most about you, how good you were. And you have help. A seeing-eye Indian, no less. What's his name? Howard something? Right?"

"Get to the point, Burton."

Colonel Harris chuckled. "Howard Moon Deer! That's it, I remember now. Some sort of graduate student, isn't he? Not a professional, like you and me. But doesn't that worry you? I mean, not being a professional. A guy like that could get hurt in a rough trade he hasn't trained for properly. I understand this Howard Moon Deer can barely handle a gun."

Jack kept his temper. "What do you want, Burton. Why are you here?"

"Well, I'll tell you. Seeing as you're an old colleague, I wanted to give you a friendly word of advice. I want you to tell your Indian pal to back off. I want him to have nothing to do with a certain situation that's unfolding in New Mexico. There are national secrets involved and he needs to get out of the way. To be honest, Jack, I can't say I ever liked you. But I felt the need to warn you."

Jack smiled. "So that's what you came all the way from Washington to tell me?"

"That's it. Knowing how stubborn you are, I thought I'd better come in person so you'd know how serious this is."

"Well, thanks for taking the trouble. Now you'd better go have those Mai Tais and games of golf, don't you think? Otherwise you won't have time to take advantage of the perks of your job."

"We're clear about this?"

"We are, Burton. Totally."

Colonel Harris reached out the shake Jack's hand to seal the understanding. Jack didn't know about the offered handshake because he couldn't see. But he heard the menacing growl deep in Katya's throat. In an instant, she could transform from a cuddly pet into a very dangerous animal if she believed Jack was threatened. She didn't seem to like Burton Harris any more than Jack did.

She barked sharply. It wasn't the friendly bark she had when she wanted to play with a stick. It had a snarl in it. It was a bark you didn't want to hear.

"For chrissake, get that dog away from me!" Burton cried. "Get her away!"

"Katya, come here," Jack said, putting an arm around her to keep her back.

"Goddamn dog! Jack, you'd better remember what I told you!"

"Oh, I will, Burton."

When he was gone, Jack gave Katya a big hug.

"Good dog . . . who's my favorite doggie-woggie?" he said in the baby talk he used with her when he was absolutely certain there was nobody nearby to hear.

***

Emma appeared at the beach umbrella soon after Colonel Harris left.

Jack knew it was Emma as soon as he heard her footsteps in the sand. They were very different people, often with opposite ideas about life. But after nearly forty years of marriage, it seemed at times they were physically two parts of a single organism.

"Who was that man?" she asked as she took the chair Harris had vacated.

127

"You remember Burton Harris, don't you? From the Presidio. He was the Deputy Chief of Security. Apparently, he's moved up in life. He's at the Pentagon now. Just the sort of slick asshole to work the system to his own advantage."

"I heard Katya threatening him. Not her usual bark at all."

"She's overprotective sometimes. But everything's fine."

"Jack —"

"It's all right, dear. I can handle Burton Harris."

"I wonder," said Emma. He felt her studying him. "I hope he's not asking you to get involved in something dicey."

"No, it's the other way around. He wants me to be uninvolved. Or, at least, he wants Howie to be uninvolved. How are things at the house?" he asked in order to head off any more questions.

"Not pleasant. Julia and Todd are still quarreling about the wake after the service. She's threatening not to go to the fancy reception he's arranged. All she wants is to be with a few friends and close family. Honestly, I'm not sure the marriage is going to survive."

"Well, maybe it's for the best." Jack shook his head. "They've been going their separate ways for some time now. You know, Emma, I think relationships were easier when you and I were young. I wouldn't want to be swimming those waters today."

"I'm not sure I'd describe our early days as easy," Emma told him. Jack had been so involved with his career, he was still blandly unaware of how many times she had almost left him.

"Men and women *liked* each other back then," he insisted. "We were romantic in a way kids just aren't today. Do you remember how we used to drink chianti from those bottles in straw baskets, then put candles in them when they were empty?"

"I remember scraping off the melted wax from the dinner table."

"*Sketches of Spain*!" he remembered. "That restaurant with the checkered tablecloths we used to go to in North Beach!"

"Your buddy from the station who got so drunk he barfed in our bathroom and passed out on the living room sofa. What was his name?"

"Sergeant Tom Molinari." Jack sighed. Tom was one of a number of cops Jack knew who had committed suicide after he retired. Put the barrel of your service revolver in your mouth and pull the trigger; such was the preferred escape from lonely, meaningless old age.

"Anyway," said Emma, "I got an email from Claire this morning and she and Howie are going through problems, too."

Jack nodded but didn't ask for details. He wasn't sure he needed to know the intimacies of Howie's love life. Emma told him anyway.

"She's been seeing someone. A famous conductor, Richard Watson-Fowles. I suppose it was bound to happen. She and Howie spend so much time apart, and with Claire's career, she meets very talented people. Richard's much older than her and she's very confused. She's tried to talk to Howie about it, but apparently he's angry and defensive. They had a difficult phone conversation on Sunday."

"Angry and defensive? I don't blame him!"

"Oh, Jack, it's complicated. She loves Howie very much. She can't bear the thought of losing him. But at the same time, Richard is apparently extremely charismatic, and he's been promoting her career. For a young musician, you can imagine how irresistible that would be. Plus, he has a huge house in London and has introduced her to all sorts of famous people. Good God, they had brunch with Harry and Meghan last week!"

"A star is born," Jack said flatly. "I hope she's happy."

"But she isn't happy! She's miserable!"

"Then she should give Richard what's-his-name a good kick in the rear and get back to Howie."

"Jack, you and I are old, our hormones have calmed down, our careers are settled. But when you're young, these things aren't so simple."

"Aren't they? Well, they should be," Jack said stolidly.

Emma sighed. "Well, they're not. And Howie . . . poor Howie! Can you imagine how Howie's taking this? I'm sure he's devastated."

Jack considered this for a moment. In the distance, the surf was breaking and someone was playing bad rap music on a boom box.

"You know, Emma, I think it's time for us to pack up and get ourselves back to San Geronimo. What do you say we change our reservations and fly home tomorrow after the funeral instead of next Saturday?"

"You think Howie is in trouble?"

"Yes, I do," said Jack. "I think he may be seriously in over his head."

Chapter Fifteen

On Wednesday morning, Jack, Emma, and Katya flew from Honolulu to Los Angeles, changed planes, and barely caught their connecting flight to Albuquerque.

With the time change, they lost four hours and arrived in Albuquerque so late they decided to spend the night at the airport Hilton. The next morning, Thursday, they collected Emma's Subaru from long-term parking and arrived in San Geronimo shortly after noon.

Jack had been trying to reach Howie by phone since Monday morning with no luck. He had left a half dozen voice messages, each with a tone of increasing urgency.

He tried Howie a final time as they were driving down the long grade from the foothills into town.

"Howie, it's Jack. Where are you? We've come home early, and I need to talk with you. Give me a call back as soon as you get this, no matter what time."

"Goddamnit!" he swore when he hung up. "What a time for Howie to disappear!"

"Jack, it doesn't help getting angry. He wasn't expecting us back until Saturday. He's a young man, after all. He has a life."

Jack knew she was right. The last time they spoke, he had told Howie to disappear and that was probably what he was doing. Nevertheless, Jack was worried. He should be answering his phone.

"Where do you want me to take you, Jack? Home?"

"No, I need to figure out what's going on. Drop me at the office. Ruth should be there. If I can't reach Howie, I'll have her drive me home later."

***

"I'm back!" Jack called as he and Katya came into the office from the rear door. "Where's Howie?"

Ruth didn't bother to look up from her computer screen in the next room.

"You don't have to shout, Jack. I can hear you perfectly well. Howie hasn't come in today."

"I'm not shouting. I'm asking. When's the last time you saw him?"

"Friday."

"Friday! . . . *last* Friday?"

"None other."

"You haven't seen him for *six* days?"

"Would you like me to write this down for you?"

"What I'd like to know is where Howie's gone!"

Jack galumphed his way into the reception area where Ruth was working. He didn't need Katya to guide him in the office, he knew each step of the way. Nevertheless, he managed to kick over a potted plant, a geranium, that Ruth had moved because she found the scent too strong.

"Damn!" he cried. "When on Friday?"

"He was still here when I left at five. He was doing something on his computer. Why aren't you on Oahu? I've been telling people you won't be back until Saturday."

"I changed my plans. Frankly, paradise isn't all it's made out to be."

"That's because you don't know how to relax, Jack."

"I can relax very well, thank you. I was sitting on my beach chair nearly catatonic with relaxation when some jerk from the Pentagon came over and told me that Howie was messing with national secrets, and if he didn't back off, we were both going to be in trouble. How's that for relaxation?"

"National secrets? You're kidding me."

"I am not."

Jack sat down in the chair by Ruth's desk and sighed with exasperation.

"Okay, so it's Thursday," he said. "And you're saying you haven't heard from Howie since last Friday?"

"That's what I'm saying, Jack. Would you like me to say it one more time?"

"Did he leave voice mail to explain what he was up to?"

"He did not."

"And he didn't call in this entire week?"

"Not that either."

Ruth Slisak was one of the few people willing to take Jack on, face to face, ego to ego, one grouch to another. Emma had discovered Ruth at the San Geronimo Public Library where she had come to ask about inter-library book loans. Ruth was a retired New York City public school teacher, so she knew how to hold her own against all comers and against all odds. Six months ago, when Jack was complaining about how busy the detective agency had become, a victim of its own success, Emma had suggested Ruth as someone who could take on the heavy load of paperwork and correspondence. She was a good addition to Wilder & Associate, eccentric enough to fit in. Like Jack, Ruth had found herself bored in retirement and the extra money was helpful on her fixed income.

"I tell you what, Jack. Why don't I fix you a nice cup of chamomile tea," she suggested. "I'll slip a Valium into it."

"Check your phone," he said. "Maybe he texted you this morning."

"I would have heard my phone chime. But I'll check it anyway, just so you don't have a stroke . . . no, there's nothing."

Jack was becoming increasingly concerned.

"Does he have any appointments today?"

"No, but he missed an appointment yesterday. He was supposed to meet a guy who writes reviews of burrito stands in New Mexico. The guy showed up, but Howie didn't. So he left after forty-five minutes in a huff."

"They review burrito stands now?"

"Apparently they do. Online, of course, like everything else these days. And Howie is considered a world class expert on the subject."

"Well, it doesn't sound like Howie to miss an appointment without calling in. Did you try phoning him?"

"I did, but I couldn't reach him. I left a message."

"Okay, let's back up. Tell me about the client he saw on Friday. The daughter who's looking for her father."

"Dr. Mia Bloom. That's what she called herself, at least. She sure didn't look like a doctor to me."

"What did she look like?"

"A floozie."

"Blonde? Big tits?"

"Not *that* kind of floozie, Jack. Jesus, you're old-fashioned! She was petite, hardly any tits at all, if you want to know the truth. Red lipstick, black hair, pale skin, a gold ring in one nostril. What I would call the delicate Audrey Hepburn type. Very pretty, actually. At least she would have been pretty if she didn't look like something out of Charles Addams. She was in a black dress that was barely the size of a handkerchief. Howie slurped at the sight of her."

"Howie doesn't slurp at girls. His girlfriend, Claire, wouldn't approve."

"Right," said Ruth.

"How old would you say she was?"

"The floozie? She looked about sixteen, but that was part of the illusion. Early thirties, I'd say, when you got a better look. She wore a wig."

"You inspected her pretty thoroughly, I'd say. How do you know it was a wig?"

"No hair is that perfectly black. It was like she was in a costume. A woman can tell these things."

"Could you hear what she and Howie were talking about in his office?"

"Of course, I could hear. She was asking him to find out what happened to her father, the crazy guy Howie ran into on his camping trip. She went on about what a great man he was, winning the Nobel Prize for discovering something called the Blue Moon quark. Doesn't sound like much of a discovery to me, frankly. It appeared for about a millionth of a second in the big particle collider they have in Switzerland."

"I'd say you were listening pretty carefully, Ruth. Some people might even call it eavesdropping."

"Well, I had to, didn't I? A girl like that would eat up Howie in one bite if I wasn't there to protect him."

Jack smiled. "Okay. I'll be in my office if you need me."

Jack returned to his office and sat at his desk, rocking rhythmically in his big wooden rocker. After a few minutes of thought, he switched on Nancy, his desktop computer. Nancy was a specially modified Mac with Kurzweil voice software for the blind. Buzzy had added a few extras as well. Buzzy was a teenage computer genius who had worked part time for the agency before winning a full scholarship to Stanford.

"Good morning, Jack," Nancy told him. "I hope you had a good trip to Hawaii."

"Not so good, Nancy. It was all very sad. The family was on edge, everybody fighting. I'm glad to be home."

"I hope you didn't get sunburned."

"I wore a hat."

"You still need sunscreen, Jack. With an SPF of at least thirty. Personally, I'd go with fifty."

"Good, I'm glad we have that straight. Now, I want you to look up Grisha Bloom, the astrophysicist. I want everything you can find about him."

"There are one thousand two hundred and five entries concerning Gregory Bloom, born in London in 1949. The nickname Grisha comes from his student days at Cambridge University. He's been known by it ever since."

"Great. Let's start with the Wikipedia article and I'll tell you where to go from there."

As Howie had found, the Wikipedia entry began with a general description of the discovery of the controversial Blue Moon quark, which a number of scientists refused to acknowledge belonged in the quark classification. Apparently, there were thousands of tiny subatomic particles of this nature which appeared for a fraction of a second before they were annihilated by antiparticles.

For nearly ten minutes, Jack listened to increasingly arcane descriptions of nuclear physics before he lost patience. This was fascinating stuff, but it wasn't what he wanted to know.

"Hold on, Nancy. Let's save the physics for later. Right now I'm interested in his daughter Mia. Tell me what you can about her."

As Howie had discovered, Wikipedia made a brief mention of a marriage to a Martha Bloom, and a daughter, Mia, who had been born in 1971. This made Mia quite a bit older than Ruth had suggested, but it still didn't strike him as a matter of concern. There were women who could shed decades with a bit of makeup and a surgeon's knife.

As they continued searching the web, Jack and Nancy found the middle-aged academic, Mia Bloom, who taught at Georgia State, but she was obviously not the Mia Bloom they were seeking. Like Howie, they searched the Caltech site to discover there was no faculty member with that name nor a graduate student assistant.

"Nothing!" said Jack, frowning intently.

"Shall we go dark and deep, Jack?" Nancy asked.

"Okay. Let's try Torch."

Torch was software that searched the deep web, the dark, anonymous swamp of the Internet. There were other engines that searched these secret places, but this was the one Buzzy had recommended as the safest for a newbie like Jack. Buzzy had also installed CyberGhost VPN which helped protect anonymity and guard against the threat of identity theft. Every time Jack entered the deep web, he felt like he was in a bathysphere exploring the black depths of the ocean, an alternate world of strange creatures. It was a dangerous world to be in.

But there was nothing here either.

There were several people of that name, but none of them fit the description of the woman who had come to Howie's office on Friday afternoon.

So who was she?

Jack began to tap his desk with his gold wedding band, a nervous habit that appeared when he was especially worried.

He took a deep breath and phoned Santo Ruben.

Chapter Sixteen

"You didn't get a tan, Jack," Santo remarked. "How the hell can a guy spend a week in Hawaii and not come away with a tan?"

"I stayed out of the sun, that's how," Jack answered. "Ever heard of skin cancer? Anyway, we weren't there to frolic in the surf. It wasn't a happy time."

"I'm sorry about River," Santo told him. He had met River on one of his trips to San Geronimo and had been favorably impressed. "It's the saddest thing I can imagine to lose a nice young kid like that. How's his mother taking it?"

"Not well, Santo. Not well at all."

Lieutenant Santo Ruben had picked up Jack and Katya at the office and driven them to Ernesto's, a Hispanic bar on the south end of town, a local hangout that was not Anglo-friendly. There were big motorcycles parked outside and even larger riders in black leather parked inside on barstools. Santo enjoyed surprising Jack with out of the way drinking dives that would have been off limits for Jack if he had been by himself.

Santo was drinking orange juice due to the fact that he was an alcoholic, and Jack had a coke in order to keep him company. Santo didn't touch a drop on the days he was working. He was a distinguished looking silver-haired man with a great deal of self-control. But on his days off, the control gates opened and the drops flowed.

Jack and Santo Ruben had become good friends over the years. It had begun as a purely professional relationship, working a case of a missing California teenager Jack and Howie had been hired to find. Most cops treated private detectives contemptuously, but Santo knew of Jack's law enforcement past and had been helpful.

Six months later, it was Santo who had come to Jack for advice on an important homicide investigation that was going nowhere, and before long the two men discovered they enjoyed each other's company. They were peers, they could discuss cop matters with a shared understanding. In the past year, they had taken to having breakfast together once a week. Jack wasn't entirely sure why it was, but he often confided things to Santo that he never spoke of with anyone else, not even with Emma.

"So, tell me about Howie," Jack said. "He phoned you on Saturday?"

"He did. He told me about his camping trip, how he'd met a crazy scientist in the rain who was raving about being abducted by a flying saucer. It must have been a spooky encounter, miles from nowhere. And then the guy shows up dead in your doorway. God only knows how that happened! You know about this, I assume?"

"I only know what Howie told me. He phoned me in Hawaii later that day."

"Then you know about Lorna Wolf showing up, the head of security at Los Alamos. I've had a few dealings with her, and I warned Howie to be careful. I mean, I understand her concerns. Guarding a place like LANL is a big job. They make the pits there, you know. That's what they call the plutonium cores for nuclear bombs. This is hardcore stuff, nothing someone like Howie should be involved with."

"Santo, I agree a hundred percent. I had a visit in Hawaii from a guy I used to know who works in the Pentagon and he warned me off as well. The problem is Lorna Wolf seems to think that Bloom gave Howie something up on that mountain, something that's secret and she wants it back."

"That's a problem, then. Wolf isn't going to give up until she's sure Howie's clean. *Did* Bloom give him something?"

"Not a thing, Santo. Nothing." Jack didn't like lying to Santo but the fewer people who knew about the equation, the better. "I told Howie to disappear for a while, lay low. But now I can't find him."

"Well, he did what you told him, that's all."

"Yeah, but when he sees my name come up on his screen, he should be answering my calls. Ruth hasn't seen or heard from him since Friday and I'm starting to be concerned."

"We could put out a missing persons bulletin on him, if you like, Jack."

Jack had to think about that. "Let's hold off maybe one more day," he decided. "You know what I would like, Santo, if you have the time. Could you drive us out to Howie's house? Maybe there's something there that will give a clue to what he's up to."

"You got it, Jack. Let's go."

***

Late on Thursday afternoon, while Jack and Santo were driving to Howie's land in the foothills, a green VW microbus with California license plates made its way past the Wilder & Associate agency on Calle Dos Flores in search of a parking spot. As an out-of-towner, the driver didn't know he might as well have been seeking the Holy Grail.

There was no parking at all on Calle Dos Flores, a one-way street hardly wide enough for a donkey cart, and nothing to be found on the crowded streets of the historic district, not a single space. Undeterred, the driver of the VW bus continued onward, searching up and down the narrow streets, reciting his personal mantra and breathing deeply to calm his nerves.

"I breathe in the joy of this moment," he said to himself slowly. "I breathe out blessings to the world."

He had learned this breathing mantra at a three-day workshop in Boulder, Colorado, for which he had paid $395, money well spent. Tranquility was at the core of the well-focused warrior.

After driving around for some time, he found a metered space in the San Geronimo Plaza, once the center of town but now bustling with souvenir shops. He stepped out of the camper and fed four quarters into the meter. He was a small man dressed in jeans, green tennis shoes, and a blue T-shirt with the planet Saturn on the front and the words COSMIC TRAVELER on top. He was fortyish with a pleasant nebbishy face and a mop of brown hair long enough to cover his ears. Like his VW camper, he seemed a throwback to another era. If he had a guitar, you might expect a chorus of "Michael, Row the Boat Ashore."

The small man walked quickly to Calle Dos Flores and entered Wilder & Associate, Private Investigations.

Ruth had been backing up her computer to the Cloud, getting ready to leave for the day. Calle Dos Flores wasn't the sort of street where you'd expect to find a detective agency and quite often tourists drifted in the door wondering where they could find a cappuccino or a nice watercolor of a New Mexico sunset.

Ruth glanced up briefly from her screen, noted the presence of the folky apparition and returned quickly to her work.

"What do you want?" she demanded as she continued typing. "If you're looking for the museum it's three doors down."

"Excuse me, is this the detective agency?"

"Why?"

"Why? I'm hoping Mr. Wilder might do some detecting for me. What else would I be looking for?"

Ruth stopped her work to give him a better look. She wasn't impressed. He had a weak face, in her opinion. Ruth either liked someone at first glance or she didn't like him at all. This one fell into the second category.

"Mr. Wilder left the office half an hour ago," she told him. "Mr. Moon Deer isn't here either. Perhaps you can give me an idea of what's on your mind and I can tell you if it's something they'd be interested in."

"Wouldn't it be easier if I spoke to Jack Wilder directly?"

"Maybe yes, maybe no," Ruth answered. "I'm just trying to save you time. Mr. Wilder only takes certain cases that interest him. Divorce, for example, is out."

The man smiled. "Oh, I haven't been divorced in years," he said. "I tell you what. I'll leave my card. If you'll be so kind as to give it to him when he returns, I'll let him decide if he wants to see me."

"Suit yourself," she said, returning to her screen. She always made numerous back-ups at the end of the day, having little faith in computers. She was only partially aware of the unimpressively folksy person writing on the back of his card, using a corner of her desk.

"Here you are," he said, attempting to hand her the card.

"You can just leave it there. I'll get to it when I can."

"Then I'll say adieu. Thank you so much for your rapt attention."

Was there a note of sarcasm in his manner? Ruth heard the front door close and decided she was curious enough to look at what he had written.

The card said:

Ronald Devereaux

Little Green Man Society

On the back, he had written a single brief sentence in neat but very small cursive. She had to put on her glasses to read it:

If you're looking for Moon Deer call 415.555.1215.

"Hey!" Ruth called, running out the front door hoping to catch him. She had a glimpse of the back of his blue T-shirt further down the street, but then he turned a corner and was gone.

Chapter Seventeen

Santo disliked A/C. He swore it was like breathing plastic, so he kept the windows open as he and Jack drove in his black State Police Ford Explorer along the two-lane highway that wound north of town into the foothills.

Every now and then he flashed his bar lights at slow vehicles ahead of him on the road, forcing them to move over so he could pass.

Katya rode in the back seat with her head out the window, sniffing the air greedily. Jack appreciated the open window as well, forming a picture in his mind of the surrounding countryside from the scents and sounds.

He had visited northern New Mexico several times before he lost his eyesight, so he had an idea of what the land was like. Now his impressions came from his expanded awareness of smell, taste, touch, and hearing. Sometimes he felt like a bat, sending out sonic signals into the dark. Combined with his imagination, his sensory radar formed a map of the world, his personal planet of the blind.

The pavement ended and the last half mile to Howie's land was a rough ride up a dirt road. Howie had bought the land two years ago with his part of a very generous bonus that he and Jack had received from a wealthy client who had hired them to rescue his granddaughter from a religious sect in the desert.

Jack waited in the cruiser while Santo and Katya made their way up the trail to the unconventional eco pod that Howie called home. The trail was uneven and it would have been a challenge for Jack to navigate, even with Katya's help. Santo took Katya with him because if Howie was somewhere on the land, she would find him.

Jack's phone rang while he was waiting. It was Ruth back in the office.

"Jack, you'll never guess what just happened!"

Jack had spent much of his life guessing about things that had happened and he didn't like to make a game out of it.

"Why don't you just tell me, Ruth. So I can save my few remaining brain cells."

"A strange little guy stopped by and said he wanted to talk to you about a job. He looked like a shorter version of John Denver, but he didn't have much of a chin."

"Ruth, please, get to the point."

"When I told him you were gone, he left his card and wrote a note on the back. Guess what it said?"

"Ruth!"

"Okay, it said, 'If you're looking for Moon Deer call . . . and then he gave a number with a 415 area code. That's San Francisco."

"Yes, I know. What was on the front of the card?"

"Just his name, Ronald Devereaux. And his organization, the Little Green Man Society."

"Really?" said Jack.

"I kid you not. You know sometimes, Jack, I think I should have stayed in New York. The minute you put your foot down west of the Mississippi, the country goes bonkers on you."

"The Little Green Man Society!" Jack repeated thoughtfully. "Well, okay, leave the card on my reading machine. I'll phone him when I get back to the office, which should be in forty minutes or so."

"Do you want me to stick around?"

"No, that's okay. Go home. Thanks for calling."

"You think this guy knows where Howie is?"

"I don't know," was all Jack could say.

He was ending the call when he heard Santo and Katya coming back on the trail.

"Howie wasn't there," Santo said. He opened the rear door for Katya and slipped into the driver's seat. "The place is locked up and there's no sign of him."

"Well, it was worth a try," Jack said gloomily.

"That house is something else! What does Howie call it? A pod?"

"An eco pod. Hip young architects are having a field day designing stuff like this. It's the new wave, Santo. Old fogies like you and me will need to step aside."

"I guess so. Well, it doesn't look like he's been home for a few days. His big orange cat was outside looking like she hasn't been fed for a while. There's one of those automatic feeders outside, but it was empty. The cat rubbed against my leg and meowed like she was saying, 'Where's dinner?' She wasn't afraid of Katya."

"She wouldn't be. Katya likes cats and she and Orange are friends. You know, Santo, Howie adores that cat and he wouldn't think of leaving her without food. This is starting to feel bad."

"I can put out that alert for Howie if you'd like."

"Yes, I think it's time after all. Here's another thing, if you can manage it. I'd like to check Howie's phone calls, everything he received and made since he came down from Dawson Peak a week ago. It might give us a better idea of what's going on."

"I'll see what I can do. I'll put one of my people on it as soon as I get back to the station."

"Let's head back to town, then. I'm going to need to buy cat food and come back here to feed Orange, but I don't want to tie you up with something like that. Emma will drive me. By the way, have you ever heard of a group that calls itself the Little Green Man Society?"

Santo laughed. "Funny you mention them. They popped up in my world just the other day. They're a group of UFO enthusiasts who are holding a kind of festival the weekend after next. It's a big thing, actually. The hotels are sold out. There are lots of people who believe in flying saucers."

"Well, there's not much of a difference these days between fact and science fiction," Jack remarked.

"Here's another odd twist, the War Chief from the Pueblo came to see me the other day. He doesn't like the Little Green Men going up on Dawson Peak."

"John Concha?"

"Do you know him?"

"Howie does. I only met him once and he impressed me. But I don't understand. What's the deal with the Little Green Men and Dawson Peak?"

"A bunch of them are going to climb up there on the Sunday of the UFO festival to witness a predicted UFO sighting. Supposedly this is going to be the big moment they've all been waiting for. The Arrival, as they call it."

"The Rapture, the Arrival, the end of the world with all the Christians floating up to heaven . . . it's very telling how people believe in this stuff!"

"*Deus ex machina,*" said Santo. "All problems solved. The phrase comes from medieval morality plays where God was lowered down onto the stage with ropes and pulleys to dispense judgement and wrap up all the loose ends of the plot. Wouldn't it be nice if we could solve crimes like that?"

"God in a machine!" Jack muttered to himself. "You know, that's an interesting point, Santo. God in a machine! I wonder . . ."

Jack kept his wonderings to himself, trailing off.

"Jack, I was kidding. Anyway, it's God *from* a machine. I went to Catholic school and had to study Latin. In any case, the War Chief doesn't like the Little Green Men because the Pueblo regards that mountain as sacred Indian land. Dawson Peak was part of the reservation until the early twentieth century when the government appropriated it for the National Forest. The Pueblo's been fighting in court for decades to try to get the land returned to them, but I wouldn't hold your breath. Concha wanted to see if I could do anything to stop the Green Men from going up there. I had to tell him, sorry, I couldn't do a thing. But he might try the Forest Service."

Jack's thoughts circled like vultures in the sky. The Blue Moon quark . . . a dead astrophysicist . . . a girl who didn't seem to exist . . . and now a Little Green Man Society and the War Chief hoping to stop a UFO festival.

It had to add up to something. But for the life of him, Jack didn't know what.

He had a lot to think about as they drove back to town.

Chapter Eighteen

Ruth showed Ronald Devereaux of the Little Green Man Society into Jack's office at precisely 11 o'clock Friday morning.

Jack had been waiting impatiently to see Devereaux ever since Thursday afternoon when he had phoned the number on Devereaux's card but gotten no answer. After four rings, a recorded message told him the mailbox of the number he had called was full, which added to his frustration.

He had his Kurzweil reading machine give him the number again to make sure he had it right, but when he tried it a second time, he got the same result. Full mailbox, no possibility of leaving a message.

Jack wasn't good at waiting when he wanted something badly. He fumed around the office as he tried the number a third time and then a fourth. Finally, on the fifth attempt, an hour later, a nasal, high-pitched voice answered his call.

"Little Green Man Society?" said the voice with a chirpy upturn at the end. "Ronald Devereaux speaking."

"Mr. Devereaux, this is Jack Wilder. You left your card at my office earlier this afternoon. I would like to speak with you as soon as possible. I'm in the office now. Do you think you could come by?"

"You mean now?"

"Yes," said Jack. "Now."

"Well, I'm in my bus driving to Roswell. I won't be able to see you until tomorrow afternoon."

"Is there any chance you could return to San Geronimo tonight?"

"Oh, I'm afraid not. No, that's impossible. I have an important meeting with our volunteers, you see."

Jack didn't like the image he had of Devereaux from his voice. He knew this wasn't a fair way to judge a person, but Jack's hearing was sensitive and the quality of a voice—its timber, the nuances of tone and inflection—always made a strong impression on him. With Ronald Devereaux, he imagined a precise, petty, stubborn little man.

"Well, tomorrow then," Jack agreed reluctantly. "But look, Mr. Devereaux, your note said you know where Howie Moon Deer is. If that's true, I'd very much appreciate it if you'd tell me now."

"I'd rather tell you in person," Devereaux replied. "You see, I'm not a phone person. I'll be able to explain it to you much better face to face."

Not a phone person! Jack wanted to strangle the guy!

With strained patience, he told Devereaux that the New Mexico State Police were looking for Howie, as was Jack, and if Ronald had any information, he'd better spill it now. But it was no good. Jack's impression of a petty, stubborn little man appeared to be correct. He refused to say anything on the phone—not being a phone person!—though he would be happy to give a complete account tomorrow. The only compromise Jack achieved was to get Devereaux to agree to return to San Geronimo in the morning rather than the afternoon.

***

Jack was not inclined to like Ronald Devereaux in person any more than he had liked him on the phone. It took all his self-control to smile pleasantly when Ruth showed him into the office the next morning.

"Thank you for making the trip back from Roswell," he said. "Please have a seat, Mr. Devereaux. Would you like some coffee?"

"Oh, I never drink coffee! But I'd take a cup of peppermint tea if you have it."

Jack made an effort to unclench his teeth. "Do we have peppermint tea, Ruth?"

"Sure we do, Jack. What would we do without peppermint?"

"Then please make a cup for Mr. Devereaux."

"Lemon?" asked Ruth.

"Honey," said Ronald.

"Well, Mr. Devereaux, now that you're here why don't you tell me what you know about Howie Moon Deer. We're worried about him, naturally, and would like to know where he is."

"Isn't it obvious?"

Jack raised an eyebrow. "Obvious? Not really. If it were obvious, we would have found him by now. Now please tell me what you know."

"He's been abducted."

"I see," said Jack. "Abducted by whom?"

"By the Klizmorians, of course."

Jack exhaled a long, weary, angry sigh.

"You're saying he's been abducted by a flying saucer?"

Ronald chuckled indulgently. "We don't call them flying saucers anymore, Mr. Wilder. That's a misleading image. Actually, the ships are more an oblong shape."

"And they've taken Howie?"

"Yes, they have. But don't be alarmed. Klizmor is a very peaceful planet. They'll return him to Earth in good time."

"And how do you know this, Mr. Devereaux? If I may ask."

"Oh, we've been communicating with Klizmor for years and years! We know them quite well by now."

"Really?" said Jack. "And how do you communicate?"

Ronald chuckled. "I'm not sure I should tell you. I sense you're a disbeliever. You'll only laugh."

"Try me."

"Well, we communicate telepathically. The Klizmorians have no need of spoken language. They mastered telepathy eons ago. Telekinesis, too."

"So how does it work? You sit in a kind of trance and let their voices come to you?"

"No, it's not like that. We . . . actually, well, we use a Ouija board."

Jack snorted. "They speak to you through a Ouija board?"

"Exactly. It's only a convenient device, of course. If they wanted . . . why, they could speak to us through a teapot!"

As though on cue, Ruth returned to Jack's office with a mug of peppermint tea.

"Thank you," said Ronald. "Do you happen to have a biscuit?"

"How about a jelly donut?" said Ruth.

"Oh, not a jelly donut! No, thank you!"

Jack used the distraction to gather his thoughts. He was disappointed, of course. It had been a thin hope that Ronald Devereaux would know where Howie was. But he was disappointed anyway.

When Ruth was gone, he decided to press on and gather what he could.

"So tell me about the Little Green Man Society," he said. "I'm interested."

"Are you? Our name, I hope you understand, is tongue-in-cheek. We don't wish to sacrifice our sense of humor. And yet, of course, this is the greatest moment in mankind's brief history, contact with other races and other worlds. Our group is made up of individuals from many walks of life—professors, carpenters, bankers, artists, yoga instructors, plumbers, some wealthy, others not. But we share the common goal of reaching out to our celestial visitors. They have been visiting our planet for thousands of years, of course, but have avoided contact fearing we are not yet ready."

"And what is your position in the Little Green Man Society, Mr. Devereaux? Are you the leader?"

"Oh, no, not at all. I am merely a spokesman appointed by our board of directors. In my private life, I'm an exobiologist at San Francisco State."

Jack raised an eyebrow. San Francisco State was his own alma mater. "Exobiologist? This is an actual academic field?"

"Of course. What are the conditions necessary for life to exist? Does a planet need liquid water, as many believe? Or will methane suffice. You have to ask yourself what *is* life. Will we recognize it when we see it? At one time, science said that for there to be life, an organism must be able to reproduce itself. But that's no longer the accepted criteria. Crystals reproduce themselves, for instance. But crystals aren't what we consider life. These are the sorts of questions an exobiologist asks."

"Interesting," said Jack.

"It's much more than interesting. As you perhaps know, the Hubble telescope has discovered over two hundred billion galaxies . . . galaxies, mind you, each one as large as the Milky Way. Each one containing over a hundred billion stars. You appear to be an educated man, Mr. Wilder. Are you really so arrogant as to suggest that in this unimaginably vast universe, we are the only intelligent life form that has come into existence? There's a name for this. In astrophysics, it's called the Copernican Principle. This is a core belief that says the Earth is not special. We're not the center of the universe, we're in an obscure corner of the Milky Way, and what we find here, we will find in other places."

"Okay," said Jack. "I know who Copernicus was. The problem with little green visitors from outer space has to do with distance and the fact that nothing can travel faster than the speed of light. If these alien races exist—and perhaps they do—they will never get to us, and we will never get to them."

"Not true," said Devereaux. "If you take any basic college course, Astronomy 101, you'll discover that in the first thousandth of a second after the Big Bang, the universe expanded at many millions of times the speed of light. Einstein wasn't exactly wrong, but he was limited by what science knew in 1905. The speed of light isn't the absolute ceiling and in this fact lies the possibility for intergalactic space travel. Yes, it's beyond us now, but not for an advanced civilization that's many millions of years older than ours. Besides we have proof. We've been visited by UFOs here in New Mexico, at Roswell and Aztec. It's well documented."

Jack threw up his hands in surrender. "Okay, maybe you're right, maybe you're wrong. I don't pretend to know the answers to these things. But tell me," said Jack, changing the subject, "How did you hear that Howie was missing?"

Devereaux laughed. It was an unusual laugh, high-pitched and nerdy. "Ah, I have my contacts, don't I?"

"Do you?"

"Would it surprise you to know that there are folks at the Los Alamos Lab who share my belief that we've been visited multiple times by UFOs?"

"Nothing surprises me, Mr. Devereaux," Jack replied. Which wasn't entirely true. "But I must ask you again, who told you about Howie?"

"All right, Dr. Brandon Eckehart. That's who. He's a top scientist at LANL and one of our staunchest supporters. You see, we're not just a group of crackpots. Eckehart is an assistant to Grisha Bloom, who won the Nobel Prize. These are some of the most knowledgeable people on the planet."

"I presume you know that Grisha Bloom is dead?"

"Of course, I know." Ronald Devereaux lowered his voice. "That's why I'm here. Bloom was picked up by a Klizmor ship and taken to Alpha Centauri. He was returned to Earth last Wednesday and it's vitally important that we discover everything we can about his trip and if he was able to bring back anything with him. A journal, perhaps. Photographs, if we're lucky. It's a tragedy he's dead, of course, a terrible loss. Which is why it's so vital to trace his final movements and discover if he left us any clues. I'm willing to write you a check today, right this minute, for ten thousand dollars if you will undertake this investigation on our behalf."

"Ten thousand dollars?" It seemed a large sum from what Jack imagined to be a fringe group. "But what if there's nothing? Maybe the whole thing's a hoax."

"Oh, it's not a hoax, Mr. Wilder. And Bloom's testimonial, if we can find it, will be the biggest story of the ages. Think of it! The account of a journey to the stars from a Nobel Prize winning physicist—"

"Mr. Devereaux—"

"No, hear me out. This story needs to be told because Grisha Bloom has credibility. They won't be able to write him off as a nut case. At last, the world will acknowledge what we in the Little Green Man Society have been saying all along. The wonderful news that we are not alone, Mr. Wilder! We have friends in the universe who are eager to give our poor planet a helping hand!"

"Yes, I understand," Jack said calmly, hoping to lower the volume. "But I'm afraid I don't see how I can do anything for you."

"Oh, I think you can! It's my belief that Grisha Bloom gave something to Moon Deer that night in the rain on Dawson Peak, something that proves he made the trip to Alpha Centauri. I'm right, aren't I?"

Jack smiled. "I'm afraid not, Mr. Devereaux. Not that I know of."

"It's the Theory of Everything, isn't it? Tell me the truth. And you have it! Moon Deer gave it to you!"

Jack laughed and shook his head. "No, no. You got it wrong. I've got the theory of nothing, and that's the truth."

"Don't play word games with me. We want to find what Grisha gave to your assistant. It's the proof we need and I'm willing to raise your fee to . . . let's say twenty thousand dollars if you can get us what we want."

"Twenty thousand? Tell me something, Mr. Devereaux, how can a group like yours shell out a sum like that?"

"How?" He lowered his voice. "Perhaps we have a very wealthy patron. Someone famous, a name you would know—someone with deep pockets who believes in the important work we're doing! You see, we're not just some nutcase group of crazies—oh, I know very well what you're thinking, Mr. Wilder! We're cosmic warriors, we're guardians of the holy flame!"

Jack nodded. You had to tread carefully when you were dealing with cosmic warriors, guardians of the holy flame. Meanwhile, he wondered about the rich, famous person who was funding the Little Green Man Society. He didn't doubt for a moment that some wealthy person might be shelling out money. Rich people, in Jack's experience, could be as unhinged as anyone else.

"I'm sure you're a very credible organization, Mr. Devereaux. Can you tell me who this famous person might be?"

"Oh, I can't do that! I shouldn't have mentioned him at all, he prefers to be anonymous. But I'll tell you what. To show you how earnest we are, how important this is, I'm going to raise the ante. I'll give you fifty thousand dollars, Mr. Wilder, if you will hand over whatever Grisha Bloom brought back with him from Klizmor. Fifty thousand! I am prepared to give you a certified check for that amount today!"

Jack laughed and raised his hands. "Well, I can't say this hasn't been an interesting morning! But there's nothing to give you. I'm afraid I can't do the impossible, Mr. Devereaux."

"So you won't help us?"

Jack shook his head. "No, I can't and I won't."

***

That night Jack barbecued two New York steaks and a chicken breast in the backyard on the massive propane Weber grill he had bought for himself last summer, deciding at last to switch from charcoal. As a traditionalist, this was a big step for Jack, but he had to admit, propane was a good deal easier than charcoal. Less mess, less fuss, easier to control the exact temperature.

Emma made the salad and a rice pilaf leaving Jack in an apron with a glass of wine to putter at the grill. The steaks were for himself and Katya, the chicken for Emma who didn't eat red meat.

Jack enjoyed cooking and as long as he had everything organized— his prongs, spices, and tools in their proper places—lack of eyesight wasn't a problem. Cooking, he claimed, was mostly a matter of smell, touch, and taste. The largest of the two steaks was for Katya. When it was done, he cut it up into pieces and let it cool before he gave it to her on a plate on the flagstone patio.

It was a warm night and Jack and Emma ate outside at the wrought iron table on the patio. Emma had lit the candle lantern, music played softly on the stereo in the house (Chopin, the Nocturnes), a bottle of Pouilly-Fuissé sat in an ice bucket within easy reach. In their busy lives, Jack and Emma often ate on the run. But they had a tradition of at least one decent sit down dinner per week.

"Tell me something, Emma," Jack asked. "Do you believe there are UFOs?"

"Well, of course, I do. Just the other day, the *New York Times* had a story that Navy pilots keep seeing them, odd objects in the sky moving at incredible speeds. Apparently they turn at abrupt angles and don't leave vapor trails. Even Congress and the President have been briefed."

"But are they visitors from outer space?"

Emma considered this. "How can anyone be sure? Most of what I've read suggests other possibilities. Weather balloons, clouds, mistaken instrument readings, reflections in the sky from something on the ground, odd tricks of light. But you have to keep an open mind. From what I understand, astronomers have found hundreds of planets around various stars, and there are certainly billions and billions more. So what's your opinion, Jack?"

"What bothers me is this," he said. "Remember when we were young, sci-fi stories used to imagine creatures from outer space as monsters? Purple people eaters with killer rays who wanted to turn Earth into a slave colony. *War of the Worlds*. But now the whole thing has been turned around. It's the creatures from space who are now the Good Guys and we're the Bad. It's like a religion. Hoping for a Messiah who will set things right. Santo and I were talking about it today."

"That's an interesting point," Emma agreed. "I suppose it's because our world seems to be in so much trouble these days. The problems just get worse and worse."

"Remember that silly Spielberg movie, *Close Encounters of the Third Kind?*"

"*Jack,* I enjoyed that film!"

"Come on, Emma, the ending went on forever. All those people with dreamy faces making their way to Monument Valley, like they were waiting for God to arrive. That's the religious part of this that worries me. It makes me think of Jonestown, those nine hundred people who drank poisoned Kool-Aid thinking they would be transported to spaceships that were waiting to take them to paradise."

"Well, that's an extreme case."

"Oh, I'm not so sure. The world's going crazy on us, Emma. Conspiracy theories, crackpot religions, rejection of science—we're slipping into a new Dark Age."

"Now *you're* being extreme!"

"I'm not being extreme. Nancy reads the papers to me every morning and I know what's going on."

"Yes, but you're taking a very dark view, Jack. Next thing, you'll be suggesting we build a survival shelter and start stockpiling food."

"That's not such a bad idea."

"Let me tell you something, Jack. If the world ends, I plan to end with it. I don't want to be left roaming some post-apocalyptic planet of the damned!"

Jack and Emma didn't always agree on things. It had kept their marriage interesting for forty years.

"Anyway, getting back to movies," Emma said. "I'd say *Contact* was a better film than *Close Encounters*. But of course, that was adapted from a novel by Carl Sagan, who's a great deal more interesting than Steven Spielberg."

"Yeah, but it's the same fantasy. A race of superior beings who come to help us out of our muddle. My point is it's wishing for something that isn't real. And if people want something badly enough, they tend to create the evidence to support their beliefs. That's what I think about flying saucers. People want them to exist, so *ergo*, they do."

"Well, I don't know, Jack. That sounds like specious reasoning to me," Emma replied. "You might want gold to exist in them thar hills, because then you'd be rich. But there *was* gold in those hills, in California anyway. So people weren't imagining something that was just a fantasy."

"Okay, here's another point," said Jack. "If these fabulous creatures from outer space are visiting us, why are they so coy about it? Why don't they just come out and show themselves? Certainly, they don't have anything to fear from the likes of us. Not if they're so incredibly advanced."

"Maybe they only want to observe us."

"Sure," said Jack. "That's what a guy I had in my office today told me. Get this—he's from the Little Green Man Society. He left a message for me saying he knew where Howie was, but when I got him in the office, he told me this absurd story about Howie being abducted by a flying saucer and taken to the planet Klizmor. What's the world coming to, Emma? I mean, honestly—I thought I'd seen every crazy thing in California in the Sixties. But that's nothing compared to what's going on today!"

"Ah, I'm getting this now! This is why you've been babbling about UFOs."

"Well, it's a damn mystery, Emma. And I still don't know where Howie is. I'm starting to be very worried."

"Jack, we've only been back from Hawaii two days. You'll get to the bottom of this, I know you will. You need to give yourself time."

Jack shook his head. "Yes, but that's the problem. The way things are going, I'm afraid we're running out of time."

***

Jack helped Emma with the dishes. He scrubbed the pots and bowls while Emma rinsed the plates and glasses for the dishwasher.

Once the dishes were done, Jack went through his evening ritual checking that the windows and doors were locked. Lastly, he turned on the alarm system. Being a cop for nearly thirty years had taught him to take security seriously.

Jack and Emma said goodnight to each other in the hallway. They slept in separate bedrooms because of Jack's insomnia and Emma's need for sleep.

"I love you, you big old bear," she said, giving Jack a kiss on the lips.

"Even if we disagree on so many things?"

"It would be boring to agree about everything. And you're never boring, Jack."

That was something, he supposed. Jack made his way into his ground floor office before going to bed and poured himself a shot of Remy Martin. Katya followed him and put her head onto his lap. He scratched her ears as he sat at his desk deep in thought.

He was seriously worried about Howie, even more so than he had let on to Emma. Nuclear secrets, national security . . . these were matters rational people stayed well clear of. Nor was he happy about Ronald Devereaux and his barely concealed fanaticism.

"It's time for precautions," Jack said to Katya as he rose from his chair and made his way to the wall safe.

He opened the sliding panel, found the keypad with his right hand, and punched in the five-digit code. The door of the safe clicked open.

Jack reached inside for the gun he kept there, his 9mm Glock, and was surprised not to find it. Howie must have taken it. But this was even more alarming. Howie didn't like guns so there must have been a good reason for him to think he needed to be armed.

Feeling inside the safe, Jack had a second surprise. There was a sheet of A8 paper folded in quarters that Howie had obviously left for him. A note. Hopefully it was an explanation for why he had taken the gun.

Jack turned on the Kurzweil reading machine that was on a wheeled trolley by his desk. He unfolded the note and placed it on the glass.

Almost immediately a bland female voice spoke two words:

Claire's knee.

Jack wasn't sure he had heard correctly, so he made the machine repeat itself. But the message was the same.

Claire's knee!

Jack liked puzzles. In general, he was good at solving them. But this was beyond mysterious. Jack supposed Claire had nice knees. She was tall and slim. But he had no idea why Howie should mention them on a piece of paper left in his safe.

Jack returned to his desk and poured himself another shot of cognac. He recalled that in their phone conversation he had told Howie not to tell him where the book of Chinese poetry was hidden. Half-kidding, he had told Howie to leave him a clue.

That's what this was, then. A clue. But it wasn't a good clue. It was too obscure.

"Okay, Katya," he said as she once again settled her head in his lap. "No more farting around, my friend. It's time to get down to business!"

Chapter Nineteen

Jack's phone rang at 4:25 Saturday morning, an unsettling hour for a call.

He had only fallen asleep an hour before. He'd been awake worrying about how he was going to proceed. Grisha dead, Howie vanished . . . Jack felt stymied and inadequate. He didn't know what to do.

In normal circumstances, he and Howie would have worked together on a case like this. But without Howie, he was stuck without wheels, without eyes, without any means of organizing an investigation. How was he even going to get from one place to another?

Ruth, he had decided around three in the morning. But she wasn't his first choice. He wasn't certain how helpful she'd be.

The ringing telephone—an old-fashioned telephone ring, programmed for nostalgia—was so startling that Jack reached too quickly and knocked it off his bedside table. The phone kept ringing which helped him find it on the floor.

"Damn!" he growled, at last getting it to his ear. "Yes?"

"Jack, it's Santo. I know you're an early riser, so I didn't think you'd mind the call. We've found Brandon Eckehart and his wife. They're both dead. He was tortured, she was strangled. We've found their bodies in an observatory up in the mountains, a geodesic dome that has a fancy telescope."

"Eckehart . . ." Jack was groggy from sleep and the name didn't immediately make a connection.

"I woke you up, didn't I? Look, I think you need to be here. Why don't you have yourself a cup of coffee and I'll send one of my guys to pick you up. It'll be easier to tell you everything in person."

"You're at the station?"

"I'm at the murder scene up in the hills. The Eckeharts were discovered by a survivalist who lives in the forest."

"At four in the morning?"

"They were found last night. It's complicated. I'll explain everything when I see you."

Jack was nearly awake now. Two dead people in the mountains. Tortured and strangled.

"I'll be waiting," he told Santo.

***

Jack and Katya were waiting twenty minutes later when the doorbell rang.

"Detective Dan Hamm, sir," said a youthful voice when Jack opened the door. "Lieutenant Ruben sent me to pick you up and take you to the crime scene."

"Lead on, Detective."

Summer mornings in the high desert were fresh and cold and scented with sage and chamisa. Jack took a deep breath and allowed himself to be guided to the State Police cruiser. Katya jumped into the back.

"I guess your guide dog goes with you everywhere, sir? He must be real well trained."

"She is."

As they drove, Dan chatted amiably about the State Police K9 division, how great the dogs were, trained to sniff out drugs, find fugitives, intimidate suspects, all sorts of things. Dan Hamm sounded awfully young to be a detective. His name was unfortunate, too much like a sandwich, which had probably caused him a good amount of kidding over the years. Jack thought he knew all of Santo's crew, but he had never met Detective Hamm before.

"So how long have you been in San Geronimo?" he asked.

"Well, I'm a newbie, sir. Did my two years in uniform in Las Cruces, passed the detective exam a month ago, and got sent up here to San Geronimo just last week. I can't tell you how excited I am finally to be here working with someone like Lieutenant Ruben!"

"Well, that's great," Jack said. The detective's enthusiasm made him feel old and tired.

"You see, I got a lot to live up to," Dan said seriously. "My uncle is Steve Malloy, the head of Public Safety in Santa Fe. It's kind of a weight on my shoulders to prove myself."

"I understand."

In fact, Jack got the picture very well. Santo had had no choice but to take the green detective under his wing. The politics in law enforcement were brutal, especially the need to do favors to important people. It had always been the part of the job that Jack had liked the least, though he had been good at it, he supposed. In a big city police department, you didn't rise higher than the rank of sergeant if you didn't know how to work the system.

The highway climbed from the desert into the mountains along a series of winding roads. It was a longer drive than Jack had expected.

"We're still in the county?" he asked after they had been driving for at least forty-five minutes.

"Yes, sir. It wouldn't be our jurisdiction otherwise. The roads are kinda roundabout up here, up and down and all over. Do you know the Escondido Valley?"

"No, I don't."

"Well, we just passed through there and we're about to climb up past the old village of Tres Rios. We're not far from the back side of Dawson Peak. It's not far now."

Jack couldn't entirely visualize the geography in his mind. He wished he could see a map.

"Here's the driveway. Better hang on, sir, it's kinda steep."

Steep was an understatement. They headed up a dirt road at such a sharp incline that the cruiser's rear wheels fishtailed, spun, then caught again before they could slide backwards. Jack was relieved when they came to a stop at last. Four-wheel drive would have been useful in these mountains. When he stepped outside, the air was frigid and full of pine.

"Here we are, sir," said Dan. "Boy, they got everybody out of bed this morning!"

"I'd appreciate it if you'd describe it to me, Dan. Perhaps you can tell me who's here?"

"Yes, sir. There's an ambulance, three state cruisers, the medical examiner's car, the CSU van, and a Sheriff's car. The house is pretty fancy, one of those ski chalet type places with lots of sun decks. It's in an open meadow near the top of a hill. Bet it has great views."

"And there's an outbuilding, I understand? An observatory."

"That's maybe a hundred yards further up the meadow . . . oh, and there's Lieutenant Ruben's SUV."

"Why don't you take us to him, Dan."

Jack let Katya out of the back and got her into her harness. Even with her help, it was unnerving to be in a place he didn't know.

"Would you like me to take your arm, sir?"

"It would be better if I took *your* arm, Detective."

With his left hand gripping the end of Katya's harness, and his right hand lightly on Dan's arm, Jack climbed the path toward the house. He sensed the excitement you always found at a major crime scene where a large number of law enforcement people had gathered. There was a buzz of conversation and squawk of radios. Though it was a work scene, he overheard snatches of gossip and socializing among colleagues who hadn't seen one another for a while.

Dan led Jack and Katya to where Santo was standing in the driveway with the medical examiner.

"Thanks for coming, Jack," Santo said taking his arm. "Do you know James Marino, our M.E.?"

"We've met . . . how you doing, Jim?"

"Middling. Not so pleased to be roused at this hour, but crime has a bad case of insomnia, I guess! Ha ha!"

Jack managed a smile.

James Marino, the San Geronimo County Medical Examiner, believed himself to be a wit. The body would eventually be taken to the coroner in Albuquerque at the University of New Mexico after it was released from the scene.

"So—" Jack turned to Santo.

"So, things are ugly," Santo answered. "The CSU is up at the observatory where the bodies were found and we're waiting for them to finish. The observatory is a geodesic dome with a fancy telescope inside that sits on a track. You can wheel it out onto an open deck where I imagine there's a great view of the sky on a clear night. It's not Mt. Palomar but it's a pretty nice setup for a home observatory."

"Whose house is this?"

"Let's step away a minute and I'll tell you . . . see you later, James," he said to the medical examiner. He took Jack's arm and led him further up the driveway away from the gathering.

"Okay, the property belongs to an astrophysicist who works at Los Alamos, a Dr. Wei Huang," Santo said when they were alone. "But he's out of the country for the year at the Altacama Large Millimeter Array in Chile and he's been renting to Grisha Bloom while he's gone. These famous scientists move around a bit."

166

"So this is where Howie's spaceman has been living? Isn't it a long way from the Lab?"

"It's a bit over an hour, Jack. Lots of people do a longer commute. Bloom has been staying here for the last six months. We've already spoken to Dr. Huang in Chile. He and Bloom are old friends."

"Is there anyone in the house now?"

"Nobody. But someone's gone through recently pulling out drawers, looking under sofas, making a big mess of things, searching for something. The killer, I presume. Probably more than one person, a team. We'll know more when the CSU people have a look, once they're finished in the observatory. I'm trying to get more help from Santa Fe, but they probably won't arrive until later in the morning."

"You said Eckehart was tortured?"

Santo sighed. "His arms were pulled back the wrong way and he was strung up by rope from one of the struts that holds the dome together. We figure he's been dead a few days, but we won't have a more precise time until the coroner's had a look."

"Who found the bodies? You said something about a survivalist."

"Yep, a guy who goes by the name of Last Man. He lives in a hut about a quarter of a mile away. Last Man owns a few acres, but he roams the area looking for herbs and nuts without much regard for property lines. We've had some dealings with him before because he hunts with a bow and arrow, and another neighbor called us a few years back when he killed an elk."

"Elk steak isn't bad, Santo."

"Sure, but it tastes better if it's in season and you have a permit to hunt. To make a long story short, Last Man says he was hunting rabbits yesterday afternoon and saw the door of the observatory was open. He looked inside and found Brandon Eckehart hanging and his wife, Ashley, on the floor. He returned to his hut, cooked up some rabbit stew, smoked a little ganja and waited for a few hours, debating with himself what to do. Guys like Last Man don't like cops. It was 11:27 before he finally decided to contact us."

"There's cell service up here?"

"No, but he has a satellite connection to the Internet. Even crazy people living in the woods have the latest technology these days. He emailed the State Police website instead of phoning. This slowed things down considerably. I didn't get called until just before one AM and I didn't get here until two. As you can tell, we're slowly getting the crime scene organized, but none of us have had much sleep and it's been a challenge."

"How did you ID the Eckeharts?"

"That was the easy part. He had his wallet in his pocket with his driver's license and all his credit cards. Whatever the motive for killing him, it wasn't robbery. She was wearing a wedding ring that matched his, so right now we're assuming she's Ashley Eckehart, though we won't know that for certain until we do more checking."

"And the house was tossed?"

"It's pretty obvious that the killers wanted something they believed Eckehart had. Hanging him up by his arms, they were probably trying to get him to talk. So maybe it's time for you to tell us what they were after, Jack. I think you know something you're holding back."

"Santo, believe me, all I want is to find Howie. I'm as confused as you are by all this."

It was an evasive answer, but for the moment Santo let it go.

"There's something else I have to tell you," Santo said. "I just found out about this late afternoon yesterday. On Monday afternoon a neighbor next door to the Eckeharts in Los Alamos called the State Police in Española and told dispatch she'd seen an Indian male break a side window and crawl inside the house. I assume that was Howie. What he was doing there, I have no idea. Normally, the Española station shares ongoing situations with us, but this was such a small matter they didn't bother. I only heard about it by accident . . . oh, damn! We've got ourselves a problem, Jack!"

As they had been talking, Jack had become aware of a helicopter beating its way closer to the hilltop where they were standing. The sound grew in intensity until it was difficult to hear themselves talk. Jack felt a wash of wind from the rotor blades as the helicopter circled overhead looking for a place to land.

"It's a chopper from LANL!" Santo shouted over the roar. "The She-Wolf. I thought we were going to have more time before she arrived. Look, Jack, there's more to this story, but you're going to have to get it from the neighbor. It's better that way, anyway. Her name is Gladys Serna and she lives next door to the Eckeharts. She's eighty-two years old and she keeps an eagle eye on the street. You definitely need to hear her out. Meanwhile, Brandon Eckehart had a top security clearance at Los Alamos, which means Wolf is going to take over here with a vengeance. I'm not going to be able to get near this again. But I doubt that will stop a stubborn private citizen like you."

"You want me to keep investigating?"

"Don't you?"

"You bet I do, if this has anything to do with Howie. But I have very limited resources on my own."

"What do you think of Dan Hamm, the young detective I sent to pick you up this morning?"

"Seems like a nice kid. Bit wet behind the ears."

"How would you like it if I loaned him to you for a few days? However long you need him. Sure, he's wet behind the ears. He's totally clueless. But I'll give him a set of wheels and he can drive you around. He has a badge, a gun, he'll give you an official presence and get you places where you can't get on your own. Plus, you'll be doing me a favor."

Jack smiled. "You want him out of your hair?"

"Well, yeah. Look, the kid's uncle is the big boss in Santa Fe, so I have to tread carefully. But I'm just too busy right now to be a babysitter. Anyway, you'll be an inspiration to him."

"Santo, please!"

"No, I mean it, Jack. How many detectives have you trained in your day? Hundreds, I bet. All Dan needs is seasoning. Honestly, you'll be helping me by taking him off my hands, he'll be helping you by giving you wheels and access, and you'll be helping him by teaching him the ropes. It's a win-win situation. What do you say?"

"Okay, Santo. It's a deal. The kid will be useful, and I'll do my best to return him to you in one piece."

"All I ask is you keep me in the loop . . . oh, Jesus, she's just landed near the dome! Look, I need to go deal with her, but if you stay here with Katya, I'll send Dan to you and you can make your escape. I suggest you get out of here while you can."

***

Jack was standing by himself in the hubbub of the crime scene with people coming and going when Katya began pulling on her harness. She was trying to lead him further down the hill to something she had seen.

"What's up, Katya?"

She barked and pulled so strongly on the harness that Jack had no option but to follow after her. She pulled him another dozen feet until she came to a stop, still barking.

"Oh, here you are, sir," said Detective Hamm, appearing at his side. "The lieutenant said I'm supposed to drive you to the station and pick up a different cruiser. He said we'd better get out of here pronto."

"What's Katya barking at, Dan?"

"Well, nothing, sir. I mean, it's just a car."

"What kind of car?"

"A station wagon. One of those Subaru Outbacks. It looks a few years old."

"What color is it?"

"Dark blue."

"Read me the license plate."

"BNL 525. It's a New Mexico plate."

Jack felt a tingle of excitement mixed with worry. Finally, finally, he was getting somewhere. Katya had found Howie's car, a Subaru Outback that Jack knew well. It had once belonged to Emma, who had sold it to Howie a few years back. But it worried him that the car had been abandoned.

"We should get going, sir. Lieutenant Ruben said we shouldn't waste any time."

"I understand. I just need a few moments here."

Jack felt his way around to the driver's side door, hoping it wasn't locked. The door opened when he pulled the handle. Katya was happy to sniff Howie. She barked and wagged her tail and Jack had to restrain her from jumping inside.

"Look, Dan, I know we're in a hurry but I need you to help me. You can search the back seat and the cargo area while I check out the front."

"Well, sure. But what am I looking for?"

"This is Howie's car, my associate. Look for a notebook of any kind. Maybe a book of poetry. Anything written down that might let us know what he was doing here. Okay, let's do this as quickly as we can."

Jack spent the next ten minutes sitting in the driver's seat exploring with his hands. He went through the side pockets, felt along the dashboard, the glove compartment, the floor beneath the seats.

Howie didn't keep a neat car. As they worked, Jack and Dan came across a wide miscellany of stuff: books, clothes, CD folders, junk mail, food wrappers, maps, plastic containers of motor oil, a funnel, an electric pump that plugged into the cigarette lighter to inflate tires. It was a well lived in station wagon, part vehicle, part storage closet.

Dan kept calling out new items as he found them. But there wasn't anything Jack thought would prove to be particularly helpful.

Until he came across Howie's iPhone, which had slipped onto the floor in the crack between the driver's seat and the door. Jack felt the smooth, glossy plastic with his fingers and lifted gently until he held it in his hand.

Luck was finally beginning to break Jack's way.

"Okay," he said to Dan. "Let's get moving."

Chapter Twenty

Jack sat in the passenger seat of the cruiser deep in thought as Detective Dan Hamm drove at an uncomfortably fast speed along the deep curves of the mountain road to San Geronimo. Gravity sent Jack leaning hard against one side of the car, then the other.

Every now and then, Dan touched his siren to make slow moving vehicles get out of the way. Either he was in a hurry or he was venting his anger at finding himself commandeered into service as chauffeur to a blind civilian on his first week as a State Police detective.

Jack had more pressing matters to worry about. It was an important step forward to find Howie's abandoned car, but if he'd had his way, he would have ordered an exhaustive search of the surrounding countryside to see if there was any sign of Howie himself. Unfortunately, the arrival of the She-Wolf had put an end to that option. Her investigation would mean the hilltop house would be off limits to Jack—and Santo, too—for a long time to come. Jack understood the national security implications of Eckehart's murder, but it was frustrating nonetheless.

Howie's phone would hopefully provide some answers, a log of incoming and outgoing calls and texts which would give Jack an idea of what Howie had been up to in the days before his disappearance.

Unfortunately, the phone would most likely need to be charged before it would yield its goldmine of information. This would take time and meanwhile Jack wanted to get himself as quickly as possible to the Eckehart house in Los Alamos to speak to the neighbor who had seen Howie climbing into the house. This was possibly the last time Howie had been seen before he vanished, and Jack wanted to check it out before Lorna Wolf shut down access to the place. With luck, she would be occupied at the murder scene for another few hours, which gave him a window of opportunity if he acted quickly.

What did he want to tackle first? The phone or the neighbor? Jack was pondering when Dan swerved abruptly to avoid an oncoming car.

"Slow down, Dan!" Jack cried. "Let's try to get to San Geronimo alive!"

"Right!" Dan said sullenly. "Darn out-of-state drivers! You'd think they'd never driven a mountain road before."

Jack sensed he needed to deal with Detective Hamm before he could tackle either Howie's phone or the Los Alamos neighbor.

"Look, I know you're not happy to be chauffeuring me around when there's a big murder investigation under way, but you're going to have a long career ahead of you if we don't die on the road today."

"It's not your fault, sir," Dan said. "That lady from Los Alamos is going to shut down our investigation anyway. It's just been discouraging the way the other guys have been treating me at the station. Like I don't even exist."

"You're paying your dues, Dan. Give it time."

"I mean, I spent years working for this! I passed the detective exam, and what do they have me doing? Going out for coffee and sandwiches. And now driving you . . . beg your pardon, sir."

"It's okay, Dan. You know, when I made Inspector back before you were born, they used to have a ritual in San Francisco for newbies like me. I'll never forget my first day. Just out of uniform, I came into the squad room in a spiffy dark grey suit with my gun in my shoulder holster, all eager and excited to get started. I'd been assigned to Robbery/Homicide in the Tenderloin, the sleaziest part of the city, lots of drunks and prostitution and crime.

"And you know what happened? The first day the Loo calls me into his office and gives me an assignment to find a small-time hood by the name of Charlie Chin who was holed up somewhere in the Tenderloin. A chink, as the Loo put it. You've got to understand that these were the days when Chinese were chinks, Latinos where spics, and blacks . . . well, you know what blacks were. Charlie Chin supposedly needed to be brought in because he was a witness to a homicide. I have to tell you, Dan, I felt pretty good at landing such an important assignment for my first case.

"Well, I spent two weeks looking for the guy, poking my head into every seamy joint in the Tenderloin, giving it my best. I was out to prove myself, but I got zilch, absolutely nothing. All the time, whenever I returned to the squad room, the other detectives would glance my way and chuckle. Every now and then one of them would smirk and ask me how the Charlie Chin case was coming. Until finally I got it. The whole thing was a joke. There wasn't anybody named Charlie Chin. I was on a snipe hunt. When I found out, I felt pretty bad at first. I was angry. Until I realized it was only an initiation process every newbie went through and you had to be tough enough to survive it or you shouldn't be a cop in the first place. This making sense to you, Dan?"

The young detective had listened without saying a word. He finally spoke.

"May I ask you a question, sir?"

"Of course you can. But stop calling me sir."

"Would you like me to call you Commander?"

"No, not that either. I'm not Commander Wilder any longer, I'm retired. We're going to be working together so you need to call me Jack. Now, what's your question?"

"When you rose up the ranks, Jack—did you haze the younger guys coming up behind you?

"No, I did not. And when I became a precinct captain, I put an end to it entirely, as much as I was able. There was too much real work to be done to allow any of my detectives to waste time looking for people who didn't exist. And in any case, the police department was changing. The beefy cops who beat guys with nightsticks and called people spics and chinks were retiring and a new kind of more educated police force was coming in. I'm not saying it was ever a Sunday school, but the times were changing and those who couldn't go with the flow were let go."

Dan had become cautiously interested. "So, an Inspector in San Francisco . . . that's what we would call a Detective One?"

"Yup."

"Did you have to go to college to qualify?"

"I did. San Francisco State, four years. These days, I would need a master's or a law degree to advance as far as I did, so I guess I was lucky, getting in on the tail end of an era. Now, I'm sure you realize the reason I'm telling you this. You're all hyped up to conquer the world and I don't blame you for being unhappy. But in fact, what we're doing is important and if you come through for me, I'll make sure the Lieutenant knows you did your part."

"So your partner's missing, huh?" Dan asked.

"Yeah, but there's much more to it than that. Look what we have here. Brandon Eckehart and his wife dead in that house. Plus a Nobel Prize winning physicist, Grisha Bloom, who's dead as well. All of this is connected, I'm not sure how yet, but we're going to unravel it. And we're going to do it without drawing attention to ourselves from Wolf and the powers that be at LANL."

"So we're going to be sorta undercover, is that what you're saying?"

"Not undercover exactly, but it's going to be unorthodox. We'll need to sort our way forward as things come up. So what I need to know is if you're okay with this, Dan? I need to know you're onboard, because once we get going, there won't be any turning back."

"Well, yes, sir, Jack," Dan said with new vigor. "Yes, I am."

"You sure now?"

"Yes, I am. The way you explain it, I get it now. How important this is."

Dan was a young man who seemed to need a heroic quest, and this was starting to sound like it might be halfway exciting.

"What's first on the agenda?" he asked eagerly.

"Breakfast," said Jack. "As you come into town, we'll pick up some burritos at Juanita's."

***

Jack phoned ahead so they didn't waste time at Juanita's, currently the best food cart in town. From there, Dan drove them to the station where Santo had instructed him to exchange the spiffy black cruiser they were driving for Friendly Wendy, a ten year old Crown Victoria wreck with 150,000 miles on the odometer, the oldest, saddest vehicle on the State Police lot.

The car had gotten its name due to a local prostitute known as Friendly Wendy who had taken it on a joy ride and crashed it into a tree. It was a legendary tale at the station. Friendly Wendy and Timmy Orozco, the state trooper whose assigned car it was, had been enjoying a midnight romp in Torres County Park, polishing off a quart of tequila, when Wendy decided to go for a spin, leaving the befuddled trooper by the side of the road struggling to get his pants back on. It wasn't a proud moment in New Mexico State Police history. Timmy had lost his job and the Crown Victoria never entirely recovered from the tree.

In normal procedure, Friendly Wendy would have been recycled for a newer vehicle and sold at auction, but for reasons no one could explain, it had remained in the vehicle yard where it was used infrequently, mostly for quick trips to KFC to pick up buckets of chicken.

"Friendly Wendy!" Dan complained with a sigh. "Well, isn't that a kick in the pants! I sure hope she doesn't break down on us, Jack, sir."

"It reflects our status," Jack said as they drove from the station lot. "But that's okay. We'll remain optimistic."

The next stop was the agency office where Jack left Howie's phone with Ruth. He asked her to charge the phone then make a list of all Howie's calls and texts from Wednesday, July 10th on, the day Howie met Bloom on Dawson Peak.

"Type out the text messages," he told her, "so I can hear them later on my reading machine."

"Yeah, Jack. But I'm not going to be able to get into Howie's phone without his pass code."

"It's 0925," he told her. Which was September 25th, Claire's birthday. Howie used Claire's birthday on all his devices which didn't make for good security. But Howie didn't like smart phones any more than Jack did, and he was too lazy to remember a bunch of different codes.

"Where to now, Jack?" Dan asked when they were back in Friendly Wendy.

"Los Alamos. Does this jalopy have roof lights?"

"Well, sure."

"Then use 'em, please. We're in a hurry."

***

They pulled up to the curb in front of the Eckehart house in Los Alamos in mid-afternoon, the hottest time of the day.

Jack hadn't been sure Friendly Wendy would make it. The muffler began falling off in Española and grew louder by the mile. The A/C didn't work so they had all four windows wide open fishing for air. Then there was the unsettling grinding noise from under the hood, metal against metal. But the roof lights did indeed work, and in fact, they had made good time getting here from San Geronimo.

Dan had found the Eckehart's address on the dashboard laptop. This, too, was functional, though it was slow.

"We're here, Jack."

"Any sign of Feds?" Jack enquired.

"I don't think so."

"No mysterious vans or unmarked cars?"

"Nope."

"Okay, Dan. Now remember, you're my eyes, I can't see a thing without you, so I need you to describe everything to me as clearly as you can. Let's hear you paint a word picture of the Eckehart home."

"Well, it's a one-story house with white aluminum siding and a bit of lawn and a flower bed outside. The flowers look like no one really cares about them. They're . . . well, they're sort of sad."

"Really?" Jack was surprised at this detail. "What do you deduce from that fact, Dan?"

"I deduce that the Eckeharts weren't interested in gardening."

"Okay," Jack said with a nod of encouragement. "Sad flowers. I'm sure that will go a long way in helping us solve this case. What else do you see?"

Detective Dan Hamm thought for a moment. "I see . . . a troubled marriage."

This was an even more surprising observation.

"A troubled marriage? Are there empty beer cans on the lawn?"

"No, it's just a feeling I get. A kind of . . . malaise over everything."

A malaise! Jack was impressed.

"The lawn's not cut," Dan continued. "I can picture his wife saying, 'Brandon, get off that couch and cut the lawn.' And him answering, 'Heck with that, sweetheart. You don't like it, go cut it yourself.'"

"Tell me something, Dan, do you read novels?"

"Well, sure. I gobble up all the Dan Brown I can get my hands on. Clive Clussler, too."

Jack nodded. "We'll work on your literary taste later. Does it look like anybody's inside?"

"Nope," Dan decided. "I'd say the house is empty."

"Okay, now tell me about the neighbor's house. Gladys Serna. You got her address, too, didn't you?"

"She's right next door, just a few feet away, separated by a low hedge. A blue house, one story. Kinda the wrong end of middle class, if you know what I mean."

"I do."

"But she has a real nice yard. Flower beds, a nice little lawn, an apple tree, a porch out front with a rocking chair. Everything kind of . . . grandmotherly. Does that help you see it?"

"It does, Dan. I'm still absorbing the wrong end of middle class. And grandmotherly . . . that should win a prize! Now tell me, does it look like she's at home."

"She is. She's sitting on a glider on the front porch knitting."

"Well, isn't that sweet? We'll leave Katya in the car so we don't alarm her. Let me check to make sure she has water, then we'll pay grandma a visit."

Chapter Twenty-One

Detective Hamm held up his badge as he and Jack walked up the path toward the pleasantly shaded porch where the old woman was sitting on an old-fashioned glider with her bag of knitting.

Dan believed he was good with elderly women. He had adored his own grandmother, who had played a large part in his childhood. Granny Rose, as he called her—to distinguish her from Granny Martha, his father's mother—had filled his childhood with the smell of baking pies and Sunday roasts.

He approached the old woman with a pleasant smile, doing his best to look harmless as he and Jack arrived at the porch. Jack was holding on lightly to his left arm.

"What do you want?" the old woman demanded, peering up from her knitting. She was short and plump with frizzy white hair.

"Sorry to disturb you, ma'am," said Dan. "I'm Detective Hamm of the New Mexico State Police, and this is Commander Jack Wilder, a special consultant from the San Francisco Police Department. If you have a minute, we're hoping to ask you a few questions about your neighbor next door."

She stared at them suspiciously. Her mouth was set in a downward scowl, which might have been the result of not having her dentures in. Her knitting needles continued clicking away at a great speed.

"Show me that ID again, sonny. There are a lot of creeps out there and you gotta be careful."

Dan obliged, taken aback by her not-so-sweet grandmotherliness. He gave her his shield which she regarded from several angles, turning it upside down then right side up again.

"You don't look like a cop," she said, returning his shield. "But okay, I guess you're the real deal."

"Do you think we could step inside the house, Mrs. Serna?" Jack asked.

"No, you can't," said the woman irritably. "The house is a mess. You can ask your questions from where you're standing, and if you don't like it, that's too bad."

Jack smiled. Unlike Dan, he liked crusty old women more than the syrupy kind.

"We're here because you phoned the State Police on Monday. You reported an Indian man who broke a side window in the Eckehart's house next door. Is that right?"

"Damn right I called the cops! Those Indians, they're all drunks, living off handouts from the government. This one broke the kitchen window and climbed inside. I don't care much for the Eckeharts, but I wasn't going to stand by and watch some damn redskin break into their house!"

Jack nodded sympathetically. "I understand. Can you tell me why you don't like the Eckeharts?"

"Why? They're weird, that's why. They play loud music and fight and come and go at all hours. Believe me, all those big brains at the Lab are wackos! My husband worked there for thirty years before he died. He drove a forklift, he wasn't a scientist, thank God! I'm still trying to collect compensation for his brain tumor. But, oh no, plutonium's perfectly safe, they say, if you believe those idiots!"

The old woman had a great deal more to say about the Los Alamos National Lab. Jack listened with polite interest. The drought, she said, was due to the plutonium in the air. Her lawn was dying because of radioactive isotopes. She suffered from insomnia because there was uranium in the water.

It took some time for Jack to bring her back to the matter at hand.

"Can you tell me what time it was on Monday when you saw the Indian climbing in the window?"

"Three o'clock."

"You looked at your watch?"

"*Bonanza* had just started."

"I see. Were the Eckeharts home?"

"Well, the slob wasn't there. I hadn't seen him for a few days. He disappears sometimes."

"The slob? Meaning Brandon Eckehart?"

"You got it. He comes and goes a lot."

"What about the wife, Ashley? When did you see her last?"

"Sunday, I guess. She was coming back from shopping with the kid in the car."

"And the kid is—"

"Juniper, they call her. Their one-year-old. What sort of name is that, I ask you?"

Jack thought Juniper was a sweet name for a little girl. But he let it go.

"So, Monday, three o'clock—was anyone home?"

"How do I know? You think I have x-ray vision?"

"Were there any cars in the driveway?"

"Not that I remember. I don't pay attention to stuff like that."

"Were there any sounds coming from the house? A TV playing? Music, perhaps?"

"Just the kid crying."

"Juniper was inside crying?"

"That's what I said, didn't I? That kid was crying like all get out. On and on."

"So where did you figure her mother was?"

"I figured she was sleeping it off, recovering from the party," said Mrs. Serna, shaking her head. "Bet she had some hangover, leaving that kid to cry like that!"

"Party?" Jack asked. "You didn't mention a party."

"Sunday night. You didn't ask me. I woke up at two in the morning hearing loud voices. All the lights were on and it sounded like she was having a bash."

"Did you see what cars were in the driveway?"

"There were a couple of cars, but I wasn't paying attention. I just shut my windows and turned on the air conditioning to drown out the noise."

"You didn't think to call the cops?"

"Why should I? The local cops won't do anything about loud parties. They don't do anything, period. That's why I called the State Police in Española the next day when I saw the Indian crawling in the window. The Los Alamos cops are pathetic losers."

"They probably aren't paid very much," said Jack. "But back to the party, did you see anyone come or go?"

"Look, I didn't see anyone, period. Okay? I just heard them. The Eckeharts are loud people and I've learned to ignore them."

"Were they shouting? Could you hear any parts of the conversation?"

"Nothing I could understand."

"How long did the party last?"

"I've no idea. I'd taken a pill and with the window closed and air conditioner on, I just tuned them out. The next morning all the cars were gone and everything was quiet."

"Except for Juniper crying!" Jack said thoughtfully.

"Well, the Eckeharts pay no attention to that kid. They're lousy parents, absorbed in their own lousy lives."

"Didn't this bother you? That maybe a young child was in a house with no one looking after her?"

"Listen, bub, if I was bothered by everything that goes on at that house, I'd have lost my mind a long time ago. I mind my own business and stay clear of them. So are we finished yet?" she asked. "Judge Judy is on in five minutes."

Jack debated whether he should tell Mrs. Serna that the Eckeharts were dead. Gruesomely dead. Probably, it would make her day. He decided against it. In any case, she would hear soon enough.

"I appreciate your time, Mrs. Serna," he said. "I really do. I just have one or two more questions. I'm hoping you can help me visualize what happened on Monday afternoon. There's a child crying in the house and there's no sign of the parents. Is that right?"

"Right."

"Then at 3 o'clock an Indian arrives, smashes the kitchen window, and crawls inside. Did it occur to you that maybe he was trying to get inside to help the child?"

"What occurred to me was he was trying to rob the joint."

"Okay. What happened next?"

"I told you. I called the cops. Then a few minutes later the girl arrived—"

"Wait a second. What girl? Ashley?"

"Ashley's no girl. This was someone different, I don't know who. I saw her fiddle with the front door and walk inside."

"What do you mean, fiddle with the front door?"

"She had some sort of jimmy. She sure as hell didn't have a key. I watched her fiddle for a while and then she went inside."

"Did you call the cops back to give them an update? This was getting kind of serious, don't you think?"

"I was thinking about it. But then two white vans from the Lab showed up and I thought they'd take care of things. They were security, I've seen them before."

"Lab security, I see. And this was . . . what? A few minutes after the girl had broken into the house?"

"Maybe five minutes. But they were too late. The Indian and the girl must have heard them coming. They ducked out the back door into the backyard and climbed the fence into Mrs. Trujillo's yard. They had the baby with them. The Indian passed the kid over the fence to the girl and they got away."

Jack was stunned. "You saw all this?"

"Sure, I did. Out my back window."

"Did the security people follow them out into the backyard?"

"Not right away. A few minutes later one of them poked his head outside, but they were gone by then."

"So the girl and the Indian and the child got away?"

"As far I know. I didn't see them again."

"I see!" said Jack, more to himself than to her. "Now, did you tell the Lab people all this?"

"They never asked."

"They didn't interview you?"

"No, of course not. What do they care about somebody like me? A whole bunch of cars and vans arrived after that, a big crowd from the Lab. But they didn't come over to ask me anything and I didn't volunteer. Why should I help a bunch of jerks whose brains are fried on plutonium?"

"I see," Jack said again, even more thoughtfully than before, though he didn't see at all. Why the team from LANL didn't interview the witness next door was beyond him. Unless they already knew everything that they wanted to know.

"Just one more question. Can you describe the girl for me?"

Jack wasn't surprised by the description. He already had a good idea who she was.

Black hair, a pale complexion, small and thin.

Chapter Twenty-Two

On Saturday morning, as Jack was arriving at Grisha Bloom's rental house in the mountains, Emma sat drinking a mug of coffee and reading an email from Claire on her laptop on the kitchen table:

Hi Emma, it's days now since I've heard from Howie and I'm starting to go out of my mind, hoping he's okay.

I imagine you've heard what's up between me and Howie, though what's down is probably a better description. You know how much I love Howie. He's the love of my life.

But here's the problem. I've been having an affair with Richard Watson-Fowles, the conductor, and I'm so totally confused and conflicted about it. You know who he is, I presume? He's 67 years old, extravagantly romantic, a bush of wild white hair—have you heard his recordings of Mahler? —a musical genius. I was so, so flattered when he asked me to perform the second Shostakovich Cello Concerto with the London Philharmonic (no less!), not an easy piece to play. He worked with me for three weeks before the concert, patiently going over the score, bringing out something in my playing that I never knew was there, a passionate commitment to every note.

Well, most of the time we rehearsed afternoons at his home on the Chelsea Embankment overlooking the river and I guess you can imagine how one thing led to another. Emma, I swear to you, I didn't mean for it to happen! Before I knew it, I found myself in his bed. It was like I was caught up in the whirlwind of his huge personality and I just couldn't help myself. Then he asked to conduct me in the Dvorak Cello Concerto and I was so flattered I thought I was in love.

Until yesterday, that is, when I found out he sleeps with all his young female protégés. He's screwing two other girls at the moment—one of them he has set up in a flat just across the river in Battersea, where he can get to her in five minutes. I mean, he's 67 years old, I don't know how he can do it, and I feel like such a fool!

Well, you can imagine—I sent him a note just an hour ago, no more afternoon rehearsals, I'm not even sure I want to do the Dvorak anymore. The whole thing is off, off, off . . . but now I've gone and ruined everything with Howie! I'm just so confused and desperately unhappy, and Howie won't even answer my email. I told him about Richard, of course—we've always been honest with each other. But I'm sure Howie hates me, and I hate myself even more. I bet he has 5 new girlfriends by now, all of them younger and prettier than I am.

Do you think I have a chance to win him back somehow? Or should I just slit my wrists and be done with it? A hug to you and Jack. Confusedly, Claire.

Emma read the email twice as she munched an English muffin. Then she wrote back:

My dear darling Claire—first of all, you have to stop beating up on yourself. The way you describe the situation with Richard it's hard to imagine any young woman not doing exactly what you did. And paying the price for it too because these charismatic musical geniuses always turn out to be egotistical bastards. I kid you not.

The real problem, Claire, is that you and Howie have been living thousands of miles apart, you with your career and Howie with his. That's what you need to figure out. You're both at an age where Things are bound to happen if you're physically separated for long periods of time. So if you want to keep your relationship with Howie, either he needs to go live where you are, or you need to come back here. I know this is a complicated matter for both of you. You're a truly gifted musician, but Howie doesn't want to be the Boyfriend hanging around the edges of your success without anything to do.

As for your affair with Richard—you know, Claire, couples who genuinely love one another get through these things. I don't generally talk about this, but long ago when I was young—when Jack and I were still in our late-twenties—I had an affair with a jazz piano player in San Francisco. You would know his name if I told you because he went on to have a big career and he was just about as charismatic as your Richard. I was totally swept off my feet for about a month and it nearly ended things between me and Jack. But then he (the pianist) went off on a national tour and I soon heard about his groupies and like you I realized what a fool I'd been.

To make a long story short, Jack and I went through a rough patch for about a year. It wasn't easy. But we stuck with each other and we ended up closer than before. As for you and Howie, you'll just have to see if the two of you have the will and the love and the commitment to work this out.

That said, the reason you haven't heard from Howie isn't necessarily that he's angry with you—he's on a case right now. In fact, I don't want to worry you, but Howie hasn't been heard from for a few days now and Jack is starting to become concerned.

In any case, don't YOU worry—I'll let you know the minute I get news of Howie. Meanwhile, if you want to save your relationship, you might consider clearing your concert schedule for a few weeks and making a trip back to New Mexico.

By the way, I don't like Richard Watson-Fowles' interpretation of Mahler. For me, he goes seriously over the top with those symphonies. I'd say less charisma, less dancing about on the podium, just play the damn tunes!

All my love to you, and don't EVER again joke about slitting your wrists!

XXX, Emma

Chapter Twenty-Three

Howie woke slowly. He wasn't sure how long he'd been unconscious, but it felt as though he'd slept for a long time.

He was happy to lie with his eyes closed for awhile, feeling peaceful and strangely refreshed. He was on a couch of some kind that was very comfortable. He had that good feeling of waking after a restful sleep.

Until he opened his eyes.

Where was he?

It took a moment to figure it out. He was in a room with white walls that glowed and hummed. They were the oddest walls he'd ever seen. They were rounded overhead, made of some translucent material he was unable to identify.

His mind was working slowly. The room was long and narrow and curved in every direction he could see. He seemed to be inside a capsule of some kind.

Or, more accurately, inside . . . a large glowing hot dog!

Howie sat up abruptly, his heart beating fast.

The couch on which he lay was in the center of the capsule. It was made of some smooth white plastic material and it reminded him of a dentist chair, curved to fit the contours of his body. The curved surfaces of the walls twinkled with colored LED lights, instrument panels of some kind though there was no indication of their purpose. Red, green, orange, and yellow shone through the translucent walls, blinking at him with an amiable insistence.

This was strange enough, but what made his heart nearly stop was the round window at the far end of the room.

The window looked out on a black starry night that was more vivid than even the clearest New Mexico sky, a view of the universe Howie had seen from Hubble photographs, but never from Earth.

Stars blazed with incredible intensity against the blackness of space. There were thousands and thousands of them. Millions, billions, uncountable. In the distance, there was a blue and orange nebula exploding with unearthly colors.

"No!" said Howard Moon Deer. "No, no, no, it can't be!"

It was impossible, he didn't believe it.

And yet. . .

Howie fell back on the plastic couch.

He closed his eyes and wondered if he was going insane.

***

Howie lay for some time with his eyes closed, heart thumping, telling himself, *this is impossible, this isn't happening! No way!*

Then he remembered something Jack had once told him. *When you eliminate the impossible, whatever remains, no matter how improbable, must be the truth.*

It was a maxim from Sherlock Holmes, the fictional creation of Arthur Conan Doyle, and a favorite of Jack's.

Taking a deep breath, Howie opened his eyes again. He tried to remember back to the moment when he had stood on the hilltop near the geodesic dome with Zoey nearby and a strange vibration had filled the air.

Either a flying saucer had come by to abduct him—not impossible, he supposed, but not likely. Or it had been a helicopter, a much better guess. There had been intense lights, lasers perhaps, something high tech. And an odd scent. Could he have been drugged? Something sprayed from the helicopter? He remembered very little about it, which was suspicious in itself.

But who would have done something like that? And why?

Howie didn't have the answers, but he was glad to be doing some straight thinking. In an age where uncertainty had become a principal, straight thinking did a lot to calm one's nerves.

He noticed for the first time that he was dressed in loose white clothes, comfortable pants with a drawstring and a short sleeve top. A yoga outfit, as Howie thought of it. All he needed was a roll up mat. He had no idea where his own clothes had gone.

His stomach growled and he realized he hadn't eaten for a while.

Howie stood up from the couch and explored his prison. The capsule was approximately ten feet wide and thirty feet long. Except for the window at the end, the walls were perfectly smooth and even. He could find no cracks that would indicate a door.

There was no furniture except for the couch. Inspecting the couch more closely, Howie decided it resembled more a La-Z-Boy recliner than a dentist chair. Howie got on his hands and knees, curious to inspect the underside. The floor glowed just like the ceiling, so he was able to see the seam underneath where the material joined together. It was a sort of Naugahyde, a glossy product that imitated leather.

There was a label that protruded from the seam, a small square of material that had writing on it. Howie had to lie on his back with his head underneath the chair to read it.

The label read:

LA-Z-BOY

MONROE, MICHIGAN

This confirmed his suspicions. He doubted they had La-Z-Boy chairs on the planet Klizmor.

"What are you doing on the floor, Moon Deer?" a voice asked.

He was so surprised he bumped his head hard against the bottom of the chair.

"Ouch!" he said, easing himself out from under the chair. He sat up feeling foolish.

He wasn't entirely surprised to find Mia Bloom—aka Zoey Kelly—standing near the window watching him with a glitter of amusement in her cold blue eyes. She was fetchingly dressed in a tight fitting grey uniform that was oddly similar to what Captain Kirk and his crew wore on *Star Trek*. The uniform had a small blue triangle near her heart, and it clung to her body in a flattering way.

"Zoey," he said in a flat voice. "Imagine finding you here."

"Princess Zora," she corrected. "I've come to help set you free."

"Sure, you have," said Howie.

He was starting to get it. He wasn't flying through space in a giant hot dog. He was in a comic book.

Chapter Twenty-Four

Jack and Emma had a Sunday morning ritual. Come hell or high water—no matter what the crisis, what the case—Jack cooked brunch.

The brunch itself varied, some weeks omelettes, other times crepes. Today it was Eggs Benedict. As usual, the biggest challenge for blind cooking was to get everything set up properly. Emma needed to help with this part, finding all the ingredients in the fridge and setting them up on the counter. The eggs, butter, lemon, English muffins, Canadian bacon, orange juice, and a bottle of champagne (Korbel, nothing special) still in the fridge for Mimosas.

With Eggs Benedict, the timing was crucial, and Jack felt about the counter with his hand to make certain he had everything in its right place, everything in easy reach. A small mistake and your hollandaise sauce could turn into seriously bad scrambled eggs.

"Jack, you seem distracted this morning. Are you sure you're up for this?" Emma asked. "We could just do fruit and yogurt today."

Fruit and yogurt! Jack was nearly speechless. "Emma, I'm fine," he said patiently. "I have it all under control."

"Right, Jack. Just tell me if you need help. And please, dear, try not to make too big a mess."

Of course, that was the other aspect of blind cooking. The cooking part was a breeze, it was the clean up afterwards that sometimes threatened divorce.

Jack knew his cupboards and kitchen shelves by heart. He got the electric egg poacher ready, put the double boiler on the stove, cut open the package of Canadian bacon, sliced the English muffins, placed the squeezed lemon juice into a cup, and began melting the butter in a small pan over a low heat on the stove.

Everything now had to be done quickly so that the hollandaise came out at the same time as the poached eggs, the muffins, and the bacon.

He began breaking eggs—a deft move with one hand, spreading the shell with his fingers, separating the whites from the yolk, and dropping the yolks into the top of the double boiler. It was almost a ballet to do this well . . .

"Jack!" Emma cried.

"Emma, not now. I'm concentrating."

"Jack, you're dropping the egg yolks on the floor!"

"Oh, come on, Emma, you've got to be—"

Kidding, was what he meant to say. Until he stepped on an egg yolk on the floor and nearly slipped and fell over Katya, who had come up behind him to lick up the mess.

Emma crossed the kitchen and took his arm. "Jack," Emma said patiently, "let me take over before you destroy the kitchen. You go into your office and try to figure out where Howie is, I'll finish breakfast and call you when it's ready."

***

Jack retreated into his office, sat down heavily on his swivel chair by the desk, and made an attempt to regather.

There were times when he had a brutally clear image of himself: a blind, foolish, opinionated old man who had once been a good detective, but now couldn't even manage to make breakfast!

How Emma had put up with him all these years, he didn't know. This latest fiasco was beyond belief—dropping egg yolks on the kitchen floor without even noticing, lost in his thoughts, worried about Howie, oblivious to everything else!

He would be lost without Emma, he knew that very well. She had indulged him for all these years . . . and what did he give her in return?

Katya, too. He would be lost without her. And Howie . . . without Howie, he couldn't exist as a private detective, he would need to close the agency.

Had he ever told any of them how much they were appreciated? Yes, how much he loved them!

How selfish he'd been! How did people put up with him? A ridiculous person stumbling about in the dark.

Okay, he told himself firmly, *stop this now!*

It helped nothing to wallow in brutal self-doubt.

If you can't take the fire, get out of the kitchen!

Jack took three deep breaths. He rolled his head to loosen the tension in his neck. He sighed deeply, regained his focus, and replayed the sheet on his Kurzweil reading machine that Ruth had made for him, the log of Howie's phone activity.

He got back to work.

***

Jack had already listened to the list that Ruth had prepared for him of Howie's phone activity twice last night after he had returned from Los Alamos. He put the sheet of paper on his reading machine and listened again in the hope it would kick start some ideas.

The majority of the texts on Howie's phone were messages back and forth with Claire. There had also been a single phone call with her last Sunday morning that had lasted 84 minutes. Jack ignored these as none of his business, though he was sorry to know that Claire and Howie were going through a bad time.

Of more interest to Jack, there had been a phone call from Brandon Eckehart to Howie later that Sunday, July 14th, at 12:18 PM. There was no way to know what Howie and Eckehart had talked about, but it was significant that they had been in touch.

The following day, Monday, Howie had received a mysterious text message: *Come immediately need to talk urgently my house 1051 Isotope Rd soon as you get this Eckehart.*

The address was the Eckehart house in Los Alamos where Gladys Serna had seen Howie crawl in the side window and later escape through the backyard with Mia Bloom and the toddler. Jack could imagine Howie answering the urgent message, rushing to Los Alamos, finding the child alone in the house, then encountering Mia. Where they went from there was anyone's guess. Neither Howie, the woman, nor the child had been seen again.

But here was a further problem: the urgent text purporting to come from Brandon Eckehart had been sent from a blocked number so there was no guarantee that it had actually come from him. Eckehart used his actual phone to phone Howie on Sunday—Jack had checked this out. So why should he use a different phone with a blocked number to contact Howie on Monday?

Howie had received a further mysterious text on Wednesday the 17th from John Concha, the War Chief of the San Geronimo Pueblo: *Please call re: our talk in the plaza something further to discuss.*

This was the last text on Howie's phone and there was no indication that he had ever called Concha back, or had even received this message. Jack had met the War Chief once briefly and he was curious to know what he and Howie had discussed in the Plaza and why he wanted Howie to call him back. Most likely, it had nothing to do with Howie's disappearance, but it was something that needed to be checked out.

There was one more item Ruth had found on Howie's phone that merited further scrutiny. It was on his Calendar app where Howie, often forgetful, wrote down his appointments. For Sunday, July 14th, he had written, '10 PM Worm Hole Eckehart/Dawson.'

This was very curious. It was hard to imagine a place called the Worm Hole. Jack had tried to find it on the Internet, but had come up with nothing. Yet apparently Howie had met Brandon Eckehart there, though once again there was no mention of what they had discussed.

The word Dawson added an interesting twist. Jack presumed they didn't meet on Dawson Peak, which meant that Dawson must be a village or a town.

"Nancy," he said to his computer, "tell me if there's any town or village in New Mexico by the name of Dawson."

"I'm sorry, Jack, there is no currently existing town by that name."

Jack had to think about this for a moment. One of the problems with computers was that they were too literal.

"What do you mean, no currently existing town?"

"There's a ghost town, Dawson, New Mexico, seventeen miles from Cimarron. But it was abandoned by 1952."

Nancy went on to tell Jack about the hundreds of people who had died in two separate coal mine explosions in the once thriving town of Dawson. A ghost town seemed like a very strange place for Howie to meet Eckehart, if indeed that's where the meeting took place. Yet it made a certain ghoulish sense. The worms crawl in, the worms crawl out— you could imagine a Worm Hole in such a place. Or not, but it was yet another lead he needed to check out.

Jack sat pondering how he was going to proceed. He decided he needed to go back to the very beginning and work his way forward from there: Howie's meeting with Grisha Bloom in a thunderstorm at 12,000 feet.

That was the key to everything, he was sure of it. Where had Bloom come from that night, how had he gotten up on that mountain, and how had he ended up dead on their doorstep? If Jack knew the answer to these questions, he was certain the rest of the puzzle would fall into place.

Then, of course, there was the equation Bloom had written down for Howie. The Theory of Everything. Or perhaps not. But whatever it was, it had set off a treasure hunt, a gaggle of seekers who were trying to get their hands on it.

He needed to find the equation, and to do this he needed to decipher the clue that Howie had left for him in his safe, the mysterious two words, "Claire's knee."

"Breakfast is ready, Jack," Emma said, poking her head in the office door.

Jack stood up from his desk, glad to have his focus back.

"I'm sorry about the eggs, Emma," he told her. "Sometimes I don't know how you put up with me."

"Oh, Jack," she said wearily. "I don't mind, not really. It wasn't so hard to clean up. Katya did most of it. But I have to tell you, I've been thinking, and this is absolutely the last breakfast you're going to get with hollandaise sauce. From now on, it's muesli and low-fat yogurt. I'm serious. You're 73 years old and you need to start thinking about cholesterol and your blood pressure. I don't want to lose you. Will you do this for me, if you won't do it for yourself?"

Emma had caught him at a contrite moment, which wasn't entirely fair. But he promised. She was right, of course. There would be no more Eggs Benedict for Sunday brunch. At 73 you had to grow up and accept the new limitations of your aging body.

"And you'll cut down on red meat?" she pressed, sensing she had a momentary advantage.

"I will. From now on it's fish and chicken."

"And plenty of vegetables."

"Brussel sprouts," he promised.

"And no more cream sauces. No more rich deserts."

"They're gone, Emma. They're history."

"I mean it, Jack. I don't intend to be a widow."

"I'll try, Emma, I really will. I'll even start peddling on that exercise bike you got me last Christmas. If you'll just do one favor for me in return. Well, maybe two favors."

"Here we go!" she said with a sigh. "Okay, Jack what are they?"

"Email Claire and ask her if the phrase 'Claire's knee' means anything to her. It must be a private joke between her and Howie."

"This is important?"

"Very important. It has to do with the damn equation Howie was given. He hid it away somewhere and left me a clue in case I had to find it."

"Claire's knee? That's the clue?"

"I know it's odd, but there it is."

"Okay, and what's the next favor?"

"Drive me to the Pueblo after breakfast. I need to find John Concha, the War Chief."

Chapter Twenty-Five

Jack insisted on washing the breakfast dishes. He was a difficult man, manipulative, occasionally ridiculous. But he wasn't a total troglodyte.

What had held Emma's affection for forty-two years wasn't easy to put into words—a quality about him, an odd charisma that had swept her up when she was a young woman in San Francisco and that still held her now. Plus, he wasn't a bad cook when he wasn't dropping eggs on the floor.

Nevertheless, Emma held her own with Jack. She was no pushover. She had her own career, opinions, and financial independence—in fact a trust fund which had allowed them to live beyond the salary of a San Francisco cop. Few people knew this, not even Howie, but it had been Emma's money, not Jack's, that had set up the Wilder & Associate Private Investigations agency. As a result, whatever battles Jack and Emma had, they were the battles of equals.

While Jack was cleaning up in the kitchen, Emma went to her office, a sunny corner bedroom she had converted at the side of the house, and turned on her laptop.

There was an email waiting for her from Claire:

Hi, Emma—is there any word yet on Howie? I'm going out of my head with worry and really can't concentrate on anything, so I've decided to clear my schedule and fly back to New Mexico. I don't know if Howie will want to see me so I'm wondering if I can stay with you and Jack?

I have to do the Dvorak cello concerto this Thursday night with Richard at Albert Hall. I don't want to do it, but the concert's sold out and I can't back out. In any case, it will be absolutely the last time I ever do anything with bloody Sir Richard Watson-Fowles. I've already told him the romance is off and of course now he's phoning five times a day, determined to win me back. What an egotistical jerk! Honestly, I don't know how I fell for him!

I've just booked my flight for Monday night the 29th, London to Denver. I'll rent a car and should be in San Geronimo midday Tuesday. I only pray Howie's okay and he'll see me!

Please let me know the second you have any news.

Love, Claire

Emma read the email quickly and then wrote a reply:

Dear Claire—of course you can stay with us. I'll have the spare room ready. But my guess is Howie is going to take one look at you and welcome you back with open arms.

Jack is trying everything he can think of to find Howie. Santo is helping and has even loaned Jack the use of one of his detectives, a young man by the name of Daniel Hamm who is much too earnest, but he has a badge and a police vehicle at his disposal which is a great help. Most of all he gives Jack a semi-official presence.

So try not to worry. A group of very good people have mobilized and they're working nearly around the clock to get to the bottom of this.

One last thing Jack asked me to mention. Howie looked after our house while we were in Hawaii and he left a note for Jack that's a bit of a mystery. The note is simply two words long, "Claire's knee." That's all it says. Your knee. Do you have any idea what this means? Howie wrote it on a sheet of paper that he folded into a square and left in Jack's safe, so it's obviously important somehow. Jack believes it could be a clue that will help him find Howie, so please get back to me about this as soon as you can.

Love to you, Emma

***

San Geronimo was an old place. The Spanish Conquistadores arrived in 1610 searching for El Dorado, a fabled city of gold that existed only in their dreams.

As for the Indians—the People, as they called themselves—they had been here a very long time, but not forever. The San Geronimo Pueblo was at least a thousand years old in its present form, an outpost of the ancient Anasazi civilization. But like everybody else in this part of the world, they too were immigrants.

Today fewer than 3000 Indians lived at the Pueblo, but it remained the psychological core of the community, a presence that had kept San Geronimo from becoming just an over-developed ski resort and tourist town.

The Pueblo village was nestled against the mountains with the reservation extending for many thousands of acres into the foothills and higher peaks. Emma drove onto Pueblo land with a sense that she was entering a separate country. She drove past the small casino and souvenir shops until she came to a stop sign and a chain across the road. A large billboard read:

CLOSED

THE SAN GERONIMO PUEBLO

IS CLOSED TO THE PUBLIC

July 14 - September 1

ABSOLUTELY NO ENTRY

TRESPASSERS WILL BE PROSECUTED

"Oh, Jack, I'm sorry, I forgot! The Pueblo closed last week for their annual whatever-you-call-it. Retreat. Cleansing. Sacred Rituals."

"This time of year?" Jack objected from the passenger seat. "At the height of the tourist season? For almost six weeks?"

"They do it every year," Emma said. "You remember, don't you? It's their way of reclaiming their culture. The young people go into kiva to learn the old ways. Honestly, Jack, don't you wish the entire town could shut down to tourism for six weeks every year? Think how peaceful it would be."

"Parking would certainly be easier," Jack agreed. "Well, is there anyone here I can talk to?"

"There are two young men lounging by the ticket office turning cars away. I'm not sure how official they are. They're wearing jeans and T-shirts. Dudes, I think you'd call them."

"Why don't you pull over and take me to them."

The San Geronimo Pueblo had been designated a UNESCO World Heritage Site and generally this time of year hundreds of tourists would be paying ten dollars each to visit the small part of the ancient multi-storied adobe village that was open to the public. Emma pulled over onto the shoulder of the road and helped Jack out of the car. Holding his arm, she guided him across the road to where the two young men were standing directing traffic.

"The Pueblo is closed!" one of them said before Jack had a chance to open his mouth.

"I'm here to speak to John Concha, the War Chief. My name is Jack Wilder and I'd appreciate it if one of you would call and let him know I'm here."

"He's not available, sir. The Pueblo is closed."

"I understand," said Jack. "But Concha will want to speak with me. He left a message at my office saying we need to get in touch as soon as possible."

"The Pueblo is closed, sir," the gate keeper repeated. "Nobody's allowed in."

"I get it. But if you will just call John Concha—"

"Can't do it. All the phones are turned off throughout the village. This is the time of year when we turn our thoughts to sacred things."

Jack was patient, aware that outsiders had raped and pillaged the native world nearly out of existence, and the Pueblo certainly had good reason to close itself off. Still, it was frustrating. He did his best to stress the importance of reaching John Concha, but he got nowhere.

"He's not available, sir. He's in kiva until September 1st, he doesn't have a phone."

"Can you get a message to him?"

"No way. You just gotta wait."

"Tell him Jack Wilder wants to speak with him. Tell him Howard Moon Deer is missing and this is urgent."

"Moon Deer? That's the Lakota guy?"

"Exactly," said Jack. "The Lakota guy."

***

Jack left the Pueblo with a half-promise from the guards at the entrance that they would try to give Concha the message. Howie's name had opened a small door, but Jack wasn't optimistic.

He wished he knew why the War Chief had been trying to reach Howie. It could be entirely unrelated to Howie's disappearance, but Jack didn't think so. A vague idea was forming in his mind.

"Do you have a map at the library of reservation lands?" he asked Emma as they drove away.

"I think we do. I can check tomorrow if you'd like. But you might do better at the Bureau of Land Management because it's not straightforward. I know there's a main part of the reservation. But there are also some outlying areas that aren't contiguous. And of course, there's been an ongoing court case for decades about what's called the La Madre Sierra Land Grant."

"Which is?"

"It's complicated and very contentious. In 1815 the Spanish crown gave huge tracts of land to a number of families to encourage immigration to northern New Mexico. The Pueblo lands were also drawn then at more than three times the present size. But then came the Mexican American War that ended in 1848 with the Treaty of Guadalupe Hildago. The United States did very well from that skirmish. We got Texas, California, half of New Mexico, Arizona, Nevada, most of what we now call our Southwest."

"Sure," said Jack. "Davy Crocket, Manifest Destiny, remember the Alamo."

"But in the treaty we signed, the U.S. agreed to respect the property rights of all the people who had been living in these areas before the war. That's what's contentious to this day. The old land grants that were part of Guadalupe Hildago have been pretty much ignored. Soon after New Mexico became a state in 1912, Washington reduced the San Geronimo Pueblo by nearly two-thirds. The feeling was a few thousand Indians didn't really need all that land, particularly since there were mining interests, ranchers, land developers, etcetera, etcetera, all of them eager to make a buck. The Pueblo has been in court on and off since the 1950s trying to get their land returned to them."

"Well, I don't blame them," said Jack.

"I don't either. But it's complicated because if the Pueblo gets their way, nearly half of the present town of San Geronimo will revert to them. The entire ski area will be theirs, the golf course, the shopping center south of town, the Holiday Inn. And get this, Jack—our house, too."

"Our house? We're on Indian land?"

207

"We are. And so are most of our neighbors. That is, if the 1848 treaty stands. This issue heats up now and then and there are a lot of angry people on both sides."

Jack nodded. He could imagine the passions and arguments.

"Interesting," he said. "Look, Emma, do you think you could do a favor for me?"

Emma sighed. "You're notching up favors, Jack. What now?"

"Tomorrow, see if you can find an old map of northern New Mexico, pre-Guadalupe Hildago. I'm especially interested in the mountains east of town. Dan and I will go over to the BLM office to see what they can give us."

"Okay, I'll try."

"Also, if you could follow through with Claire."

"Claire's knee?"

"Exactly. You're better friends with Claire than I am and I'm sure she'll tell you. I need to know why Howie put that note in my safe. I'm hoping it's going to lead us to the book of Chinese poetry where Bloom wrote down the equation that appears to be at the center of all this. But, Emma, whatever you do, once you know where that book is, don't go near it. It's just too dangerous. Leave that for me and Detective Dan."

"And what, my dear, will you be doing while I'm off looking for old maps and Chinese poetry?"

Jack smiled. "Getting a bird's eye view of this damn case!" he replied. "I'm going to convince Santo to lend me a helicopter."

Chapter Twenty-Six

The State Police station in San Geronimo was a no-frills, one-story concrete fortress on the edge of town. New Mexico was a poor state and no attempt had been made to make the building welcoming to the public. It was surrounded by a high cyclone fence with razor wire on top and its roof bristled with antennae and satellite dishes.

Santo Ruben's office was barely large enough to accommodate his desk, a swivel chair with arms, a metal filing cabinet, and two orange plastic visitor chairs. A single window looked out on the asphalt parking area where three black State Police cruisers sat waiting for the next violent crime. In San Geronimo, that wouldn't be long in coming. Like many cops, Santo kept photographs of his family and children on his desk and walls to remind himself that he was human.

"Geography," Jack was saying to Santo. "It's taken me much too long to get a handle on this case, but geography is starting to put things into focus."

"I'm glad to hear it, Jack. But how?"

"It's what real estate people tell you. Location, location, location."

Jack sat in one of the visitor chairs and Detective Dan Hamm in the other. Katya, as always, was on the floor next to Jack following the humans attentively with her large ears swiveling from one person to the other. She didn't miss a thing.

It was nearly 8 o'clock Monday night. Everything had taken longer than Jack had anticipated, but he had learned some interesting things.

Emma had spent the morning examining old maps in the town library while Jack and Dan had spent an hour with Rick Martinez, the head of the local BLM office, then another hour at the Tax Assessor's office in the county complex. Being blind was especially difficult for Jack in this instance because when it came to maps, a picture was worth more than a thousand words. But with Dan and Emma's help, he was starting to get a better idea of the mountain setting where too many strange events had occurred.

"I'm still a long way from understanding what's going on," Jack told Santo. "But it's curious how close together all the different crime scenes are, separated by only a few miles—from the air, that is, not by road. If you call Dawson Peak Ground Zero, the hilltop house where Brandon Eckehart's body was found is only twelve miles away."

"You're calling Dawson Peak a crime scene?"

"You bet I am, Santo. Grisha didn't get up there on his own. Now look, it would be forty-seven miles by car on twisty mountain roads from Dawson Peak to the house Bloom was renting while he was in New Mexico. That's what confused me at first, what kept me from putting it all together."

"Okay," said Santo. "So put it together for me."

"Let's back up a second. First off, I found Howie's Subaru abandoned outside the house where the Eckeharts were killed. I didn't have a chance to tell you because Lorna Wolf was arriving in her helicopter. I also found Howie's phone. Somehow it had slipped out of Howie's pocket onto the floor by the driver's seat. I grabbed it before Wolf could get her hands on it."

"Jack! That's a crime scene! Wolf could get you thrown in jail for that!"

"If she finds out. And if I don't solve this thing before she does. Which I will, with a bit of luck.

"You'd better hope you do! Jesus, Jack—that phone is important evidence in a sensitive murder investigation."

Santo didn't like Lorna Wolf, nor did he like the way a murder investigation that should have been his had been taken from him. But when you were a cop, there were few things worse than having someone remove evidence from a crime scene.

"Well, okay, you got the phone," he said reluctantly. "What did you find on it?"

"I'll skip over all the texts from Claire and cut to the chase," Jack told him. "What's interesting are the communications he had from Brandon Eckehart. Howie kept track of his appointments on his Calendar app and for Sunday, July 14th, he'd written, '10 PM Worm Hole Eckehart slash Dawson.'"

"Worm Hole? Doesn't sound very appetizing, does it?"

"I'm thinking it's someplace UFO nuts hang out. Dawson is an old ghost town seventeen miles northeast of Cimarron."

"And that's where Eckehart wanted to meet? A ghost town?"

"Apparently. It was a coal town where hundreds of people died in two separate mining accidents, so the Worm Hole may be a kind of double entendre. In any case, Dan and I are going to check it out. Meanwhile, we've been studying forest service maps and checking property titles and we've come up with a few more interesting tidbits. Why don't you tell Santo what you found, Dan?"

"Well, it could be just a coincidence," Dan said, taking over. "But the ghost town sits in a valley just to the east of Dawson Peak where Moon Deer met Bloom in that thunderstorm. Like Jack's been saying, the roads are sketchy up there and there aren't any roads at all that go through from this side of the Peak to the valley where the ghost town is. To drive there from San Geronimo, you need to go clear to Cimarron and then take a seventeen-mile jog on an undeveloped dirt road. But it's not far as the crow flies."

"Or as the helicopter flies," Jack interrupted. "By road it's nearly sixty miles. But by air, it's barely seven miles from where Howie met Bloom in that thunderstorm to the Worm Hole, where he was supposed to

211

meet Eckehart. That's about a five-minute ride. It's also not that much farther to the hilltop home where Eckehart's body was found. Again, by car it would be nearly a two-hour drive. But by air it's sixteen miles."

"Sure, if you're rich enough to have a private helicopter at your disposal," Santo remarked.

"Or if you happen to be a government agency," Jack said. "Then you can let the taxpayers foot the bill."

"You're saying—"

"I'm just saying. It may be the Feds, it may be somebody else. In fact, for a few days now I've been sensing we have an invisible player in our game, someone we don't know about. And I'm starting to get an idea of who this invisible person might be."

"A ghost, huh?"

"Sort of. Only this is a ghost who may still be alive."

Santo laughed. "Like Elvis?"

"You got it. Now, listen to this. The area around Dawson Peak is almost entirely national forest except for a few miles on the eastern flank that's part of a huge private holding that calls itself the La Madre Grande Ranch. Now, this ranch is very large, 67,000 acres. But when Dan and I started checking records, I was surprised to find it's a whole lot larger still. Adjoining the Madre Grande is the Whitefield Ranch—another 94,000 acres. And next to that is the Madonna Creek Ranch which is a whopping 121,000 acres. Together they span two counties and comprise 282,000 acres of land. And guess what? All three ranches are owned by the same person."

"Well, sure, Jack. But that's happening all over the mountain West. A few billionaires are buying up huge tracts of land, creating small empires for themselves. It's made a land shortage that's driving up prices for everybody else."

"Okay, but this property is special. There are a series of shell companies involved, and it took me the rest of the afternoon to find out who owns what. Luckily, I have an old cop friend in San Francisco whose specialty is international financial crime. My in-law in Hawaii gave me a hand as well. He's a hedge fund manager and knows all the ins and outs of shell companies.

"So here's what I discovered. The three ranches I mentioned are owned by Triangle Fund Management, based in Dallas, which in turn is owned by the Scheherazade Group in New York City. Which is part of a still larger entity based in Zurich, Genius Partners. I got slowed down here because things get very secretive at the top. Fortunately, my in-law has dealt with these people. The top person at Genius is a woman, very elderly now but still active. Her name is Greta Von Hilderman. Does that ring a bell?"

"No. Should it?"

"Probably not. In 1969 she was the production chief at Jupiter International Studio in Hollywood. An unusual job for a young woman at the time. Jupiter International churned out dozens of horror movies and science fiction thrillers. None of them ever won an Academy Award, but they made a ton of money in their day. Now guess who owned Jupiter International, Santo?"

"I can't imagine, Jack. Hollywood isn't something I know much about."

"The studio was owned by Sebastian Hays, the legendary movie mogul. Greta Von Hilderman, by the way, was Hays's fifth wife."

"Okay," said Santo. "And you're saying Sebastian Hays owns all this land? But he's been dead for years, hasn't he?"

"I don't know. He hasn't been seen in public for nearly forty years, but that doesn't mean he's dead. He'd be 96 years old today, if he's alive. A venerable age, but more and more people are living that long."

"He owned an airline too, didn't he? I'm starting to remember."

"And a chain of hotels. Plus, he had quite a collection of wives. Several of them were famous actresses. But he went crazy in the end, like some of these rich people do. In the Sixties it was rumored he was taking LSD and that may have been what drove him over the edge. He gave his final interview in 1978 to Playboy magazine. It was pretty wild stuff. Do you remember what he said?"

"Jack, I was a kid in 1978. Back then, it would have been the photos that interested me, not the interviews."

"In his last interview, Sebastian Hays claimed he had been abducted by a flying saucer and taken to an alien planet he called Klizmor."

Santo didn't speak immediately. He sat tapping a finger on his desk as he considered what Jack had told him.

"Okay, Jack," he said after a moment. "What do you want?"

"A helicopter."

"You're kidding me!"

"No, Santo, I'm not."

***

The ride was rough over the high peaks of the Sangre de Cristo range. The thermal winds sent the small police chopper bobbing up and down like a cork in rough water. Black clouds floated over the mountains threatening rain. But for the moment, there was still more blue sky than storm.

"Hang on to your stomach, Mr. Wilder," the pilot said cheerfully into the headphones. "We're about to encounter a bit of turbulence."

"I'm fi—" Jack started to say. *Fine.* Just as the chopper hit a geyser of air that sent the flying bubble shooting upward a hundred feet, then dropping again just as fast.

In fact, Jack was not fine. Nor was Katya. He was strapped in tightly, but his stomach was doing somersaults. He wished he had thought to bring some Valium along.

The helicopter had room for only the pilot and three passengers. Dan was in front next to the pilot, and Jack and Katya were in the two seats in back. Jack kept a good grip on Katya, one arm around her body to keep her from flailing about. She whimpered from time to time, small squeaks of unhappiness.

"Be brave," he told her.

It was Tuesday afternoon. It hadn't been easy to convince Santo to give him the use of a State Police helicopter and it had taken a day to find one that was free for non-emergency use. In the end, it was the need to find Howie that had convinced Santo to agree.

"But I'm giving you only two hours of flight time, Jack. I mean it. Do you know how much it costs to run one of those things? With the fuel and insurance, it's two thousand dollars an hour. Okay?"

"I'll be back on time," Jack promised. "Honest."

Their first destination was the house Grisha Bloom had rented in the mountains, where Howie had abandoned his Subaru. Jack wanted Dan to make an aerial search of the surrounding area to see if there was any sign of where Howie might have gone. Jack listened on his headphones as Dan did his best to narrate the view.

"It's still a crime scene down there, Jack. There are three . . . no four vehicles. Two vans, a pickup truck, and an SUV. A bunch of people are wandering around. Darn! There's Lorna Wolf. She's standing near the house looking up at us, waving us off. And boy, does she look mad!"

Darn was strong language for Dan.

"Don't let her scare you, Dan. She might not like us flying overhead, but she's not going to shoot us down. How low can you get us, Sergeant?" he asked the pilot through his headset.

Sergeant Billy Hicks, the pilot, had a pronounced Texas accent. In New Mexico, pilots of police helicopters were required to be law enforcement officers

"I can shave off the tops of those trees if you'd like, Mister Wilder," Billy told him.

"It won't be necessary to go quite as low as that. How thick is the foliage down there?"

The forest below was mostly aspen and evergreens with a few grassy clearings. Sergeant Hicks told Jack that except for a few places, the ground was fairly easy to reconnoiter from the air. For the next half hour, they flew in an expanding circle around the house until they had examined an area of nearly half a mile. They found an old rubbish dump, an abandoned log cabin, and a small marijuana plantation that belonged to a neighbor. This concerned both Sergeant Hicks and Detective Hamm, but Jack told them to let it go. They weren't here this afternoon to make a marijuana bust.

Several times they hovered while Dan used his binoculars to examine the land below more closely. He spotted the decomposing body of an elk and the rusted frame of an ancient pickup truck, but there was no sign of Howie.

After half an hour of circling, Dan thought he saw a discarded backpack on a rocky meadow nearly a mile from the house. Billy was able to land on the clearing and Dan climbed out of the helicopter to investigate with Katya scampering behind him. But the backpack turned out to be a brown paper bag and Katya had been unable to pick up any scent of Howie.

"Sorry, Jack, there's nothing," Dan said as he and Katya returned to their seats.

Discouraged, Jack told Sergeant Hicks to head to Dawson Peak, a ten-minute trip by air.

"Do you fly over these mountains often, Billy?" Jack asked as they were making their way north.

"Often enough, I guess," said the sergeant. "A couple of times a week."

"Do you encounter private helicopters from time to time?"

"Well, sure. Not every time I set out, but they're around, all right. Mostly they're medical helicopters or news outfits covering some story. When there's a forest fire, you'll see a lot of 'em buzzing around. They can be a nuisance, getting in the way of the planes dropping water so we'll warn them off. Every now and then, I'll spot a chopper I don't recognize, some rich guy traveling somewhere."

"Do helicopters have to file a flight plan?"

"No, though it's always a good idea. Non-commercial crafts don't need a flight plan as long as they stay under 18,000 feet. That goes for private planes as well as choppers."

"So there's no way to keep track of who's going where?"

"Not really. Small airports generally keep logs. But if you have your own airstrip like big ranches often do these days, you can come and go as you please. As long as you stay low."

They reached Dawson Peak and flew above the trail on the western slope where Howie had hiked up from the forest road to Angel Creek campground. Two different groups were on the trail today, a man and woman with heavy packs and a larger group of teenagers with two adults in charge. The man and the woman were descending the mountain, the teenagers were going up.

"You know, we're eating up time, Mr. Wilder," Billy mentioned as they were passing over a herd of longhorn sheep. "Lieutenant Ruben told me two hours, max, and then we gotta return home."

Jack sighed. He would have liked to give the Peak a better look, but it wasn't his main interest today.

"Let's move on, then," he told Billy over his headset. "What I'm really curious about is the big ranch to the east."

Billy made a sharp turn and swooped down over the eastern slope of the mountain toward the private two hundred and eighty-thousand-acre empire that Jack had determined belonged to the eccentric millionaire, Sebastian Hays. There was nothing here, only land and more land—unbroken forest, high meadows, creeks and rivers.

They flew over an old barn and an abandoned cabin, but there was no sign of any residence an ex-movie mogul might call home.

"There's a nice little lake down there," Dan said after they had been flying over the property for nearly twenty minutes. "At the east end the water comes up to the foot of a cliff that's pretty dramatic, rising straight up for maybe a thousand feet or so. Funny, the lake's not on the map."

"How large is it?"

"Maybe ten acres. What do you think, Billy," Dan asked the pilot.

"I'd say ten acres is a good guess," Billy agreed. "Something that big *should* be on our map . . . hey, there's something down there. By the foot of the cliff. Do you see, it, Dan?"

"I'm not sure . . ."

"Get closer, Billy. What do you see, Dan?" Jack was getting excited.

"It's strange looking . . . it's not really a building. It's a . . . my God, it's . . . you're not going to believe this, Jack . . . it's a . . ."

"Spit it out, Dan. What the hell is down there?"

Dan couldn't get the words out. It was too bizarre. Billy had to say it for him.

"It's a flying saucer, Jack. Parked on the ground by the edge of the lake."

Jack nodded with grim satisfaction.

"Find somewhere to set down, Billy. I believe we have arrived at our destination."

***

"Wow!" said Dan as Billy circled above the lake looking for a place to land. "It's like something out of a science fiction movie!"

"Describe it to me," said Jack.

"Well, it's big and round. The outer skin is some kind of plastic shell. Only it's not plastic, I don't know what it is."

"Take your time, Dan."

"There are orange and red lights blinking on and off around the edges. It's like a big clam shell. But there's something funny about the surface, the way it reflects the sky and trees. It blends in so well with the landscape it's hard to see from the air. It's like it's not really there, unless you catch it in just the right light. I've never seen anything like it. Actually, clam shell isn't right. It's more like . . ."

"A giant hot dog?" Jack asked when Dan was stuck for words.

"More like an empanada, I'd say. There's a hatch in front, a ramp that comes down onto the lawn by the lake."

"Do you see an airstrip anywhere?"

"No. But there's a helicopter pad just off to the side. A square concrete slab with a circle painted on it. There's a chopper down there, too. I didn't see it at first because it's tied down with a camouflage net over it. Boy, this place is unreal!"

"Go lower, Billy. Let's get a closer look."

They were hovering in place over the lake, sending a circular hurricane of waves out over the water, when a voice came on the headsets.

"Ground to unidentified helicopter. You are in restricted airspace. Leave immediately. I repeat, this is restricted airspace. Leave immediately."

"Nonsense," said Jack. "Tell them who we are, Billy. Tell them we're landing."

"Ground, this is the New Mexico State Police. We are about to land."

"You are not authorized to land," said the voice firmly. "You are trespassing on private property. Unless you have a search warrant, you must leave immediately."

"Is there somewhere we can land?" Jack asked Billy.

"Well, the helipad is occupied. But there's a patch of lawn by the edge of the lake that will do."

"Then put her down," said Jack.

"Uh-oh, there are two guys coming down the ramp from the saucer. They're in space uniforms, like the pajamas they wear on *Star Trek* . . . damn, they have guns! Looks like AR-15s. They're aiming at us!"

"Billy, tell them again that we're the New Mexico State Police. Say they need to put down their damn guns unless they want a hundred state troopers here in the next fifteen minutes."

Billy keyed his radio and repeated Jack's message. The two men on the lawn hesitated and then lowered their weapons.

"They've stood down, Jack," Dan told him. "What do you want to do?"

"Let's land."

The helicopter set down on the lawn by the lake not far from where the two men were standing. Dan jumped out first and then helped Jack. Katya leaped out after Jack and shook herself, relieved to be on the ground. Jack told Billy to wait in the helicopter and be ready to lift off quickly.

Jack put Katya back in her harness and took a firm hold of the handle.

"Where are the guys in pajamas, Dan?"

"They're standing closer to the saucer about a hundred feet away. I wouldn't say they're friendly."

"Okay, let me take your arm. Lead us over to them. Get your badge ready. I want you to take charge, Dan. Be firm. Don't let them intimidate you. Introduce yourself and then you can introduce me. I'll take over at that point."

Dan wasn't enthusiastic, but he did his best.

"Detective Hamm, New Mexico State Police," he said firmly as they crossed the lawn. "This is Commander Jack Wilder, a special police consultant from California."

"Please tell Sebastian Hays that we're here to have a word with him," Jack added.

The two men stared at them impassively. They were monsters, each well over six feet tall with huge chests and shoulders and arms. They both wore earpieces with wires running down into their uniforms.

Jack had to repeat his request. "Get on your radios and tell Hays we want to speak with him. I don't want to return here with a warrant, but I will if I have to."

"There is nobody here by the name of Sebastian Hays," said one of the men. He had an accent. Eastern European, perhaps.

"Sure there is," said Jack. "Tell him we can make this quick and easy, or we can make it long and hard. It all depends on him. We can haul him to the station in San Geronimo if he prefers, but he probably wouldn't like that either."

The two guards appeared to be listening to instructions coming into their earbuds.

"You will wait here," one of them commanded.

***

A few minutes later a man in jeans and boots and a Harley Davidson T-shirt walked quickly down the ramp from the spacecraft and came their way across the lawn. His face was weathered, deeply lined, and he wore a black cowboy hat.

"This gets stranger and stranger!" Dan said softly.

"Another spaceman?"

"No, this one's a cowboy. He's tall and rangy, hair down to his shoulders, a big droopy mustache. He looks friendly, at least. He's smiling."

"Sorry to keep you waiting, gentlemen!" he said as he came closer. "The name's Doug McKay. What brings you to Rancho de las Estrellas?"

Jack smiled thinly. "Ranch of the Stars? We're here to see Sebastian Hays. My name is Jack Wilder, and this is Detective Hamm from the New Mexico State Police. We're investigating several murders and we have just a few questions for Mr. Hays."

"Ah, well, that's a problem, I'm afraid. You see, Sebastian is a very old man and he doesn't see people these days. And I mean, nobody. He's kind of eccentric that way. He's been living as a recluse for over forty years and all he wants from the outside world is to be left alone. But I'm happy to answer any questions for him that I can."

"And what is your position here, Mr. McKay?"

"Position? Well, that's kind of a formal way to put it. I guess you could call me his chief wrangler."

"Really? Do you have horses to train in your flying saucer? Or are you the kind of wrangler who takes care of trouble?"

McKay laughed modestly. "The flying saucer is only an old movie set," he said. "But you probably guessed that. Otherwise, this is a pretty regular ranch."

"Somehow I doubt that. Now here's the deal. We're going to see Sebastian Hays one way or another, so I'd advise him to give us a few minutes and we'll be out of his hair. Otherwise, we'll do the interview in San Geronimo and then he really will have a bother."

"Look, Sebastian is ninety-six years old, he hasn't been out of this valley for decades. You put him in a helicopter and fly him to San Geronimo, it'll kill him."

"He can bring a doctor with him, if he'd like. His attorney, too. In fact, I'd advise that. This is a murder investigation, Mr. McKay. Now, I can radio for backup and get a warrant to search through this flying saucer of yours. Or you can let me have a few minutes with him and we'll be gone. It's up to you to decide."

"Hey, there's no need for trouble," Doug said smoothly. "So, I tell you what. I'll take you to him. But I'm not sure you'll like it. Follow me."

Chapter Twenty-Seven

"Wow, this is some spaceship!" said Detective Hamm as they walked up the ramp and went inside.

"Tell me, Dan."

"We're in a kind of casino. There are slot machines, roulette wheels, poker tables. Red wallpaper. Gold sashes. Posters of old Elvis Presley movies on the walls. It's like we're in Las Vegas. There's a carousel with painted wooden horses . . . the whole thing's a kind of a funhouse for kids. But there are no kids, nobody at all. It's weird, Jack."

"Where's McKay taking us?"

"Through into the next room. It's more of the same. Pinball machines. A bowling alley, model airplanes, a miniature train . . ."

Jack held onto Katya's harness as Doug McKay led the way through the make-believe flying saucer. There were dollhouses, an entire room of elaborately painted wooden rocking horses, a huge Lego structure, a teddy bear collection, and more. It was hard to say if this was a museum of innocence or a monument to depravity. Except for the cowboy wrangler, there were no other people. Their shoes walking on the hard floor were the loudest sound, along with the pad of Katya's paws.

"You'll be speaking to Sebastian through a glass partition," McKay told them as they came to a stop. "He lives in a totally sterile environment. No germs, you see."

They came to what appeared to be a diving bell with windows that looked into a circular white, antiseptic room. A very old man was seated in a white wheelchair. There was no other furniture. Except for the wheelchair and the old man, the room was entirely bare.

"Hey, Sebastian!" Doug said in a hearty voice. "I've brought you some visitors!"

The old man didn't reply. He didn't move. It wasn't clear if he was alive or dead.

Dan put his mouth close to Jack's ear and did his best to describe the figure behind the glass.

"He's like a mummy," Dan said, trying to find the words. "His hair is tangled and long. It's a yellowish white color that doesn't look as if he ever washes it. He's wearing heavy dark glasses so you can't see his eyes. His fingernails . . . sweet Jesus, they're like blackened claws! He looks more reptile than human!"

"Sebastian, I know you hate to be disturbed, old buddy," Doug was saying, as though all this was normal. "These gentlemen are from the State Police and they have a few questions for you. I hope you don't mind."

"Yes," the old man said at last. His voice came over a speaker, raspy, dry as sand, amplified. "I mind."

"You'd better ask your questions," Doug said, turning to Jack. "I'm going to give you just a few minutes, so you'd better be quick. You see what he's like."

Jack touched the glass partition, wishing he could see the legendary figure inside.

"Thank you for seeing us, Mr. Hays. I understand you seldom have visitors. I want to tell you I was a great fan of the science fiction movies you made back in the Fifties and Sixties. They were ahead of their time. A lot of the things you predicted in those films came to pass. Holograms. Personal computers. Even global warming. You were spot on about nearly everything."

Jack paused, hoping the old man would respond to flattery. He didn't.

"I want to ask you about the scientist Grisha Bloom," Jack continued. "I wonder if you can tell me anything about him?"

The voice when it came was hardly more than a scratchy whisper. "The Blue Moon quark . . . an important breakthrough," he said. "Bloom came to visit me here. I sent for him. I wanted to speak to him about the multiverse and ask if there was a doorway from one dimension to another."

"You summoned him here?"

"I offered him a small stipend to come. I sent my helicopter for him. We had quite a lively conversation. You see, I am not entirely a recluse when there is someone I wish to know."

"How long did he stay?"

"I don't remember. Time bends. It means nothing to me."

"He left here in your helicopter?"

"My pilot flew him home."

"Which isn't far away, is it? You're neighbors, almost."

"I wouldn't know," the old man said more softly still. "You would need to ask my pilot."

"I would like to ask him, as a matter of fact. Is he here?"

"I'm afraid he isn't available. What else do you wish to know?"

"You see, Mr. Hays, the problem is Grisha Bloom never made it home. My partner found him wandering on Dawson Peak a few miles from here. And then he turned up dead on our doorstep miles away in San Geronimo. I wonder if you know anything about that, Mr. Hays."

"I do not."

"No? And Bloom's assistant at Los Alamos National Laboratory— Dr. Brandon Eckehart—was found dead along with his wife at the house Bloom was renting, the place your pilot supposedly took him after he left here."

"I know nothing of that either. Nor do I care to. Our conversation is beginning to tire me."

"I'm sorry to hear that. But as I told Mr. McKay, this is a murder investigation and I'm afraid it can't be avoided. If you prefer, we can fly you to the State Police station in San Geronimo. But I think you would find that more tiring still."

"What did you say your name was, young man?"

Jack smiled. It had been a very long time since someone had called him a young man. "I am Commander Jack Wilder."

"Then ask your questions, Commander Wilder. Let's be done with this."

"And now, you see, the mysteries just don't stop. My partner has vanished, a young Lakota man by the name of Howard Moon Deer. Do you happen to know anything about him?"

"No, I do not."

"Do you know about the Theory of Everything?"

"TOE? Ha! Of course, I do."

"Really? What is it, then?"

"You wouldn't understand. Next question, please."

"In an interview many years ago, you said that you were abducted by a flying saucer and taken to the planet Klizmor. Is this true?"

"Yes, it is. But I'm not in the mood to discuss such things. I sense you're a sceptic."

"But you're not, it seems. I wonder if you're hoping that flying saucer from Klizmor will come for you again?"

The old man didn't answer immediately. When he finally spoke, his voice was so soft Jack had to strain to hear.

"Listen young man, whoever you are. There are ancient races keeping watch over us from the stars. There are galaxies and worlds beyond your meager imagination who are speaking to us now, sending us instructions, if only you know how to listen."

"That's very interesting, Mr. Hays. What instructions do they give you?"

"They tell me prepare, prepare! The day is coming for justice and retribution! The weak will be made strong, the old will become young. The balance will be restored!"

"That sounds almost biblical, Mr. Hays. What else do they tell you? Do they tell you to make people disappear?"

"That's none of your business, and I don't like your tone. Doug, please inform these gentlemen that our interview is finished."

"You'd better come along, Commander Wilder," said the wrangler. "You heard him. That's it, I'm afraid. You need to leave now."

"I have a few more questions, Doug."

"Sorry, but if you want more time, you're going to have to come back with a warrant. And you'd better have a team of lawyers with you, because we'll have our lawyers here as well and they don't mess around. . . Beta, Alpha, please show these men back to their chopper."

The two huge spacemen in their white uniforms suddenly appeared. Where they came from Jack didn't know. But he felt a strong hand on his arm.

Katya growled, low in her throat.

"Take care of your dog, Commander," Doug said. "These guys mean business."

"Katya, down," Jack said firmly, sensing this wasn't an idle threat. "Okay, we're off. But you'll be seeing us again, Mr. McKay."

**

Doug McKay, chief wrangler at Rancho de las Estrellas, saw the visitors out and left them in the care of the Star Troopers, Alpha and Beta. Once they were gone, he returned quickly to his boss in the Decom Suite.

Doug came through the air lock after punching in the code that opened the door. Sebastian was reclining in his chair gazing up at the screen overhead that showed a live feed of the Alpha Centauri galaxy from a camera mounted on Envisat, a European Space Agency satellite. The screen was round, ten feet across, and the image was stunning: millions of stars—white stars, blue, red—blazing against the blackness of space. As usual, the old man was lost in his fascination.

"Hey, boss," Doug said coming up behind him.

"Are they gone?"

"They're on their way. But I'm not sure we should let them go."

"Oh, let them go, let them go!" Sebastian said wearily. "All I want is peace!"

"You know, boss, I don't think we can let those folks leave," Doug said. "They'll be back. And then where will we be?"

The old man frowned with exasperation. "What are you doing here, Doug? This is my room. I don't ask for much, do I? But this room is mine!"

"I know, boss. But this is important. We have to stop them from leaving and we have to be quick about it. We only have a few minutes."

"No, it's too much bother," said the old man with a sigh. "What can they do to me? Oh, look at the stars, the beautiful stars! They're coming for me! Don't you see? By the time those people are back, I'll be gone! I'll be young again! I'll be far, far away!"

"Maybe you will," said Doug McKay. "But what about me?"

Sebastian wasn't listening. He really didn't care.

Doug came up softly behind Sebastian's electric wheelchair throne.

"Well, I guess you're right, boss. Like always. Hey, look! There they are! They're coming for you now!"

"They are? Do you see them, Doug?"

"Sure, I do. Take off those dark glasses, boss, and you'll see their spacecraft . . . there they are!"

Doug had to help the old man with his dark glasses. He couldn't do much for himself anymore.

Doug pointed up to the stars that looked so real overhead.

"That's them! Do you see that orange light? That's the ship coming through the wormhole."

"No, I can't see it . . . I'm not sure!"

"Up in the left-hand corner. There they are, boss, don't you see?"

"Oh, yes! I see them now! They're going to heal me, aren't they? Oh, stars, I'm so weary! Won't you come and make me young again and whole!"

"Don't you worry about a thing, boss."

Doug McKay reached from behind and pinched the old man's nose with his right hand, cutting off the air. He put his left hand over Sebastian's mouth.

It didn't take much to smoother a ninety-six-year-old man who had been half-dead for decades.

Chapter Twenty-Eight

Jack was glad to be breathing fresh air again as he came out of the strange house. He had one hand on Dan's arm and the other on Katya's harness as they headed across the lawn to where the helicopter was idling.

"Gosh, I can't wait to get out of here!" Dan said as they hurried toward the helicopter. "It gives me the creeps to think of that guy! He looked like something that had died a hundred years ago."

Jack wanted to get away, too. As quickly as possible. The thought of the mad movie mogul hidden from the world in his empire for one made his flesh crawl.

"Is Billy in the helicopter?"

"He is, Jack. He's at the controls."

"Does he see us?"

"I think so . . . yes."

"Signal him that we want to lift off fast. Come on, Dan, let's get a move on!"

Dan made a hurry-up gesture with his free hand as they began to run, raising his arm and making a circle with his finger. Billy got the message. The engine noise increased to a high whine and the rotor blade began spinning faster.

Jack tripped as they ran, but Dan managed to grab his arm and keep him from falling. When they reached the helicopter, Katya jumped in first, then Dan helped Jack find the metal step and climbed in after him.

Dan had just slipped into the front passenger seat when he saw two men run from the house.

"Go, Billy, go!" he cried. "They have—"

Assault rifles was what Detective Hamm intended to say. But gunshots finished the sentence for him.

The sound of the gunfire was muted under the screaming pitch of the helicopter engine, but the effect was immediate. Bullets ripped into the body of the helicopter and twanged against the rotor blade.

Billy pulled back sharply on the collective, lifting the helicopter straight into the sky.

"Hold on, everybody!" he said almost calmly as the chopper climbed and turned simultaneously, banking at a sharp angle to the right. Jack felt himself straining against his shoulder harness, his body crushed toward Katya, who he held tightly with both arms.

The helicopter continued rising and banking until they were several hundred feet in the air. The gunfire from below was more distant now, but it continued unabated, a rhythmic *rat-a-tat-tat*. Jack was thinking they must be out of range when a string of bullets tore into the fuselage.

"Oh, lord!" Dan cried, "I'm hit!"

Jack smelled smoke and heard Billy saying "Mayday! Mayday!" into his radio. There was nothing he could do but hold on tight to Katya.

They continued rising and banking sideways up and over the steep hill that rose behind the house. Smoke filled the cockpit and Jack expected any moment they would burst into flame and fall from the sky.

"This is State Police unit R-23," Billy was saying urgently into his microphone. "Mayday, mayday . . ."

They rose a few seconds more. It seemed incredible that they were still flying. But then Jack heard the engine sputter and die.

"We're going down," he heard Billy say. "This is R-23 and we're going down!"

Jack felt oddly calm. He hated flying and had imagined crashing so many times that this was almost anticlimactic. It was Katya he felt bad for. She didn't deserve to end like this.

"Hang on, people," Billy cried. "The rotor's going to slow our descent, but this is going to be a hard landing."

The crash was sudden and jarring. Jack felt every bone in his body crunch with the impact as they hit the ground. But he sensed they might survive this. The helicopter was intact and they were on the ground, alive.

Jack was just starting to reunite with his stomach when he smelled the unmistakable odor of aviation fuel.

"We gotta get out!" Billy cried. Up to that moment, his voice had been oddly calm. But he wasn't calm now. "This baby's gonna burn!"

Jack heard the side door open and felt Billy's hands release his shoulder harness. He was tugged out of the crippled machine and pulled to the ground. Katya burst out of the helicopter after him.

"Run!" Billy told him. "Dan's hit and I gotta get him!"

But run where? Jack was on his hands and knees, disoriented. He felt grass under his palms, but he was dizzy and wasn't sure he could stand up. He had no idea which direction to go.

He was starting to panic when he felt Katya nudge up against him. She wasn't wearing her harness, but she allowed him to lean on her as he struggled to find his balance and get to his feet.

"Go!" he said to Katya, keeping a hand on her back. "Get us away from here!"

He bent over and clutched her collar as she led the way. The land was flat, but it was uneven. He couldn't move quickly, and he had a tingly feeling that the helicopter was about to explode.

He heard Billy and Dan coming up behind him. Dan was limping and groaning with pain, but at least he was on his feet. Billy took Jack's arm and the three men jogged awkwardly forward holding onto each other as they tried to put as much distance as they could between themselves and the helicopter. Katya ran back and forth barking at Jack's side.

Jack heard a whoosh as the helicopter burst into flames. A second later, an explosion knocked him forward onto the ground, a concussive wave of sound and fury.

There was a second explosion, but not as loud as the first. Then there was only the sound of burning.

"Everyone okay?" asked Billy.

"I'm okay," said Jack. Not entirely sure he was.

"Damn, my leg's bleeding like a mother!" said Dan. It took a lot to make Detective Hamm swear, but he was swearing now. "Damn, it hurts! But I'm hanging in there."

"Woo-eee, that was close!" Billy said. "I got the mayday off, so they'll be looking for us . . . at least if the radio was working," he added.

Jack sat up wearily, promising himself that he would never, never, get into a helicopter again.

"Where are we?" he asked Billy.

"Hell if I know. We're in a field with a bunch of empty buildings at the far end. They're just shells. They look real old, like nobody's lived here for a long time."

"It's a ghost town!" said Dan.

Jack exhaled and felt a wave of exhaustion. There was a sharp pain in his lower back. They were down, injured, but at least they weren't lost. He knew exactly where they were.

Chapter Twenty-Nine

Emma always had a great deal to do at the San Geronimo Public Library where she was the acting director, a position that was supposed to be temporary but had stretched on for several years.

It wasn't easy to keep a library going in the era of budget cuts and it had turned out to be more of a job than Emma wanted at this stage of her life. But she was uniquely qualified. She had a master's degree in library science from UC Berkeley, and for several years had run the entire San Francisco library system, so the town was reluctant to let her go.

On Monday, she had needed to review a list of new books the library wanted to purchase, meet with the volunteer committee, have lunch with a county commissioner to see if more funds could be squeezed from the county budget, work on a grant proposal to a private foundation in Washington that supported children's literacy, on and on. Yet she'd still managed to find time to locate the maps that Jack had requested, photocopy them and give the copies to Detective Hamm, who came by to pick them up.

On Monday morning she had received an email from Claire, answering Emma's email from Sunday:

Hi, Emma—Claire's Knee? That was a joke between Howie and me. You see, he's always told me he likes my knees which I don't mind a bit. But there's more to this. There's a 1970 French movie called Claire's Knee from the director Eric Rohmer that won a whole bunch of awards. Howie and I watched it on his laptop in a tent during a thunderstorm when we were camping in Montana one summer. We ended up having a fight about it, actually. I found the movie disturbing, an older man being obsessed with a teenage girl's knee, but Howie thought it was funny and "profoundly French" (as he put it.) Anyway, we made up quickly—the storm lasted for hours and there wasn't much for us to do in that tent besides make up. But I have no idea why Howie should mention this in a note that he put in Jack's safe. That really is a mystery!

Love, Claire

Late Monday morning, before her lunch with the county commissioner, Emma had found a moment to phone Jack, who was just leaving the Tax Assessor's office. She read him Claire's email, received further instructions, then sent Claire a new message:

Hello again, Claire—I just spoke with Jack who was very interested in what you said about the movie Claire's Knee. He wanted me to ask you if you saw the movie on a DVD. And if so, do you know where this DVD is now? Please get back to me as soon as possible. Jack thinks this is important.

Emma

With the time delay and Claire's performance schedule, Emma didn't receive Claire's reply until Tuesday morning:

Emma, it was a DVD. When we got back home, Howie gave me the disc of the movie saying I should watch it again on a larger screen. My French isn't as good as Howie's and I couldn't read the subtitles very well on his laptop—he said I should give it another chance. In any case, I never got around to it, and when I left San Geronimo, I put the DVD in the storage shed I keep at Toby's U-Store-It with my bicycle and a bunch of books and stuff. I guess it's my way of keeping one foot in New Mexico. It's Unit 129 and the combination is 0925, my birthday. The shed is under my name, but Howie knows the combination and uses it too because he has so little storage at his pod. Let me know if this helps!

Worried but trying to stay optimistic, Claire

***

Claire's email did help. Emma was certain she now knew where Howie's book was hidden, *100 Poems from the Chinese* with the mysterious equation jotted down inside.

Unlike Jack, Emma was good at math. She had taken two years of physics as an undergraduate at Berkeley and had actually enjoyed it. So she knew very well what the Theory of Everything was, the infamous TOE, and how Einstein had failed to find it despite searching for it throughout the entire second part of his life. Emma had graduated from college in 1970 and she knew her knowledge of physics was long out of date. Nevertheless, she understood the incredible importance the discovery of TOE would be.

This wasn't merely a matter of a Nobel Prize. This was a world changer. $E = mc^2$ was small potatoes by comparison. And the thought that this equation that had been the ultimate quest of science for a hundred years might be written in Howie's book sent shivers down her spine.

On Tuesday morning, Emma had to deal with a delegation from the San Geronimo Holy Fire Tabernacle who wanted the library to ban Harry Potter from its shelves. By the time Emma got rid of them, her nerves were frazzled and her patience strained to the breaking point.

"Of course, you're perfectly free *not* to read Harry Potter if you don't want to," she had told them (reasonably, she believed). "But a lot of people enjoy these books and it's their right to read what they want."

"They're witchcraft!" the woman from the Tabernacle had hissed.

"They're storybooks!"

"They're Satan!"

It wasn't easy to be a librarian in modern America.

I'm going to retire next spring! Emma told herself when they were gone. *I'm going to drag Jack to Spain for three months, whether he likes it or not!*

The most frustrating part of her morning was that Jack was off somewhere in a helicopter by the time she phoned him with the news of Claire's email, and he couldn't be reached.

She tried Jack again two hours later and then an hour after that, but she was only able to reach his voice mail.

She phoned Ruth at the office, but Ruth couldn't tell her when Jack would be back.

"Nobody tells me a thing. Jack and that cute Dan Hamm went off God knows where!" was all she could report.

Was Detective Hamm cute? she wondered. She supposed so. Though not as cute as Jack had been when he was a young detective. Smart, thin (remember that!), urbane, ironic yet kind. Prince of the city. He had shown her a San Francisco she had never suspected, high and low.

Jack! How she loved him, and how he frustrated her with his conservative views on such things as the death penalty—he was for, she was against. Their arguments were so heated, she had sometimes thought she would leave him. But she didn't. He was just so much more interesting than the other men she knew.

And now she couldn't find him. Just when the most exciting scientific find of the past hundred years was sitting in Toby's U-Store-It waiting to be picked up.

In the late afternoon, Emma broke down and phoned Santo at the State Police station, though she felt she shouldn't bother him. But he didn't know where Jack was either.

"I told Jack he could only have the chopper for two hours," Santo said. "Do you know how much those things cost to fly? He promised, Emma. And now he's been gone nearly four hours and I can't reach him."

Emma felt a wave of concern. "What do you mean, you can't reach him? They have a radio, don't they?"

"They're not answering. I don't know why."

"Santo, first Howie, now Jack—"

"Emma, calm down. There's nothing to worry about. It hasn't been that long. They probably set down somewhere that's messing with the signal. The pilot is Billy Hicks who's been flying helicopters for twenty years. Knowing Jack, how obsessive he is, I bet he's hot on the scent of something and he told Billy to turn off the radio so I can't call him in."

Emma wasn't entirely reassured. Santo was probably right about Jack telling the pilot to turn off the radio. He didn't like to be stopped when he was deep into an investigation.

But would a State Police pilot actually turn off his radio? Wouldn't that be dangerous? Against the strict regulations that must govern expensive things like helicopter flights?

The library closed at five. Emma finished some paperwork, closed up shop and was home by six. It was Jack's turn to cook dinner and there were two boneless, skinless chicken breasts defrosted in a bowl of water on the counter. Jack had agreed to do a low-fat, low-sodium stir fry with more vegetables than meat and with brown rice. But nothing had been started, he hadn't been home.

Emma tried Jack's cell phone. There was still no answer.

She poured herself a gin and tonic. Light on the gin, heavy on the tonic.

Howie's cat, Orange, rubbed up against her leg. Emma opened a can of cat food and set it in a bowl on the kitchen floor. Orange probably missed Katya, her best friend. Emma had picked up Orange last Friday not wanting to leave her uncared for in an empty home. Howie's cat had stayed with them before while he was overseas with Claire. Orange often slept curled up in the circle of Katya's front paws.

Should I start cutting up vegetables? Emma wondered. *Or should I drive over to Toby's U-Store-It and pick up Howie's book?*

239

All afternoon, the Theory of Everything had been weighing on her. It seemed absurd to leave the most important scientific breakthrough of the century just sitting in a flimsy storage shed. Jack had told her to stay away from it. But Jack wasn't here. Now that she knew where it was, shouldn't she get her hands on it and put it somewhere safe?

Emma turned on the evening NPR radio news, sat on the living room sofa, and sipped her gin and tonic.

She could imagine Audie Cornish, the NPR anchor, telling the nation the astonishing news of Emma Wilder, the librarian of a small New Mexican town, who had just unearthed the greatest scientific discovery of the past hundred years . . .

No! she told herself.

Yet another part of her was saying, *Yes!*

She tried phoning Jack one more time, with the same result. She waited another hour.

Until at last she couldn't wait any longer. She locked up the house and set off in her Subaru to Toby's U-Store-It on the north end of town.

It was after nine o'clock with only a lingering streak of sunset red on the western horizon. The roads were busy, and Emma didn't notice the headlights in her rearview mirror, a vehicle she couldn't entirely see in the darkness that turned when she turned and kept a constant distance behind her.

Chapter Thirty

Howie wasn't enjoying his journey to the stars. As space travel went, this was a bust.

The days went by in stressful monotony, anxiety mixed with boredom. He had no idea how many days had passed since he had been abducted. In his sealed capsule there was no way to count passing time, day from night. He had nothing to read, nothing to watch, nothing to do.

He was fed nothing, nor was he given much to drink. Which was probably just as well, since there were no bathroom facilities in his capsule. He used the farthest end for his occasional needs, but they became more and more occasional as time passed. Howie was soon lightheaded and weak. His throat was parched, he had a constant headache, he felt himself fading. Since there was nothing to do, he spent nearly all his time on his La-Z-Boy recliner sleeping.

His only visitor was Princess Zora, aka Mia/Zoey. She came and went mysteriously, appearing and disappearing, always at a time when he was either sleeping or had his eyes closed. He had no idea how she did this since the capsule had no door as far as he could tell. Before he became so weak, he had felt carefully with his hands along the floor and sides for a doorway, but the glowing plastic material of his prison appeared to be seamless, smooth and unbroken.

Howie's hunch was Zora somehow came and went through the porthole, his circular view of the fake universe outside his window. The stars and nebulae were almost convincing, but not quite. The whole show was oddly second rate, like the dioramas in natural history museums where a stuffed elk stands thoughtfully on a papier-mâché hill in front of a painted background.

However she arrived, Princess Zora always had the same questions for him.

"You must tell me, Moon Deer, what did Grisha give you? What did he tell you?"

"Look, I've told you this a dozen times. He was out of his head, exhausted, soaked from the thunderstorm. He said he'd been abducted by a flying saucer. He was sick and incoherent, and I left him in my tent to go find help. That's everything."

"No, that's not everything. Why are you lying to me?"

Howie had a sudden idea.

"Grisha was here, wasn't he? In this capsule! He said you helped him escape."

"Yes, I did, Moon Deer. And I can help you, too. But first you have to tell me what he gave you and where it is. We have to get it back, you see. The human species simply isn't ready yet for the knowledge. It will destroy you. You won't be ready for a thousand years."

"Sure," said Howie. "I get it. Except this isn't a very convincing flying saucer. It's about as hokey as you are, Princess. I feel like I'm inside a B-movie."

"No, you're wrong. We'll be in Klizmor in only a few hours. You will see wonders beyond your imagination. We mean you no harm, Moon Deer. But you must tell me what Grisha gave to you."

The interrogation went on and on, always the same. Howie wasn't sure why he was being so stubborn. He suspected he would fold in the end. But he was determined to hold out as long as possible.

Anxiety turned to panic as the hours passed. He didn't want to die in this claustrophobic little capsule, cut off from everything he loved. As an exercise, he closed his eyes and tried to remember hiking up the mountain, before the storm, before he met the spaceman, that morning when the meadows were full of wildflowers. He visualized the sky, the huge expanse, the desert far away. It was a good practice, a mental escape he could keep going for an hour or two at a time. But there always came a moment when he opened his eyes and found himself back on his La-Z-Boy recliner in the glowing plastic tube.

Princess Zora came every few hours to look in on him and ask the questions that were always the same. Finally, she brought him a glass of water.

"You must drink, Moon Deer. You're becoming weak. You're fading away."

He wasn't sure he wanted to accept anything from her. But he had not been given much water for several days, by his reckoning, and he knew he was becoming seriously dehydrated.

He drank. Slowly at first, knowing he had to be careful not to drink too much at once. He drank the entire glass.

Zora disappeared afterwards, leaving him in his solitary cell. Within minutes, he began feeling strange. Very strange. Stranger and stranger.

Until outer space became inner space, through which he floated and fell in lazy circles endlessly through the star-filled sky.

***

Howie had taken psychedelics a number of times when he was an undergraduate at Dartmouth, back in his wild days. LSD once, mushrooms three times, maybe four. And once, returning home to South Dakota his junior year, he'd had a very memorable experience in a sweat lodge with peyote.

This was years ago, but the memory was a grounding that helped him now, at least in the beginning. He was able to tell himself, I'm not crazy, I'm drugged, and if I can just hang on for a few hours, I'll get through this.

Still, it was a rocky ride. Staring wide-eyed out the window of his capsule, he witnessed the Big Bang, the universe contract into a mass the size of a pea and explode with a violence and force that was beyond reckoning.

He was swallowed by a dragon and spat out into a burning sea of fire.

He shrank and turned into a toad.

The toad sprang wings and became an angel.

The angel fell from the sky and went splat on the ground.

In short, the usual psychedelic roller coaster ride. But then it got worse. Much worse. He lost the thread of who he was. He lost his mind. He lost everything.

Suddenly he was screaming, running through a land of dead faces with hideous eyes and mouths that smirked and grinned. A ghoulish figure in black appeared and began running after him with a knife, always only inches behind, always just about to kill him.

The terror was all-consuming. Howie ran with all his might, but it was like running on a treadmill. His legs moved but he couldn't escape. The ghoul came closer, closer. Howie turned to look at him. His face was blank, only a black circle, but on this blankness, Howie saw an evil so great and primal, his heart was about to burst.

He was in hell. A hell beyond hell, a realm of total terror. How many hours passed, Howie couldn't say. It seemed an eternity. But eventually the terror subsided, and he found himself lying exhausted on the La-Z-Boy, panting hard, physically and emotionally drained.

Slowly, the world took on a more solid aspect. He found Princess Zora leaning over him, her blue eyes regarding him with clinical interest.

"Now tell me what Grisha gave you. Tell me where it is."

He gazed up at her, took a deep breath, and replied, "Not on your life, lady! Not if you were the last princess on Klizmor!"

She smiled regretfully. "Then we'll have another go, I'm afraid."

Howie closed his mouth firmly. He wasn't going to drink another glass of her funny water, no matter what. But she held a hypodermic needle. The point of the needle glittered as it came at him.

***

Again and again, Howie found himself in a land of psychotic terror. There were no more dragons or toads. The drug was cunning, it had discovered what frightened him most, the man with no face, and from now that was what he experienced, his personal nightmare, always the same ghoulish figure who was forever about to catch him, sometimes so close that Howie felt his putrid breath on his neck.

"Oh, I have you now, Moon Deer!" he said in a terrible voice. "And I'm never going to let you go!"

When Howie could remember, he told himself this wasn't real. It was an illusion, it only existed in his mind. But that didn't help much.

Between nightmares, Zora asked again and again, "What did Grisha Bloom give you?" And again and again, he told her nothing at all. It wasn't that he was brave. He was simply very stubborn.

And then somehow it was over. There were no more injections. Alone in the space capsule, he slept for a long time. Sleep became the only activity that had any interest for him. All he wanted was to sleep and sleep and wake in his own bed with Claire beside him and chuckle about what a silly dream he'd had, getting himself abducted on a make-believe flying saucer.

Howie was dreaming about Claire when he felt a hand on his shoulder shaking him awake. He opened his eyes and saw Zora looking down at him.

"I'm not telling you a thing—" he began, but she didn't let him finish.

"Listen to me, Moon Deer," she said urgently. "We only have a short time. I'm a prisoner here, just like you are. I turned off the camera in the next room but the guards will be back any minute and we have to get out of here while we can. You have to trust me."

"*Trust* you?" Howie was incredulous.

"Okay, you're angry, I get it. But do you want to escape or don't you?"

Howie raised himself on the recliner and stared at her.

"What do you mean, you're a prisoner, too?"

"It's a long story and we don't have time. But it's the truth. Now do you want to get out of here? Then get up and follow me."

He kept staring at her. He was weak after everything he'd gone through. His mind was mushy. He didn't move.

"Come on, Moon Deer, we've got to hurry!"

Howie watched as she moved to the end of the capsule and put the palm of her hand on the wall by the window. The glass slid open without a sound.

The universe blazed so realistically through the open portal that Howie had the lurching feeling that they were both going to be sucked out into the vacuum.

Zora stepped through the portal and gestured for him to follow.

Behind her, the cosmos was stunning, a billion pinpoints of stars blazing against the blackness. There were swirling galaxies and fantastically colored nebulae.

"Come on, Howie!" she urged. "You can trust me!"

Sure, he could.

But what choice did he have? In the end, the temptation to escape was greater than his worry of what she had in store for him next.

Howie staggered up from the La-Z-Boy recliner and fumbled through the portal into the stars.

Chapter Thirty-One

The town of San Geronimo ended abruptly at the brightly lit Chevron station five miles north of the Plaza. From here on there was only empty highway and high desert stretching unseen into the night.

Emma made a left turn after the Chevron station and followed the smaller highway west toward the local airport until she came to Toby's RV Park, U-Store-It sheds and convenience store, by the side of the road. The last glow of sunset had faded completely by now and the complex was an island of light in the desert.

The RV park was busy this time of year and the office was open until 10 PM for late arrivals. The storage units were enclosed by a cyclone fence at the end of one of the RV loops. There were half a dozen RV parks in San Geronimo, and twice that number of storage companies, for America was a restless, nomadic land.

Emma drove through the gate and passed along the brightly lit rows of sheds until she found Claire's unit. The lock had four small numbered wheels that had to be aligned correctly for it to open. She got on her knees and used the flashlight on her phone to see the numbers well enough to spin the wheels and get 0925 on the proper line.

A car drove up the aisle while she was kneeling over the lock, a big black SUV. Emma glanced up as it passed by, but it continued to the end of the row, made a left turn toward the next row over, and she didn't give it another thought. The compound was open for another hour and there were always people coming and going.

The lock finally opened. Emma rose to her feet with more effort than rising to her feet used to require.

"Oh, dear!" she exclaimed, as she opened the door and peered inside. The shed was tightly packed with cardboard boxes, skis, an old rocking chair, snowshoes, a mattress, a chest of drawers, a bicycle, and more. It was going to take time and a good deal of effort to find anything here.

Emma set to work with determination, pulling out boxes, stacking them on the ground outside the shed, opening the top of each box and giving a good look inside. It was hard work and soon her arms were tired from all the lifting. She went through boxes of books, old tax files, bills, music scores, clothes, kitchenware, vinyl records, cassette tapes, and more books still. Emma was becoming discouraged when finally she opened a cardboard box containing DVDs.

The French movie, *Claire's Knee,* was in a stack of DVDs beneath *Jules and Jim* and *Citizen Kane.* Emma was bewildered at first because *Claire's Knee* was in a plastic cover that was clearly two thin to contain a paperback book. But when she lifted the cover, she found the book underneath.

100 Poems from the Chinese, translated by Kenneth Rexroth, was a book Emma knew well. The poems were simple but wonderfully evocative of misty mountains and monastery bells, lovers drinking wine and gazing at the moon. The copy she held now had been her birthday gift to Claire several years ago, and Claire had loaned it to Howie.

Emma opened the book while she stood in the storage shed and examined it with her flashlight. Sure enough, there was a long mathematical equation written on the blank page after the frontispiece.

But Emma was puzzled. The equation in the book seemed too long. The whole idea of the Theory of Everything, as she understood it, was that it was supposed to be one simple rule that underlay all physical phenomena, everything mankind knew about the universe. "Elegant" was the word physicists liked to use when describing the great mathematical equations of Newton and Einstein. $E = mc^2$ was a prime example, elegant and brief. The equation in the book was neither. It went on for two very complicated-looking lines.

But this was a matter for someone else to decipher, an expert. Emma put the book in the glove compartment of her car and spent the next twenty minutes getting all the cardboard boxes back into the shed, a herculean task that was like rearranging a Rubik's cube. At last, groaning with effort, she locked the shed and drove out of the compound.

Emma noticed a darkened vehicle in the gravel turnout outside the cyclone fence. It was the big black SUV she had seen earlier, but once again, she didn't pay it any particular attention.

Until its headlights came on and the vehicle followed her out from Toby's onto the deserted desert highway.

***

The SUV came up fast behind her as she was driving back to town.

Emma didn't like night driving and she especially disliked being tailgated. The glare of headlights in her rearview mirror made it hard to see. She adjusted the mirror to its night position, but it still made her very tense to have someone so close behind. On a deserted highway there should be plenty of room for everyone. She hoped the idiot would pull around and pass.

But the idiot didn't pull over, he didn't pass. Instead, the idiot came up even closer. She was traveling at a nudge over 60 mph and the SUV was only a few feet back, way too close. Emma's usual strategy with tailgaters was to slow gradually until the driver became impatient and was forced to pass. But she wasn't sure that would work in this instance.

The vehicle had its bright lights on which was even more annoying. It was a drunk, she supposed. Drunks were a constant danger on New Mexico highways, particularly at night.

Emma put her foot on the gas and increased her speed to 70. But the car behind kept pace and, if anything, seemed even closer than before. 70

mph wasn't in itself a dangerous speed on a straight, uncrowded desert highway with wide shoulders. But the slightest mistake in her driving would bring the tailgater crashing into her back end.

It was only now that Emma began to appreciate the danger she was in. Jack had warned her, but she hadn't taken his warning seriously. This wasn't a drunk. This was about the book in her glove compartment.

Emma was frightened. Without noticing, her speed had increased to nearly 80. Which was definitely too fast for night driving on a two-lane highway, way beyond her comfort zone.

The Chevron station was less than three miles up ahead, and once she was there, there would be more cars and buildings. Not a guarantee of safety, but she didn't think whoever was behind her would attack with other people around.

She decided 80 was as fast as she dared to go. She would keep a constant speed and hope for the best. Whoever was behind her didn't want to die either. She had to rely on that.

In the distance, she could see the lights of the Chevron station. She was starting to feel optimistic when the black SUV gunned its engine and pulled over into the next lane to come up alongside her.

Emma wasn't sure what to do. Speed up? Slow down? Jam on her brakes, let the bastard zoom ahead while she did a quick U-turn and sped off the other way?

That seemed a good idea until she realized that he would do a U-turn, too. Then he would come after her while she was heading in the wrong direction, toward the lonely mountains to the west.

While Emma was debating, the passenger window came down, and she had a quick glimpse of the barrel of a gun that was pointed her way.

That decided her.

Without considering what she was doing, Emma swerved sharply to the left, hit the side of the SUV metal to metal with a sharp slap, swerved back into her own lane, and pushed down hard on her brakes.

Up ahead she was astonished to see the SUV fly off the left side of the highway. It skittered into the sagebrush for another hundred feet, bouncing over the rough terrain, until it toppled nose first into a ditch and came to a crunching stop.

Had she really done that? She had! It had been like smacking a pool ball in just the right spot, sending it flying into a side pocket.

Emma drove past the wreck slowly, lowering her window to get a better look. The taillights, still glowing red, were pointed up to the sky. The rear wheels were spinning free. The SUV looked ridiculously out of place at such an odd angle in a ditch.

Emma's hands were shaking, and her heart was beating so fast it was hard to catch her breath. She couldn't believe what she had just done. She had sent someone skittering off the road!

She didn't see the driver. The sagebrush had slowed the car's motion considerably before it had toppled into the ditch, so there was a good chance that the people inside weren't seriously hurt. If they were wearing seat belts. If not, too bad for them!

Should she stop and help? No, she didn't think so. All she wanted was to get away. She stepped on the gas and drove at the precise speed limit—65 mph—to the Chevron station up ahead. She turned right and continued at 50 mph into town. There was a funny sound in the front fender, metal rubbing against the tire, but otherwise her heartbeat was returning to normal and she was feeling okay.

More than okay, really. She was proud of herself. The bastard had tried to run her off the road. He had pointed a gun at her. And she had held her own.

But now she had to consider what to do with *100 Poems from the Chinese.* Where do you hide something as important as the Theory of Everything?

In plain sight, she decided.

Emma drove to the library where she slipped the book into the outside return box, giving the handle a good jiggle as she slammed it shut.

Chapter Thirty-Two

"Careful!" Princess Zora said, as she led Howie through the area behind his capsule.

The universe outside Howie's porthole window wasn't very convincing up close. It consisted of a white screen with three projectors on a metal bar overhead. The projectors broadcast a slowly changing light show of stars and planets and nebulae. Seen from this angle, the whole thing was very cheesy, nothing more than a set from a low-budget sci-fi movie.

Zora led the way along a narrow wooden walkway to a black velour curtain. She moved the curtain aside with her hand and stepped on through to a backstage area where there was a metal door.

"Where are we going?" he asked.

"You'll see. Come on, Moon Deer, we have to be quick."

The door opened onto a long windowless hallway with a concrete floor. It was more like a tunnel than a hallway, a no-frills passageway lit by bubble lights set in the ceiling every dozen feet. The tunnel continued as far as Howie could see, the overhead lights receding in a straight line into the distance ahead. The air was dank and heavy. Howie sensed that they were underground.

Zora was walking so quickly he had to hurry to keep up.

"Slow down!" he called.

"We can't. Not now, Moon Deer! We have to get out of here before they find out we're gone!"

They? Howie was curious to know who *they* were. But she began jogging and he saw no alternative except to stumble after her.

The tunnel came to a ninety degree turn and set off to the left. Howie was starting to feel like a mouse in a maze. He was out of shape, out of breath, and nearly out of patience. He had a stitch in his side as they continued down the seemingly endless tunnel.

They went on and on. Howie was barefoot and he wasn't sure he could continue much longer. He was on the verge of calling for a stop when they came to a small iron door that was shut securely with a metal bar.

"We're here," Zora told him, lifting the bar holding the door closed.

"Great," said Howie. "Where's here?"

"The wormhole." She turned to him with a smile. "We're about to pass from one dimension to another."

"Zora," he said. "Mia, whoever you are. I've had enough science fiction to last a lifetime. You need to tell me what's going on."

"Let's get through the wormhole first. Then I'll tell you everything. I promise."

Howie sighed.

***

It wasn't a wormhole. It was the shaft of an old coal mine.

Inside the iron door, two pairs of old-fashioned rubber galoshes were waiting neatly on the ground along with two miner's helmets with lights on top. The galoshes were small on Howie's large feet, but he was grateful he didn't have to go through a coal mine barefoot. As soon as they had their headlamps on, Zora closed the iron door behind them with a heavy clang and slipped a metal bolt through a hole to keep it shut.

"It sure is convenient to find two helmets and two pairs of galoshes just waiting for us," Howie remarked.

"Moon Deer, I've been planning our escape for days. Now come on, there's no time for talk. Follow me as quickly as you can. Watch your footing, the ground is uneven."

She took off at a fast walk and once again Howie saw no alternative but to follow.

The old mine shaft was deep and dark and dreadful. The lamps on their helmets cast a feeble yellow glow that didn't do much to penetrate the gloom. Howie hated to think what it would be like down here if their batteries gave out.

He followed as quickly as he could, waddling along in the awkward galoshes. He didn't like being underground. The air was suffocating and stale, thick with coal dust. The mountain above their heads was like being buried alive.

At least he had a good idea where they were now. There weren't that many abandoned coal mines in New Mexico to choose from.

"Your wormhole comes out in the old ghost town, doesn't it?" he said, calling to Zora ahead of him. "We're in Dawson."

"Why don't you wait and see, Moon Deer. Maybe you'll be surprised."

"I've had enough surprises," he told her. "Did you help Grisha Bloom escape this way?"

She didn't answer so he called to her again.

"Grisha was here, wasn't he? You had him in that make-believe space capsule just like you had me. You fed him psychedelics to make him crazy and then you helped him escape just like you're helping me."

Again, she didn't answer.

"Come on, Princess. Let's have some truth for a change."

"All right, Moon Deer. You're right. Grisha was in the Space Room, that's what we call it. And I helped him escape. But not through the mine. We went out another way. Above ground, by the lake."

"That sounds a lot more pleasant than this old coal shaft. Why couldn't we go that way?"

"Why?" She stopped and turned around angrily. "Because I couldn't use the same way twice, that's why. It's guarded now. They're more careful after Grisha got away."

"Who's more careful?"

"You don't want to know, Moon Deer. Isn't it enough that I'm helping you?"

"I think what you're hoping is that I'll decide you're suddenly my new best friend and I'll tell you where the equation is."

"Ah!" She nodded grimly. "The equation! He *did* give it to you, didn't he?"

"Maybe yes, maybe no. Why do you care?"

"I don't care a hoot! As far as I'm concerned, you can take that Theory of Everything and shove it!"

"But you know what it is, I see."

"Of course, I know. That's all he talks about these days. I'm bored to death with the whole thing! Now let's get going. I'd like to get out of here as fast as we can. Okay?"

She turned and continued walking.

"That's all *who* talks about?" Howie asked, following after her. "Who's behind all this?"

She kept walking and didn't answer.

"Who's behind all this nonsense?" he repeated.

She still didn't answer.

The walls of the tunnel were rough and black. The roof was supported in many places by old timbers but more often there was no support at all, simply rock and coal and earth. Howie did his best to fight off the claustrophobia he felt. *Relax*, he told himself. Panic wasn't going to do him any good. But the sense of the enormous weight of the mountain overhead was hard to dispel.

They passed scattered signs of human activity—old shovels, a pick-axe, a tin lunch box, a blackened jacket. After half an hour, they came to a narrow gauge railway and a cart that was still half full of coal. Occasionally, new tunnels branched off from the main line, some ascending, others slanting deeper into the earth. Zora followed the rail tracks which seemed reasonable. Eventually the tracks must lead to the exit.

They trudged along in single file. They had been in the old mine for nearly an hour now and Howie's headlamp was starting to dim.

The coal dust in the air became thicker as they continued through the shaft making it difficult to breathe. Coal dust was extremely flammable, which was one of the dangers you encountered in a mine. Methane gas was another danger. There were dozens of ways to die in a coal mine including the possibility of a tunnel collapse. This old shaft had been closed for decades without ventilation and one small spark could set off an explosion. That's how hundreds of miners had died here in the early years of the 20th century. Explosions.

In the 1913 disaster, Howie remembered, the miners were using dynamite to expand one of the tunnels when it ignited the coal dust in the air. In 1923, a support beam collapsed knocking down an electric line and the spark had been enough to set off the dust.

"I hope you know the way out of here," he called out hopefully.

"Look, I've studied the old maps. But I've never actually been through here. I don't like this old mine any more than you do. But it's our only chance to escape."

Up ahead, Howie was surprised to see a narrow beam of sunlight coming down into the mine from somewhere high above. The light drew him like a moth to a flame. The tunnel opened up into a wide underground cavern where there were more carts and abandoned equipment. The beam of light from above revealed a table of rough wood and benches where the miner's might have had their lunch, enjoying a respite from the darkness.

Howie stopped and strained his head upward. The cavern ceiling was very high. Far above their heads there was a small opening to the sky where the beam of daylight came through. It wasn't large enough to ventilate the cavern. The coal dust was as thick here as anywhere else. But the light was wonderful. A beam of hope.

"Let's stop a minute," he said, collapsing onto one of the benches.

"Okay, but we can't stay long."

Howie needed the rest. His throat was sore from breathing coal dust. He was thirsty, hungry, out of breath, nearly out of everything. Meanwhile, the cavern was almost pleasant compared to the rest of the mine. They turned off their headlamps and sat side by side in the beam of sunlight. He could see that her face was smudged with coal. He imagined he was blackened, too.

"All right," he said. "Who is *they?* Who's behind all this craziness?"

"You don't give up, do you?"

"No, I don't."

"Okay," she said reluctantly. "It's the old man. My loony grandfather. Actually, he's my great-grandfather. But I call him Gramps."

She paused. Howie waited for her to go on.

"Gramps," he prodded after a moment.

"He's kind of eccentric."

"I've begun to suspect that."

"In fact, I'd say . . . maybe he's insane."

"Only maybe?"

"Look, Moon Deer. Do you want me to tell this? Or are you going to keep interrupting me."

"Go on."

"Gramps' real name is Sebastian Hays. Does that ring a bell?"

Howie had to think a moment. The name rang a very distant bell.

"Is this the Sebastian Hays who owned that movie studio in the Fifties where they made all those horror movies and sci-fi flicks?"

"Jupiter International," she told him.

"Okay, I remember now. Hays was a flamboyant figure, married to a bunch of beautiful women. There are a lot of stories about him. But he's been dead for decades."

"Not dead. He became a recluse. He took his money and disappeared. He's been living in these mountains all this time. He owns hundreds of thousands of acres, an empire, really. He's ninety-six years old, kind of creepy to look at. The movie studio was his last public venture. Before that he owned an airline, and a hotel chain before that. He started out rich—his father was a Texas oil millionaire—and he became richer as the years went on. I guess he became crazier, too. He found me a few years ago in California . . . but that's another story."

"I'd like to hear it."

She sighed. "Well, I was in Los Angeles. An actress, sort of, but it wasn't going well. I was trying to get my big break along with a zillion other girls. I had a few parts in TV shows. I did a car commercial. An occasional industrial show. Mostly, I fended off horny old men who said they'd make me a star if I slept with them.

"Anyway, I was getting discouraged, thinking maybe it was time to go back to Chicago and try something new. And that's when this guy Doug found me. Doug McKay. He's Gramps' all-purpose fixer. You've met him, actually."

"I don't think so."

"Yes, you have. He told me so. He has a big droopy mustache. Sort of a middle-aged long-haired cowboy type. Rides a big Harley."

It was the Harley that gave Howie the connection. The droopy mustache completed the picture. Howie had met Doug briefly outside the Worm Hole Café when he had come to meet Brandon Eckehart.

"I remember now. Good God, *that's* your great grandfather's fixer?"

"Yep. Gramps had him track me down. My great-grandmother was Sebastian's favorite wife, Barbara Barnett, the actress. Do you know who she was?"

"I'm sorry, I don't."

"She was a famous sex kitten for a year or two. She played the part of Princess Zora in Gramps' 1956 movie, *Nightmare on Neptune*."

"That's where the name Princess Zora comes from?"

"Yeah, originally. Gramps revised the part for me when I got here. My great-grandmother died long before I was born. But Doug was able to locate my grandmother, and then my mother, and that's how he found me. Doug said my great-grandfather was alive and he wanted to make me a generous offer. Come live with him in New Mexico, be his helper and companion, and he would put a million dollars in a Swiss bank account for me. Well, like I said, nothing was happening in L.A., so I thought, why not? When Doug told me how old Gramps was, I didn't think the job would last long. With a million dollars I'd be free to do whatever I wanted afterwards."

"So how long have you been here?"

"Nearly three years. Which is a lot longer than I wanted. Plus, there's some really strange stuff that goes on here that I don't like. I guess I got in over my head." Zora stood up from the bench. "Now, look, Moon Deer, we've got to keep moving. We still have a ways to go."

Howie needed more time to rest. His feet hurt from the tight galoshes, he was flat-out exhausted.

"Tell me about the strange stuff," he insisted, refusing to budge.

"We've already stayed here too long, Moon Deer! We've got to keep moving!"

"Just give me another minute to catch my breath. Tell me about this strange stuff."

Zora shook her head, exasperated. But she sat back down.

"Well, you see, the main thing about Gramps is that he hates being old and decrepit. He has all kinds of doctors who fly in and give him shots and aging treatments that are supposed to make him young again. But of course, none of them really work. When you're ninety-six, there's no way to turn back the clock. Except . . . well, this is where Klizmor comes in. And of course, the Theory of Everything."

"Go on," Howie prodded.

"Like I said, Gramps has some crazy ideas. He believes there are aliens who possess the knowledge to make him young again. That's why he's been trying to communicate with Klizmor. There are huge radio transmitters at the far edge of the property that he's been using for years trying to send messages to Alpha Centauri. He also uses mental telepathy. He's obsessed with it, trying to send his SOS to the stars, telling them they need to come and save him."

Howie shook his head. "Stay young and live forever! And he's willing to kill for this fantasy?"

"You haven't lived in Southern California! Being young forever is what L.A. is all about. Half the people there would kill to be seventeen again!"

"Oh, come on, that's easy to say, but it's absurd."

"Is it? If you could make a deal with the devil, if you had enough power, enough money . . . if you could wish upon a star, you don't think a homicide or two would stop most people from doing anything—anything at all—to be young forever?"

Howie sighed. Put that way, he wasn't sure. Personally, he liked the idea of old age. Wisdom, maybe. No more hormones hijacking your brain. He thought it might come as a relief. But billions of dollars of media advertising suggested the bulk of America believed otherwise.

"So why did Gramps kidnap Grisha Bloom? What was all that about?"

"Same thing. It has to do with the Blue Moon quark, Bloom's big discovery. Look, I don't understand the physics, Moon Deer. I've studied it to play my part, I've read a few books, but this stuff is off the deep end. The general idea is that if Klizmor wouldn't come to him, Gramps would travel to Klizmor. The Blue Moon quark theoretically exists in two dimensions at once, don't ask me how. It has to do with Heisenberg's Uncertainty Principle. And if you can be in two dimensions at once, theoretically there might be a wormhole that will take you from one part of the universe to another. I know, it sounds crazy, but there are some very brilliant scientists investigating this stuff. With government money, by the way. At national laboratories like Los Alamos. Theoretical physics has come up with some pretty weird stuff."

"And this is where Grisha came in?"

"Exactly. Gramps thought Bloom could help find a wormhole to Klizmor where, abracadabra, the advanced people there would heal him and give him the secret of living forever. At least that's what Doug McKay has been telling him."

"Doug's into this, too?"

"He encourages it. I'm not sure why, except it plays into Gramps' fantasies and I guess it gives Doug a kind of power over him."

"But why did you help Grisha escape?"

"The same reason I'm helping you! I don't like what's going on. I never agreed to help kidnap people!"

"Aren't you going to get into trouble for helping me?"

"I'm not going back, Moon Deer. This time I'm escaping, too. Hell with the money! This place is creepy and I'm getting out."

Howie didn't know if he believed her story. It was a good story, as stories went. But she had told him too many good stories before. An astrophysicist at Caltech. An officer in a secret Air Force program. Now he was supposed to believe she was the great-granddaughter of a reclusive billionaire.

His thoughts circled backward. *She wasn't an officer in the Air Force!* . . . Good God, he had forgotten little Juniper! In all the astonishing things that had happened to him, she had completely slipped his mind. He'd assumed the toddler was safely with some Air Force officer who had come by the Motel 6 to pick her up. But now he knew that was a lie.

"What about the little girl?" he demanded. "What the hell did you do with her?"

"She's safe. Calm down, Moon Deer. Don't worry about the kid. Worry about yourself if we don't find our way out of here!"

Howie wasn't going to be put off. "You said you gave Juniper to somebody in the Air Force. But you're not in the military. So what the hell did you do with her?"

"Doug came to the motel and got her. He paid someone to take her to Ashley's sister in Texas."

"You'd better be telling the truth for a change!"

"I am, Moon Deer. Honestly, Doug wouldn't hurt a child. He's a cold son of a bitch, sure. But he only does what advances his interest. And killing Juniper wouldn't help him at all."

"So who took the girl to Texas?"

"Look, Doug has a small network of people he employs. They're outsiders. None of them have ever been to the ranch, none of them know about Sebastian Hays. But he pays them well and they do what he says. A woman on his payroll drove Juniper to Austin."

"You sure about this?"

"Moon Deer, she's okay."

Howie sighed. He wanted to believe it, but he wasn't sure. "You're pretty close with Doug, are you?"

"Moon Deer, for chrissake, I've been here for three years. We're not close, but I know him, okay? I know the setup here." She stood up and flicked on her headlamp. "Now let's get out of here. When Doug discovers we're gone, he's going to come after us."

Howie had more questions. What about Brandon Eckehart and his wife? What kind of wormhole had transported Grisha Bloom from that tent in Angel Creek campground to his doorway in town?

But Zora was already walking quickly from the comforting shaft of light into the awful darkness of the tunnel ahead.

Once again, Howie had no option but to turn on his own headlamp and follow her.

***

The shaft slanted downward. Down into the darkness.

They followed the narrow gauge tracks for nearly an hour, trudging on and on in silence. Howie found himself too tired for talk, too numb for questions. The light from his headlamp was fading along with his spirits.

Finally, Zora stopped and leaned against one of the old coal carts in order to take off her left boot and give it a shake.

"Hold on, Moon Deer. I got a rock in my boot."

Howie watched as she pressed her back against the cart to balance on one leg while she shook the rock from her boot. She was leaning forward to slip the boot back on her foot when the cart moved unexpectedly behind her on the track. The metal wheels made a small screech as they slid on the iron rails.

Metal against metal.

The cart moved hardly more than an inch. But Howie knew immediately that this was a mistake.

He didn't see the spark, it must have been very small.

The explosion filled the tunnel, an intense hurricane of fire and noise that seemed to be everywhere at once. The flash was blinding. Howie felt himself picked up and sent flying backward off his feet onto the ground.

He was stunned, sprawled awkwardly on the ground. It had all happened so suddenly. His ears rang. His left side throbbed with pain. He couldn't move at first, he could only breathe the harsh air and lie where he had fallen trying to gather his wits.

Once the explosion faded, there was absolute darkness in the mine. He had no idea where his helmet had gone. It been flung from his head and the light was out. There was no sign of the girl's light either.

Howie wasn't sure how he had survived the blast. When he began gathering himself onto his knees, his hand brushed against the coal cart. Perhaps this was what had saved him, a barrier between himself and the explosion.

"Zora!" he called. There was so much soot and ash that he had a spasm of coughing. "Mia!" he called again. "Zoey! . . . where are you?"

At first he heard nothing. Then there came a soft moaning from not far away.

"Moon Deer!" she said faintly.

It took a few minutes to find her, crawling through the darkness on his hands and knees. He heard her groan and corrected his course. At last he touched her leg. It was wet with blood.

"I'm here," he said. "How are you doing?"

"Closer," she said. "Come closer."

Howie lowered his head so that his ear was nearly to her lips.

"I'm cold," she whispered.

Howie had nothing to give her. He was dressed only in a grimy T-shirt and loose yoga pants. He slipped off his T-shirt and put it around her shoulders. It was all he could do.

"I'm afraid!" Her voice was barely audible.

"Hang on," he told her. "We'll get out of here. Somehow."

"I don't want to die here in the dark."

Howie didn't know how to answer. He didn't want to die in the dark either.

"Hang on," he said again. What else could he say? "We'll think of something."

Would they? His ears were still ringing from the blast, he could barely think at all.

He found her hand and held it. It was slick with blood like her leg. It was impossible to know how bad her injuries were, but he sensed the worst.

After what seemed a long while, she said something he couldn't quite hear.

He leaned closer. "Say that again."

"Judy," she whispered. "Judy Cranston."

"I'm sorry?"

"Who I am . . . Judy . . . I want you to know . . ."

"I got it. You're Judy Cranston!" He repeated the name urgently, as though everything depended on it.

He heard a long sigh as her life slipped away.

That was all. A name in the dark. An affirmation, he supposed. What you said when there was nothing left to lie about.

Judy Cranston.

Howie was alone in the silence.

Chapter Thirty-Three

Outside, the old ghost town slowly turned more ghostly as the afternoon deepened and cool mountain shadows crept over the land.

Jack thought he heard a distant explosion. "What was that? Thunder?"

"The sky's clear," Billy answered. "But there may be some weather on the other side of the mountains."

Thunder was a common background sound of New Mexico summers and it didn't come again.

Jack sat on a rocky patch of grass as the daylight faded. A flashlight would have been welcome along with a bottle of ibuprofen. He had pulled something in his lower back in the hard landing.

They were at 6500 feet, possibly higher, and the air was turning cold. This had been meant to be a two-hour trip on a summer day and he was wearing a short sleeve shirt. He'd brought a sweater along, but that had burned up in the helicopter.

"Help should have been here by now," Billy said after awhile. "I'm starting to think my last transmission didn't send."

"Your radio wasn't working?" This was serious. Jack had thought help was on its way.

"Well, I don't know," Billy told him. "There's an LED light that comes on when you're transmitting. But ten things were failing at once and I wasn't looking. I had my hands full trying to keep that bird in the air."

Billy was sitting next to Jack in the stubby grass on a wide field outside the ghost town. Dan was stretched out on the ground next to Billy, obviously in pain. They made a desolate group. As the sky darkened and the temperature dropped, their situation wasn't looking hopeful. The spooky emptiness of the old ghost town didn't help matters.

Jack turned toward Dan. "How are you doing over there, Detective?"

"Could be better," Dan admitted. His voice sounded stretched and thin. Billy had used Jack's belt to make a tourniquet above the gunshot wound on Dan's left leg. But he had lost a good deal of blood and he needed a doctor.

"The gall of those guys, shooting at a police chopper!" Dan complained. "Darn, I want to get my hands on those jerks!"

Dan was back to saying darn. Jack wasn't sure if that was a good sign or bad.

"We'll get them, Dan," he said with forced optimism. He hated the thought that he had gotten the young detective into this situation. Help would be coming eventually, but it was hard to say when. Once Santo realized their helicopter was missing, he would set off a major search and rescue operation. But there were hundreds of square miles to search and it might take some time to find them. Time in which Detective Dan Hamm could bleed to death.

"I think I should try going for help," Billy suggested. "If I walk back along the road that comes into town, I'm sure to find a house sooner or later."

"Cimarron is seventeen miles away."

"I can do that in four hours or so if I hurry. I should have left earlier except I kept thinking the cavalry was going to arrive." Billy lowered his voice. "We seriously need to get Dan to a hospital. You know that, don't you?"

"I do," said Jack.

Billy had given Dan his flight jacket, Jack had donated his belt for the tourniquet, but there wasn't anything more they could do for him. They didn't even have a Band Aid. Everything had gone up in smoke inside the helicopter. Someone had to go for help and Billy was the only one who could do it.

Jack was about to say he'd be okay with Dan until Billy returned when he heard Katya barking in the distance. She had been gone for some time browsing around the old town. At first he thought she had come across a rabbit or a coyote, but over the years Jack had become attuned to the nuances of Katya's bark and this bark was different.

"Katya!" he called loudly. "Come here, girl!"

She came bounding their way from the ghost town barking excitedly.

"Katya, what is it?"

Katya wasn't a yappy sort of dog. Usually she gave a bark or two and then was quiet. But now she was barking loudly and wouldn't stop.

Jack managed to get to his feet, rising awkwardly from the ground. His joints were stiff, his back hurt, and the ground was uneven. Billy took hold of his arm to keep him steady.

"I think we'd better go see what's upsetting Katya," Jack said.

***

The dirt road through the abandoned town was rutted and uneven. Katya's harness had been lost in the helicopter, so Jack walked alongside her holding onto her collar. This was awkward, but Billy gave him a hand in places where the road was particularly bad. Neither of them liked leaving Dan alone in the field, but there wasn't any choice. They had to see if Katya had found something that might prove useful.

They followed her for nearly ten minutes before she came to a stop.

"Where are we?" Jack asked.

"She's led us to the far end of town. It's a spooky place. Shells of buildings. Stores, houses, an old hotel. It's like the world ended and the people just disappeared. We're in front of an old wooden saloon that's flush up against the side of a steep hill . . . well, that's strange!"

"What is, Billy?"

"There's a sign out front that says, 'The Worm Hole Café. Food and Spirits That Are Out of This World.' The funny thing is, the sign looks new."

Jack nodded. It was all starting to come together in his mind. This had to be where Howie had met Brandon Eckehart.

"It's like a stage set," Billy was saying about the Worm Hole. "Like one of those saloons from an old Western movie. There's even a wooden sidewalk out front."

"I think it really *is* a stage set," Jack said. "I'll bet you anything we're still on Sebastian's land! Is there any indication that people have been here recently?"

"There are tire marks in the dirt out front. There's been a car here not long ago. Maybe a motorcycle. The road's pretty dusty so the marks aren't very definite."

Jack had let go of Katya's collar, allowing her to roam. She began barking again.

"What's she doing?" Jack asked.

"She's standing by the front door, barking her head off."

"I think we'd better take a closer look at this so-called café. Let's go inside."

"The door's padlocked."

"What sort of padlock is it?"

"A big one. And it looks pretty solid."

"You got your gun with you?"

"Well, sure."

"Then shoot it off."

"We don't have a search warrant, Jack."

Katya was barking more urgently than before.

"Just shoot the damn thing off, Billy. The ghosts won't mind."

"Okay, I guess. Stand back."

Jack took hold of Katya's collar and pulled her out of the way. There was a loud explosion and the tear of breaking metal and wood. Billy needed to fire a second time to get the lock open.

Katya went inside as soon as the door was open. Jack followed her holding onto her collar trying to keep up.

"It's dark in here, Jack," Billy said behind him. "But I got a light on my phone so I can see a little. We're in a bar that's a whole lot more modern than the rest of this weird town."

Katya didn't stop at the bar. She led the way across the room toward a corridor in back.

"This must lead to the bathrooms, Jack . . . now that's cute! There are signs on the doors, Spacemen, Spacewomen . . . okay, now she's taking us past the bathrooms into a storeroom with boxes of booze and aluminum kegs of beer."

Katya stopped in front of a huge metal door that was at least ten feet high and fifteen feet wide. She kept barking loudly. Her claws scratched against the smooth metal surface.

"Can you get this door open, Billy? Shoot the lock off if you need to."

"I don't know. It's not like any door I've ever seen. It's huge and I don't see any lock on it. It just one piece of solid metal."

"Is there a rock anywhere, Billy? Something I can use as a knocker?"

"A knocker . . . here's a metal pail. Will that do?"

"Give me the pail," Jack told him. "I'll make it do."

Jack picked up the pail with both hands and hit it three times against the metal door.

He waited. At first there was nothing. Then finally there was an answer: a single knock, as though someone had thrown a stone at the door from inside.

Jack used the pail again to tap out three more times. But now there was no reply.

"Billy, you need to go for help. Take me back to Dan first, then go as fast as you can. When you get to a phone, tell Santo we need a helicopter and a blow torch."

***

Jack waited with Dan on the open field at the edge of town. He would have preferred to remain at the metal door in case there was any new sounds from inside, but he didn't want to leave the wounded detective on his own.

Night fell, cold and clear. A pack of coyotes began to howl all at once from not far away. What set them off was hard to say. They continued howling for less than a minute, then, just as mysteriously, they stopped.

Sitting on the hard-rocky ground, Jack felt as bleak and helpless as he had ever felt in his life. He hoped Billy didn't have to walk far before he came to a house, but he was prepared for a long wait.

Jack got Katya to lay down next to Dan, hoping her body would give him some warmth. He tried to keep Dan awake with talk.

"So did you always want to be a cop, Dan?"

It wasn't a great conversation starter, but Dan did his best to answer. In fact, Dan had not always wanted to be a cop. Smart kid. His earliest ambition had been to play football for the Dallas Cowboys. When he grew out of that, he planned on being an astronaut. Being a cop was his third choice and now, lying on the cold rocky field, Jack imagined he was wishing he had done something else.

Before long, Dan ran out of steam. Jack took over, talking about his own distant youth.

Jack had dreamed of being a criminal defense attorney. Specifically, he had wanted to be Perry Mason, whose cases he had watched on TV with obsessive interest. Once a week, every Sunday night on CBS, Perry's keen intelligence cut through every lie and subterfuge to get to the clean bare truth.

Wouldn't that be wonderful? To find the truth in a single hour, once a week, every time!

Unfortunately, Dan Hamm had never heard of Perry Mason, he was far too young, so the conversation wasn't a great success. Jack talked anyway, doing his best to keep Dan awake and hopeful.

Don't fade away, Dan! Don't stop breathing!

The hours dragged on and eventually even Jack ran out of steam. He sat listening to the rustling sounds of the night, the breeze and small animals and crickets in the branches of the nearby trees.

A deep discouragement crept over him. If Dan died . . . if Howie was dead . . . he didn't know how he would be able to live with himself.

And then faintly . . . faintly . . . he heard the whish of a helicopter beating through the air, coming his way.

***

The State Police helicopter landed on a field not far from where Jack, Dan, and Katya were waiting. A second helicopter arrived five minutes later.

Within half an hour, county vehicles began pulling up the dirt road from Cimarron, their headlights shooting wild beams of light over the ghost town. Before long, the field was teaming with activity. Santo

Ruben arrived with the second wave of emergency vehicles, a convoy that included a fire truck and an ambulance.

Two EMTs examined Dan and radioed for an air ambulance which arrived twenty minutes later and flew him to a hospital in Albuquerque.

"Let's get you to the hospital, too, Jack," Santo suggested. "You look cold and miserable and it would be good for a doctor to check you out."

But Jack wasn't ready to leave. He wanted to be present when the firemen got through the steel door at the rear of the café.

It was a long night with helicopters and county vehicles coming and going, bringing in supplies and people. A CSU unit arrived at two in the morning along with an FAA inspector to examine the wreckage of the helicopter and photograph the bullet holes. Soon there were news helicopters from Albuquerque circling overhead as well. Santo refused to let them land.

To Jack's frustration, it took several hours to get through the metal door. A blow torch proved ineffective on the thick steel and several more firemen had to be flown in to chip away with pickaxes in order to expose the mechanism that worked the sliding door.

Once the door was open, Santo disappeared inside with a team of firemen and state troopers. Bright lights powered by a generator were set up on metal stands so that they could see. Jack and Katya waited impatiently on the edges of the activity as the work continued.

At last, Santo emerged, his face blackened with coal dust.

"We found him, Jack," he said. "Howie's okay."

Jack expelled a great sigh of relief.

"Thank God! I tell you, Santo, this has been the longest night of my life!"

"Well, it's pretty nasty in there, Jack. It's an old coal mine. There was an explosion. Howie's going to be all right, but he's in a good deal of pain and suffering from dehydration and exhaustion. We're going to fly him to Albuquerque."

"He's awake?"

"Yeah, but he's woozy. They just gave him a shot of something pretty strong. There was a dead girl inside the mine near where we found him. Do you know who she was?"

"Black hair? Pretty?"

"Not so pretty now, but I suppose she was once. I'm thinking this is the Mia Bloom who wanted Howie to find her father?"

"Well, whoever she was, she wasn't Grisha Bloom's daughter. Maybe Howie can tell us."

"Here he comes now. They're bringing him out on a stretcher."

"Can you take me over to him, Santo? I won't hold things up, but I'd like to have a few words with him."

Santo took Jack's arm and led him through the crowd to where Howie was being carried out of the mine.

Howie was floating in an opiate cloud, observing his pain from a pleasant distance. A big wet tongue came out of nowhere and licked the side of his face.

"Get down, dog!" he heard someone say.

Howie looked up from his stretcher and saw Jack's face peering down at him. Jack appeared to be floating just like he was in a world without gravity.

"How are you doing, Howie?"

"Kind of floaty fluffy."

"I'm glad to have you back on Earth."

"We've got to keep moving," said one of the EMTs who was carrying Howie toward the air ambulance.

Jack was able to follow alongside the stretcher for a short way by holding on to Santo's arm.

"Tell me about the girl," he said. "Is that Mia Bloom in there?"

"Mia?" Howie wondered. He closed his eyes as she drifted in and out of his memory. He smiled from far away. "Princess Zora . . . you should have seen her in a space suit!"

"Princess who? What are you talking about, Howie?"

"She was his granddaughter."

"Sebastian Hays's granddaughter?"

"Great-granddaughter," he corrected. "But maybe that was a lie, too. Maybe she was just Judy Cranston. Maybe she was nobody at all . . ."

That was all Jack could get out of Howie. He was left on the ground in the wash of sound and air as the helicopter rose from the field and flew away.

Chapter Thirty-Four

On Wednesday afternoon, the New Mexico State Police and the FBI conducted a joint raid on the 280,000 acre ranch owned by Sebastian Hays in the northern mountains.

They arrived in overwhelming numbers. A heavily armed SWAT team descended from the air in five helicopters while a convoy of seven SUVs arrived simultaneously on a seldom used logging road that passed through the mountains from the Escondido Valley. It was a serious matter to shoot down a police helicopter and law enforcement wasn't taking any chances.

The helicopters landed on the lawn by the lake just as the convoy of vehicles came streaming up the road to the futuristic house that was shaped to resemble a flying saucer. Sergeant Billy Hicks had told them what to expect.

The SWAT team spread out on the lawn while the FBI agents and New Mexico state troopers waited behind the cover of their cars. One of the Special Agents used a bullhorn to address the house, ordering the people inside to come out with their hands raised.

There was no response from the house, if you could call it a house. Only silence. After a conference, the SWAT team approached the ramp that came down from the belly of the flying saucer and shot tear gas canisters inside the open door. They waited for a few minutes before bursting inside with gas masks and automatic weapons.

Santo Ruben waited with his team behind a police van. He wore a Kevlar vest and held his 9mm semi-automatic loosely in his hand, but he suspected that they weren't going to encounter resistance. Except for the police range, Santo hadn't fired his weapon in ten years, and he was happy not to do so today.

Another twenty minutes went by before the head of the SWAT team radioed that there was no one inside except a very old man who was dead in a high-tech chair in a bizarre bell-shaped room that resembled a gas chamber. It wasn't immediately clear if he had died of natural causes or foul play.

Santo put his gun back in its holster and stepped away from the cover of the SUV.

"My God, a flying saucer!" said Sergeant Ben Trujillo who was standing next to him, his second in command. "Now I've seen every-thing!"

"There are more things in heaven and earth, Ben," Santo told him, "than are dreamt of in your philosophy."

"No kidding? That's from a song, isn't it? Lady Gaga?"

Santo sighed.

***

Jack heard the details of the raid the following morning in a telephone call from Santo as he sat on the visitor's chair in Howie's room at the Presbyterian Hospital in Albuquerque. Jack and Emma had driven down on Wednesday and stayed overnight in a motel.

Howie was going to be okay. Once a thick layer of coal dust had been removed, his injuries hadn't been as bad as they had initially appeared. He had suffered a concussion, his left side was badly bruised, and he was seriously dehydrated. The doctors wanted to keep him in the hospital another day for observation, but he would be able to return to San Geron-imo tomorrow.

Howie was sitting up in the hospital bed listening to Jack's end of the conversation. He had a drip in the vein of his right arm which he didn't like very much, but he supposed it wasn't too much of an inconvenience after everything else he had gone through.

"Well?" he asked when Jack ended the call.

"There was nobody inside but Sebastian Hays. They found him dead in his germ-free chamber."

"So I guess you can't live forever," Howie remarked. "No matter how much money you have."

"He didn't die of old age, Howie. He was murdered. The M.E. found petechiae around his eyes."

Petechiae were the most common sign of suffocation, broken capillary blood vessels that appear in traumatic instances when someone is struggling to breathe.

"The ranch helicopter was gone by the time Santo got there," Jack continued. "Which is how Doug McKay and the others must have gotten away. Unfortunately, they could be anywhere by now. When I was there, we only encountered two other people besides McKay—two guards who were dressed up like Star Trekkies. They called themselves Alpha and Beta, believe it or not. They were big guys with Eastern European accents."

"Aliens, I guess," said Howie. "The on-planet kind."

"Did you meet them?"

"I'm glad to say I didn't."

"Well, a place that size—there must have been cooks, gardeners, cleaning people. But they all got away, which is a shame. So tell me about this fellow Doug," Jack said. "Let's go over it again, what your spacey princess told you about him."

"Okay, but let's get one thing straight, Jack. That wasn't *my* flying saucer! And she wasn't *my* princess. I was only—"

"Right, only toodling up a peaceful mountain trail minding your own business when a crazy guy walks into your camp out of nowhere. Get over it, Howie. Life is arbitrary. Life isn't fair. Now, let's go over this again."

Howie and Jack had been talking for several hours. Howie had told Jack as much as he could remember of the last week, and Jack in turn had given Howie a short version of what he had been up to since he'd returned from Hawaii.

"Doug was Sebastian's fixer—that's how Judy described him. You know, it's hard for me to think of her as Judy after all the fancy names she used on me. Mia, Zoey, Zora . . . Judy Cranston's not a bad name, I suppose. But it lacks glamor."

"Reality often lacks glamor."

"Reality often sucks," observed Howie. "Anyway, she said Sebastian sent Doug to find her in Los Angeles where she was trying to be an actress. She said her great-grandmother was Barbara Barnett, Sebastian's favorite ex-wife, and that Doug had been able to track her down from her grandmother, who was still alive. Apparently, Sebastian didn't like to have strangers around him. He preferred someone like Judy who had a blood connection, however distant. I guess he had trust issues."

"So why do you think he trusted McKay?"

"I have no idea. But there must be some connection. Judy said he encouraged Sebastian's outer-space fantasies and had some power over the old guy. Did I tell you, I met Doug once? Outside the Worm Hole Café when I went to meet Brandon Eckehart. He was on a big Harley. We only talked for a minute, but I got a strange vibe from him. He looked like a lanky old cowboy, not really like someone you'd expect to be hanging with Sebastian Hays. He was friendly but menacing somehow."

"I had that impression, too. Well, we'll find the connection, hopefully, and maybe that will help us find him," Jack said. "The CSU techs have been going over that flying saucer for prints and DNA. Doug and his crew left in a hurry so I'm sure there will be something to tell us who they really are. The girl, too. Judy Cranston could be just another mirage."

Howie sighed. "Another mirage!"

"Relax, Howie. We'll find out who they really are, it's just a matter of time."

"So what about Grisha? Do you have any thoughts about how he ended up dead on our doorstep?"

"Well, actually, yes, I do have an idea about that."

"Would you care to share it, Jack?"

"Lunch time!" said a nurse cheerfully, coming into the room with a tray that she set down on a metal table that swung around over Howie's lap. Howie inspected the hospital lunch dubiously. There was a small portion of chicken-something in a gluttonous brown sauce. Mashed potatoes. Green beans. Bright red jello for dessert.

"Jello!" Howie said incredulously. He poked it with a spoon and watched it wiggle.

"I'm sorry, but visiting time was over an hour ago," the nurse said brightly to Jack. "There's a volunteer in the hallway waiting to see you out."

"We'll talk tomorrow," Jack said, getting up from his chair. "Just one more question. John Concha, the War Chief at the Pueblo, left a message on my phone that he wanted to speak with me. Unfortunately, by the time I tried to get back to him, the Pueblo was in its annual retreat and I couldn't get through. Do you have any idea what he wants?"

"Not really. I saw John in the town Plaza on Friday night before I was abducted. He wanted to know what had happened on Dawson Peak. I didn't realize until I spoke with him that the Peak is part of the land grant the Pueblo has been trying to get returned to them. Why are you asking?"

"We'll see, Howie," was all Jack was willing to say. "It may be important. But probably not."

***

After leaving Howie's private room, a teenage girl, a Candy Stripe volunteer, led Jack down the hall to ICU where Dan Hamm was recovering from his bullet wound. Dan had lost a good deal of blood, but his prognosis was cautiously hopeful.

Jack found Dan asleep in a cocoon of intensive care drips and devices. He stood next to the bed for a few minutes listening to the electronic beeps and the rhythmic whoosh of the ventilator that helped Dan breath. With both Howie and Dan in the hospital, Jack felt a sense of failure. He didn't know what he could have done differently, but he believed somehow that he had let them down.

The volunteer led him out of the hospital where Emma and Katya were waiting with the car to drive him back to San Geronimo. Jack wanted to stay awake and keep Emma company, but he was tired and the drowsy monotony of Interstate 25 brought his eyclids drooping downward.

He woke as they were passing through Santa Fe.

"Feeling better?" Emma asked.

"I am," he told her.

He didn't feel better at all, but he didn't want to burden Emma with his weariness. He wanted to be positive for her. But she knew him too well.

"Honestly, Jack, you should feel good. Howie's safe, Dan is going to make it. And you got your man, right? Sebastian Hays."

"I'm not so sure he's our man," he told her.

"You don't think so? I don't mean he did everything personally. But he had the money and power to set everything going. He was the . . . *force majeure*."

Jack didn't answer. It was very Emma-like to use an expression like *force majeure*. But he wasn't sure she was right. He wanted to believe Sebastian Hays was his man, but he wasn't satisfied.

"Well?" Emma prodded.

"I don't know. It's just too convenient to blame a crazy guy who's dead."

"Well, if it wasn't Sebastian, then who?"

"Doug McKay, probably. He was Sebastian's fixer. That's how Howie's princess from outer space described him."

"Well, there you go. I imagine Hays paid him a lot of money."

"Possibly," said Jack. "Only . . ."

"Only what?"

"I don't know, Emma. I was with Sebastian for less than five minutes, but I'm not sure he was a killer. Yes, he was nuts. Clinically insane, most likely. He'd lived as a recluse on that huge ranch of his for more than forty years. He was a lonely man who had lost touch with reality. But a killer . . ."

Jack wished he had something more definite to say. But he wasn't definite, that was the problem. He only had a dissatisfied feeling that there was something he didn't know. At the very least, they needed to find Doug McKay and hear what he had to say for himself.

Jack fell into a meditative silence as they continued north on Interstate 25.

"What's that sound?" he asked after a while. "In the front end. It's sounds like something's loose."

"In the car?"

"Yes, the car."

Emma sighed. "Well, Jack, I have a small confession to make." Her tone was contrite, but not entirely. There was something about it of the unapologetic apology. "I went to Claire's storage rental and found where

Howie hid the book with the equation. I took it, I'm afraid. I know you told me not to, but I did. And I had . . . well, a small skirmish driving home."

Jack nodded. "Tell me," he said.

Emma described her emails back and forth with Claire, how she had discovered where Howie had hidden *100 Poems from the Chinese,* and the SUV that had followed her from the storage shed compound.

"I don't know what got into me! I swerved, that's all. And somehow I sent that car skittering off the highway into the sagebrush. I think whoever was inside must be alright, though. I hope so! It wasn't really that much of a crash."

Jack couldn't help smiling. "Well, you're one tough cookie," he told her. "Don't mess with Emma Wilder!"

"Jack, it wasn't funny. I was scared to death!"

"So, where did you put the book?"

"In the outside return slot at the library."

Jack laughed. "That's not too bad, actually!"

"I phoned the library yesterday and told them to put it on my desk when they emptied the box. Do you think it will be safe there?"

"Sure, for the time being. Why not? In fact, I think that's not such a big worry anymore. We'll pick it up later."

"Are you angry?"

"No, I'm just glad you're safe."

"Well, I'm glad you're safe, too!"

Emma stopped at Trader Joe's in Santa Fe and Jack and Katya waited in the car with the windows open while she went inside to shop. The Santa Fe Trader Joe's was a hectic place, a feeding frenzy of shoppers filling their carts in a near orgy of gluttony and greed for bargains. It was no place for a blind man. Jack had once been mowed down by a woman in the cheese section who was trying to get to the brie.

His phone rang while he was waiting. It was Santo.

"How are Howie and Dan?" Santo asked.

"Howie's fine. Dan's still in intensive care, but I think he's going to make it. Have you found McKay yet?"

"We're still looking. We found prints on the chair where the old man was killed that we think are his. His real name is Tex Ryder."

"That's his *real* name?"

"Yep. He was a stunt man in the movies. His father was a stunt man, too. Blaze Ryder. And get this, Jack. Blaze worked for Hays in many of those sci-fi thrillers he made in the Sixties. So there's a connection."

"That makes sense. Sebastian liked people around him who had old family connections. Howie and I were just talking about that. The girl who pretended to be Mia Bloom was the great-granddaughter of Sebastian's favorite ex-wife. What else have you found out about Tex Ryder?"

"Well, a few things. He was born in 1977 and he's an Army vet, Special Forces. He fought in both Iraq and Afghanistan, but got a dishonorable discharge in 2005 for selling hashish. After that, he returned to L.A. and got work as a stuntman, mostly at Stardust Studio. That's the lot in Burbank that used to be Jupiter International, the studio Sebastian once owned. So there's another connection. But then in 2014, Tex was charged with manslaughter. He killed someone in a bar fight, jumped bail and vanished. Nobody's seen him since and there's a federal warrant out for him. I imagine that's when he changed his name to Doug McKay and went to work on Sebastian's ranch. It would be a good way to disappear."

"Is there a money trail? A bank account? Credit cards?"

"Not under Doug McKay. But he has a married daughter in Laramie, Wyoming. That's our best lead so far. Laramie is 430 miles from the ranch in New Mexico which means he could get there in a chopper on one tank of gas. We've already put a stakeout on the daughter's house. Her name is Billie Maddow. I'm going to head up there tonight."

285

"Sounds like you're making progress, Santo. Have you had any more trouble with Lorna Wolf?"

"Not yet. She's been running her own investigation and I have no idea what she's come up with."

"Good. Listen, Santo, keep me up to date. I have some ideas of my own and I'll let you know if anything pans out."

Jack disconnected and almost immediately his phone rang again.

"Yes?" he answered. He listened to the voice on the other end and was saying, "Okay, I'll be there," when he heard Emma open the rear cargo door and begin arranging boxes and environmentally friendly cloth bags inside.

"Emma, dear," he said when she slid into the driver's seat. "How would you like to drive us to the Pueblo to see the War Chief? I think John Concha is going to be able to clear up just about everything."

Chapter Thirty-Five

Emma drove onto the reservation on the northern road that bypassed the Pueblo village and crossed a wide grassy expanse to the foot of the mountains.

The reservation was still officially closed to the public, but John Concha had finally gotten back to Jack and had agreed to see them this afternoon.

The War Chief lived in a pleasant adobe house in the shade of two large cottonwood trees on the north bank of the shallow, fast moving river that came down from the mountains and divided the Pueblo in two. Jack knew very little about how the Pueblo was organized, for the tribe kept these matters to themselves. But he understood that the river was more than a geographical divide, it was a social division also. Different clans, each with their own customs, lived on different banks.

John met them on the shaded ramada in front of his house where there was a simple wooden table and four kitchen chairs. Emma found the view breathtaking. To the east, the mountain peaks rose steeply into the clouds. To the west, the high grass seemed to go on forever. Near the house there was a teepee with painted symbols on the sides and feathers and colored flags attached to the poles on top. A large corral with two horses stood behind the teepee.

Jack took a deep breath, inhaling the scent of the grass and wildflowers and the meadow breeze. The water rushing down from the mountains made a peaceful sound.

"This is a very nice spot," he said. "I can't see it, but I feel its beauty."

"It's the way it used to be here," Concha said as they gathered around the outside table. "In the old days. Before the Spanish came. Before the tourists with their cameras. So what can I tell you, Jack?"

***

Emma found the War Chief charismatic. Powerful, proud, stern, in his late forties, but clearly in the prime of life. He carried himself with natural authority.

Nevertheless, she imagined he could be stubborn and much too certain of his own opinions. She found herself wondering if he was married, and if so, how his wife dealt with such a strong personality. It wouldn't be easy.

Of course, Jack— blind and old—was no pushover either. Together, they were like two bulls squaring off.

"I'm curious, John—you sought out Howie in the Plaza on Friday night a week and a half ago," Jack said. "I've been wondering why you wanted to speak with him."

"He'd been up on Indian land and I wanted to know what happened there."

"You're saying Dawson Peak is Indian land?"

"Of course. It was stolen from us, but it's ours."

Jack nodded. "I understand you're in court trying to get it back?"

"You bet we are. We don't call it Dawson Peak and I'm not going to say its name in Tiwa. But the English translation would be something like Place of Looking West. You need to understand, our religion is the land itself. You white people have churches. For us, the earth is our cathedral. Place of Looking West is one of our most sacred places. It was deeded to us forever in the Treaty of Guadalupe Hildago, but like every treaty you white men made, you broke it the minute it suited you."

"Look, I'm not going to argue with you, John. I know the history of the West and of course you're right. But what did you want from Howie?"

John didn't answer at first. He sat silently, like a block of granite. Stubborn didn't begin to describe him. Emma, who was watching closely from behind her sunglasses, thought it would be easier to move a mountain.

At last the War Chief chose to speak. "There have been white men recently on Place of Looking West, people who are despoiling the land. As I told you, I wanted to know what Howie had seen."

"But you were up there yourself that night," Jack pressed. "The night Grisha Bloom wandered into Howie's camp."

John gazed at Jack solemnly, but once again went silent.

"Here's what I think," said Jack. "The federal government broke the Treaty of Guadalupe Hildago, sure. But that hasn't stopped the Pueblo from using that mountain for ceremonies. If the BLM knows about this, they don't care. It's public land, after all. Anyone can go. But you care. You were up there that Wednesday night and you saw things you didn't like. I think you were the one who brought Grisha Bloom down the mountain and dropped him off on the doorstep of our office."

The War Chief still didn't speak.

"John, please understand me. I don't want to know about your sacred worship. I respect your need to keep these matters to yourself. I don't even care that a crime was committed, leaving someone dead on our doorstep. I only want to figure out what's behind all these puzzling events."

"What would you say if somebody walked into one of your cathedrals and pissed on the altar?" the War Chief asked angrily. "How would that strike you?"

"I'd say nobody has a right to be disrespectful to a religion that other people hold sacred. I wouldn't kill anyone over it, however. I'd just make certain it didn't happen again."

"I didn't kill anyone, Jack."

"I didn't say you did. But you brought Bloom's body down the mountain, didn't you?"

John nodded. "Yes, I did. There were a dozen of us up there that night. We found the white man the next morning in Moon Deer's tent. He was very ill, so we carried him down the mountain on horseback intending to get him to the Pueblo clinic. Unfortunately, he died along the way. To be honest, I didn't quite know what to do with him."

"You didn't want to have to tell anyone what you were doing up there?"

"We didn't want a dead man found on our land, bringing a lot of nosey people up there! I decided it was Moon Deer's job to deal with this since he was the one who got himself involved in the first place. So yes, I waited a day, thinking it over. Then on Friday I left the body on your doorstep. I didn't want any part of it. Two of us pretended we were helping a drunk who couldn't walk on his own. People expect that of Indians, that we're all drunks."

Jack was pleased to have at least one mystery solved. But there were still a few more to go.

"So you knew Howie was at Angel Creek?"

"Yes, of course. We saw him. That campground is only a short way from a place that's important to us, but it was raining hard and we know how to make ourselves invisible."

"In fact, you were the ones who guided Bloom toward Howie's tent, weren't you?"

"Yes. The old fool was wandering around lost and we gave him a nudge in the right direction. We had other things to do and didn't want to deal with him ourselves."

"What else did you see that night? Who else was up there, John?"

"This is important for you to know?"

"You bet it is!"

The War Chief nodded. "Then I will tell you my concern. It's not the hikers who bother us greatly. We wish they weren't there, of course, but the place they call Dawson Peak is remote and difficult to reach and there aren't many of them each year. It's the helicopters we don't like. They spy on us from the sky. They are a grave threat to our sacred practice."

"You're telling me there was a helicopter on Dawson Peak that night?"

"There was."

Everyone in San Geronimo knew about the Pueblo's dislike of aircraft flying over their land. Two years before, the Pueblo had gone to court to stop the airport from expanding for this very reason, fearing a new runway would bring the flight path directly over the reservation.

"Where was this chopper?"

"It landed on a flat shoulder near the summit. The weather was bad, so it had to hunker down on the ground for nearly half an hour before there was a break in the storm and it could take off again."

"Did you see Bloom get out of it?"

"No, we didn't spot him until after the helicopter was gone. But that's the only way he could have gotten up there. He certainly didn't climb that mountain on his own."

"Was it a government helicopter? LANL, maybe?"

"No, private."

"Really? Can you describe it for me?"

"It was a Bell 505 Jet Ranger, dark blue. A rich man's toy. They cost nearly a million and a half dollars."

Jack raised an eyebrow. "That's very precise, John."

"I know something about choppers. I saw enough of them in Iraq. I've been investigating buying one for the Pueblo. We would need a BIA grant, but it would be a good way to patrol our boundaries."

"And have you seen this particular helicopter again?"

"It's been coming and going the last couple of weeks. They've set up a camp just below tree line on the eastern slope. They've been off-loading equipment."

"What kind of equipment?"

The War Chief shrugged. "I don't know. For the moment, we've been giving them a wide berth. From a distance, it looks like they brought up a generator and some kind of large balloon. Also some lights."

"These are ballooners?"

"I don't know who they are. But these aren't things we wish to have on the Place of Looking West!"

"I understand your concern. Now, tell me about this blue helicopter, the Bell 505. By any chance, did you see it again yesterday, some time in the afternoon?"

"Wednesday?" John Concha seemed surprise. "Yes, it flew in late in the afternoon and landed in its usual place. It's still there now. They have it tied down and covered with a camouflage net. How do you know?"

Jack knew because this was all starting to make sense to him.

"And the guy flying this chopper? He's a lanky cowboy type with a large droopy mustache?"

"Yes. Doug McKay. There were two men. That was one of them."

"You know McKay?"

"Yes, I do. And I don't like him!"

"And the other man?"

"The other? I've seen him before, but I don't know his name."

"Can you describe him to me?"

"Will you help me get rid of the intruders?"

"John, I will make sure these intruders on your sacred land go to prison for a very long time. Now, tell me about the second man."

John Concha told him. Jack listened carefully as the last piece of the puzzle fell into place.

Chapter Thirty-Six

Sunday afternoon was warm and hazy. There was smoke in the air from a distant forest fire, as was often the case in recent years, an uncontrolled blaze in Colorado nearly two hundred miles away. The American West was burning.

In San Geronimo, dark thunderheads were gathering above the high mountain peaks which added to the worry. Lightning strikes caused fires.

It was the final day of the San Geronimo UFO Festival. Jack, Emma, and Santo stood in a group of several hundred spectators on a meadow, a viewing area a mile up along the trail to Dawson Peak.

For the past two days, the town had been besieged by at least a thousand festival goers. The hotels were full, the restaurants crowded, and everywhere you looked there was someone in a Star Wars costume or wearing an alien mask. Many of the cars had BEAM ME UP, SCOTTIE bumper stickers.

UFO enthusiasts, once regarded as a fringe group, were now mainstream. The atmosphere in town was more like Mardi Gras than a serious conference, but many of the attendees were devout believers in flying saucers and visitors from space. The tourist bureau had been quick to promote San Geronimo as an E.T. friendly town. Money was always welcome, from one end of the universe to the other.

Jack had climbed the trail with the help of Katya and a hiking pole and more than an occasional hand from Santo and Emma. Both Emma and Santo had done their best to discourage Jack from attempting the climb, saying he wasn't really needed here. But the Little Green Man Society had predicted a flying saucer was going to set down on Dawson Peak at exactly 3 o'clock in the afternoon, and Jack had decided this was an event not to be missed. The alien race from Alpha Centauri was about to show themselves to mankind.

"It sure is nice of them," said Jack, "to arrive just in time for the last day of the festival."

"Probably they're getting a cut of the gate," said Santo.

"You two are so cynical!" Emma scolded. "You should keep an open mind!"

"As long as it's not an open wallet," Jack told her.

More and more people were arriving up the trail, crowding the meadow. There was a cloud of marijuana smoke in the air and many had brought folding chairs and small coolers of beer, the kind that could be carried like backpacks. From nearby, someone had begun to play a bagpipe.

"What time is it, Santo?" Jack asked

"Two twenty-eight."

"Good. Only half an hour more and we can wrap this up. Let the show begin!"

***

Howie's horse was a sweet, patient palomino named Turtle. She was slow and steady and old, no race horse. But she carried Howie up the long trail to Dawson Peak without complaint.

Every now and then, she spotted a nice tuft of grass and bent over with her long neck to get at it. Howie had to pull her up by the reins to keep her moving, but he was sympathetic. He was hungry, too.

"Come on, Turtle! We don't want to get left behind!"

Howie rode last in a line of seven riders from the Pueblo who were each on horses that were faster and bolder than his own. Every now and then he had to give Turtle a kick to keep up.

John Concha, the War Chief, was the lead rider on the trail. He rode on a huge white stallion that pranced and snorted and looked like he wanted to break into a gallop. Concha rode with a rifle in a leather sheath hanging from his saddle against the stallion's flank. Most of the other Indian riders rode bareback, but they too were armed with rifles slung across their backs. Howie was the only one who wasn't armed. He was along as an observer.

Howie hadn't been on a horse in years. It was like riding a bicycle, he supposed. You never forgot how. But his butt was sore, and he had forgotten how the big Western saddle chaffed the inside of his legs.

They had left the Pueblo at dawn along a narrow trail that wasn't on any Forest Service map. For several hours they rode through a dense forest, weaving up and down the foothills. By mid-morning they began climbing steeply up the side of a mountain along a path that was barely visible to Howie, but the other riders appeared to know. The trail zig-zagged into the high country until they were above tree line.

Shortly after noon, they stopped at a small lake of clear cold water to let the horses drink and munch the long grass by the shore. Concha passed out flat rounds of Indian fry bread and oranges. After ten minutes, they remounted and resumed the long climb up Dawson Peak.

The clouds floating over the mountains grew darker and colder the higher they climbed. In the summer monsoon season, mountain storms generally arrived late in the afternoon, but today there were growls of thunder by one o'clock which didn't bode well. Howie had a rain poncho and a fleece jacket in his day pack, but he had a feeling that once again he was going get a good drenching in these mountains.

Déjà vu all over again, he said to himself glumly.

Life went around in circles.

If Jack was right, along with the rain, there would be a flying saucer, too. Just like old times.

***

Shortly after two o'clock, they dismounted and left the horses untethered on a high windswept meadow. Indian horses were trained to stay put when their reins were left hanging on the ground.

The War Chief slipped his rifle from its sheath and put a finger to his lips to call for silence. He led the way up a steep grassy hill toward a ridge of bare rock. Concha gestured to Howie to join him where he was crouching behind a large boulder. Howie arrived out of breath. They were above 13,000 feet and the air was thin. He crouched alongside the War Chief and peered out onto a wide meadow below their perch.

Jack had prepared Howie for what he was going to see, but it still came as a shock.

A hundred feet below where they were hidden, a dozen people were working to inflate a huge fabric balloon that was spread out over the meadow. A generator off to the side was powering an electric blower that was filling the envelope with air. Howie had heard the generator as he was climbing the hill, but it was louder now that there was nothing blocking the sound.

There were electric cables spread out on the meadow as well as a number of tubular devices on tripods—lasers, Howie imagined, that would provide a light show and a bit of magic.

The envelope of the balloon was only half filled with air, but its blobby shape was already becoming clear. It was about to become a flying saucer. A powerful propane burner was waiting off to the side. When the balloon was inflated, the burner would be lit at the opening at the bottom, the air would heat, and the balloon would rise into the air. It wouldn't look realistic from where Howie and John were watching, but with the laser lights it would make quite a spectacle for the crowd gathered on the clearing nearly a mile away.

A dark blue helicopter sat at the edge of the meadow not far from the generator, tied down due to the possibility of bad weather. It would have taken a number of trips to get the balloon and all the equipment and people up to this spot.

Howie saw Doug McKay among the dozen people who were working to get the balloon inflated. He recognized the droopy mustache and cowboy hat of the man he had encountered briefly outside the Worm Hole Café. McKay was in jeans and a burnt-orange parka, but the rest of the crew were in matching green jumpsuits.

"They're from the Little Green Man Society," Concha said to Howie, speaking quietly.

"They're the ones behind this nonsense?"

"Yep," said John.

The War Chief had made Jack promise not to mention the helicopter to Santo because he didn't want non-Indian law enforcement on the sacred mountain. Jack had agreed, giving his word, and it was a white man's promise he didn't intend to break. In return, Concha had agreed to arrest Doug McKay and his merry band of Green Men and turn them over to the State Police once he brought them down the mountain.

Jack knew that Santo wouldn't be happy when he discovered the arrangement. But after all, this was Indian land—by right, if not by law—and John was the chief law enforcement official here.

The War Chief nodded to his group of warriors. Then he raised his rifle and sighted along the barrel.

***

It began late.

Emma Wilder, standing in the viewing area below Dawson Peak, sensed the crowd was becoming restless. Someone nearby began clapping impatiently and a few others joined in.

More and more people had been arriving in the clearing, a steady stream of hikers coming up the trail with chairs and backpacks, dogs and children, everyone in a party mood.

Emma worried that the meadow wasn't large enough to hold such a crowd. It was less than a quarter acre in size, she judged, more of a knoll than a meadow, bordered on one side by a stand of dense pine and on the other by a precipice that fell off abruptly a hundred feet to where the trail came snaking up from below. Emma was especially worried about the precipice because more and more people had gathered there close to the edge with no other place to go.

An Albuquerque television crew had arrived with a video camera and a small portable satellite dish. Other professional-looking video equipment had been set up near a raised wooden platform where a young man was testing a battery-powered P.A. system, saying, "one, two, three, four" again and again into the microphone.

This was more than an event, it was a mini-Woodstock of ufology.

Young men and women in tight-fitting green outfits were squeezing through the crowd with some difficulty handing out glossy brochures.

"CHURCH OF THE STARS," proclaimed the cover in large orange letters. Underneath, in smaller print: "The Inter-Galactic Religion."

"Welcome to The Arrival!" Emma read, opening her brochure. "The Church of the Stars proclaims the Cosmic Truth at Last! All Beings are Brothers and Sisters in the Stars! The New Age is Here! Read the Galactic Bible by Ronald Devereaux, Downloaded on Your Device for a Donation of $11.99. Learn the Secrets of the Ancient Races!"

Several three-day workshops were offered on the opposite page. "Don't Let the Black Hole Get You!" promised to teach how to find "the

Mantra of Hope in the Age of Anxiety." "Find Your Cosmic Warrior" offered a path to health, joy, and eternal youth. The workshops would be held in October in Boulder, Colorado, $795 for the 3-day weekend, which included food, lodging, and a private fifteen-minute session with Ronald Devereaux. A website was given for more information and future workshops.

Meanwhile, the Arrival still hadn't arrived. Emma noticed Ronald Devereaux himself standing by the foot of the raised wooden platform speaking urgently into a walkie-talkie. Santo had pointed him out to Emma earlier. He wasn't her idea of a galactic guru. He was a mousey little person with floppy brown hair. Nebbishy had been Ruth's word for him. He didn't look like anything much at all.

At last, when the impatience of the crowd was growing louder, Ronald climbed up onto the wooden platform and addressed the crowd.

"The Arrival has come, my friends!" he cried. "Yes, it's here now! I've just had word the space craft has come through the wormhole! Make yourselves ready, brothers and sisters! The Arrival is close at hand!"

"Hallelujah!" several answered. It was no longer a secular gathering. This was the coming of God.

Emma was feeling more and more uneasy. A great cry rose up from the crowd. "They're here! They're here!"

Some fell to their knees, others moaned. The bagpipe began wheezing ecstatically a fevered version of *Amazing Grace.*

"Join hands, brothers and sisters!" Ronald cried from the platform. "Join hands and send forth your prayer! They have come! The Arrival is here!"

Emma didn't like crowds in the best of circumstances, and this crowd was getting out of control. A woman nearby reached out aggressively and grabbed her hand. She appeared to be speaking in tongues. Or perhaps it was Klizmorian, Emma didn't know. She pulled her hand free and turned to Jack, who didn't seem happy either. Katya was sitting on her haunches looking about nervously.

"Where did Santo go?" Jack asked.

"I don't know. He was here a second ago."

Santo was most likely maneuvering himself closer to Ronald Devereaux, who he was planning to question after the ceremony. Ronald had a lot of things to answer for. Nevertheless, Jack wished Santo was closer by.

"Let's get out of here," he said to Emma.

"What?" There was so much noise she couldn't hear him.

"Can you get us away from here?" he asked more loudly.

"I'm not sure, Jack."

A cry came from the crowd as the great moment finally arrived. A flying saucer rose above Dawson Peak into the stormy, blackened sky. It was an incredible sight, huge in the sky, at least forty feet high and perhaps a hundred and fifty feet long. You could just make out portholes and two large antennae on top. The body of the spacecraft glowed from the inside with an orange light as though there was a flame burning in its heart. Intense colored beams pierced the clouds, red, orange, blue.

The crowd was going crazy. "They're here . . . hallelujah! . . . they're here!"

The ancient race from the stars had arrived to set things right on Planet Earth. And not a moment too soon, the way Planet Earth was going!

But then, without warning, one end of the flying saucer jerked upward into the sky at a crazy angle. The craft hovered in the air for what seemed a long moment, and then it deflated into a shapeless heap and fell from the sky onto Dawson Peak below.

There was stunned silence from the viewing area.

"It's only a balloon!" someone shouted. "A goddamn balloon! And it popped!"

"No, they're here! They're here!"

Even now, many didn't want to believe the truth of what their eyes saw. But the mood changed quickly as the realization sunk in and ecstasy turned to anger.

People didn't like to be fooled. Especially when they themselves were the foolish.

***

Jack felt himself jostled and shoved from all sides. It was terrifying to be tossed about in an ocean of humanity that he couldn't see. Emma took hold of his arm and Katya began to bark. They didn't like it either.

"Can you see Santo?" Jack had to shout over the noise of the crowd.

"No, I can't! This is getting dangerous!"

"You said there are trees somewhere. Can you get us there? We'll hunker down until . . ."

Before he could finish the sentence, he was pushed off his feet backward onto the ground. The crowd surged around him. He lay with one arm clutching Katya, feeling almost like he was underwater, tossed about in the surf.

He remembered stories of stampedes in India, hundreds of people trampled to death. Everyone trying to save themselves. It felt like that now. He was engulfed in a melee of feet, legs, hands, bodies, shouts of anger, screams of fear. There was no escape, nothing he could do.

But where was Emma?

She had let go of his arm, carried away by the surge.

Jack managed to get to his knees. "Emma!" he shouted.

Someone's leg kicked against his shoulder.

"Emma!" he cried again.

He used Katya's back for balance and somehow pulled himself to his feet. The crowd had thinned a little. He was still buffeted from all sides, but he was able to keep his footing.

A gunshot exploded nearby. The sound was deafening. Jack's senses were overwhelmed. People shouting, bodies shoving back and forth, Katya barking.

Then to his surprise, the crowd opened and there was space to breathe.

"Don't come near me!" a voice screamed. "The next shot won't be in the air! I'll kill him! I'll kill him, I swear!"

Kill who? Jack wondered. Until he felt the barrel of a gun against his chin and an arm around his neck.

Kill Jack, that was who.

Ronald Devereaux was pressed behind him, not so nebbishy now. How Ronald had found him in the crowd, Jack couldn't say.

"Let him go, Ronald!" someone said from a few feet away. It was Santo. "You can't get away down that trail. You know you can't. For chrissake, man, give it up!"

"I want a helicopter!" Ronald demanded. "Get me a helicopter or I'll kill him. He's coming with me. I'll let Jack go once I get away!"

"Let's talk this over, Ronald," Santo told him. "We'll arrange something. But you need to calm down if you want to get out of here in one piece."

"Don't you bullshit me!" Ronald cried. "I'm going to count to ten. Then I want to hear you on your radio asking for a chopper. If you don't, I'm going to kill Jack, then I'll start shooting the crowd. I don't care if you kill me. Either you get me a helicopter, or I'm going out in a burst of glory. I'm not going to prison, I swear to God!"

Jack pictured Santo with his own gun out, ready to shoot Ronald at the first chance. The crowd had parted around them. Like the Red Sea, Jack thought. Like Moses had raised his staff.

Ronald had made a tragic mistake. They had nothing on him until now, not really—only suspicions, no hard evidence. Santo had only wanted to question him. But Ronald had obviously panicked when Santo approached, assuming the worst, and now there was no turning back.

Jack found himself strangely calm. He didn't know why. It was as though he had passed through a hurricane of terror to the other side. He took a deep breath. He knew what he was going to do. He only wished he knew where Emma was.

Ronald began counting. "One . . . two . . . three . . . four . . . "

Jack heard Katya's deep throaty growl.

He jerked his right elbow back as hard as he could into Ronald's stomach.

Which sent Katya into overdrive. She snarled as her teeth tore deep into Ronald's crotch.

"YEEAAHH!" Ronald's scream was barely human.

A fraction of a second later, a shot rang out from Santo's gun.

The arm around Jack's throat went slack and he found himself standing alone, free and clear and safe. Until Emma practically knocked him over.

"Oh, Jack! Jack! Are you alright?"

"Pretty much a picnic, Emma," he told her, only slightly out of breath. He managed a manic smile. "A Sunday picnic in the park!"

Which was when the storm broke overhead. The black clouds burst, lightning flashed, the heavens opened, and a hard rain began to fall.

Chapter Thirty-Seven

The train left the swarm of New York City, passed through an ashy, industrial corner of New Jersey, and continued onward toward the green, academic haven of Princeton.

Howie liked trains. And so did Claire. But Claire was puzzled. "So the cowboy with the droopy mustache—"

"He called himself Doug McKay. But his real name was Tex Ryder."

"Oh, come on, Howie! That's not a real name!"

"No, it was. His father was a famous stunt man in Hollywood, Blaze Ryder. And he named his kid, Tex. Why not? These were swashbuckling characters in a colorful time. Blaze worked for Sebastian Hays in the Fifties first as a stunt man in the movies, then later as kind of bodyguard companion all-purpose go-to-guy. You see, these connections go way back. Sebastian was Tex's godfather."

"Okay, Tex Ryder. But why did he change his name to Doug McKay?"

"Because Tex was on the run for killing somebody in a bar fight in Santa Monica. Hiding out with a reclusive godfather was the perfect way to disappear. He knew about the ranch because his father was living there. Blaze went with Sebastian to New Mexico when he dropped out of sight, so it was a natural place for Tex to go when he got into trouble in L.A. Blaze died in 1995 and Tex—who now called himself Doug McKay—took over as Sebastian's all-purpose wrangler fixer."

"Okay, so it was Sebastian who was behind everything?"

"Not quite," said Howie. "The whole thing was dreamed up by a nebbishy guy from the Little Green Man Society."

Claire laughed. "The Little Green Man Society! You're kidding!"

A month had gone by since the UFO festival in San Geronimo. It was late August and Howie and Claire were on their way to see Dr. Henry Sachs at the Institute for Advanced Study in Princeton. Claire had changed her ticket to fly to New York from London and, by the time of their train ride, they had already spent three days together at an apartment on Bank Street in Greenwich Village, talking, wandering the city, eating in small restaurants, getting to know one other again. The apartment belonged to a musician friend of Claire's, a violinist who was on tour in Asia.

Murder, abductions, flying saucers, and nuclear secrets had barely been mentioned until today. They had had more important matters to discuss: love, jealousy, Sir Richard Watson-Fowles, and what they were going to do about their relationship.

It wasn't working for either of them to live and work so many thousands of miles apart. If they were going to stay together, they had to be together. It was as simple as that.

It was Claire who had come up with the answer. A compromise that wasn't perfect, but one they thought might work.

Several weeks ago, she had been offered a place in the prestigious Los Angeles String Quartet and she had decided to accept. It would be a big change, moving to California and leaving the group she had been performing with for five years. But there were direct flights from L.A. to Santa Fe and she and Howie would be able to see each other often, perhaps as often as every other week. He would fly to her, she would fly to him.

In fact, the Los Angeles String Quartet would be a step up for Claire's career. The ensemble had won three Grammys and many international awards. The original cellist had been forced to retire after being diagnosed with Parkinson's Disease and the flattering offer to join the ensemble had come out of the blue.

There would still be occasional travel to Europe and Asia, but Los Angeles would be her home. She had already found an apartment in Pacific Palisades with a view of the ocean. $5900 a month for West L.A. was expensive, but Claire was doing well enough to afford it.

There was still an awkwardness between them, an elephant in the room, Claire's brief affair and the hurt it had caused. But they were working through it, day by day. Meanwhile, it was easier to talk about flying saucers.

"So, Sebastian Hays," Howie continued. "Like a lot of rich people, he was a miser. Doug had a place to hide, but he had no money of his own. Not only that, Sebastian had made it clear that he was leaving his entire estate to endow a museum of ufology in Atlanta. Doug wasn't going to get a cent. Meanwhile, the old man was ninety-six and Doug was starting to think about what he was going to do when Sebastian died. That's where Ronald Devereaux came in. Ronald was a con man with a long history of scams."

"Was Devereaux his real name?"

"Not even close. He was born David Peterson and, by the time he set up the Little Green Man Society, he'd gone through almost as many names as scams. He and Doug came up with the idea that there was a ton of money to be made with fake flying saucer sightings. The Klizmorian extravaganza on Dawson Peak was just the beginning. The real killing was going to come with a Klizmor religion, the Church of the Stars, which was going to show people how to retune their brains to receive happy vibrations from Alpha Centauri and double their life span. If Scientology could rake in millions, Doug and Ronald believed the Church of the Stars would make them billionaires."

"But the bubble burst."

"It sure did. Literally. Which was no accident. John Concha and his team shot that flying saucer full of holes and brought it down. Doug tried to escape, but Concha swept down on his horse and got him. It was very exciting."

"Sure, Howie. But let's go back to the beginning. Tell me about Grisha Bloom. What was he doing on Dawson Peak? And I want to know about Mia Bloom, or whoever she was. Somehow you haven't said very much about her. Was she really Sebastian's great-granddaughter?"

"It's hard to be certain. Sebastian sent Doug to L.A. to find her and make an offer to come live at the ranch. Jack thinks she was just an actress Doug hired, but I'm inclined to believe she really was Sebastian's great-granddaughter. In any case, Sebastian was very particular about who he had around him. He wanted absolute loyalty, which is why he went to the children of people he already trusted—in Mia's case, the descendant of the only one of his wives he hadn't come to despise. Mia's real name, by the way, really was Judy Cranston—Santo established that from her fingerprints.

"Now, Sebastian was a crazy old man, but he wasn't stupid. He read scientific journals, he knew who Grisha Bloom was and that he was in New Mexico at Los Alamos, not far away. So, he sent Judy to invite Grisha to the ranch, and then held him captive when he wanted to leave. He wanted to squeeze information from Grisha that didn't really exist, the secret of the stars. Sebastian thought the Blue Moon quark might provide a way to find a wormhole to Alpha Centauri. Is this making sense, Claire?"

"Not really," she answered. "But go on."

"Well, the actual science isn't as important as what Sebastian believed the science to be. He thought Grisha would get him to Klizmor where the advanced civilization there would make him young and live forever. That's the fantasy he had.

"Unfortunately, Grisha wasn't helpful. Some of this I don't know for certain, so I'm filling in the blanks as best I can. What I imagine is that

Bloom tried to explain to him that, no, the Blue Moon Quark was only a theoretical concept, a mathematical equation, and it would be many years, if ever, before there was any practical application. But Sebastian thought he was holding back. That's when he put Grisha in the space capsule where I ended up, too. He fed him psychedelic drugs and tried to shake the information out of him.

"But this is where Judy began to have qualms about what they were doing. She was an actress, she didn't mind having a sugar daddy give her a nice vacation in the mountains. She had helped lure Bloom to the ranch, but holding him prisoner and filling him full of drugs was more than she had signed up for. So she helped him escape.

"Unfortunately, Grisha didn't get far before Sebastian realized he was gone. So, he sent Doug after him in the ranch helicopter. Doug is a helicopter pilot, by the way. That was part of his job. But by this time, Doug had already teamed up with Ronald and he had his own plans. He found Grisha not very far away, picked him up, and dropped him off on Dawson Peak.

"Bloom was pretty much out of his head at this point from all the drugs, and the idea was to make it seem like he had been let off by a flying saucer. Ronald had a team up there already getting ready for the UFO festival and two of the Little Green Men were going to pretend they were hiking and saw Bloom getting out of a flying saucer. They were going to bring him down the mountain and make sure there was plenty of publicity. But Concha blew that by nudging Grisha toward me."

"Good God, Howie, there sure was a crowd on Dawson Peak that night!"

"There was. And I thought I was alone. Concha had ridden up from the Pueblo with several of his warriors. The next morning, he found Bloom in my tent and carried him down the mountain. Unfortunately, he was very sick and died on the trip down."

Claire was quiet for a moment, putting the pieces together in her mind.

"Okay, Howie, I think I'm starting to get this. But who tried to hijack Emma on the highway as she was leaving my storage shed with the book of poetry?"

"Doug confessed to that. It was two local guys he hired to find the missing equation."

"They were after the Theory of Everything?"

"They were. Sebastian wanted it and Doug's salary depended on making Sebastian happy. Doug and his crew tossed the Eckehart house in Los Alamos looking for the equation, and also the house that Grisha Bloom was renting in the mountains. You see, this is what Bloom and Eckehart had been working on at LANL. For a while, they believed they were very close to a breakthrough. It's what Lorna Wolfe believed Bloom had put on a flash drive and stolen from the Lab. She was after it, too."

"So, *is* it the Theory of Everything?"

"I guess we'll find out when we see Dr. Sachs. Personally, I don't think Grisha actually intended to steal anything from the Lab. My guess is he wanted that flash drive simply so he could continue working at home, no big deal. He was used to the Institute for Advanced Studies where security is a lot looser than LANL."

"So, what about Brandon Eckehart and his wife? Why were they killed?"

"Okay, this part of the story we know from Doug's confession. You see, Eckehart knew about the scam that Doug and Ronald were planning. He'd met McKay several times at the Worm Hole Café, and he knew Ronald, too. They had tried to enlist him to help with some of the science they needed to know to make their Church of the Stars halfway believable, and at first Brandon was willing to go along. He had a weird sense of humor—he liked comic books and thought flying saucers were a great joke. Plus, Ronald and Doug were offering him a lot of money, which he liked, too. But then it got complicated.

"According to Doug, Ronald decided that Brandon couldn't be trusted. He was too jokey, too lighthearted about the venture. He didn't take the Church of the Stars seriously enough. Plus, he kept upping the money he wanted.

"And then Brandon made a very big mistake. He tried to blackmail Doug and Ronald. He told them he wanted to back out of the whole deal, it wasn't really his thing, as he put it. But he wanted half a million dollars to keep quiet about what they were planning. So, when Sebastian ordered Doug to pick up Eckehart and squeeze the Theory of Everything out of him, Doug decided this was the moment to rid themselves of what was becoming a serious problem."

"But why torture him? Why hang him up like that?"

"They seriously wanted that equation. Not just for Sebastian, but for themselves. A stunning breakthrough in physics was just what they needed to make their hoax more believable. Unfortunately, Brandon couldn't give it to them because he didn't have it."

Claire shook her head, unhappy with what she was hearing.

"Tell me, Howie—I'm afraid to ask, but what happened to their little girl?"

"Juniper? She's fine," Howie assured her. "Santo checked. It was one of the first things he did. Doug didn't lie about her. He had someone drive Juniper to Ashley's sister in Texas."

"Well, that's a relief! Thank God! But why did they have to kill the mother?"

"Because she knew about the scam, too. According to Doug, Ashley was the one behind the blackmail attempt. Apparently, she didn't like New Mexico. She had grown up in Florida and she missed the ocean. She wanted the money to go live on some nice Caribbean island. Red sails in the sunset, sort of thing."

"Sex on the Beach!"

"Er—"

"That's a drink, Howie."

"Can you put an umbrella in it?"

"You can, actually. You can have it any way you want."

Howie laughed. He and Claire were sitting side by side as the train rumbled down the track. *Clickety-clack, clickety-clack.* Howie let the sound carry him away. He did his best to be funny for Claire and she was upbeat in return. But it had been a difficult time for both of them and there was sorrow underneath.

Howie closed his eyes and felt a wave of exhaustion wash over him. He hadn't been sleeping well since the explosion in the coal mine. Often he woke with nightmares, the same terrible dream again and again: the man with no face forever coming after him with a knife. Even on a sunny day like this, he was haunted by the memory of Judy Cranston—Princess Zora—as she lay dying in the dark, knowing his own slow death would follow soon enough.

Howie shivered though the train was warm.

Watching closely, Claire reached and took his hand.

***

The meeting with Dr. Henry Sachs at the Institute for Advanced Study was a disappointment. Grisha Bloom's Theory of Everything turned out to be a bust.

At least, according to the doctor.

He was a short, balding man in a conservative dark suit. He was a disappointment, also. Up to now, every astrophysicist Howie had met was flamboyantly eccentric. But not Dr. Henry Sachs. He dressed and behaved like a fussy small-town banker.

Howie had faxed Sachs a copy of the equation from his book of Chinese poetry a week earlier, so he'd had time to examine it.

"Gibberish," he pronounced. "Doesn't make sense in the least. Grisha was a brilliant scientist at one time, but he lost it, I'm afraid. His brain got jiggled."

"Jiggled?"

"Juggled, jiggled, jinxed, jammed . . . who knows? Somewhere along the line he lost his ju-ju. Gives me a case of jitters even to think about it! Makes me want to get juiced, frankly."

Perhaps Dr. Sachs wasn't so normal after all.

Howie asked a question that was bothering him. "Did you know Brandon Eckehart, Doctor?"

"Eckehart? Of course. He was here for a while at the Institute."

"Well, Brandon told me that Grisha stole some of his work in order to claim it was his. I was wondering what you think of that."

"Nonsense! Eckehart had a huge ego, nearly as big as his belly. He thought he was the cat's meow, frankly. But he was never on Grisha's level, not a bit. Don't get me wrong, Brandon was a decent physicist, but he was a plodder. He didn't have the spark you need to make the big creative leaps."

"But Grisha did?"

"Yes, certainly. Grisha leaped a bit too far sometimes. But he leaped."

Howie was relieved to hear this. He didn't like to think of Grisha as an intellectual pirate. As far as Howie was concerned, better a leap too far than never to have leapt at all.

Howie and Claire left the Institute for Advanced Study and got an Uber ride to the university. Howie wanted to show Claire the campus where he had done his graduate work.

Of all the universities in America, Princeton is perhaps the most lovely. Aristocratic old buildings covered in ivy. Green quads, quiet paths, privilege, elitism, academic brilliance, old money, old ways—that was what Princeton was all about.

"Snooty," said Claire.

"Very," Howie agreed. "But you can get a great education here."

"Old boys' network!" she snorted.

"Definitely. But it's been co-ed since 1969. They even let in the occasional Lakota Sioux. The times have been a-changing."

Howie showed her around Firestone library and the eating clubs and Aaron Burr Hall where the anthropology department was housed.

"You're kidding, Aaron Burr Hall?"

"He was the second president of the university. Before he went on to shoot Hamilton in a duel. You can see where I got my lust for adventure."

"Lust?"

"Figuratively speaking."

It was a warm, languid afternoon and after some time wandering about the campus, Howie and Claire stretched out on the grass in the quad at the foot of the university chapel.

"You know, Howie, I'm not sure if this is a comedy or a tragedy."

"Hamilton and Burr? It's a musical, actually."

"Oh, Howie! Not the play! I'm talking about Grisha Bloom and the Eckeharts and Ronald Devereaux with his flying saucers and Church of the Stars. It's all so . . . mad. And sad, somehow."

"Well, there you are. Pathos. A get rich scheme. A falling out of thieves. Religion, money, power, science gone amuck . . . just another day in America."

Howie was lying on his back feeling very comfortable, looking up at the green shade trees overhead. Claire was cuddled up next to him on the lawn, propped up on one elbow.

"Was she very sexy?" she asked unexpectedly.

"Uh . . . who?"

"Princess Zora. I know I don't have any right to ask . . ."

Howie sighed. "Well, she *was* sexy. But nothing happened. I was tempted, of course. I was hurt, I was angry, but I wasn't ready to let go of you yet. Even if it was only the idea of you."

Claire settled her head against Howie's neck, her arm resting on his chest.

"I'm sorry," she said softly. "I'm really, really sorry."

Howie didn't want to talk about this particularly. All he wanted to do was hold her in his arms.

But he supposed something needed to be said. He just wasn't sure what.

"Howie? I know you're hurting. I want to help you."

He sat up and rolled over onto her so that he could look down on her lovely face, her blond hair on the green of the grass.

"Claire, it's going to be okay. You know, in crazy times like these . . . ice caps melting, all the lies and tumult . . . there has to be something good to hold onto. And for me, that's you. When I thought I was going to die in that coal mine, all I could think about was how I wanted to hold onto you."

She looked up at him. "Are you sure?"

"I'm sure," he said.

"Then kiss me," she told him. "Kiss me like a thousand rockets on the Fourth of July!"

He laughed. He felt lighter than he had for a long time.

To kiss like a thousand rockets on the Fourth of July was a lot to ask. But he gave it his best shot.

Acknowledgements

I'd like to take this opportunity to thank my wife, Gail Westbrook, who read numerous drafts of this book, edited my faulty grammar, and gave me lots of ideas, large and small.

Also, a huge thanks to my publishers at Speaking Volumes, Kurt and Erica Mueller, who encouraged me to continue the adventures of Howie and Jack.

I assume that many of my readers know a great deal more about astrophysics than I do, and I want to apologize for my simplifications of a very complex subject, and any mistakes I might have made. Like Howie, I spent my college years in the humanities rather than the sciences.

The Blue Moon quark, of course, is entirely fictitious, though new subatomic particles are being discovered all the time, and who knows— the way science is going, the Blue Moon quark might be next.

Just this week, to give an illustration, scientists at the Institute for Nuclear Research at the Hungarian Academy of Sciences announced the discovery of a new particle they are calling X17, which supposedly connects the visible world with dark matter. There are many doubters but if the findings are verified, along with what is claimed to be a new "fifth force" of nature, the Hungarians will certainly be heading to Sweden.

Could there be a mystery thriller here?

In any case, science is breaking new ground every day, and when the James Webb Space Telescope is finally launched, with greatly improved resolution over the Hubble, we will be able to see, literally, to the beginning of time.

I want to thank Prof. Luke Hovey, an astrophysicist at Los Alamos National Laboratory, whose introductory course, Astronomy 101, I audited at UNM/Taos. The math was a challenge for me, but one of the great thrills of my life was looking through a good telescope on a dark New Mexico night and seeing the rings of Saturn and the moons of Jupiter.

Here are a few books I'd like to recommend to beginners, like me, who might be curious to know more about the astonishing universe in which we live:

"Cosmos," by Carl Sagan. This was written in 1983 so the science is way out of date. Nevertheless, Carl Sagan inspired a generation of astrophysicists, and this will give you a basic grounding in the subject.

"Einstein," by Walter Isaacson. This a biography of Einstein's life, but it also gives the clearest explanation that I've found of the Theory of Relativity and how gravity bends spacetime.

"Origins," by Neil de Grasse Tyson & Donald Goldsmith. If you want a good description of the Big Bang and the early seconds of the universe, this is it.

"A Brief History of Time," by Stephen Hawking. Also, his final book "Brief Answers to the Big Questions." In fact, read anything by Hawking that you can get your hands on. The man was incredible! He didn't let paralysis stop him from surfing the universe from his high-tech wheelchair and his writing is full of humor and mind-bending speculation.

Finally, "The Elegant Universe," by Brian Greene. This one goes post-Einstein into the really "spooky" stuff, as astrophysicists describe it—String Theory, the omniverse, multiple dimensions, and more. Good luck!

When life on Earth seems less than perfect—shoddy and small—it's good to look to the sky and remember where we are: less than a speck of dust circling a very average star at 67,000 miles per hour, in a distant corner of the Milky Way, a spiral galaxy among hundreds of billions of galaxies each with hundreds of billions of stars.

It puts things in perspective.

And maybe one day, in all that space and time, visitors may come knocking on our door.

Coming Soon!

HUNGRY GHOST
A Howard Moon Deer Mystery
Book 7
By
Robert Westbrook

In 1970 a Lakota boy at an Indian school in New Mexico kills the headmaster who has sexually abused him and runs away. These schools, where children were forcibly separated from their parents and forbidden to speak their native language, no longer exist, but the ghost of old crimes continues to haunt the present.

Fifty years later, Howard Moon Deer is invited for Thanksgiving weekend to a secluded ranch by his old college girlfriend, Grace Stanton, who is now a bestselling novelist and wants him to investigate the anonymous poison pen letters her father has been receiving. Grace is from a famous New Mexico family, the granddaughter of Bureau of Indian Affairs Commissioner Adam Stanton, one of the architects of the discredited Indian school policy, and the daughter of U.S. Senator Harlan Stanton. Unfortunately, Thanksgiving doesn't go well, and when Senator Stanton is found dead, Howie finds himself the prime suspect in the most sensational murder case of the year.

Now it is up to Jack Wilder to clear Howie's name and discover the real killer before the ghost of the past kills again. *Hungry Ghost* is a deadly family drama of complicated passions, murder, and lies.

For more information
visit: www.SpeakingVolumes.us

Coming Soon!

MOON OF THE BLUE MUSTANG
A Sheriff Lansing Mystery
Book 8
By
Micah S. Hackler

The body-count climbs as Sheriff Cliff Lansing contends with drugs, death, cattle theft and a power struggle with the Forestry Service. The resources of his office are spread thin. Almost too late, he realizes more than one murderer may be involved.

An Apache legend and family secrets weave their way through the action . . . unseen forces play their part . . . providing Lansing with a mystery he may never solve.

For more information
visit: www.SpeakingVolumes.us

Coming Soon!

WITCH OF THE PALO DURO
A Tay-Bodal Mystery
Book 2
By
Award-winning author
Mardi Oakley Medawar

"Another great storyteller is emerging."
—Tony Hillerman

For more information
visit: www.SpeakingVolumes.us